MOVIE Star

by Lizzie PEPPER

Also by Hilary Liftin

Candy and Me

Dear Exile: The True Story of Two Friends Separated (for a Year)
by an Ocean

MOVIE Star

by Lizzie PEPPER

HILARY LIFTIN

ALLEN&UNWIN

SYDNEY · MELBOURNE · AUCKLAND · LONDON

First published in Australia and New Zealand by Allen & Unwin in 2016
First published in the United States in 2015 by Viking, an imprint of
Penguin Random House LLC

Allen & Unwin
83 Alexander Street
Crows Nest NSW 2065
Australia
Phone: (61 2) 8425 0100
Email: info@allenandunwin.com
Web: www.allenandunwin.com

Cataloguing-in-Publication details are available
from the National Library of Australia
www.trove.nla.gov.au

ISBN 978 1 76029 262 1

Internal design by Alissa Rose Theodor
Set in Warnock Pro
Printed and bound in Australia by Griffin Press

10 9 8 7 6 5 4 3 2 1

The paper in this book is FSC® certified.
FSC® promotes environmentally responsible,
socially beneficial and economically viable
management of the world's forests.

For Allison, whose struggles and gifts brought me here.

—L.R.P.

For Chris, with lifelong love and gratitude.

—H.L.

We took risks, we knew we took them; things have come out against us, and therefore we have no cause for complaint, but bow to the will of Providence, determined still to do our best to the last . . .

CAPTAIN ROBERT FALCON SCOTT
"MESSAGE TO THE PUBLIC," MARCH 1911

MOVIE
Star

by Lizzie
PEPPER

INTRODUCTION

When I first told P. J., my longtime publicist, that I wanted to write a book, she just about hung up on me. (It wouldn't have been the first time—P. J. has one way she likes to do things: P. J.'s way.) After she'd cooled down a bit, she reminded me that we'd spent the past year and a half trying to show the world that my life was completely boring and mundane in an attempt to get the press to relax its twenty-four-hour watch on me. Why would I want to stir things up again?

It was a good question, and it has a real answer, but it might not be what everyone expects.

I know that people want to hear my side of the story. I've been asked the same questions every time I've stepped out into daylight for more than seven years. *Lizzie! Lizzie! Why did you marry Rob Mars? Was it a career move or do you really love him? Is he gay? What's it like inside the One Cell Studio? Have you learned to levitate? Is it a cult? Why did you leave Rob? Did he cheat on you? Seriously, is he gay? Where's your wedding ring? Are you saving your sons from the Studio? Are you and Johnny getting back together?* And, of course, *Who are you wearing?*

I am going to answer those questions (though I'm not going to dwell on fashion). In doing so, I have no choice but to violate my ex-husband's cherished and embattled privacy. I don't do so out of spite. In fact, I'm deeply conflicted about it. A marriage that fails has surrendered on multiple levels: the smallest intimacies; the day-to-day rituals; the fundamental principles. In my case, my issues with Rob's involvement in One Cell are distinct from my issues with Rob, but it became, and is in these pages, very difficult to separate the two. What will forever be true is that I respect Rob, and I will always care for him, and I would rather not hurt him.

So why am I telling the story? Why expose Rob, and myself—and even, to some extent, our young sons, who didn't choose a public life? It's not revenge or bitterness or a desire for attention, that's for sure. I'm not trying to make my ex-husband look bad, and I'm not trying to make myself look good. I'm not trying to rejuvenate my image or pay off debts. But for the last fifteen years the press has drawn me in crisp, simple, black-and-white lines. The Girl Next Door. America's Sweetheart. Rob Mars's wife. For all the paparazzi shots and legal briefs and features that have been written about the "news" of my every trip to Starbucks (venti soy latte, if you don't know already), nobody ever writes or talks about the reasons or the reality. I feel like nobody really knows me, and, until very recently, there were some things even I didn't understand about myself.

After this bizarre, otherworldly phase of my life in which the press tried to predict, expose, and analyze every slight movement I made, I was determined to reclaim those years, to describe what they were to me, regardless of what the truth might do to my image, dammit! The right to tell my own story, in my own words, became so important to me that I made sure it was part of my divorce agreement. (I achieved this in a rather unorthodox way, but more on that later.) Now that it has settled at last, I can finally break the first commandment of celebrity: I can tell the imperfect, unpolished truth.

I'm only thirty-two, but, as they say, my life so far has been quite a journey: growing up a straight-A student in Chicago; landing a lead role on a beloved TV series before I finished high school; making movies in Hollywood; marrying a megastar; giving birth to twins; getting a divorce under circumstances I never could have predicted; launching O Naturale, my organic cosmetics line (available at a department store near you). These are the Wikipedia trappings of a Hollywood life. I'm famous for what is completely obvious about me—that's how it works—but behind the screen, behind the scenes, behind the behind the scenes, I'm human. I fell in love, as people do, and entered a marriage that I thought would last a lifetime. I've made mistakes. I've kept secrets. I've had my heart broken. I've been extraordinarily lucky, and I've had my share of struggles. Through it all, the biggest lesson I've learned is that there are no black-and-white lines. In my story, there is no he said/she said, no good and evil, no right and wrong. We are all human, complex and simple, great and small. This is a story about the choices that we each make every day, and how those choices make us who we are.

Lizzie Pepper

LOS ANGELES

PART ONE

DAZZLED

1

I wasn't really interested in the part: another helpless girlfriend—too small a role for me—but my management told me to take the meeting. It was Rob Mars after all. You don't say no to Rob Mars.

I've had a million meetings in my acting career, and I had no idea that this would be the one that would change my life forever. I walked into the room, and there was Rob. At this point I was past being dazzled by movie stars—or so I thought. But even at the Oscars, in that concentrated crowd of self-involved, hard-to-impress A-listers, Rob Mars turns heads. Celebrities gawk at him the way most people gawk at them.

Here he was. Rob Mars, in the flesh. Seeing him spun me back to my teen years, before I took the role of Lucy McAlister on *American Dream*, before all the press, the red carpets, the award ceremonies, the movies and TV appearances. Back to the days when Rob Mars was a life-size poster on my best friend Aurora's bedroom door, and we had no idea that I would ever lead a life that would have me meeting him in person, much less as a potential colleague. I would say I never dreamed of it . . . but isn't this what everyone dreams of?

Rob rose to greet me, tall and debonair, his familiar face sharper in three dimensions, as if he'd always been slightly blurry onscreen and now he was in high-def. His brow and chin were strong, elegantly framed by salt-and-pepper hair. But you know that. What I really mean is that in person his features were breathtaking, his face chiseled by destiny. And I had never noticed before how his eyebrows slanted down toward his ears. It made him look a little vulnerable in spite of the ridiculous bone structure.

"Hi, I'm Lizzie," I said, and stuck out my hand to shake his. A worry flitted through my head. Was he one of those germophobes? I hadn't done my research. Had I blown it already? But he took my hand and at the same time leaned in to kiss my cheek. Phew.

"Can I call you Elizabeth?" he asked. "You're too sophisticated for Lizzie."

I nodded dumbly. My father was the only person who called me Elizabeth. Elizabeth felt premature, but also intimate coming from Rob—as if he'd already found something in me that he'd been looking for.

"Elizabeth," he said, and smiled. That famous megawatt smile, but now it was for me.

We took our chairs, and I noticed that he was one of those people with a disproportionately long torso because sitting down he was a good foot taller than I was, and I'm five foot seven.

There were other people in the room. Six, maybe? Hard to say, I never pay much attention to entourages of agents and managers, and I was transfixed by that smile. Anyway, Rob was the one who led the conversation from the start. He talked about how much he'd admired my work, not just on *American Dream*, but in *Underground* and *The Last Hurrah*. I ate up the praise. *American Dream* was formative for me—I grew up on that show—but I didn't want it to define me as an actor for the rest of my life. Plus, these compliments were coming from one of the biggest movie stars in the world. Maybe *the* biggest movie star. Rob Mars isn't just a moviegoer's idol. He's an actor's actor. He's played good guys, bad guys, teen heartthrobs, Jesus himself, and an immortal god who rules over an unbelievably distant planet. He even sang in some musical where he played a sensitive cowboy. Anyway, my point is completely obvious to anyone who has ever stepped into a movie theater. Nothing Rob Mars ever does feels small, and it never is. All his movies over-perform. He over-performs. Whatever you think of that movie, he was a completely believable Son of God. Somehow even the cowboy musical, which was generally considered to be a flop, made millions of dollars. Meanwhile, all my movies so far had been small, offbeat indies with good reviews and mediocre-to-nonexistent box offices, and all my parts had been awkward girls with glasses and names like Ruby who just needed to accept their quirkiness before realizing that the cute lead guys loved them in spite of themselves. And now Rob Mars himself knew who I was. By name. He knew and said he loved my last film, which, as far as I could tell, had been seen by about twelve people. If nothing else came out of this meeting, at least I had that.

We chatted. He never broke eye contact. He might not even have blinked. Even stranger, he also didn't say a word about the part in his new movie, which was ostensibly the reason we were there. Where was this going? I was flattered and a little confused. But fine, if he was one of those people who liked some long, semi-personal "get-to-know-you" conversation to see if I had a brain before getting to the point, I could play that game.

"Okay, this is off topic," I said, "but I read this amazing book last week: *The Birthday Boys*. It's a fictionalization of Captain Robert Scott's failed expedition to the South Pole. He and three other men froze to death in a tent, waiting out a blizzard that they knew would never end."

"Tell me more," Rob said. A good sign. I had a morbid interest in survival stories (they could take place at either Pole, in the Andes, or in outer space so long as they involved intrepid people in inhumane circumstances fighting for their lives), and as my go-to topic of conversation they tended to separate the wheat from the chaff. Approximately half the time, my audience took the first chance to excuse themselves to get another drink. But I had Rob's full attention.

"One of the characters says it was so cold their teeth splintered. Do you think the author made up that detail—or do you think their teeth actually froze and cracked? I mean, they're *teeth*."

Rob seemed to ponder this.

Then he said, "Guys, could you . . . ?" and before he finished the sentence, the room emptied.

Now it was just the two of us. Rob sat calmly in his armchair, but I could feel his intensity radiating toward me.

"So, Elizabeth, I hear you had a poster of me on your wall?"

I cringed. He'd seen the profile in *Glam*, the one where I said he was my childhood crush. It wasn't true—the poster I had in mind was the one on my best friend Aurora's bedroom door—sometimes in an interview I panic under the pressure to come up with an answer. My real childhood crush was Alec Dumall, but since he'd just been busted for downloading child porn (hey, perhaps we'd both had crushes on each other!)—I'd had to think fast.

"Do you always read *Glam*, or do you mostly just tear out the pictures and tape them inside your locker?" I teased.

He laughed. "I like you, Elizabeth Pepper." There was an awkward pause. Or, rather, I felt awkward. Rob sat there watching me squirm, a beatific smile on his face.

"Look," he said, "I have to go. But I want to spend more time with you. Can I take you out?" *Take me out.* A date? Either a date or a mob hit. It wasn't an exaggeration to say that Rob Mars was the most eligible bachelor in the world. Aurora was going to keel over and die. But I wasn't making any assumptions.

"Sure," I said, trying to sound casual.

"Excellent!" he said, and pumped his fist in the air. Yup, a fist pump. But it was somehow okay on him, as if he'd invented it and everyone else who followed had turned it fratty and overused. "Hold on," he continued. "Let me walk you to your car." He picked up the landline and pushed a button. "I'm heading down to the lobby," he said.

He walked me out into the office hallway. One of the suits who'd been in our meeting came up to us. "All clear," he said, and vanished. Rob and I headed to the elevator bank, and it struck me that the cubicles, which had been bustling when I entered, were quiet now. The halls were empty. Even the front reception desk wasn't monitored. This was ACE, one of the biggest agencies in Hollywood. Incoming calls were always answered immediately. Yet, as we exited, multiple phone lines rang and rang.

The elevator was waiting when we got there. The lobby button was already lit. And when the doors opened and I saw that the lobby, like the offices above, was completely deserted, I finally understood what "all clear" meant. Rob walked me to the front door as if it were perfectly normal that an entire office building would shut down operations to let him pass. Because, as I would soon learn, it *was* perfectly normal to him.

"Shut up." Aurora, who had just served herself some of our take-out sushi, sat up straight.

"Well, it's not necessarily a date. He just said—"

"It is totally a date and, holy crap, we have to figure out what you're going to wear. When is this date happening?"

"I don't know. He said he'd call."

"You have to be ready!" Aurora exclaimed. "I know how this goes down. He's going to call the day of. A limo will whisk you to a restaurant, where you'll be the only people because he's reserved the whole place for the two of you. You won't have time to think. The only solution is to be fully made-up and wearing a black cocktail dress every waking moment of your life. Do you own the right dress for a date with Rob Mars? This is major." Aurora sprang up. She flew to the closet, her unruly mane of blond hair bouncing. In a blur of wiry limbs, she started pulling out dresses.

"Trying too hard," she said, rejecting a dark red silk. "Slutty . . . this could be good." She held up a graphite sparkling mini-dress. "Hel-*lo*, Lizzie!"

"He calls me Elizabeth."

Aurora tossed the dress aside. "Oh, forget this one, then."

"Can you *please* stop this makeover montage?" I begged.

Aurora threw three dresses into my arms. "Try these ridiculous little handkerchiefs."

"He might not call, you know." I dropped the dresses on the bed.

Aurora paced impatiently. "Pepper, you are impossible." She paused and closed her eyes. I waited. More was coming.

"You know that he's gay."

"Aurora . . ."

"I'm serious. I have it on good authority. My power yoga teacher is best friends with his lover."

Aurora was visiting from Chicago, where her power yoga teacher, an L.A. transplant, was her best and only source for all celebrity rumors, including plenty about me that we both knew were lies. Mostly. Okay, exaggerations. The one with the tequila shots and the Segway on the 405 is true, but I was young and I'm not proud.

"Fine. He's gay. He's also twenty years older than I am. I'm just going out with him. If he ever actually calls. And even if he does, it might not be a date—certainly not if he's gay—so who cares?"

"It is a date. I'm just saying be careful. You don't want to be a beard like his last wife." Rob had been married to Lexy Hartfield for fifteen years. Lexy Hartfield! How could I compete with her? The long, dark hair, full lips, almond eyes, and curves that made me look like a schoolboy. If Lexy was Rob's type, then I certainly wasn't. She was drop-dead gorgeous, famous for never wearing makeup or styling her hair except on set. Without the fancy dresses and professional makeup, I'm a plain Jane. (See, for evidence, any paparazzi shot of me from the past year, along with the accompanying snarky, derogatory caption.) And, if anything, I've been encouraged to play up my plainness and sensibility. Because, as my publicist never fails to remind me, I am famous for my girl-next-door character, my girl-next-door upbringing, and my girl-next-door looks. Apparently I'm famous for how undeserving of fame I am. Furthermore, Lexy was a daredevil, said to have performed all her own stunts in the action movies that made her a star. She could have any man in the world. There was no way she was a beard. Yeah, now that I thought about Lexy, I realized there was no way Rob would go for me. Easy come, easy go.

I lit a cigarette and leaned out the window to exhale. My parents were visiting the next day, and my mother had a nose like a bloodhound.

2

As always, Aurora was right. The call came without warning. But what she failed to anticipate was that it would come at seven a.m., at least two hours before what I consider to be daybreak. My phone vibrated on my bedside table as I groped for it in the dark room.

"Elizabeth. It's me."

Me. Because he knew I would know.

"Hey," I whispered, hoping my half-awake croak would pass for sexy.

"Can I steal you away?" This guy had spent too much time reading scripts.

"Um, what did you have in mind?"

"Let me surprise you. Come downstairs. Your chariot awaits."

Downstairs? He was downstairs? "I'm . . . I'm just waking up. And if this surprise is going to run past eleven, I have a few things to cancel."

"Cancel," he said. "I'll wait."

I peeked around the edge of my curtains. There he was, on the street ten flights below, leaning against a lamppost. He saw me at the window and waved. *Crap.* Did *every* moment in his life seem like it came straight out of a movie? He gestured to a limo parked outside my front door. My "chariot."

"Be right down," I said into the phone.

★

Ten minutes later I slid into the backseat of the limo. It took me a second to process that I was the only passenger. Where was Rob? "Wait!" I said to the driver. I thought there was some mistake. Maybe I'd hopped into a limo someone in my building had summoned for a trip to the airport.

"It's okay," the driver said. (His name, I would later know, was Lewis.) "He wanted me to give you this." He handed me an envelope and we started speeding toward the highway.

"Elizabeth," the neatly written note read, "I'm sorry it has to be like this, but it will be much better for both of us if we aren't seen together. Yet. Now please look out the passenger-side window."

I turned to my right and there, driving in the lane next to us, was another black Escalade with Rob sticking his head out the back window. He gave me a thumbs-up, a questioning look on his face. I smiled gamely and returned the thumbs-up. What choice did I have? I couldn't turn back now. I grounded myself by composing a text to Aurora in my head. *i am living your fantasy.* Rob's car pulled ahead of mine, and he stuck his arms out toward me, as if we were being tragically torn from each other. I couldn't suppress an internal swoon.

I still had no idea of our destination, but it dawned on me that Rob was right to arrange for us to travel separately. Nobody was following us. Nobody had whipped out their phones to take pictures. Nobody wanted an autograph. We were free. This was a feat. The tabloids had barely gotten over my embarrassingly public breakup with Johnny Flaim. (*"Lizzie's Flaim Out"*—which tabloid *hadn't* had that headline at the ready?) The moment they caught me with someone new, they would have a field day. No, I realized, I would no longer be the lead. I may have been a star, but Rob was the sun. The headline this date would have generated wouldn't have started with me. It began and ended with Rob Mars.

An hour later we arrived at a harbor, still and gray in the morning fog. I was getting hungry and hoped we were there for a romantic breakfast at some restaurant by the shore followed by a quick ride back home so I could spend the rest of the day by myself squealing loudly into my pillow, but instead we thanked our respective drivers and Rob led me down the docks to a waiting yacht. I've been on yachts before—mostly for parties—and it wouldn't have surprised me if Rob owned this one. A captain greeted us, and we climbed aboard. Rob led me to the upper deck. I caught a glimpse of the living room as we passed the main deck. It was stark and formal: black enamel paneling and white leather furniture. Up on the top deck, a bottle of champagne was chilling in a bucket. I mentally texted Aurora: *definitely a date.*

Rob poured me a glass of champagne, but instead of serving himself one, the captain came out and handed him a jugful of something green and foamy. I raised an eyebrow.

"I don't drink much," he said. "This gives me incredible energy."

Something about the preplanned champagne for me, green smoothie for him was disconcerting. What exactly was I doing here? "Are you trying to get me drunk?" I said.

He put down his glass. "Elizabeth, that is the last thing I would do. I want to know you. The real you."

"Okay, well, then I have to tell you. The real me thinks saying things like 'the real you' are kind of cheesy."

He froze and looked almost hurt. Then he stared deeply into my eyes and said, "Guilty as charged." His face broke into a smile, and suddenly Rob Mars the movie star and Rob Mars the person simultaneously merged and separated. His expressions, his smile, his manner—all were familiar to me from his movies. No actor can transform himself entirely.

But in that moment I also had a flash of recognizing the divide between who he was and what he brought of himself to his characters. I saw that—right now, at least—he was not acting for me. Then, for the first time, I allowed myself a tiny, internal "wow."

He lifted his green jug to my crystal glass. "Requesting permission to be cheesy?"

I smiled in spite of myself. "Granted."

I had assumed we were alone on board except for the captain, but we hadn't traveled far from shore when another man came out onto the deck. He wore jeans and a light yellow cashmere sweater. He looked sort of beige and featureless, like a soulless Wall Street guy on his day off, non-descript except that one of his pale eyes had a patch of brown in it. He was sucking vigorously on a mint, which I could smell as he approached. He stopped sucking, smiled politely, and then quickly, as if it were a tic, flipped the mint in his mouth with his tongue.

"Elizabeth, you remember Geoff from our meeting," Rob said.

"Of course I do." I didn't. Clearly I'd been otherwise focused or I would have remembered the mint-sucking. As I watched, the stranger opened an Altoid tin and popped two new mints in his mouth. The guy was chain-mint-sucking.

Was Geoff one of Rob's agents? Maybe this wasn't a date after all.

"Welcome aboard," Geoff said. "I won't disturb you, but I wanted you to know how happy we are to have you as our guest."

Apparently this man was my host. I automatically thanked him and complimented the boat. Then Rob touched my chin and turned it in the direction we were heading. Rising before us was an island. It was lush and green, and appeared deserted except for one enormous white stone build-ing, which cascaded like a snowcap down the highest peak of the island.

"This is Century Island," Rob said. "Geoff is kind enough to let me use it." If anyone would own an entire island, just miles off the shore of L.A., it would be Rob Mars or one of his associates. Was it even on maps?

"I've never brought a guest here before," Rob went on. "You're the first."

I liked the sound of that.

On the island, Rob and I followed an old, rough boardwalk that clung to the rocks. We came to an overlook that jutted out over the rough water below.

"Let's sit," Rob said.

"Is it safe?" I asked.

"Trust me," he said, and led me forward. Sitting side-by-side on a driftwood log (too perfect!), we were mostly quiet. I reminded myself not to romanticize the whole thing. I was on a fantasy island date with a fantasy man. I wasn't about to be seduced by all this perfection. Besides, not everything was perfect. I was freezing. Then, out of nowhere, a massive wave crashed spectacularly against the rocks, nearly sweeping us out to sea. I screamed and jumped to my feet.

"You're drenched! I'm so sorry," Rob said, wrapping his coat around me.

"I'm totally fine," I said, but as we headed back off the promontory, I slipped on the now-wet rocks.

"I gotcha," Rob said, catching me with a strong grasp. He put a sturdy arm around my waist and guided me to safety. There was a reason Rob had been cast as Jesus. He radiated supreme confidence, as if he understood the world on another level. Life, death—he walked the line without recklessness or doubt. He expected my trust, and I gave it. I leaned against him, sinking closer to this increasingly familiar stranger. Cautious though I was, and far out of my comfort zone, I suddenly felt brave, safe, or both. I had just walked out onto a cliff with this man. Where else would I follow him?

Looking back on it now, I still remember that feeling and what it triggered in me. I was a girl who'd always done what was right and best. My parents had the greatest faith and confidence in me, and I lived up to that. I was their wonder child, achieving their dreams for me without even trying. Now here was a man who opened my world in just the way I was ready for it to be opened, at just the right time. I was practically handed to him on a silver platter. As it turned out, this was true in more ways than I knew.

After a while, we climbed the road up to the fortress. Rob had called it "the Lodge," which was like calling Versailles "the Country House." Thankfully I was wearing flats (Aurora had nailed that one). "Welcome," Rob said, opening the oversize front door.

We were standing in a great room, all white, surrounded by glass walls showcasing the panoramic view. Lounge-y couches faced outward, and the centerpiece of the room, on the inside wall, was an unusual, vast stone fireplace. A massive fire blazed, though not a soul was in sight to credit with having built it. I held my hands out toward the heat, trying to stop shivering.

"This fireplace is cut into the mountaintop. See?" Rob thumped his palm on it. "It was my idea. One solid piece of rock." Then he interrupted himself. "I'm a jerk. What you need is a hot shower."

Rob led me downstairs to a bedroom. The floors were polished concrete, smooth and shiny as an ice rink. One wall was the rough rock of the mountain; the rest were glass. The room jutted out over the uninhabited wilderness of the island. All the furniture was white and gray, and on the dresser was a steel vase, cut in jagged lines echoing the mountain vibe. In it were a dozen perfect roses.

"There's a bathroom in there," Rob said. "Take your time."

When I emerged from the shower, my wet clothes had disappeared from the bed and a white robe, which seemed to have been pre-warmed, was spread in their place. I put it on, took a picture of myself in the mirror, and forwarded it to Aurora with a text: *am at crazy private island with boy wonder. more later.* I rejoined Rob on a monolithic balcony that overlooked the harbor, where the yacht was docked next to another, smaller boat, so far down they looked like bathtub toys. Rob handed me a glass of water and took my hand. We sat watching the sun move across the sky, and my phone started chiming. Text after text, streaming in from Aurora. I slid my hand into the robe pocket and shut her down. Poor Aurora. I was torturing her.

It suddenly occurred to me that I was starving. It was after noon by then and we hadn't had a bite all day. As if someone had read my mind, a waiter appeared with a towering tray of food and gracefully slid it onto a table. I started to thank the man, but he disappeared before I could say a word.

"Don't worry about it," Rob said. "I want to pretend it's just us." There was clearly a staff up here—a chef, this waiter, someone who kept everything spotless and warmed bathrobes for guests—but from the utter silence you never would have known it.

The tray before me was spread with delicacies. On one side was a block of ice, carved with rocky edges and a flat top. Was I wrong, or did a narrow path winding up the side look exactly like the path we had climbed to get here? On the peak, exactly where the Lodge would be, was an architectural arrangement of sashimi and an artistic smear of wasabi. I raised my eyebrow. "We're supposed to eat the Lodge?"

Rob deftly picked up a bite of yellowtail with his chopsticks and popped it in his mouth. "I just ate your bedroom. Now where are you gonna go?"

On the warm side of the tray were small bowls of miso soup, tender bites of lobster somehow cooked with foie gras, and squid tempura. It was so over the top that it came all the way around again and tasted like comfort food.

For the first time that day, Rob and I sat face-to-face and talked. We covered unexceptional first-date ground—the annual ice-cream socials in his hometown (Hudson, Ohio), my frustration with this phase of my career, and our favorite places in the world. But what stood out to me was how easily the conversation flowed. He did more of the questioning, to be sure, and I did more of the talking. Here was a man who could have any girl he wanted. If I wasn't right for him I wasn't going to pretend otherwise. On the contrary, I did everything I could to emphasize the ways we didn't match. Where he was supremely confident and unflappable, I was overly cautious; a bit cynical; serious, but sometimes brazen. He persisted nonetheless. In a way, weirdly, that was what convinced me we belonged together.

A few hours later another boat arrived at the island. We watched its passengers disembark from above, and Rob pointed out his brother, Scotty; Scotty's gorgeous pregnant wife; and Geoff's girlfriend, Patricia.

"I'm wearing a robe. They're going to make assumptions," I said.

"Your clothes are probably ready. Let's check your room."

Indeed my clothes were back on the bed, now dried and folded—maybe ironed, from the look of them. Somewhere in this fortress was a roomful of Oompa Loompas cooking, washing, ironing, and God knows what else. I wondered just how carefully they were watching me. Before I went into the bathroom, I took one of the red roses out of the vase on the dresser. I broke it halfway up its stem and left it on the table. When I came out of the bathroom, two minutes later, there were a dozen perfect roses once again in the vase. There was no sign of that broken rose. No sign, in fact, that I'd been there at all.

By the time I returned to Rob, the new guests were sipping cocktails in the great room. Rob introduced his older brother as "the handsome Mars." Apparently when they were growing up Scotty had been the high school's star football player, a top student, the pride of the family. Even now, having taken a backseat to his movie star brother, Scotty radiated charm and self-confidence.

"I never watched your show; I must be the only one," he said.

"Oh, don't worry!" I said. "It's actually refreshing not to be confused with my character. People are constantly telling me that I shouldn't have set the family house on fire. I'm, like, *'It's a TV show.'*"

"Didn't I hear something about how you got the part? Something about how you didn't have to audition?"

"It wasn't like that exactly," I said.

Rob jumped in to tell the story, which had been reported in practically every feature ever written about me. He'd obviously read up on me, and he wasn't afraid to show it. "She turned down the audition for *American Dream* because her grandmother was dying."

The media constantly reported that I skipped the audition to be at my grandmother's deathbed. It was a better story, but it wasn't accurate. "Actually, she was just in the hospital," I said. "It was a massive stroke, and nobody thought she'd make it. But the doctors didn't know Granny."

Rob went on, "She wasn't about to leave her grandmother for some lousy lead in a network series. The showrunner, Steve Romany, gave her the part of Lucy McAlister anyway. Sight unseen."

"Actually, we'd met before," I explained. "And my mom sent him a tape of my high school play."

"Now I remember," Scotty said approvingly. "How honorable of you to set aside your dreams for your family."

"Thank you," I said. "I hope I haven't changed."

"Not if everything Rob has told me about you is true," he said.

I raised an eyebrow. Rob jumped in. "You embarrassing me already, dude?"

"Apparently he's heard all about me," I teased.

"Don't butt in," Scotty said to Rob. "We're getting along just fine without you." Rob threw up his hands and backed away in mock surrender.

Then, just to me, Scotty said, "I really want Robby to find someone. It's been six years since he and Lexy split up, and it's so hard for him to meet people."

"Seriously?" I said. "It's hard for Rob Mars to meet women?"

A long, rough-hewn table stretched out from the fireplace like the line of an exclamation point. Dinner had magically appeared on it: The Oompa Loompas at work again. Rob rematerialized at my elbow and guided me to a chair between him and Scotty. I was relieved. I hadn't talked to Geoff's girlfriend, Patricia, yet, but her mouth was set in a thin line and I had her pegged as an ice queen.

Rob had told his brother about me. I knew what that meant—or thought I did at the time, because I was still operating on the standard Boy Meets Girl protocol. In that manual, Boy Tells His Brother About You translated to: Boy Has a Crush on You. I was flattered, and talking to Scotty made Rob seem more like a typical vulnerable guy looking for love, with the added complication of being The Biggest Freakin' Movie Star in the Whole Wide World.

On my other side, Rob was talking to Geoff about an island in French Polynesia. "Rapa is a tiny dot in the middle of the ocean," he was saying, "three hundred miles from the closest island. The fruit I ate there was the best I've ever tasted. It's out of this world." Rob turned to me. "You don't realize how much pressure civilization exerts until you truly escape it. God, you would love it, Elizabeth. I hope to take you there someday."

Rob, who could go anywhere in the world, longed for the isolation of far-off lands. This bit of knowledge might have appealed to my sense of adventure. Or at the very least caused me to consider what it meant that this man had a thing for islands. But to be honest, all I heard was the word "someday." I made a mental note for Aurora. Rob was the opposite of my ex Johnny. Johnny couldn't commit to seeing me later the same night, much less "someday" in the vast and unpredictable future.

After dinner, the other guests made their excuses and turned in early. I smiled inwardly. It felt like they were conspiring. They wanted to give me and Rob a chance. Once again I got the sense I'd just passed a test that I hadn't even known I was taking.

The sun had dropped below the horizon, its fiery wake still blazing the sky. Rob took my hands in his. "Elizabeth, I'm having an amazing time. That boat is at our disposal. We can head back whenever you want. But I want to ask you if you're willing to stay here with me to-night."

Aha! There it was. He expected me to sleep with him on our first date. He'd shown up at my apartment without calling first, transported me to a secret island without telling me where we were going, and now he thought I would just hand it over? But of course he did. Because who *wouldn't* sleep with Rob Mars on the first date? I had to admit that he'd gone to a lot of trouble for a guy who could just walk into any bar in the world, snap his fingers, and have his choice of the hottest women around. Still, I wasn't about to give in. So what if he was Rob Mars? I wasn't any-one's conquest.

"Rob, this is so fantastic. You, this place, all of it. But I have to get home! I didn't plan . . ."

"Don't worry," he interrupted me. "You'll have your own room. We're not there yet. I'm very attracted to you, but I respect you too much to proceed with anything but caution."

"Do you always speak in . . . road signs?" He was just too perfect. I couldn't buy it. I needed him to crack.

"You want to know what I'm really thinking?" he asked, and now he was close, leaning against the wall to make himself closer to my height, his voice low and flirty.

"I think so," I said. Then he put his hand around my neck, pulled me toward him, and kissed me. And for every ounce of cynicism in my body, even knowing how gag-inducing these next words sound, I have to admit that an electric charge ran through me. I know, I know, but cut me some slack. There was a glorious sunset. I was alone on a balcony overlooking an island with a man who had been named *Glam*'s Sexiest Man of the Year more times than I knew. I was standing on my tiptoes to reach him, clean, warm, and buzzed, and that first kiss threw me completely under his spell. When we finally came up for air, I stood there, dizzy and dazzled, until Rob said, "P.S. I'm not gay." We laughed, and all the distance between us—our ages, our Hollywood status, the fact that he was the one calling the shots, the totally ridiculously over-the-top setting—it all evaporated and we were two regular people who wanted to know each other. And that's what the whole prolonged date was like. Moments that were normal and mundane and just like anyone else could have been experiencing, surrounded by events and situations so far outside the realm of normal experience that, after an entire day, it got hard to tell which was which. Living that way for months, or years, only made that distinction fuzzier.

But that night, in the moment of our first kiss, the extreme and ordinary met in a flutter that brought a flush to my cheeks. I'm always too cautious. I haven't missed a night of flossing since I got my first and only cavity in 1994. Three friends have extra sets of my keys, just in case. So what if I was going to miss my Pilates class in the morning? So what if tomorrow turned out to be the day my dream script arrived by messenger and I wasn't the *very first* girl next door to read it and respond to my agent? So what if my doorman silently noted my walk of shame the next day? I was tired of being so relentlessly well behaved. All that responsibility looked good on the outside, but I secretly knew that it was just fear. Fear of making a mistake. Fear of taking risks. Fear of the unknown. I felt safe with Rob. And I wasn't even going to sleep with the guy! It was time to be spontaneous for once in my life. This was an awesome, once-in-a-lifetime date and I wasn't ready for it to end. "Okay," I said.

"Okay . . . ?"

"Okay, I'll stay."

Rob saw me to my room, and it was hard to leave him, but it was what we both wanted. I clung to the knowledge that he would be there again in the morning, because I already didn't want us to be apart. We parted at my door. Walking back down the hallway, Rob tripped and caught his fall. Then he turned back and saw me watching him.

"Damn," he said. "You saw that."

"Aha," I said. "You're not perfect."

He swooped back toward me, took me up in his arms, and spun me around, with a deep, unforgettable kiss. "Am I a movie star again?" he asked.

"I like the you who stumbles. The one who doesn't get it on the first take," I said. He put his hand to his chest, thumping it against his heart. "Get out of here, cheeseball," I said, giving him a little push back down the hall.

I closed the door behind him, went to the bathroom, and stood looking at myself in the mirror. My hair had dried curly and was in desperate need of product. His stubble had chapped my chin. I stuck my tongue out at myself, giggled, then hid my face in my hands like a stupid teenager.

Holy smokes, this was actually happening. Then I crawled into the bed—high-thread-count, down pillows galore—and finally called Aurora.

That trip to Century Island was and still is sacred to me. It reminds me that I fell in love with Rob for real, for who he was and how we were together. Rob played gods and romantic heroes onscreen, and there was a reason he was so good at it. He was remarkably present. When we were together, he was completely in that moment and that moment alone. We were the only two people in the world. He believed in us, and I believed in him. Anything seemed possible. Sheer joy. An unimaginable love. Eternal life while circling an unbelievably distant star.

3

Rob liked to say that he put the pedal to the metal in our relationship. I liked to say "Please don't use car metaphors to describe us." In the beginning, every day was a step forward for us as a couple. Right after we returned from Century Island, he sent me two dozen long-stemmed red roses. The note just read "Yours." Roses have never been my favorite flower. So Hallmark-y. But they fit with Rob's unrelenting romanticism, which was slowly dismantling my cynical resolve. What was so bad about having a man send me the type of flower most symbolizing love? I decided to let myself enjoy more, judge less.

He called several times a day, just to see what I was doing. He texted me: *Here's what has been going through my mind all day: Elizabeth. Elizabeth. Elizabeth. Where is Elizabeth right now? What is Elizabeth doing right now? When will I see Elizabeth again? Elizabeth. Elizabeth.* Aurora joked that I was being stalked by the most famous man in the world.

Most of my previous relationships—okay, both of them—had begun with tipsy fumbling that escalated into hot and hurried sex. Rob, on the other hand, prepared for our first night together as if it were already an anniversary. One night at my apartment we were on my couch, making out.

He whispered in my ear, "We know this is going to happen." We rolled off my couch onto the floor. "We know it's going to be incredible," he said. He paused to look at me, and every hookup I'd had told me exactly what he was going to do next—but then, to my surprise, he stood up and helped me to my feet. "So why not make it one of a kind?"

I leaned in to him, my arms around his neck, my hips sealed to his, still in the moment. "What did you have in mind?" I whispered.

"My plane." Then he was gone, leaving me rumpled and alone. I looked at the clock. It was just before midnight. My Prince Charming was afraid of turning into a pumpkin.

A week and one private jet ride later, I called Aurora. I had to tell her—our friendship history mandated a full report of every sexual encounter—but this time was different.

"Definitely not gay," I told her.

She squealed. "I. Need. Every. Detail."

"It was great," I said.

"That's it? Crap."

I didn't tell her that having sex with Rob for the first time was unlike with any other lover I'd had. At first I'd had my doubts about the plane: Would the crew know? Would it be cozy and romantic, or was it stunt-sex? If people caught colds from breathing the air on commercial airlines, what would I catch having sex on a private jet? How much of my relationship with Rob Mars was destined to take place in exotic locales?

We boarded at a private runway in Malibu. As I met the pilot and the crew, I scrutinized each of them. Did they know why I was here? How many times had he brought women on board for this very purpose? Were they secretly laughing at my naïveté? Keeping score? But they kept to their tasks, friendly, with blank military precision. One snicker and they'd be fired.

Rob led me to a closed-off room that was outfitted like an elegant, minimalist hotel room. (Yes, there was a bed. That had been one of my unspoken requirements.) I lay back on the pillows, kind of figuring we'd get right to it.

"Slow down there, Lizzie," Rob said. "FAA regulations say we gotta sit in our seats for takeoff."

Oh. Right. There were two big white leather lounge chairs that looked funny with their regulation airplane seat belts, like those women who wear business suits and stockings, then cap off the look with sneakers for the walk to work. The pilot's voice came on, but instead of making any formal announcements, he just said, "You guys ready?" I looked at Rob. He raised his eyebrows at me.

"Ready?"

I nodded, and Rob pushed a button on the arm of his chair, sending our affirmation to the pilot. We were off.

I don't kiss and tell, but I will say that I, Lizzie Pepper, am an official member of the Mile-High Club (though as Rob pointed out we were a lot higher than that). It didn't escape my notice that I was joining a much more elite club at the same time: lover of Rob Mars. Maybe the grand production of the private plane took some of the pressure off him. If Rob Mars wasn't a stud, world markets would crash. But it was only afterward when I finally appreciated where we were. In bed, still entwined, we gazed out the four oversize oval windows at a blue, blue sky. Then I saw what Rob had wanted. We were alone, suspended above reality, cradled by a miraculous machine, floating in a strange balloon of luxury and danger. We had escaped the weight of the world. This was the isolation that Rob craved. He was right; it was worth it.

I didn't tell Aurora the specifics of that night. I didn't tell her about Rob saying to me, "I've looked down at the world from this plane hundreds of times, and every time it clears my head. But you've gone and made it foggy again." And I didn't tell her that every night since, Rob and I had fallen asleep with him wrapped around me like a blanket, and that all night long he kept his hand draped over my waist or his feet tangled in mine. In the morning when I woke up, the first thing I saw was his dark eyes, wide open, inches from my face, as if he'd been watching me sleep all night long. I most certainly didn't tell her that he had confided in me about the gay rumors, telling me the details of his sexual past. Those stories are his, and I will always respect his privacy on that count. What was most important to me was that he was honest with me, and that he trusted me with his secrets. I kept them from Aurora, and that was a first.

Rob had a house in Brentwood and a house in Malibu. Brentwood was a comfortable estate that Rob seemed to use as a crash pad when he had to be in L.A. for more than one day in a row and didn't feel like commuting back to Malibu. But in those first few weeks we were mostly in Malibu, where his house was on a private beach. The entrance was at street level, and the house went six stories down from there to the shoreline—built into the rock on the street side and open to the Pacific on the other. Every morning Rob brought lattes out to the balcony and the two of us sat reading scripts, pausing to share a line or to gaze out at the ocean. Of course, the difference was that Rob rejected every script he read, while I called my agent to discuss each one: It had little to do with how much I loved a particular part. There was only one Rob Mars, but at any given moment there were at least ten Lizzie Peppers, just off their own *American Dream*, and I felt the dark fear of actors everywhere: Each day in which I didn't land a part further convinced me I would never work again.

But when I looked up, the perpetually blue sky would wash away the shadows, drawing me back into the Hollywood fantasy: strolling on the dunes, being served by a private chef, staying in bed until the sun was high enough to hit the western-facing windows, and having your choice of parts, the hottest scripts with the finest directors in the business already attached, or willing to sign on if you were on board to play the starring role.

One of the biggest adjustments was something that at first felt like a small detail: Rob's household staff. They tried to stay out of our way, but there were a lot of them, and they came in twos. Two drivers. Two chefs. Two gate guards and two bodyguards. It was easy to get used to not lifting a finger. What was harder was the lack of privacy. Anticipating our needs meant being available, which meant being . . . around. When I went to the bathroom, I locked the door and felt stupid about it, protecting myself from the people who kept us safe.

After I'd been in Malibu about a week, a masseur showed up.

"He usually comes every day I'm in residence," Rob said. "I just wanted to update his nondisclosure before he met you."

Rob returned from his massage wearing a white terrycloth robe, his skin shiny with oil. "Joseph has his table set up in the spare room in the gym," he said. "Enjoy."

That, at least, is what I heard him say. There was, in fact, a door in the back of the gym that I'd never noticed before, but I found it locked. I knocked, but nobody answered. When I texted Rob—too lazy to run upstairs—he clarified that the masseur worked in the spare room *next to* the gym. (Oh, the problems of being fantastically wealthy—how do you name all the rooms in your palace?) The locked room, Rob told me, was his private office. I remember finding it something of a relief to know that the staff didn't have access to every nook and cranny of his life. I went next door and got the best massage of my life.

Afterward, sipping cucumber water on the back deck, my whole body felt like Jell-O. *a girl could get used to this*, I texted Aurora.

Our relationship was still a secret. I had always practiced standard celebrity discretion: baseball hat, sunglasses, nondescript clothing. I avoided paparazzi hangouts. My agency was across the street from Barneys, a perfect crosswalk for lazy paparazzi, so for the last couple of years almost every magazine shot had me carrying a Barneys bag. Otherwise, when the cameramen did find me on the street, which happened at most once a month, I posed quickly and they left. With the glaring exception of my recent breakup with Johnny, which had plunged me into a salacious spotlight for what I hoped would be a brief hell, my encounters with the press were mundane and routine.

But Rob lived on another plane of celebrity. I was known; he was worshipped. Where I got free designer purses, he got monthlong vacations in private châteaus. Where I had one incompetent stalker who constantly showed up at an apartment I hadn't occupied for five years, Rob had fans of *The Son* who were so convinced by his performance that they showed up in droves with photos of dead loved ones, wanting Rob to confirm the status of their souls. While I was walking red carpets at movie premieres, he was at the White House, watching his latest movie with the president, *at the president's request.*

Once discovered, our romance would be big news in the gossip magazines. We'd have to go public at some point, but first we wanted some time to enjoy our privacy and, though it was unspoken, to be sure the relationship was serious enough to warrant the media onslaught. Sneaking around was fun when it meant going shopping after dinner, with his assistant calling ahead and having the boutiques open just for us. We entered restaurants—certain restaurants only—through back entrances and dined in private rooms. What was missing was spontaneity. There was no taking walks, no popping out for pizza, no window-shopping. And we couldn't have a good old-fashioned movie date. Rob had screening rooms in both of his houses and a subscription to first-run movies. We could see anything we wanted, but only at home. Believe me, I wasn't complaining.

To me all the conspiring was a new adventure, but for Rob it was a normal, if inconvenient, way of life. One Sunday after we'd been together for only a couple of weeks, we had spent the day paddleboarding and sipping iced tea on the deck. After dinner I realized I needed tampons. Ordinarily I wouldn't have mentioned it to a guy I was dating—I'm not a prude, but I can tend to my own bodily functions, thank you. At Rob's, however, I didn't know how to handle it.

Rob was running on the treadmill, looking out at the ocean.

"Um, Rob? I assume you don't keep a stock of tampons for your lady visitors."

He chuckled. "No . . . you're in need?"

"I'm afraid so."

He stopped the machine, grabbed his cell, and started sending a text.

"Wait," I said. "What are you doing?"

"Asking Jake to pick some up for you." Jake was his assistant, a twitchy mouse of a man who never made eye contact.

"Seriously? I don't want Jake buying tampons for me," I said.

Rob paused. He seemed utterly bewildered by my words, as if I had just told him there was an armchair on his head. "What did you have in mind?"

Good question. I couldn't just drive to the store. The Malibu Country Mart was swarming with paparazzi, all of whom knew I didn't have my own Malibu pad. They would follow me to find out where—and with whom—I was staying. Nor could Rob Mars be seen buying tampons. Obviously. We stood there looking at each other for a moment. Here we were, with all the riches of the world at our disposal, and *we couldn't pop out to get a box of tampons.*

"Didn't Jake say it was his sister's birthday tonight?"

Rob nodded, and started to text. "It's too bad, but what can we do? This is an emergency."

It wasn't an emergency. It was a completely normal incident that became an "emergency" because of our ridiculous situation. But it was my new life.

A moment later Rob's phone dinged. He turned to me. "Regular or super?" he asked.

I buried my head in my hands in embarrassment. "Regular."

4

Rob and I had only been dating a month when I was due to host a benefit for LifeHeartTruth, an addiction recovery center that I'd picked as my requisite signature cause. We couldn't attend as a couple, not yet, but Rob had asked ACE to put him on the list. "So I can admire you from afar," he said. I wasn't sure his attendance was a good idea, mostly because I didn't want him to see what awaited me on the red carpet: the lowest level of paparazzi trash, all thanks to my exboyfriend.

Johnny Flaim and I had been together for a year and a half, and we'd broken up in an image-shattering public flameout only four months before I met Rob.

Like plenty of musicians—okay, all musicians—Johnny was a party boy. Which is the upbeat, non-libelous way of saying he had a drinking problem. (Now that he's been to rehab, I don't need to equivocate.) At first maybe I liked the idea of having a wild boyfriend—it was a way for me to break the rules without actually having to take any risks. But his boozing quickly got in the way of our relationship. Call me a prude, but I had no interest in pounding shots until three in the morning, and I didn't want to spend the first half of every day recovering from the night before. For a while, I just let him keep that part of his life separate from me—like a hobby. But, inevitably, his little hobby escalated into disaster.

We'd broken up just before Thanksgiving. I was finishing up my movie *Man of Her Dreams*, doing reshoots of a few critical scenes at the Grove, a popular outdoor mall in the middle of West Hollywood. The director, Olson Nelson, had decided he didn't like the lighting in a key scene, where I first recognize my love interest—a man I've never met but have been dreaming about night after night. I chase him down, only to have him treat me like a stranger.

During the last scene of the day, the one where my would-be love (Luke, played by the very sweet Matt Wilson) spurns me, Johnny showed up, drunk and belligerent. It was four in the afternoon; we had been working since daybreak; we were running late (costing the production God knows how much) and losing our light; and the director was blaming everyone but himself.

"Let's get it this time. Please, Lizzie," Olson said. Then we were rolling.

"I already told you, I've never seen you before in my life," Luke said.

"Just hear me out," I said, reaching to touch his arm.

He flinched and started backing away. "Look, whoever you are, you've got the wrong guy."

"You love crossword puzzles, and graffiti, and dogs," I said. "Especially little ones, even if it's less manly."

That freaked Luke out. How did I know these private details? "Leave me alone!" he said, pulling out his phone. "I'm calling the police!"

And that's when Johnny tackled him.

The rest of the sorry mess that ensued is available for viewing on your lowbrow media outlet of choice. Matt's black eye (which, on top of the needless pain and suffering, delayed production and triggered at least three insurance lawsuits). Olson diving into the fray (out of anger, it should be said, not honor). Me, hysterical, trying to pull Johnny out of the pile. And, worst of all, the clip of me that will live in perpetuity: mascara running down my face, screaming in a voice I don't recognize, "We are over!" A public breakup. This is what I had become right before I met Rob: the messy, angry, overexposed ex-girlfriend of a bar rat. The tabloids were in tawdry heaven for a good two weeks. Ever since, I'd been lying low while Johnny dried out at—you guessed it—LifeHeartTruth.

Tonight, the most sleazy press element would be hovering outside the benefit, hoping that Johnny would show, our paths would cross, and they would score pay dirt: a repeat performance. But Rob wanted to come, and I couldn't say no, given what his presence would mean for LifeHeartTruth.

We had to arrive separately to keep our relationship secret, but it was a blessing in disguise. Rob didn't have to witness the storm of questions about his predecessor. *Is Johnny here tonight? Is he clean? Will you get back together? Johnny says he did it for you, Lizzie. Can you comment?* I was doing my best to fend them off, but then, when I was only halfway up the red carpet, I heard a murmur ripple through the lunging cameramen. *Rob Mars—at the back door.* Miraculously, the sea of cameras parted as they rushed around the block in hope of seeing the man they had no idea was my new boyfriend. And then I realized what lay ahead. Soon, so very soon, I would be free from this bullshit. Rob Mars was the solution. The moment we went public, the spectacular news of my perfect media darling of a lover would leave my relationship with Johnny in the dust, and I could rebuild my image as a serious actor.

Inside, as I made the rounds, it was surprisingly titillating to peek over at Rob, who, though he was oblivious to it, was the sun around which the event revolved. Attendees tweeted even the smallest interactions with him. After that night, #LifeHeartTruth exploded and the resulting donations funded the center's new wing. So I guess it was worth it.

Rob and I had been together for a month. We were two normal people in the early stages of a promising relationship. Except that Rob had really nice houses, and we were in hiding in them. It was obvious that this couldn't go on indefinitely. One morning we met at ACE to plan our coming out before we were busted. I thought it would just be me; Rob; his brother, Scotty, who handled a lot of his press; and my PR rep, P. J., but we came up the agency's service elevator and were led to a boardroom full of people, all from ACE except for Scotty, P. J., Geoff, and, inexplicably, Geoff's girlfriend, Patricia, whom I still hadn't heard utter a single word.

To my great embarrassment, the room applauded the two of us, as if our relationship were a deal that had come through. Then Rob's agent, Matthew Brau, went through an impossibly detailed agenda: locations, scenarios, favors, exclusives, existing commitments, my wardrobe, whether we had purchased any form of birth control in any traceable manner, and God knows what else.

The first topic of discussion was reasonable enough: Where and when would we let the cat out of the bag? The Cannes Film Festival was only a couple of weeks away, in mid-May. Revealing our relationship on the red carpet, where everyone could photograph us at the same time, in a civilized fashion, would mean we controlled the story. It was all about controlling the story. Plus, the press would play nicely with the movie Rob would be promoting there—not his new movie, *Firing Squad*, but a documentary that he had coproduced on the exploitation of underage Indonesian fishermen in Australia.

Somebody, whose name I never learned, stood up to present magazine exclusives that had *already been negotiated*. In short order, the team established who would have which elements of the story, in what order, what the payments would be, and how the photo approvals would be spelled out. When P. J. started to question some of the language around the approvals, Matthew Brau turned to her and said, "We're working from boilerplate here," and shut her down.

This went on for a while. Rob must have seen the look on my face. He leaned over and whispered to me, "I'm hungry. Let's blow." It was music to my ears. When we slipped out of the room, nobody even noticed.

There was one thing I had to do before we went public. My ex-boyfriend was just out of rehab, and I didn't want anything to throw him off track. I had to tell Johnny about Rob before he saw it in the news.

Oh, Johnny. He was still very much in my heart. It sounds strange, but in some ways falling in love with Rob made me miss Johnny more. Johnny and I were the same age, and when we were together, we were at exactly the same point in our respective careers. We'd hit early stardom and we were ambitious. We both were constantly in demand—him for concerts, me for new projects—but we both struggled to figure out the best next move. Life was a grand adventure, with moments of daring and drama, and Johnny and I were in it together. Meanwhile, Rob, though older, more experienced, and more successful, put me up on a pedestal. He brought flowers every time he saw me. He surprised me with extravagant gifts. I felt like a princess. But, in a way, all that adulation kept us further apart from each other. Would we ever have what Johnny and I had? Would we ever be best friends? Or was I destined to feel like an honored guest in Rob's wonderland?

Johnny didn't pick up my call. I left a message saying that I had something I needed to tell him. On the phone the night before, Aurora had walked me through every possible scenario. "Sound grave," she'd said, "so he knows you're not trying to get back together."

"Don't worry," I added on the voice mail, "I'm not pregnant." Aurora had thought of that, too.

He called back a half hour later.

"This is awkward," I said, "but I wanted you to hear it from me first. I'm seeing someone."

"Okay . . ." he said.

"It's kind of serious. And I think because of who it is, we're all going to be in the tabloids again."

He sighed. "Just say it, Lizzie. I can take it."

"Rob Mars." There was a silence. Then he guffawed.

"Seriously?"

"Seriously."

"But you *have* a dad."

"Yeah, but Rob's way hotter than my dad."

Johnny laughed, and I suddenly missed him horribly.

"Okay, so that's why I'm calling," I said. "I apologize in advance."

"Thanks for the heads-up," he said. "I guess you can't do better than the Son of God."

"You're the only person I've told." That wasn't quite true, but I wanted to make sure he thought that I'd be able to pin any indiscretion on him. "Please don't tell a soul until it's out."

"You have my word," he said, and I knew that, so long as he stayed sober, he was good for it.

We talked a bit longer, about nothing, to pretend the heartbreak wasn't there. Then he said he had to go. "Be happy, girl."

"You too," I said, and hung up quickly. A sob tightened my chest, but I stifled it. Now Johnny knew, and he hadn't tried to stop me, and that proved I was doing the right thing.

5

We arrived in Cannes the afternoon before our first event—the premiere of *Fisherboys*. Our villa was nestled in the hills right above the center of the city. In the distance, the Mediterranean stretched for miles. Between the sea and the landscaping at the edge of the pool, I could see a bit of the harbor, and the rooftops of the stores that lined La Croisette. I felt the pull of the town—the house was relaxing and beautiful, but, looking below, it seemed like I was missing out. Then Rob said, "Come here, I want to show you something." He led me up to our bedroom. It was white and airy, with a big sliding glass door opening to a balcony above the pool.

"Close your eyes," he said.

I complied, and felt his hands drape something heavy around my neck. He turned me toward the mirror, then said, "Now look."

It was a diamond-encrusted heart-shaped locket, and it practically blinded me.

"Rob—" I started to protest.

"You can wear it tomorrow, on the red carpet," he said.

Oh, right. This necklace wasn't just for me. It was also for show. ACE had put him up to this. "Is it a loan?" I asked.

"Only if you don't like it," he said.

Aurora had always been a diamond girl. You wouldn't think it to meet her—she worked at a nonprofit and always wore jeans and her wild hair back in a tight bun. But she'd been planning and replanning her engagement and wedding since high school. The engagement ring alone had evolved from a simple round diamond solitaire to a vintage deco design. (I had to be kept up-to-date in case a boyfriend—though currently nowhere in sight—called me for advice.) To me, diamonds were like red roses and champagne and strapless dresses, and, for that matter, expensive purses. They were overrated, impractical, and, in the case of champagne and strapless dresses, not particularly good at doing the job for which they were intended. Diamonds were so clear and cold. They seemed almost cruel. I mean, if you were going to spend thousands of dollars on a jewel, shouldn't it at least have a little bit of color? Those were the arguments I made to Aurora, who desired nothing more than a two-carat rock on her finger. But if I admitted it to myself, the real reason traditional images of romance made me uncomfortable wasn't just because they were cliché, but because I was afraid they would never be mine.

Rob, standing behind me, leaned down to kiss my ear.

"Elizabeth, don't make this complicated. I love you. This is no big deal. It's a shabby representation of my love."

"Did you pick it yourself? I mean, was it your idea or did they come up with it in the boardroom?" I had to know if he was imitating his movies, or—even worse—taking advice from the agents. Rob was so . . . perfect. I still couldn't believe he was for real.

Rob looked hurt. "That's harsh."

"I just need to know."

"It's me, Elizabeth. Nobody tells me what to do. Period. And my advisers know that my love life is out of bounds."

It wasn't—I'd been at that meeting—but I knew what he meant. There was a line, and he was the one who had drawn it. Reassured, I looked in the mirror, and the multiple stones in the necklace caught the light of the sun, casting little rainbows all over the room. I gasped. Now I saw it. Diamonds hid their colors like secrets, ready to spill at the smallest provocation. They contain and reflect. They absorb their surroundings and throw them back, transformed. Maybe I'd been wrong about diamonds. I looked up at Rob. His eyes shone, and I decided that I could wear a heart of diamonds after all, because wearing it meant believing in him.

But not in front of everyone. Rob and I were going to be all over the press. What I wore would be scrutinized. Was I really going to parade down the red carpet with Rob Mars, wearing a new one-of-a-kind bauble? This necklace was a statement that I didn't want to make.

"It's beautiful," I said. "Thank you." I leaned over and gave him a kiss. "Can we walk through town first, before the red carpet? Tomorrow morning? In jeans?"

This fairy tale we were living, which all seemed too good to be true—I wasn't ready to flaunt it. I'd seen that roomful of advisers meticulously plan out every last detail of our unveiling. I was now proposing that we upend all of that. What would my boyfriend say to the idea? There was a pause—a tiny pause, but a pause nonetheless—before Rob grinned. "Let's do it."

Tomorrow, I knew, everything would change. I walked over to the balcony door and looked down at the town below. I'd always liked to live and visit places where you didn't need a car. To go for a run and see people in the midst of work, dogs snuffling at street corners, children twirling at the end of parental arms. To stroll to a restaurant for dinner and afterward, best of all, to walk home in the darkness so the evening's conversation wasn't halted by the slam of a car door but was allowed to flicker out in the quiet night like a spent candle. Tonight, maybe, I could stroll through Cannes. Certainly not with Rob, but maybe alone. I could eavesdrop on the sounds of the village, get lost on the unfamiliar streets. After tomorrow . . . never again. I remembered, back in L.A., how one night at my apartment I'd popped out while Rob was napping to surprise him with frozen yogurt when he woke up. When I told him what I'd done, he'd said, "Enjoy it while you can." I was just beginning to realize what he meant. Privacy required hiding from the world. And as soon as we let go of that, we would live in a fishbowl. Either way, we were trapped.

"This is an incredibly fancy jail, isn't it?" I said.

Rob walked over and stood behind me, looking at the same view. His body felt like a solid wall behind me. Then he reached forward and traced my faint reflection in the glass door.

"See yourself, Elizabeth?" he said.

I nodded.

"You're beautiful. But the woman I love goes deeper than that. They can capture your image as much as they want, but they will never have you." He hugged me tightly, and I felt his strong body soften into mine. "You are always free."

"So can we go for a swim?"

He glanced up at the hills to the right of the window, and I knew he was evaluating the security issues.

"Not until tomorrow."

I remember feeling light-headed when our car dropped us at La Croisette, the shop-lined boulevard that runs along the waterfront in Cannes. Rob and I loved each other, and there was no reason to hide a moment longer. We started to walk down the street together, and for a few precious moments I had what I wanted: I was strolling in a charming French village with my lover on my arm. Just an anonymous couple being quiet and boring and happy.

How many minutes passed? Three? Maybe five? I don't think we had time to say a word about the weather (which was gorgeous) or to glance in a shopwindow. All I remember is Rob bending down and whispering in my ear. "Brace yourself," he said, "it all starts now," and tucked my arm firmly under his elbow.

The landscape around us, a moment earlier shaped by the white rectangles of buildings, triangles of blue sky, the long slope of the beach, and the graceful lines of palm trees towering over the boulevard, was suddenly a seething block of bodies, each face obscured by what looked like a gas mask. Cameras. The paparazzi had found us.

"Lizzie! Rob! Over here, over here!" I slid my hand down Rob's arm, finding his fingertips. I thought we would stand there for a moment, posing and smiling, but Rob suddenly strode forward, directly toward the crowd. I scurried to keep up with him. The flashes came continuously now, and I forced a smile. Why wasn't Rob pausing? I wanted us to pose for the photos and be done. But instead we hurried down the street.

Revealing our relationship on the red carpet had one benefit that was now all too clear. The red carpet was always lined with rope to hold the paparazzi back. Now, with no such restraints, the men in the front of the swarm surged forward, planting themselves maybe five feet in front of us to get their shots. But the photographers behind them continued to push forward. The front cameramen struggled to stay standing, and for a moment it seemed like the mob would bear down on us. Rob stopped abruptly, putting his arm around me protectively. I huddled into him, anticipating the crush. *We didn't think this through*, I thought. *I shouldn't have interfered. We should have stuck to the original plan.* Then, from nowhere, two huge men appeared in front of us, arms spread wide: a barricade.

"Back, everyone, back. You'll get your shots." The crowd responded instantly, seemingly as relieved as we were that by some miracle these two bodyguards had taken control. A radius emerged around us; the sky reappeared; I realized that I'd been holding my breath, and exhaled deeply.

Half a block farther, Rob took me around the shoulder, gave me a tight half hug, and whispered, "This way!" He steered me in a sharp right turn, and there, idling next to us, was a limo with an open door. Our car. The "miracle" bodyguards slid in after us. The door slammed, and everything was quiet. I leaned back into the leather seat. Rob winked at me and smiled. "Perfect, Elizabeth!" He held up a hand for a high five. I'd been wrong. Rob knew this turf far better than I. He had made sure that the casual appearance I'd asked for was as planned as the red carpet would have been. It was choreographed down to the minute. I just hadn't been in on it. But instead of feeling belittled or betrayed, all I felt was gratitude. It was as if the karmic universe had said, "Let's let Lizzie get her way just enough to see that she was wrong, and she won't question us again." And it worked.

Sitting in the car, I knew that even as we caught our breath the photos of us were traveling through virtual space, being sold and distributed to news outlets across the globe. With every passing second, websites, blogs, producers, former costars, family, friends, the bizarre but undeniable universe of hundreds, no thousands, of people who cared that Rob and I were an item was expanding. For once I was kind of excited. Sure, I hated the paparazzi. It was no fun being photographed with a wardrobe malfunction at the beach, and it had been unpleasant to see the pictures of me and Johnny in a fight at the Red Sox game. (Why must my face get so blotchy whenever I cry?) But I was happy to be with Rob, and, now that I thought of it, I didn't yet have any pictures of us as a couple. I wanted to see what we looked like together. I might even want copies!

When we got home, Rob and I hung out by the pool. (According to our respective reps, if the paparazzi found us now it didn't matter so much. Because we'd controlled the news release. Or something like that.) Anyway, I couldn't really relax. I kept reloading TMZ on my phone. So sue me for caring. Aurora and I were texting: *any minute*, I told her.

calling my mother the minute it's out, she wrote back. Then another text came in from Aurora. *don't sweat it, pepper. the web people are lowest common denominator.* Uh-oh. I tapped a search into my phone: *lizzie pepper rob*.

Search results immediately came up on my phone. Lots of them.

```
Lizzie Aims High, Shoots for Mars

Lizzie Pepper Cast as Rob Mars Costar: It's All an Act

Liz and Rob: Love or Money?

Rob's Tin Lizzie: Fake Love at Last
```

What the hell was this? I looked up at Rob. He was reading a newspaper, so nonchalant.

"Babe?" I said. "It's out."

He nodded. "Okay."

"I haven't looked yet . . . but I think they're saying we're a sham."

"Yeah, because I'm gay, right?"

"It's so . . . mean."

Rob put down his paper. He smiled and my heart took a roller-coaster dip. I couldn't help smiling back. He came over and sat straddling the foot of my chaise, facing me. He set my feet on top of his thighs. "Who cares what they say? We have each other."

He leaned forward and gave me a long, deep kiss. My phone dropped out of my hand to the patio. I started to pick it up. "To hell with that," he said, pulling me back toward him.

I left the phone where it fell. Still, we went inside to have sex. We weren't idiots.

Later I read the articles. They were worse than I'd anticipated. The tabloids had indeed decided that our relationship was all an act. A business deal. We didn't love each other. Rob was gay. I was a status climber. Depending which "news" outlet you read, our "love" was orchestrated by One Cell Studio to prove that Rob, their best-known practitioner, was straight; or the relationship was a ploy for him to promote *Firing Squad* and for me to promote myself in general. Running alongside the ludicrous stories were the photos of us taken on La Croisette a few hours earlier. Rob looked like the tall, confident, handsome movie star that he was. I hurried two steps behind him at the end of his arm, like a child. My eyes were cast slightly downward, a dazed half-smile on my face. I looked like one of the Manson girls.

Rob didn't care about any of it. I wished the faceless people behind the tabloids and everyone who believed their crap could see how little he cared.

"When they don't have news, they invent it, Elizabeth. I don't blame them. It's a crappy job, but if they don't do it, someone else will."

It was a perfect response. I respected him for this attitude, but I didn't have such thick skin. The only bad press I'd ever gotten was when Johnny and I had that fight at the ball game, and when we split up. And even then I had to admit that they'd pretty much gotten it right. He was sometimes drunk and I was always miserable. We were breaking up and, unfortunately, everyone knew it. But this was the first time I'd had to read straight-out lies about myself, lies that made me sound like someone I was not.

My father was outraged. "I thought Rob's people were pros," he said on the phone that night. "I thought Geoff knew how to handle this."

Though I'd spoken to my father about my relationship with Rob, I'd never had reason to mention Geoff, the chronic mint sucker. How my dad knew that Geoff existed, much less that he might be involved in Rob's PR, was a mystery to me. But my dad hadn't built the biggest corporate consulting business in Chicago by twiddling his thumbs. Leave it to Dad to suss out the key relationships in my romance. No doubt he was worried that I was in over my head—and I certainly was.

My father wanted to know how we were going to spin this back down to earth. But when I asked my publicist, she just said, "There's no point in trying. This is what you get for dating Rob Mars. Take it or leave him."

Two weeks later, back in L.A., the press still hadn't let up. Every time we left the house, we were photographed. The photos were accompanied by the same negative rumors. Rob didn't care, but I felt like there was a shadow over our relationship and, for that matter, my image. I didn't want to be seen as a fame whore. People should know that what we had was real. This was love.

So that is what brought us to the infamous "Love of My Life" serenade on top of the car. Sigh.

Everyone already knows what happened, and I realize now how it looked to the world, but if you will, please try to see it all through my eyes: Rob and I were on our way home from a charity luncheon at Geoff and Patricia's in Beverly Hills. The paparazzi had followed us there, and now they were following us back home. Earlier that day, *Rounder* had released a particularly offensive article, listing the professional pros that being in a relationship with Rob offered me. They labeled me "career-climber Lizzie." I was quiet on the way home, and Rob knew why.

"It doesn't matter. It doesn't mean anything," he said for the umpteenth time.

"I know. You're right. But I still care."

"Pull over," Rob suddenly said to Lewis, the driver. We were on Beverly Drive, in the heart of Beverly Hills. The sidewalks were thick with pedestrians, an anonymous mix of locals and tourists. Lewis swerved sharply to the curb, and there was nearly a paparazzi pileup behind us. They slammed on their brakes, stopping in a cluster around us.

"What are you doing?" I said.

"I'm going to tell them the truth. I love you. Plain and simple." Rob threw the car door open. The cameramen were out of their cars at once, pushing closer, an eager, confused mass.

"Rob—stop!" I said, but he was determined.

"Come," Rob said, and took my arm, pulling me out after him. He lifted me up to sit on the hood of the car.

A crowd instantly gathered on the sidewalk, cell phones raised in salute, and the moment Rob climbed up to stand on the hood in front of me, they went wild. Like every girl who was a teenager when *Great and True* came out, I knew Rob's "Love of My Life" scene. His serenade of Lexy Hartfield in the bed of the pickup truck was the moment preserved in the poster that Aurora had on her bedroom door, the scene that had won the hearts of girls across America. It had been replayed on entertainment TV ad nauseam when he and Lexy got married. And now it was happening to me.

Rob started crooning "Love of My Life."

"Oh my God, stop! You ridiculous person." I stood up next to him and rose on my toes to kiss him, not a little bit desperate to shut him up.

He put an arm around me and we faced the crowd. He said, "Let me introduce the love of my life, Elizabeth Pepper!"

And just like that, I was christened with a new, sophisticated brand. Lizzie Pepper, girl next door, was all grown up and worthy of Rob Mars. Henceforth, I was to be Elizabeth Pepper. Frankly, I had no idea people would make such a big deal about it. My real name had always been Elizabeth. It was on all my credit cards and checkbooks. It felt a bit too formal and un-me—Aurora teased me for it—but Rob liked it, and I thought I'd get used to it. I was a woman now, even if I didn't exactly feel like one.

Rob leaned down and whispered in my ear, "I love you." You saw that happen on YouTube, but what you didn't know was that it was the first time he had told me he loved me. I mean, he'd talked about his love for me, as in "I don't mind having people see that we love each other," but this was the first time he had said those three words, simple and direct. Leave it to Rob to save it for a dramatic moment.

We pulled apart and paused for a moment, looking into each other's eyes. I saw my sweet Rob, willing, wanting to give me the world. He loved me with all his heart, and those grand gestures were the only way he knew to express it. Swept up in the moment, I forgot the pedestrians, the paparazzi, the slightly precarious car hood. All I wanted was to show Rob that he didn't need to try half this hard. I took his hand and pressed it to my heart. How did I think people would respond? Well, if I'd thought about it, I would have assumed that everyone would recognize the love that connected us.

And so it was awful when the world decided that what they were seeing was the exact opposite.

So much for countering the negative response to our Cannes debut. Instead, the press was brutal. Poor Rob, he bore the brunt of it. People didn't believe it was a spontaneous act of love. They called him a manufactured brand, a robot attempting to play the role of a man in love. The YouTube meme, the talk show sketches, the political cartoon showing the president sitting on a car while the House speaker sings to him. For the life of me, I could not see what they thought was so bizarre. Rob shrugged it off. "We can't win," he said. "Next week they'll love us again."

Needless to say, my father, who called us the very next day, was apoplectic. He raged at Rob, who stayed on the phone with him, serious and focused, saying, "Yes, sir," every so often until my father had exhausted himself. Not the best first impression a boyfriend's ever given my dad, but (thanks to Johnny) far from the worst. Afterward, Rob told me that, with all due respect, my father would forget it as quickly as everyone else.

"Ha," I said. "You don't know my father."

As I've said, Rob has pretty thick skin. But I don't. Having people be so merciless toward us, something changed in me. One night I was sitting at the kitchen counter with my laptop, reading the comments on a particularly scathing *Glam* piece ("Lizzie Pepper Drops Name and Personality"), when Rob came up to me, closed the laptop, and took it to the study.

"Hey!" I followed him. Sure, it was a waste of time, but that didn't mean I wanted him to confiscate my computer like I was a naughty child.

"It's enough," Rob said. "As soon as you let go, you'll realize how little it matters." He took my hand and kissed every finger. As he did, he spoke, saying one word between each kiss, "I have you. You have me. Our love is everything."

That was the moment of decision for me. I had watched carefully as Rob rode out every aspect of the debacle with aplomb. He was so inscrutable. He seemed above it all, immune to public opinion, free of any self-doubt. At times he really did seem like the too-perfect robot the vicious press had labeled him. *Was* he for real? It was time for me to make up my mind. Would I trust this man? Would I take him at face value? Was his calm reserve an empty shell, as the media would have it, or was it really possible that this wasn't all an act, that he was the same strong, confident prince all the way to the core?

I chose to have faith in Rob. While the rest of society was full of mean-spirited judgment, Rob just kept right on loving me. In my prior relationships, I'd been the stable one, the rational one, the decision maker. Compared to Rob, I was the inexperienced child who had so much to learn. It felt like a load off my shoulders.

His certainty anchored me, and yet he wasn't too good to be true. Rob wasn't a perfect lover, smooth and cinematic. He was sweaty and trembling and questioning and vulnerable. There was a deeper Rob, I needed to believe, one he still hadn't let me fully see. I caught glimpses of it in our most intimate moments. Our bed felt like a little boat on a stormy sea, where it was us against the elements. If we had to cling to our vessel, isolating ourselves from public opinion and judgment, waiting for a change in tides, or charting a course to foreign lands, so be it.

"You're right," I said. "We don't need Hollywood. We make a perfect universe of two."

The next weekend, I moved in with Rob.

6

The only work I had managed to line up for the summer was an appearance on *Apartment 3J*. Guest-starring on such a popular sitcom was a stopgap. It was taking far too long for me to get a movie, and meanwhile the media was trashing me. A guest appearance would bolster my image in the gap before *Man of Her Dreams* was released in November.

The part wasn't hysterically funny, but at least it had some depth. I was playing Benji's long-lost high school girlfriend—his first love—so I essentially got to play two characters: a hopelessly-in-love teenager in his flashbacks to high school, and a current-day woman who'd outgrown puppy love. I was psyched to work with Colin Anthony (who played Benji). He carried that show, as far as I was concerned.

The first day of rehearsals went well, when we played our googly-eyed high school selves. But the next day we were working on the second act, when he tracked me down at my law firm and I had to spurn him. For some reason I wasn't nailing the character. The director kept telling me to warm her up. "How can I 'warm up' rejecting him?!" I wanted to shout back, but instead I just smiled and thanked him for the thought and then kept doing it the only way that made sense to me.

That Thursday night we started shooting before a live audience, and

I still had no plan for how to fix my performance in the second act. Then, after the first-act break, I heard a buzz on the set. Rob had appeared to surprise me, a huge grin on his face. We slipped into my dressing room, and I wolfed down some craft services mac and cheese.

Rob asked me how it was going. I told him I couldn't find the balance between outgrowing my relationship with Benji and being a cold bitch.

"Do you love me?" he asked.

"Totally," I said.

"But what about Justin?" My *American Dream* boyfriend, both in the show and off camera, as everyone knows.

"What about him?"

"Don't you still love him?"

"No!"

"Of course not," he said. "You love me. But doesn't the twenty-year-old you still love him, in some bittersweet, wistful way?"

I thought about Justin. My first kiss—first onscreen, then off—my first love. On *American Dream* we worked sixteen-hour days, but there were awkward chunks of downtime between takes, when they reset lights and we were at loose ends. Justin had been my salvation.

"Let's explore!" he'd say. I'd resist, afraid to stray too far from the set. But he'd drag me away, into the rolling Tennessee hills if we were shooting outside, off into a corner of the former city hall that served as the family mansion, and, once, on the soundstage, up a series of ladders to a nosebleed catwalk the lighting crew used only while in safety harnesses. We smoked cigarettes until we set off the smoke alarms, then hid up in our aerie, undiscovered, until the excitement died down.

Our adventures inevitably turned romantic, and there was nothing better than sneaking off to make out in a former courtroom or coming back from a "nature walk" with leaves in my hair and a blush on my cheeks.

I thought about who I'd been with Justin: not just Lizzie Pepper, but the first-time-in-love Lizzie Pepper. A once-in-a-lifetime version of my-self, glowing with the new feeling of connecting with another person. In the middle of getting notes from the director, a glance from him spread warmth through my body. His hand on the small of my back was every-thing to me. When I walked, my fingers twitched in the air, remembering the sensation of his skin.

Years had passed since then. I was over Justin, rationally and emo-tionally, as much as I ever would be, but I would always feel nostalgia for the heights of romance I had discovered with him.

"There!" Rob interrupted my reverie. "That was it. I saw it on your face. First love ends but never dies. Go there."

When I returned to the set, we shot the scene on the first take.

That night, back home, I thanked Rob for helping me. "Is that how you connect with each of your characters? Find something from your life?"

"It's not quite that simple. Mostly I have to credit One Cell. What practicing at the Studio has done for my acting is incredible."

There it was.

It was so casual, so thrown away that I'd nearly missed it. But none-theless, there it was.

In the four months that we'd been dating, Rob had only mentioned the One Cell Studio a handful of times, and only in the most dismis-sive, don't-even-ask-me-about-this manner. And yet I knew how impor-tant, how present, it was in his life, not just from the tabloids and rumors, but in the many times a week he would go to the Studio to practice, in the meetings that sometimes filled his days, the private phone calls, the time he would occasionally spend inside that office he had behind the gym.

But really, all I knew about One Cell was what everyone knew, or thought they knew. It was a secretive, possibly cult-y meditation group whose practitioners wore simple burlap robes and, supposedly, used superpowerful magnets to channel their energy, or something like that. I often drove past its center of operations—a massive green marble mono-lith that loomed over Beverly Hills. Nobody knew what went on beyond those high, Oz-like walls. But there were an unusual number of A-list celebrities among its followers, actors whose work I deeply admired. To my mind, there was no way all of those respectable, successful people, including Rob, were brainwashed.

Aurora had half-jokingly warned me, on more than one occasion, not to get sucked into Rob's crazy cult. That never seemed possible. In fact, I'd begun to think that maybe Rob intended, for whatever reason, to keep me separate from that part of his life indefinitely.

But now, just the tiniest sliver of an opening dangled in the air be-tween us, inviting me—if I wanted—to ask Rob more about the Studio. One Cell, it seemed, was the key to my boyfriend's acting talent. And—if it really was so core to his life—it could also lead to the deeper Rob I longed to access, the imperfect Rob with doubts and needs and unmet desires, the frog behind the prince.

I waited a moment longer, then dove in.

"One Cell. The cult," I said. "What's the real story?"

"There's a lot of misinformation out there," Rob said. "But I'll let you make your own judgments. I first heard about Teddy Dillon and her brother, Luther, about twenty years ago, when they were just starting to develop the One Cell Practice. Not sure what you'd think of Teddy, but she's a genius. She has her PhD in organic chemistry, but it wasn't until she spent five years living in the desert with the Aborigines that she put the science and meditation together. My acting coach for *The Son* sent me to Teddy. Before I began practicing at the Studio, my acting was just . . .

seat of the pants. Through the Practice I learned to harness a range of emotions I hadn't even experienced *in my own life*. I was so jazzed by what she was doing that I spent six months at the first Studio in Fernhills. My involvement took off from there."

"How come I've never taken one of the classes? I mean, you've never even invited me," I said.

"You have your own set of principles. I don't want to inflict mine on you. I'm just glad you let Geoff steal me away a couple times a week to go to the Studio."

"Geoff is involved?" This was news to me, but I had never tried to understand the roles of the many people who orbited around Rob.

Rob laughed. "Wow, I'm terrible aren't I? Geoff is actually the head of PR for One Cell."

Oh my God! "Geoff is *Geoffrey Anciak*!" I was an idiot for not making the connection. Whenever the One Cell Studio was mentioned in the press, Geoff Anciak was the one quoted, usually making another futile effort to dispel the rumors of the day. When we'd gone on what I thought was *Geoff's* yacht to what I thought might be *Geoff's* island—it was all part of One Cell. No wonder my father had known who he was. Geoff was the public voice of the Studio. Naturally he would consult with its most high-profile practitioner.

Over the next couple of weeks, I watched Rob through a slightly altered lens, wondering which parts of his confidence came from the Studio, and if and when he would invite me into this part of his life.

Now that I was paying attention, I noticed that sometimes Geoff picked Rob up in his Maserati (to my credit, it never occurred to me that high-ups in an organization famous for group meditation in burlap robes would drive bright red sports cars. Only in L.A.), and, one time, he came for dinner with his girlfriend, Patricia. That night, Geoff didn't talk much; mostly he exchanged sucking on Altoids for chewing food, but after dinner he and Rob went out to the balcony, leaving me with Patricia. I tried to pry conversation out of that husk of a woman while she wordlessly knit a dreadful sea-foam green scarf. Finally, I just went for it.

"I know this is ridiculous, but I only recently realized your connection to the Studio. I'm so curious about that part of Rob's life. I'd love to hear more."

Patricia didn't look up from her knitting, but she did finally speak. "Love and self-understanding go hand in hand. Both require a commitment to the whole, in spite of its flaws—even in your darkest moments, even if it means great sacrifice. We are imperfect without, but we can always strive for balance within. This is a challenge one must choose to undertake. Rob would no more tell you to take up our practice than he would tell you to love him."

Wow. That was a lot from Patricia. I understood her message, or so I thought at the time: Rob was privately hoping I would join him in his practice, much as he hoped our relationship would succeed. Loving him—knowing him—meant doing this, and I resolved to try.

"I want to learn about One Cell," I said to Rob later that night. "It's so important to you—will you share it with me?"

"I'd love to," Rob said, "but don't do it for me. You have to come to it yourself." It was just as Patricia had said. The effect of Rob's mildness, his seeming ambivalence, was to pique my curiosity. I had to know more, to be a part of it, to be wanted. My desire for Rob and my desire for One Cell mingled, intense and inseparable.

"I'm ready," I said.

What I didn't think about at the time was the rest of Patricia's cryptic comment. What were these "dark moments" of being and love? What kind of sacrifice was required? Only looking back do I see that she was trying to tell me something. Trying to warn me.

A few days later, after almost five months of dating Rob, I found myself entering the mysterious gates of the great emerald One Cell Studio on Wilshire Boulevard. Nobody knew what actually went on in there, but there were plenty of rumors. Group meditations that went on for twenty-four hours, nonstop. Brainwashed actors chanting in unison to land each other lead roles. Families that joined the Practice and seemed to disappear into a black hole. There was so much speculation about what went on inside this impenetrable fortress that it was impossible not to feel special. Those mysterious doors were about to be opened for me. I texted Aurora, *entering the studio. stand by for intervention.*

dying, she wrote back. *tell all asap.*

will do, I promised, then shut off my phone. One Cell policy.

Instead of pulling into the circular drive out front, our driver turned into an alley and dipped down into an underground garage. He dropped us off at an elevator bank in the far back corner. Finally, I was entering the exclusive retreat. I pictured doors with immense locks and secret chambers lit by candles. A bit overeager, I reached to push the elevator's call button, but Rob grabbed my hand.

"Easy, girl. Follow me."

He opened a door to a bare metal stairwell. I wrinkled my nose. *Really?* We were going to walk up the seedy, airless garage stairs? (Not to be a diva, but I kind of have a phobia about being trapped in a stairwell—by an earthquake, fire, a stalker fan—the standard stuff.)

"Trust me," Rob said. He stepped around the stairs to a plain door. Nailed to it was a tiny brass letter. An "M."

"M for Mars?"

Instead of answering, Rob put a key into the knob. The door opened silently. "M" for Mars indeed.

"Your private door has a chintzy lock, I want you to know," I said, poking him in the ribs.

Rob chuckled. "You're hard to impress."

The cone of silence around the Studio was so powerful that I guess I really did expect the halls to be lined with robed Illuminati, carrying candles and wax-sealed documents containing the secrets to world domination. Instead, the halls were bathed in sunlight, as it turned out that the massive building surrounded a bright, grassy courtyard filled with café tables and babbling fountains. There were people having tea alone with a newspaper or in small groups. Watching these people, chatting and laughing and wiping their chins with napkins, I couldn't help but be surprised at how . . . normal it all seemed. It reminded me of those photo spreads in magazines showing celebrities doing "normal" things: One Cell practitioners are just like us! They read the sports section! They have sneezing fits! They spill water on their bagels! I'd pictured a lot of things going on behind those walls. This was never part of my image.

Rob led me to his parlor and office. (Another operational base. Just what he needed. Malibu, Brentwood, Aspen, and New York weren't enough. Because sometimes a man's in Beverly Hills. . . .) A one-way window looked straight across Wilshire Boulevard to the ACE offices. Down the block was Rodeo Drive, the high end of the high end. "Drop in for some guided meditation, then pick up some baubles at Walford Diamond," I joked with Rob. (It was a joke, but Rob definitely did just that on more than one occasion. Not complaining.)

The walls of his One Cell office were hung with photos of himself: Rob standing with groups of robed practitioners; Rob meeting the Dalai Lama; Rob accepting an award from a tall, auburn-haired woman I would later find out was Teddy Dillon, the cofounder of the Studio. Next to Rob

I recognized Geoff, and on his other side an attractive brunette. At first I didn't get it. What kind of movement was this, giving a celebrity a vanity office suite and handing out trophies?

I sat down on the couch and beckoned to Rob. He joined me.

"Thank you for finally bringing me here," I said.

"Thank you for wanting to come."

I leaned in to kiss him, and he kissed me back but he kept it chaste, turning away abruptly.

"Sorry, Elizabeth," he said, "but this really isn't the place."

I felt horrible, like I'd been trying to corrupt him. In a way I was trying to prove to myself that his love (and lust) for me was stronger than his commitment to any organization. Come to think of it, that is kind of corrupt. I apologized and then said, "Rain check?" and I got the familiar smile that told me he was mine enough.

Rob led me back out to the courtyard. On the way he showed me a simple meeting room that reminded me of the chapel in our church back home. A group of burlap-robed people sat quietly, eyes closed, while a tape played a woman's soothing voice. I caught a bit of it: "The choices you make determine your fate. One step at a time, you lead yourself forward . . ." It seemed harmlessly yogic. There were offices, a few lounges, and other empty rooms surrounding the courtyard. The "weirdest" thing was that some of the rooms had floors covered with sand. Rob explained that part of the Practice was to meditate while standing on sand or earth as a way of grounding one's energy. Also, almost everyone seemed to be wearing the same kind of necklace that Rob never took off, a simple string with a few beads. That was all! This was the "crazy cult world" that was so impenetrable and mysterious. There were no mystical totems and idols. No spiral-eyed, chanting actors. No initiation rites. No magnets. No levitating. It was situated on a multimillion-dollar property in the heart of Beverly Hills, but otherwise the place was unexceptional. It looked like a run-of-the-mill community center where senior citizens might learn Spanish and AA meetings happened every Wednesday night in a room with folding chairs and a limited supply of doughnuts. Where was the big mystery? Why was everyone so worked up about One Cell? Headlines would be made if only the press could see how mundane it all was.

I did, however, see a change in the way Rob carried himself here. He was in less of a rush, walking more slowly, stopping to talk to people along the way. He knew everyone's name and asked them personal questions, like whether a sick dog had improved and how someone's audition had gone. He seemed very relaxed, and as we made our tour I started to see why. At events he had to be on—acting the part of Rob Mars. And at home he seemed to relish the quiet. It was only on the rare occasions when we had a dinner with friends and family that I'd seen him let down his guard like this. He wasn't gossip fodder here; just, it seemed, a respected community member. I could certainly see why that appealed to him.

I had never been a joiner. My family belonged to a country club, and we went to church on Christmas and Easter, if we weren't on a holiday trip, but I had never stumbled on a particular community whose philosophy or beliefs inspired me. The closest I'd had to that was being on location for *American Dream*, with a cast and crew that became like a family, but since I was at least ten years younger than most of the other regular cast members, it wasn't exactly a community of peers.

Rob, in the little he'd told me, had said that the basis of the Studio was intense internal work that taught you a new way to be in the world. Rob was famous for having walked on coals to prepare for the role of Jesus in *The Son*. (Yes, for the record he absolutely knows that Jesus walked on water. It was an exercise in commitment, not miracles.) But what I admired most about him was more subtle. It was his total outlook— the steady confidence, his acting, the complete embodiment that made him a convincing (albeit controversial) Jesus—all this he credited to the Studio. What they called the One Cell Whole Body Principles.

So now I was trying to see how exactly all that righteous self-knowledge went down in this expensive but rather generic piece of Beverly Hills real estate. I wanted to understand One Cell. I had to, if I was going to stay serious with Rob. It was a still mysterious part of my boyfriend's life.

But it didn't turn out to be Rob who really brought me to the Studio. It was Meg.

When we walked out into the courtyard, we ran into Geoff, and a woman Rob introduced as his friend Meg. I recognized her as the attractive brunette from the picture in Rob's office. Meg was about my age, tall and slender, her hair even longer and darker than mine. With big, natural waves. It was like my hair after two hours' prep for an award show. If the Whole Body Principles could give me hair like that without professional help, then I was all in. Except hers had a purple streak down the side. Not exactly what I'd expected from a meditation devotee. She had pale, smooth skin and a dimpled smile that revealed small white teeth.

"Hey, welcome," she said.

"Thanks."

"I've known Meg a long time," Rob said. "You guys are going to like each other."

"Cool," I said. But I felt suddenly shy, like I was meeting Rob's family all over again. The four of us—me and Rob, Meg and Geoff—sat down to coffee. When the four of us were at the table together, my age difference with Rob stood out. Like we were two young women sitting there with our fathers.

When Geoff and Rob started talking, Meg ignored them and turned to me. "So, what do you think?" She gestured to the buildings surrounding the courtyard. "It can't possibly live up to the hype." Her smile was warm and slightly mischievous.

"Depends," I said. "Do I have to chant before I drink this latte?"

She shrugged. "Only if you seek eternal enlightenment. Whatever." We both laughed, and I immediately saw that we would get along. Also, although I wouldn't have been able to articulate it at the time, I was eager for a friend who understood my boyfriend's world. Meg could be my translator.

After we all had coffee, Geoff and Rob disappeared to attend to the vague and seemingly never-ending Studio business, and Meg and I got refills.

"How long have you been part of the Practice?" I asked Meg. It was weirdly easier to ask Meg than it was to talk to Rob about the Studio.

"Oh gosh, since I was a kid," Meg said. She explained that when she was eleven, her parents had moved to Fernhills in Northern California to practice with Teddy and Luther, and that she'd grown up in the small community in that town, where nearly everyone practiced at the Studio.

"I feel lucky," she said. "Growing up at Fernhills, there were no mean girls in my class—I mean, there were only four other kids my age! I never hated my mother as a teenager. I never drank or did drugs. I mean, it wasn't perfect, but for the most part it was like being part of a huge family, where everyone was a trusted friend."

That was what I'd seen in Rob. The comfort. The *trust*. "Were you allowed to hang out with people outside the Studio?"

"Sure," Meg said. "But it didn't happen a lot. We had our own school at Fernhills. Then, for part of high school, I worked in an ice-cream parlor. I made norm friends—that's what we called people outside the Studio—but I saw how different I was from other people my age."

"What made you different?" She seemed pretty "norm" to me.

"American kids learn to pass tests and please adults. They perform like circus animals and are rewarded with degrees and jobs, but they never reflect. They have no balance. And eventually they get depressed, divorced, and have midlife crises. They have no idea who they are. Before I came to the Studio, I hated school. But in our one-room schoolhouse, I was encouraged to think about my place in the world. Who was I? What did I want to achieve? What motivated me? What obstacles did I face and where did they originate? How could I bring my dreams to fruition?"

I could see the appeal. Rob had no interest in the mundane. Even when he relaxed with the paper, he read world news only, no fluff. He constantly sought to better himself and others.

"It's almost a hippie philosophy," Meg said, "but without the drugs. Or alcohol. Or free love."

"No beer?" I asked.

Meg laughed. "People get hung up on those details, but that isn't the real point. The kids at the norm high school in our town drove around all weekend looking for unlit corners where they could get wasted and forget who they were. I felt sorry for them. I don't want to sound snobby, but I guess I still do. Living by the Whole Body Principles is incredibly joyful. You learn to have perspective on yourself—your emotions, needs, desires—once you see these from a distance, you can think so much more clearly. Teenagers are supposed to be angsty and petulant, but I spent my adolescence feeling centered, calm, and confident. It was awesome." When Meg spoke, she didn't seem at all like a brainwashed zombie. She was a straight shooter—she'd grown up in this unusual world, but she had perspective on it and how she fit into mainstream society.

We'd finished our refills, and now a waiter brought us ice water. Meg jumped up and gave him a hello kiss.

"Hey, Warren."

"Hey, Meg. Where's Rob?"

"This is Elizabeth," she said. "She's Rob's girlfriend."

"Nice to meet you," he said, shaking my hand. "Welcome."

He walked away. "You kissed the waiter," I said.

"I totally kissed the waiter," she said. "I've only known him since I was five." She took a rubber band from around her wrist and swept her dark hair up into a high ponytail. "See? That's why people think we're freaks." She laughed. Her eyes were bright blue and crinkled sweetly when she laughed.

I had started playing Lucy on *American Dream* when I was seventeen. From the moment the pilot aired, I'd been famous. After that, my friends fell into two camps: those from before—the high school buddies who had "known me when." And those from after—the friends I'd made in my adult life. My old friends were trustworthy, but I didn't have much in common with them anymore—even Aurora treated me like an exotic pet. And as for my new friends, well, actors were great fun at a dinner party, but you couldn't text them without it showing up on Twitter. So, yeah, as a whole my friendships were a sad state of affairs. But here was a bright, lively woman who had a completely different life, brand-new ideas, and inside knowledge of my boyfriend's world. I was captivated.

Meg stirred her ice water with a straw. "What about that boyfriend of yours? Hasn't Rob told you anything about the Studio?"

"No," I admitted. "It's weird . . ."

"He's probably just trying not to scare you away," Meg said reassuringly. "He knows I'm a blabbermouth. This whole conversation? All part of Rob Mars's master plan." She swirled her arms in the air like a sorcerer stirring a potion.

"Okay, well, in that case will you tell me how exactly it all works? What *is* the Practice?"

"It's pretty simple, actually. Here's an example. You go to your doctor for a regular checkup, feeling perfectly fine, and she tells you she hears something wrong with your heartbeat. You have a bunch of tests, wear a heart monitor, run on a treadmill with wires attached to your chest, and finally they tell you it's an arrhythmia and you can control it with medication, but you don't have to. So all that worry and testing, and turns out you're fine. But they can fix you anyway. This kind of thing happens all the time: in medicine, in schools, in the offices of plastic surgeons. As soon as we look for problems, we find them.

"One Cell believes the opposite. If you look for solutions, you'll find them everywhere. Pause to ask yourself the most basic questions about who you are and what you want, and answers will manifest.

"You probably know that at the Studio we do group meditations. The Practice actually has three parts: Grounding, Connecting, and Energizing. Grounding is a silent standing meditation. It's kind of intense. I mean, it's harder than you think, but you really learn to feel your place on Earth, and you observe the paths your mind follows in the strict absence of external stimulation. The physical practice is a critical element. It really connects your body to your mind in a way that changes how you function in the world. You wouldn't believe it until you experience it. After that we move into Connecting, which is a guided brain journey. That's where you learn about the Whole Body Principles in a relaxed state that helps you broaden your perspective—your emotions, needs, desires. Once you see these from a distance, you can think so much more clearly. And the last part is Energizing, where we do poses that are designed to channel all those ideas and revelations from your heart and brain centers to your fingertips."

Ah yes, those Studio poses. Hollywood lore credited them for lean strength, the toned but slender bodies we all were expected to bring to every role, no matter the character.

"The best part is the 100. Have you heard of it?"

I'd heard of the 100. It was part of the Studio's cult-y lore. "Is it like group therapy?"

"Sort of," Meg said, "but it's a little more direct. You join a Core Group for the Practice, and when it's your turn, during the Grounding, your leader asks you questions—it's actually a lot more than 100 questions. Truth comes out—the truths you've been keeping from yourself. Once you've uprooted your ugliest, hardest, deepest fears and desires, you face life in a completely new way. Post 100, you control your emotions instead of your emotions controlling you." She touched her bead necklace, the one that resembled Rob's. "This is a Truth necklace. We all have them. They represent what you learn about yourself in the 100. Does this all sound dopey? I mean, I am fully aware that it's just some beads on a leather cord."

"Not at all!" So far I was impressed. It sounded less like a cult than an ambitious self-esteem-building program. No wonder Rob was so unflaggingly confident in acting and in life. "Why does One Cell get such a bad rap?"

"I always wonder that. I'm kind of too inside it to completely understand. But when people get involved in One Cell, they change, body and soul. Sometimes they devote their lives to the Practice or leave toxic people behind. Nobody likes to see their loved ones transform, especially if it means they're growing apart. Think about a woman who leaves her abusive husband. Of course he's going to hate the people or organization that gave her the strength to escape. But I really don't understand why the press goes bananas."

"Maybe because everything is so secretive?"

Meg laughed. "That's kind of a catch-22. We get a bad rap for being secretive, but we've learned to be private because we're so constantly misunderstood."

There was a pause, and Meg asked, "Should we find Rob for you? He'll be stuck in meetings forever if we don't rescue him."

We headed back inside and ran into Rob, walking down the hall toward us. "There are my girls!" said Rob. He gave me a big hug. "I missed you."

"I've been talking too much," said Meg. "You know how I get."

"Watch out, she's trouble," Rob said to me, and gave Meg a teasing smile.

"Meg's been a great host," I said.

"I knew you two would hit it off," Rob said. I remember how the old me felt in that moment, thrilled that he knew me so well. He'd picked a friend for me, and he'd gotten it right. Only later would I come to realize how carefully planned it all was.

When I turned my phone back on, there were the texts from Aurora. *how is it? r u alive? pepper? pls confirm you have not signed away yr bank account.*

not such a big deal after all, I wrote. *very hollywood but no pressure. will call tonight.*

okay, b careful!

7

"C ome on, there must be more. Did they swear you to secrecy?"

"I'm telling you the truth," I insisted. "It's nice, but not fancy. They do meditation and offer classes. It's all sort of self-help stuff, except whatever it is really helped Rob's acting."

"What about the Klan robes?"

"Optional."

"Okay, maybe that's true," Aurora said. "But, Pepper, you have to promise me, double-dog-pinkie-swear promise, that you will not shave your head and wear a robe and marry Rob in a mass wedding."

I could tell Aurora was slightly disappointed that there was nothing scandalous going on behind the walls of One Cell. Aurora was my best friend, but we'd gone in such different directions. During the six years I was working on *American Dream* she'd gone off to college, joined a sorority, and gotten a master's in social work. Sometimes our friendship seemed to center around her infinite fascination with my comparatively glamorous life. Almost like I was her own personal reality TV show—the more drama, the better.

It was funny that I was the one who'd become a celebrity, because Aurora was the star all through high school. Not only did she have the leads in all the plays, she hosted all the parties and, as a freshman, dated a senior who was objectively the cutest boy in school. I wanted to be her friend, in an idle way, like any ninth-grade girl who saw Aurora's self-assurance would. She was the kind of girl who wore a ratty colorless sweater one day and the next thing you knew all the girls were showing up in their fathers' old, stretched-out gray crewnecks. But I knew she'd never notice me: quiet, studious Lizzie Pepper.

Then, the first week of sophomore year, I had an opening. In home-room I was assigned a seat right next to Alan Mollander. Now, it was no secret that Aurora had an unrelenting crush on Alan Mollander. Here was one subtle clue: She'd written "I love Alan Mollander" on the wall in the girls' bathroom in pink Sharpie and signed and dated it every month for two years, cute (now-graduated) boyfriend be damned. On the second day of school, when the teacher asked if there were any problems with the seating arrangements, I raised my hand and said that I was having trouble seeing the board. I asked to switch seats with Aurora, whose desk was front and center. This meant that she would now sit next to Alan for the rest of the semester. As we crossed each other in the aisle, carrying our respective piles of books, she mouthed, "Thank you," and our friendship was born.

From that day Aurora acted as if she'd accrued a debt that could never be repaid. She critiqued my wardrobe; she brought me to all the parties I never even would have known existed; she found me prom dates. (If I'd worn glasses, she'd have been the one to make me get contact lenses.) Above all, she made me try out for my first school play, junior year. If anyone "discovered" me, it was Aurora.

But now our lives were the opposite of what I would have predicted. Aurora, born to be the center of attention, had gone serious and world-saving, working for a nonprofit in Chicago. I had gone . . . Hollywood.

★

Once we'd exhausted her curiosity about One Cell, I told Aurora that I wanted her to meet Rob when I brought him to Chicago to introduce him to my parents. I assumed she'd be thrilled. After all, Rob Mars was an even bigger deal in her world than he was in mine. Instead, she voiced concern.

"This is getting serious," Aurora said. "It's so fast."

"I know," I said, "But I'm happy. It's okay to just go with it so long as I'm happy, right?"

Aurora was uncharacteristically cautious. "Just make sure it isn't all on his terms," Aurora said. "He's older, successful, and used to getting his way. Don't let him push you around."

I bristled. "Have I ever let anyone push me around?" Aurora should have been happy for me, and instead she was acting like a parent. It occurred to me that maybe, just maybe, my old friend was jealous.

"Well, I seem to remember that you let me wear your red dress to the prom, even though it was clearly better on you."

"You're welcome." We hung up, promising to talk soon, but I felt the distance even more than usual.

That weekend it was all over *Rounder*: "Lizzie Gets Serious with Her 'Boy Wonder.' Rob to Meet Lizzie's Parents." I hadn't told anyone—not a soul besides Aurora—about Rob meeting my parents, but Boy Wonder nailed it: That was what Aurora and I had nicknamed Rob when he and I first started dating.

I called Aurora. "How could you?" I demanded.

"I had nothing to do with it, I swear," Aurora said.

"Please, *please* be honest with me," I said. "I know that *Rounder* can be really aggressive and might take you off guard. And things have been crazy. Maybe I've been selfish with all this Rob stuff going on. The point is, you can tell me the truth. I'm not even mad."

"Here's the truth, although I can't believe you're even asking. I never sold information or gossip or anything about you. I didn't even tell my *mother* you and Rob were dating until it was in the papers, remember?"

"I wish I could believe you," I said. "I'm going to hang up now."

Aurora called me back immediately, but I didn't answer. Her texts came flying: *it wasn't me. did u tell anyone else? rob? is ur phone tapped? i think they tapped your phone.*

We were at breakfast. Rob was reading the paper. He looked up at my phone, which had vibrated right across the table.

"Aurora?" he said.

I nodded.

"You're not answering?"

"I think she's leaking stuff to the press." I handed him my phone, open to *Rounder*.

He shrugged. "Cut her some slack. She's new to this, and the tabloids can be pretty crafty."

"I guess so."

He looked at me for a moment, reading me. "I'll get you a new phone number. One for Aurora, too, if you like. With security software. Will that make you feel better?"

It would.

That night Aurora called me on my new phone.

"Thank you, lady," she said. "I love my spy phone."

"Now nothing we say will leak to the press," I said, and I didn't have to say anything more. I didn't really want or need to know the truth. I just wanted to trust my friend again.

Then Aurora told me about some crazy date she'd gone on, where it turned out the guy worked as a professional escort, without benefits. She was weighing the pros and cons, trying to figure out if that was a deal breaker, and soon she had me laughing so hard I was crying. Classic Aurora.

There were no further security issues. I didn't know if Aurora had learned her lesson or if it was the new phones, but, for a while at least, I forgot to worry.

Rob and I spent most of August in Malibu, living the dream, as Aurora liked to say. Travel would descend upon us soon. We both had movies to promote in autumn, which meant doing press and premieres on different schedules in different locations. His was an international release, so we'd be apart for at least a month. In the meantime, we settled into what was a normal life for us. Every morning his trainer came and they worked out together in the gym above the garage. (Apparently the Studio couldn't take full credit for Rob's godly physique.) Afterward, it was my turn with the trainer. We alternated between Pilates and grueling cardio workouts. Exercise bored the crap out of me, but it was part of the job.

By the time we finished working out, the phone calls from our people were coming in. Agents, managers, lawyers, publicists. Rob was shooting multiple ads, TV and print, for a brand of scotch, international media distribution only. He never drank scotch, but (as he liked to say) for ten million dollars, he *looooved* scotch. I was developing an all-natural cosmetics line and co-launching an Elizabeth Pepper–branded workout line with Target. In the late afternoons we both had mani-pedis, or haircuts and colors, or waxing, or laser treatments to erase whatever imperfections were threatening to present themselves. I'd always had facials, but now I was systematically removing freckles and unwanted hair from my entire body.

A couple times a week we went to the Studio. Rob had frequent meetings—he was involved in the Studio's plan to expand the Practice beyond California by building a new studio in the heart of Manhattan—so I'd arrange to have lunch with Meg at the same time. Then Meg started coming over to the house to help me coordinate my life with Rob's, and pretty soon it became clear that she could manage me better than I could manage myself, so Meg became my assistant, although we never called it that. It was more like she was my very resourceful friend. Who got paid. When she was paid, how much, and by whom weren't things I had to worry about.

In late August Rob and I went to the tenth-anniversary rerelease of *An Average Man.* I remembered seeing that movie in high school, with Aurora, and not quite understanding why all our parents thought it was such a big deal. But now, to watch the movie at its star's side made me feel like a queen. The line between Rob and the protagonist he played in the film, Joe Ferris, blurred. That was my boyfriend up there, transforming from ordinary Joe to Captain Joe, world leader of the future.

Being in that theater, I knew how Kathleen Scott felt, encouraging her explorer husband, Sir Robert, to embark on the Antarctic expedition on which he would perish in a blizzard. She wasn't thinking about the dangers of that frozen world. She was imagining his homecoming, the heroic return, and what their reunion would be like. What made watching *An Average Man* so hot was knowing that later, at home, Rob would be all mine. I would lie next to the real man behind the hero—the mortal man, who in spite of his bravery still needed me more than anything else.

Little by little, as in any relationship, Rob and I chipped away at each other's mysteries. His movie star veneer faded. Aside from when I was actually watching him onscreen and that shiver of unreality came when some facial expression reminded me of Henry in *Great and True*, our relationship had nothing to do with who he was in the outside world. I watched him fixate on my five-times-magnifying mirror, discovering for the first time his own unruly eyebrows. I found out that his famously distinguished salt-and-pepper hair required three hours with a colorist once a month. I saw him freak out like a schoolgirl when, closing our bedroom curtains, he discovered a bat. I learned that he could only read scripts aloud, and needed to take a break every page or so to check his e-mail, refill his water bottle, and stare out the window. I figured out that whenever he was being asked questions he didn't want to answer, his manner stayed perfectly even but the muscles in his neck contracted in a tic that made him look momentarily like a hungry fish. And yes, world, Rob Mars's farts stank.

But in some ways I felt like I still didn't truly know my boyfriend. The Rob Mars gloss was layered thick, and I was always poking at him, trying to get him to admit being bored or lazy or in a bad mood. Didn't he ever feel conflicted or guilty about the eternal sunshine of our days? Did I never annoy him, not even when I picked at my pedicure as we watched movies? And there was one particularly vexing mystery that didn't diminish: the locked door in the gym.

Occasionally, when I was working out, Rob came through the gym and disappeared into his private office. He never stayed there long, but I did mention it to Aurora—big mistake. She latched on to it immediately, referring to it as Bluebeard's chamber. Aurora had all sorts of theories about what went on in there. One day I finally worked up the courage to ask Rob about it.

"So . . . what goes on in your secret locked room?"

Rob was running on the treadmill. The door was only feet away. Still, he looked at me blankly.

"That one," I said, gesturing toward the door. "Whatcha got in there, Bluebeard?"

"The dead bodies of ex-girlfriends who asked too many questions, of course. The smell isn't bothering you, is it?" We laughed, and I waited, expecting him to explain. Finally, he said, "It's private, Elizabeth. I think it's important for all of us to be able to maintain personal space. You should try it. The room next to the sunroom would make a beautiful study for you. Or meditation room. Whatever your heart desires."

And that was all I could get out of him. It bothered me, I won't lie, but I also accepted it. If all of Rob Mars's secrets were small enough to be contained in a single room in this house, so be it. I had a secret or two of my own, and I wasn't necessarily prepared to come clean, either. And so Bluebeard's chamber became a joke between us, one of those jokes that was wrapped around a question I half hoped would eventually answer itself.

8

My mother wanted to pick us up at the airport. She or my father always met me at O'Hare, wind or snow. I explained to her that this time, instead of coming into O'Hare, Rob and I would be arriving at a private airstrip fifty miles farther from the house, but she insisted on meeting us anyway. I'd already flown with Rob to Cannes, and to a couple of other events. We always landed at small, private airports and hopped from his jet straight into a car without paying attention to where we were until we arrived at our hotel. This time we disembarked to find my mother, wearing her standard capris and polo shirt, waving enthusiastically as if we might not otherwise find her, though she was the only person standing on the tarmac.

Rob gave my mother a hug and said something about wishing he'd brought her flowers.

"Don't be silly," she said. "They came yesterday." Sometimes Rob's assistant Jake was a little *too* on top of things.

I didn't worry about Rob and my mother getting along. He was certainly in for an easier ride than I had with his parents. His stern mother, Liesl, had worked as his father's office manager throughout Rob's childhood in Hudson, but now she was part of the Studio's administrative team. She was polite and unsmiling whenever I saw her, and I became timid and obsequious in her presence. His handsome father, Alan, whom Rob said I would have loved, had Alzheimer's and was equally charmed to meet me every time I saw him.

My mother is a cool customer. Her clique of Highland Park ladies played golf, hosted charity events, and knew their wine. If any of her friends gushed for one minute about Rob (and I'm sure they did), I knew exactly what she'd say: "He's a lucky man to have my Lizzie."

Rob and I were usually driven around in an SUV, sitting together in the back. He looked out of place in the passenger seat of my mom's little BMW. But he was at his most charming, paying close attention and asking polite questions when she pointed out her friend Sibyl's shop, the Pattersons' restaurant, and the club. To my relief his hand didn't even twitch in the direction of his cell phone—my mom would have been all over that. She was a stickler for manners.

My mother showed us to our room and left us alone to settle in.

"Was this your room growing up?" Rob asked, looking at the family photos on the dresser.

"No, it's the guest room. My room just has a single bed." We were lucky, come to think of it, that my mom hadn't put us in separate rooms, as she had the last and only other time I brought a boyfriend home. But that was five years earlier, and Justin and I had been kids.

"I want to see your room," Rob said.

I giggled, thinking about the pink princess-y canopy over the bed and the clutter of soccer trophies on the bookshelves.

"I gotta see which poster of me it was. Your high school crush," he teased.

Yikes. I was busted. "I'm not sure it's there anymore," I said.

"I'm just kidding," he said.

★

Aurora had to leave town for work the next day, so that very afternoon we met up with her at the Cantina, a Mexican restaurant with a notoriously lax liquor policy where in high school we'd consumed enough frozen margaritas for a lifetime. Just being in one of the booths made me crave an illicit cigarette.

Rob and I had jokingly categorized the different ways people reacted to his fame. Some fans led by complimenting his work—the Gushers. Others wanted nothing more than a signature on a napkin or a quick photo with him—the Collectors. Then there were those who thought he was Jesus himself—the Believers. And, finally, there was our favorite group, the people who never acknowledged that they recognized him at all—the Nonchalants. Aurora, by nature, was a Gusher. But she was desperately trying to be a Nonchalant. The result was that she overdid it, making the same conversation she would with any new boyfriend of mine. She asked if we'd met through work and where Rob was from, a polite, stiff smile on her face. I was inwardly mortified. When she went so far as to inquire whether he'd had more luck with movies or television, I mock-smacked her on the head to snap her out of it.

"Meet my boyfriend, Rob Mars. Perhaps you've heard of him. Famous movie star. *Great and True. The Son. An Average Man.* Need I go on?"

Aurora put her head down on the table. "I'm an idiot," she moaned. "It's nice to meet you, Rob, but in order for me to raise my head from this table you will have to provide me with another margarita."

"I have much more to lose here than you do," Rob said. "I'll buy you as many margaritas as it takes for you to give your approval to Elizabeth."

Aurora peeked out. "Oh my God, Pepper. He's ridiculous. I can't function."

"I know," I said. "Over the top." I squeezed Rob's knee under the table, grateful for his patience. "Now please sit up and tell him the one about the guy you dated for six months without knowing his name."

That night, after my father got home from work, my parents, Rob, and I had dinner together. We sat around the dining room table eating my mom's pot roast—my favorite—and I looked at the scene through Rob's eyes: the pockmarked oak table where I'd done all my homework, the neatly repaired wallpaper below the sconces my father had wired himself, my grandmother's collection of romantic Lladro figurines on the sideboard. Was it all too Middle America for him? But I underestimated Rob. He chowed down on the pot roast, asking for seconds as if he'd studied the script on how to win over my mother. I wouldn't have been surprised if he'd called her "Ma." He was clearly on his best behavior, and I realized he didn't just see this as an obligatory meeting. He actually cared about making a good impression on my parents.

For dessert, my mother served frozen Sara Lee cheesecake the way I've liked it since I was a kid—frozen.

I scraped away at the dessert, savoring the icy slivers of cheesy goodness. Rob, given no introduction to what was on the plate in front of him, tapped at it a few times, then carved out a cautious bite.

"I wouldn't ordinarily serve this, I'll have you know, but it's Lizzie's favorite." My mother, she of the (locally) famous homemade pies, was testing Rob. It wasn't whether he'd turn up his nose at a grocery store dessert. My father, after all, was a royal food snob. It didn't matter if Rob ate the cheesecake, made fun of it, or choked on it. What my mother was watching for—instinctively, not necessarily consciously—was how he felt about me.

Rob was staring at me with fascination. "Unbelievable," he said, shaking his head.

"What?" my mother asked.

"It's just that I've spent the entire summer trying to tempt your daughter with various decadent desserts. She turned down the soufflé at Le Meurice in Paris, for God's sake, and turns out I just needed to call you!"

That was all it took. Mom was sold. All she wanted for me was a man who was attentive to my every need, and Rob was.

But I wasn't deeply concerned about what Rob thought of our middle-American home, and my mother wasn't the one I was nervous about. It was my father. Doug Pepper, CEO of Pepper Consultants, knew what was best for me. He always had. And it would be very difficult to move forward without his approval. I'd never forget what he did in sixth grade, when, for the first time in my school career, the students were tested and broken into higher-level groups by aptitude. According to your scores, the administration might place you in advanced composition, algebra, and/or world history with the famously rigorous Mr. Hamilton. On the first day of school I brought home my schedule. When my father saw that I was in regular courses across the board, he grabbed the pink sheet away and shook it at me. "You want to live a mediocre life? It starts right here."

"But, Dad, it's fair. They tested us and put us where we belong. The teacher said that people learn in different ways, and . . ."

"And you know what I have to say to that? Bullshit."

The next day, instead of going to school on the bus, I rode in my father's car. He walked me to my homeroom classroom. As I hung my backpack in my cubby, I heard him instructing my homeroom teacher, Ms. Finley, to make the change.

All the other kids stopped to listen.

"She cannot be with *those* students," he said forcefully. "She's a *Pepper*."

"*Not really*," I wanted to say, "I'm a *Purakayastha*." The story my father always told was that my great-grandfather, upon arriving from West Bengal, was asked to spell his name aloud three times to immigration officers. That night, at the local diner, he pronounced, "Spelling is for schoolchildren. I will not waste any more time on Earth doing this." At this moment of conviction he happened to be seasoning his favorite American food—scrambled eggs. Hence "Pepper." It seemed to me that anyone whose great-grandfather offhandedly picked his name from a common tabletop spice was entitled to an average education. Unfortunately, my father did not see it this way.

Ms. Finley tried her best, but at some point I guess she figured out what I already knew about my father: He went after what he wanted, and he never, ever backed down. I'd heard him say it a million times, during deal negotiations, after poker games, and when he disagreed with a teacher who'd given me anything less than an A. *I always win.*

Effective immediately, I was in all advanced courses, and it was a nightmare. I struggled to keep up until my parents hired three separate tutors. Then every night, after soccer practice, I spent another two hours transforming myself into the advanced student my father needed me to be. By the time middle school was over, all the late nights had paid off. I took AP classes as a sophomore, and, through sheer force of Doug Pepper's will, I was a straight-A student. And then I became an actor and never went to college. Oh well.

Needless to say, if Dad didn't like Rob, we were doomed. And Rob already had a few strikes against him. First, he was twenty years older than I, much closer to my father's age than to mine. Second, my father would never condone a whirlwind romance. He had all but fingerprinted my prom date. And third, their first phone call had consisted of my father yelling at Rob for his cartop performance. Somewhere way back on the Indian side of my family, every marriage had been arranged by the parents. Even though Rob personified the success and fame that most fathers dream of for their daughters, my father was different. He did want to control my life, but in his universe there was only one planet around which everything else revolved, and it wasn't Mars. It was his creation: me.

After dinner, my father asked me to come into the kitchen to help fix everyone brandies. *Uh-oh,* I thought, *here it comes.* I silently began lining up the glasses, waiting.

"Well done," my father said. "Rob cares deeply for you. That much is obvious." I was happily surprised, but then he went on. "And, of course, there are the professional perks."

"What do you mean?" I asked.

"This is an opportunity for you, Elizabeth. Make sure you leverage your newfound visibility to promote your upcoming movie."

"Dad!" I wanted him to see me and Rob together, to validate my feelings. I wanted him to be happy for me.

"No, he's right." To my utter embarrassment, Rob was standing in the doorway. I looked from my father to my boyfriend.

"I'm sorry, Rob. My dad is overly ambitious on my behalf. I would never use our connection to promote myself!"

Rob laughed. "I know you wouldn't. And that's what makes you special. But now that we've gotten that out of the way, maybe you should."

Dad nodded. "The press is all over you," he said. "You might as well control the story." Wow, three hours into their first meeting and the two of them were really in sync.

Rob added, "Hollywood is shallow. Landing the best parts is all about optics."

"Optics, what's that?"

"You really are Lucy McAlister from Tennessee," Rob teased.

"Enlighten me, please!"

"Optics just means how things look to the general public. Everything you feel and want is completely distinct from the image you put out in the world."

What he was saying reminded me of something Meg had told me—one of the Whole Body Principles was to separate the self from the perception of self.

"Rob's cartop performance was a disaster, but people are still rooting for you. They want it to be true love," Dad said.

"And luckily, it is." Rob smiled. My boyfriend had just told my father he loved me, but this was hardly how I'd envisioned it going down.

"Oh my God, you two are lunatics. My career is just fine, thank you very much." My mother came into the kitchen and started doing the dishes.

I put the drinks on a tray and carried them out to the porch. My father and Rob followed, and we all sat down on the cushioned indoor/outdoor wicker furniture.

Rob squeezed next to me on the love seat. "Babe, you are very talented. You should have your choice of roles."

"But I *like* indie movies with offbeat scripts and quirky heroines. Do I really want to play a spandex superhero? Look at you—you haven't done a single franchise."

"I've been very lucky, but my career is the exception. The reality is, once you have a series, you can ride it for years. It doesn't keep you from doing what you love—it helps make that happen."

"I don't know what I was worried about," I said. "You two are getting along like a house on fire. What exactly are you proposing?"

My father cleared his throat. He was in his element now. Corporate tycoon by day, quietly determined manager of his daughter's career by night. I should have known that he would like Rob for my career, and that was all he needed. My father had come to the dinner already knowing what he wanted, and my father always got what he wanted. *I always win.*

My mother, obviously too curious about our conversation to finish the dishes, poked her head out. "Are these men plotting for you to take over the world?" she chirped.

"Just Hollywood," said my father. He said it lightly, but his eyes were dead serious.

By the time we returned to L.A., it had all been arranged. I would switch to Rob's agency, ACE, and my new agents would line up the lead in a franchise, pronto.

I wasn't exploiting my famous boyfriend if he wanted me to do it . . . right? And, according to the two men in my life, whatever huge movie this was would propel me into the stratosphere, where I would float alongside Rob, orbited by brilliant scripts and important directors. It would be a dream come true, just not exactly how I'd envisioned it coming to pass.

9

Two weeks later, in the middle of September, Rob and I went to St. Maarten. He told me he had a meeting and wanted to make it into a vacation, but I would soon find out that was a lie. The first clue that something was going down was when our car from the airport took us straight to a yacht club at the water's edge. Rob led me out of the car, leaving our luggage to the driver, and straight up the dock, where we boarded a yacht—a large one, or, as I would later learn it was called, a super-yacht.

The sun was just beginning to set, the water a dazzling gold. There was not a soul in sight—either by chance or design. By this point I expected the latter. As we boarded, I vaguely registered that the boat was named the *Queen Elizabeth*, but I didn't think twice about it. Sure, it's my name, but a) it's pretty common and in fact seemed like a completely unoriginal name for a yacht; and b) I still wasn't really used to being anyone but "Lizzie."

I'm not the kind of girl who's had a fantasy of what her engagement night would be like since she was young. But I'm no dummy. I've seen and acted in my share of romance movies, and the minute I stepped on deck I saw that the mood had been set. Rob had spared no expense. This was to be our big night.

Music played, classical piano. The floor was scattered with blue rose petals, which I would find out had been flown in that morning from Japan, by private jet. Dozens of white candles had been artistically placed around the cabin, wafting scent. I noticed how good they smelled, although I didn't yet know that I was experiencing a designer scent that had been developed exclusively for us and this moment.

"Wait here," Rob said, and hurried up the steps to the upper deck. A few minutes later he called out, "All ready!" and I tiptoed forward. The sky was wide and glorious, streaked with red and orange. And looking perfectly cast for this backdrop was the man who stood in front of it. My gorgeous, movie star, would-be husband.

He stood there, wearing the same boyish smile he had in the poster on Aurora's bedroom door.

In Rob's hands was a box, and in the box was a custom Walford Diamond engagement ring, a rock that probably cost more than my first apartment. My heart was fluttering. This moment! It was happening before I'd even had time to wonder if or hope that it would happen.

Rob got down on one knee and asked me to marry him. Women's hearts broke around the world.

I said yes. You don't say no to Rob Mars.

The night Rob Mars asked me to marry him was every girl's fantasy. It wasn't exaggerating to say that he was the most eligible bachelor in the world. You can see it all in the photographs splashed across every magazine the following week: The shock on my face as I step out onto the deck. The hint of nervousness as he kneels in front of me with a ring. Our arms entwined, sipping champagne afterward. The photographs say it all: Here's a couple who's truly in love, perfectly happy with each other, isolated from the rest of the world in a moment of pure intimacy. But nobody stops to wonder: *Who took those photographs?*

I said yes to Rob, dropping to my knees next to him. "Wait, we were better before," I said, standing up again. We were exactly the same height when he was kneeling. We kissed, laughed, kissed again. "Oh my God," I said. "Really? Really?" I was still processing, but Rob was a man with a plan.

"Hold that thought," he said, and pulled out his phone. I assumed he was calling his parents, but all he said was "We're ready for you."

Then he explained. We were going to sell photos of our engagement to *Rounder* and donate the proceeds to One Cell's youth education fund. No sooner had he finished explaining than people started filing up on deck. Rob's event planner, a photographer, two assistants, hair and makeup people for me and Rob, and a magazine writer. Where had they come from? They must have been hiding in one of the staterooms. I wasn't ready—I'd barely caught my breath—but I could see why he wanted it done right away. Then they'd be gone and we'd be alone again to bask in the excitement and mystery of our future. Also, as his event planner pointed out to me, we only had fifty minutes until we lost our light. Of course, it had all been perfectly timed for sunset. Not the actual engagement—the reenactment.

They scurried me back downstairs to prep me to arrive on the upper deck, have the question popped, and be surprised and elated all over again. It was like an acting exercise.

At least I have no trouble remembering the details of my engagement—I did at least five takes of it before they were sure they had what they needed. If I remember correctly, the magazine donated $100,000 to One Cell in honor of our engagement, so it was all for a good cause. And then I called my parents to tell them the exciting news.

I thought of myself as a cynic, yet when it came to love I seemed to be stuck in teen movie fantasyland. After all, my first kiss was for *American Dream*, perfectly lit. My first love was my onscreen prom date, a heart-throb who'd literally been cast for our chemistry. My first heartbreak played like an end-of-series finale, both of us, still in love, compelled to go our separate ways. After Justin, the perfectly cast love interest, there was Johnny, a classic bad boy through and through. Most girls have four years of college to lie on a dorm bed, hash through obsessions and drunken encounters, and get these clichés out of their system. Then they have their twenties for a series of near misses as they tiptoe toward the mundane realities of long-term relationships. But I went straight from youthful romance to a fairy-tale prince. Roses and diamonds, mansions and islands, Rob was everything but the shining armor: a movie star, a hunk, the catch of the century, an icon. I didn't care about his fame and success, I didn't care about money and power. And I certainly didn't go for the diamonds and roses. Rob was king of the great, romantic ges-ture—but I always saw the role of Prince Charming as a nervous habit of his, something to fall back on when he felt something he had no idea how to express. Contrived as our engagement was, it came from his bundled-up heart. I didn't need Captain Joe, the hero of Rob's classic movie. I loved Rob for what was underneath it all, for the frog I could extract from all that princelyness.

After I said yes, we called our parents, and I called Aurora.

"You won, Pepper! You won the gold medal in the Love Olympics!" she exclaimed. And then: "But the most important thing is that he loves you. I saw how he looks at you. Oh my God, I'm Rob Mars's maid of honor!"

"Oh yeah—you'll be my maid of honor, won't you?" I said.

"I thought you'd never ask."

My parents feigned surprise until my father admitted that Rob had asked him for my hand when we were in Chicago.

"He didn't!" I punched Rob's arm.

"I told him you were a grown woman, but that he had my blessing."

I knew my father too well to believe that. He could blather on about my independence and maturity, but no question he was pleased Rob had asked. And delighted to bestow his blessing on a man of such . . . achievement.

After the phone calls came the part of the evening that was just for us, the part that wasn't in the magazines.

At Rob's cue, the *Queen Elizabeth* headed out into the lagoon. Champagne and a plate of spicy shrimp appeared.

"By the way," Rob said, "I hope you like this boat. It's your engagement present." Hence her name: I was marrying the king, and that made me Queen Elizabeth.

I could only shake my head. "You sure you want to do this?" I said. "Why buy the cow . . . ?"

Rob burst out laughing, pulling me into his arms. "I want the cow. It's the best damned cow I've ever seen."

The waitstaff started bringing us food. Local specialties—some of the freshest fish I've ever had—though I also had the sensation that everything—dinner, the champagne, dessert, the view, the waiters—everything tasted better, looked more beautiful, and felt delightful simply because I was in love.

After dinner we stood together, alone, at the prow of the boat. The pink-and-gold sunset had faded, and the sky was dark, full of stars. The captain cut the engines and we floated quietly, the scattered lights of the island illuminating the harbor. I watched Rob looking out at the view. He took a breath, as if to speak, and I put a finger to his mouth.

"Wait," I said. "Don't do it."

"Don't do what?"

"Don't yell how much you love me."

"I'm going to marry you, Elizabeth, and I'm so proud I might explode."

"Okay," I said, "I get it. But this is not *Titanic*. Just keep it small."

He leaned forward and whispered in my ear in the tiniest, truest voice. "I love you. You are my heart and soul. I will love you forever."

I turned my head and whispered in his ear, "Me too."

The next day, the whole world found out. Pictures of our engagement showed us on the *Queen Elizabeth*, at the beginning of the night. Rob and I looked really happy and perfect. How could we not? The Caribbean. The roses, the candlelight, the glorious sunset, the big ol' Walford Diamond ring: It was Celebrity Wedding Package Deluxe. And, just like that, in an instant, all the bad press was over. All the flubs and missteps of the past months; all the vitriol and schadenfreude and snark; all the cynicism about our relationship just melted away. It didn't matter that, to us, they were photo-ops for charity. The media ate it up. We were "the 'It' couple of Hollywood." America's Girl Next Door and *People*'s Sexiest Bachelor of the Year. A match made in Hollywood heaven. It turned out that this was what they'd wanted all along—the perfect movie romance—me and Rob, holding hands under a rainbow, ready to start our lives together.

PART TWO

SPOTLIGHT

1

Magically, now that Rob and I were engaged, the press suddenly loved me—but they had a funny way of showing it. Starting the minute we returned from the Caribbean, I was followed by at least six photographers in SUVs every time I left the house. One particularly aggressive guy with dark curly hair must have specialized in zoom shots of dermatological conditions because he was always two inches from my nose. I nicknamed him Pops because it was easier to pretend this omnipresent man was part of some bizarre family structure than to fight for my right to walk freely to my car.

Amidst the press calls and congratulatory gifts and more than a hundred thousand new Twitter followers overnight (literally), there was an odd note that, instead of coming with the regular mail, slipped out of a stack of tabloids where it must have gotten caught and nearly lost. It was written in a long, elegant hand, and all it said was "Dear Elizabeth, I wish you all the best. 'This above all: to thine own self be true.'" I knew the line from *Hamlet*—and from the yearbook pages of at least six of my high school classmates. It was signed "Lexy." Rob's ex-wife. It was a kind enough sentiment, but, again, strange.

In addition to having ACE as my new agency, I had a new PR company,

Lotus. My longtime publicist, P. J., was out—as Rob pointed out, it made sense to work with the same people as him across the board. For "leverage." Lotus told me to just roll with the press onslaught. Eventually, the value of the photos would decline, and the attention would die down. My new hair and makeup guy, Joaquim, moved into the guesthouse in Malibu, and if I left the house, even for a coffee, he spent a half hour getting me ready.

At least twenty messengers arrived every day with hanging bags from various designers. Now that I was being photographed constantly, I was a "trendsetter." Genna, my stylist, picked my outfits for events. Meg helped me with the day-to-day and managed a spreadsheet that documented everything I'd ever worn in public, when and where I wore it, and who was there. I felt like an idiot not dressing myself, but the clothing situation had become completely unmanageable. I was expected to wear something different every day, and I had no idea what I owned anymore. Or had on loan.

One morning—a few days after my twenty-fifth birthday—Meg and I were in the Brentwood guest room, getting it ready for me and Rob to co-opt while the master was being renovated. (We were breaking through a wall to "capture"—as the architect put it—what was currently a spare sitting room so it could be my dressing room.) After we finished, I had to get ready for a lunch in Beverly Hills. I was wearing what Meg had laid out for me that morning: a hand-knit sweater and jeggings. The sweater was oversize and chunky, with dolman sleeves, a built-in scarf, and earth-toned stripes. Not something I ever would have picked for myself, and now that it was midday, the cloud cover had broken and it was too hot for alpaca, or llama, or whatever hairy yaklike beast had sacrificed its wool for my warmth. As I pulled my head out of the sweater, I caught Meg pursing her lips.

"What?" I said. "Do I look like a cow?"

"Stop it," Meg said.

"Why are you making that face?"

"It's just—do you maybe want to pose in it first?" She explained that Lotus made deals for us to be photographed in certain clothes. This was called a "trend launch" and my rate was $20,000 a pop—twice Rob's—assuming the designer was mentioned by name in a major media outlet. If not, if the item was photographed but there was no mention of the brand, then the fee dropped down a tier.

"*Twenty thousand dollars?* To wear a sweater for five minutes?" I was no stranger to freebies, but now it turned out I wasn't just getting free shit. I was getting *paid* to make use of the free shit.

"Well, not always. We drove them up pretty high on this one since it isn't exactly you." Meg wrinkled her nose at the sweater.

I looked in the mirror. "What's me?" I asked. Meg laughed, but didn't respond. "No, I'm serious," I said.

Meg took a moment. "Okay, well, I think I've heard Genna pitch you as 'urban refined'—tailored and classic, but with shoes and bags that pop." She reached into the closet and pulled out a navy silk blazer that looked like someone had taken a razor to its back. "Here, is this better?"

"But what about the twenty thousand dollars?"

"Some other day," she said, shrugging.

That $20,000 was at the back of my mind all day. It was a lot of money, but what did it even mean to me now? I never saw the bills, but we probably spent at least that much every time Rob shut down a restaurant so we could have a night out. At the same time, that kind of money could change people's lives. It could provide clean water to some googleable number of children for a year. Aurora's charity could build a school or two in Africa. And I could earn it for wearing a sweater. A dinner out; two wells in Africa (I googled it); a school.

My next thought was *Great, I'll do it*. I'll wear whatever they want—so long as the money goes to charity. I would relinquish my fashion autonomy for the greater good.

The next day when I proposed this to Meg, she just said, "Don't overthink it. They'll keep making the deals. Sometimes you'll like the product, sometimes you won't. Don't sell yourself out. There's always another opportunity."

"And what about the money?" I asked. "I want it to go to a worthy cause."

"Rob gives forty percent of his net annual income to charity," Meg said. "It adds up to a whole lot more than your trend fees." Right. So that was that. Sorry, Africa.

My birthday had passed. (A dinner with Rob. More diamonds.) I was already getting more attention than any human being could tolerate. So why did I have a blowout twenty-fifth birthday party that garnered a tabloid grand slam? (That's what Lotus called landing the covers of all three major tabloids—*Rounder, Glam,* and *Starlight*—in one week.) When Meg suggested the party to me, she gave me two reasons. The first was that now that I was a client, ACE wanted to throw me a sort of coming-out celebration. They were the most powerful agency in Hollywood, and, as my father had pointed out, it made sense to be at Rob's agency. They would do anything to make their biggest client happy, and Rob would be happy if I was happy. ACE had the power to transform my career overnight.

The second reason to have the event was that apparently Rob had already signed off on it, so it didn't really matter what I thought anyway.

It says something about Meg that when she said the birthday party would be fun, I almost believed her. Plus I needed to take my mind off

Man of Her Dreams. The preliminary reviews were trickling in, and they weren't good.

My birthday party needed a theme, because that's how celebrity party planners work. You can't just say, "Come to my birthday party," stick some candles in a store-bought cake, and call it a day. Bethamy, who did all of Rob's events, could see that I was an inexperienced hostess, so she spent hours walking me through the process, which, now that I think of it, wouldn't have taken nearly so long were it not for Bethamy's propensity for run-on sentences. As Bethamy informed me, first there had to be an idea board, and Bethamy was sure I had a favorite historical period or a tropical destination or a famous crime spree that captured my feelings surrounding my first quarter century of life, and if I wasn't sure what to pick, no worries, because Bethamy herself had the best vendors, and her parties were *transformative.* Right now she was seeing a 1920s gangster theme—Rob in a chalk-stripe suit and a Panama hat. Me in a beret and tight sweater, smoking a cigarette (I liked that part). Did that give me any ideas? I felt sure Bethamy was trying to get me to suggest Bonnie and Clyde, but I refused to bite. With fake money bags and toy guns and cigars? Did I see it? *No, Bethamy, I didn't see it yet.* A bullet-ridden getaway car? An old Ford? *Nope, nothing.* Finally I said, "I like books about explorers. Mountain climbers. Jailbreaks. The Donner party. Could you make a cannibal theme work?" That shut her up for a good five minutes.

Bethamy presented swatches for the color scheme, suggesting that séance (dark blue) and nugget (tan) were together very sophisticated, and she created an online idea board with inspirational images from centerpieces to movie stills to "floral design moments" illustrating which sexy vibe of all the sexy vibes she was planning to replicate. I didn't have to worry about anything, because Bethamy was here. All I needed to do was show up and look pretty. And get something done about my brows, according to Bethamy.

We finally settled on a theme: "Fire and Ice." Don't ask me what that had to do with me, or turning twenty-five. I picked it because if I hadn't Bethamy was pushing hard for "Prom," and I had to draw the line somewhere.

The invitation went out by hand in a red lacquer box. Inside was a black candle ("ink" was one of my secondary theme colors) in Rob and my signature scent (the one Bethamy had commissioned for our engagement). The invitation was white, with a red vellum overlay cut in the shape of a flame. It was subtler than it sounds. They had to mock up the vellum six times to satisfy Bethamy, but the results were very chic, if excessive.

Aurora flew in from Chicago for the party. It was the first time she'd seen Rob's house—any of them. (We were in Brentwood since it was more convenient to the party.) Aurora and I sat by the pool, and I listened while she ticked off the wow factors in my new life.

"And this is just *one* of the houses! Or should I say palaces. How many are there?"

"This one, Malibu, Aspen, the town house in New York, and a flat in London."

"Flat. Listen to you."

"That's what they call it!" I said.

"Free clothes . . . because rich people get everything for free."

"I donate a lot . . ."

"And servants. How many servants do you have?"

"They aren't servants," I said.

"Answer the question."

"I don't know," I said. "Each house has people. I don't even see a lot of them." The truth was that at first I tried to remember all the names, and I certainly knew the key staff members, but I got fuzzy as soon as it came to gardeners; house, car, and animal maintenance; and people who weren't full-time, like the AV guy, the second security shift, and travel staff.

"Does it feel weird, a little Marie Antoinette?"

"Sometimes. Like I can't just walk into the kitchen and get myself a peanut butter sandwich—"

"Or cake," Aurora chimed in.

"But I tell myself that if you have money, it's good to spend it. We're creating jobs."

"Yeah, the president should thank you when he gives his jobs report."

"I'll be sure to mention that when we go to the White House to screen Rob's movie."

"And parody has become reality."

Rob had lived this way for so long that he didn't notice it, so it was hard to talk with him about it. But the truth was that if I'd always said what was on my mind, I'd constantly be going around saying, "Oh my God we get whatever we want! Oh my God we can fly anywhere at any time! Oh my God how much did this necklace fucking cost?" Even if she was busting my chops, with Aurora I could at least finally acknowledge just how over the top it all was.

We sat by the pool pretending that our plastic tumblers were cut from blood diamonds and that the improved taste of our margaritas was worth whatever civil wars these goblets had funded. Then Meg came out to tell me it was time to start hair and makeup. Aurora watched her walk away.

"That's her—your One Cell bodyguard?" Aurora was referring to the tabloids' christening of Meg.

"She's not my bodyguard. She's my friend."

"I expected her to be a nun. She's hot. Does she dress like that around your fiancé?" Meg was just wearing the usual: jeans and a fashionable T-shirt.

"I have no idea what you're talking about."

"But she is in the cult, right?"

"Well, it's not really like that. I told you."

"What about those secret confessionals, where they stand in a circle, take off all their clothes, and reveal their darkest desires? Have they made you do that? Did you levitate? Light as a feather, stiff as a board." Aurora held out her arms as if in a trance.

I laughed. "If you care at all, it's called the 100, and you're not naked. From what Rob tells me, it's pretty much group therapy." But it wasn't Rob who had told me. It was Meg. Rob was still frustratingly unforthcoming on the topic of One Cell.

"Well, I still think it's creepy. I mean, you're Rob Mars. You can do anything in the world—why that?"

"Maybe that's *why* he can do anything in the world . . . One Cell really does seem to help some people." The more questions Aurora asked, the more I realized how little I still knew about my fiancé's organization.

"Well, you're not going to get sucked into it, are you?"

"The minute I drink pig's blood, you'll be the first to know."

The attire for the party was black and white. Genna had brought over ten bright red gowns—so I could stand out from the crowd—but I'd negotiated her down to a black Dior dress with a Burmese ruby-and-diamond necklace that was my birthday present from Rob. Get it, fire and ice? The tabloids said Rob had worked with Ander Walford of Walford Diamond to design it for me, but by now I knew that meant that Ander had submitted some designs and Rob had gone across the street from the Studio to pick one. Anyway, it was stunning.

Meg brought in my dress and jewelry, water for everyone in the room, and a snack. She got Talia set up to do my nails and she told Joaquim to start on hair and makeup. When Meg left the room, Aurora said, "Isn't it awkward having a friend who works for you? Or does she work for the Studio?"

"It's great," I said, shutting her down. After that Aurora left it alone, but I should have paid more attention.

The ballroom at the Beverly Hills Hotel was quite dark, lit by tall flaming torches that were definitely a fire hazard. On each table was a massive abstract ice sculpture. Everything white—the flowers, the men's shirts, the cubelike furniture, and (to my surprise) highlighted hair—all glowed in the black lights. But, I noticed, only natural teeth responded to the light, so everyone with porcelain veneers (about half of the women) had dark-looking teeth. I silently gave thanks for my excellent childhood dentist, Dr. Glass.

I spent the duration of the party trapped in one spot, being greeted by guest after guest. Meg stood next to me pointing out important guests: "Diabolical Eyebrows over there—that's Jameson Whitely—he directed *Son of God*" and so on. At some point I noticed Aurora waiting patiently for my attention, and I slipped over to her side. She handed me a Bellini. The signature cocktail of the evening was a Dizzy Lizzie, in my honor, but Aurora knew I couldn't stand bourbon. I gave her a thankful squeeze.

"My shoes are killing me. And I'm so sorry I haven't been able to hang with you," I said. "This is ridiculous."

"Don't worry about me! This is your night," she said. "But one question: Do you think there will be toasts? I promise I won't embarrass you . . . too much. Maybe just a small mention of the time we crashed a wedding, picked up Siobhan and her boyfriend, then drove all night to see Siobhan's brother launch his wooden ship on Lake Michigan."

"Oh God no," I said. "It's not that kind of party. Save it for the wedding!"

We were interrupted by Teddy Dillon, the head of One Cell, and Aurora was gone.

Not five minutes later, people started clinking their glasses with spoons and rings, and Rob climbed up on the stage, holding a cordless microphone. He looked handsome in his Prada suit, and the room quieted immediately.

"It's really dark in here," he said. Everyone laughed, not that it was particularly funny, but Rob can hold a crowd in the palm of his hand. "You probably think this is a deeply sophisticated party, but really we're just trying to hide the fact that you're standing in a high school gymnasium." More laughter.

"I want to thank everyone for coming, and I ask you to raise a glass to my beautiful fiancée, who is out there somewhere. I hope." Uproarious laughter. He raised a hand to his forehead and surveyed the crowd. A spotlight appeared, circling until it found and instantly blinded me.

"Ah, there she is. Elizabeth, can you come up here?"

As I walked toward him, someone switched out my half-gone Bellini for a Dizzy Lizzie. Damn. I stood at Rob's side, and, though it was too dark to discern the faces of our guests, the dim light reflected off a sea of cell phones, all raised up, their flashes signaling like a fleet of ships seeking harbor. Hashtaglizzieandrob, officially trending. Strangers, most of them, making news of this moment, of my birthday, of my life. They wanted something from us, all of those people. I'm an actor. I'm supposed to love the spotlight. But I was terrified of disappointing them.

I focused on Rob as he toasted me, noticing the way his brow furrowed and eyebrows slanted up and in when he was being sincere. Or wanted to sound sincere. After all, I'd seen him rehearse that same expression of sincerity in the bedroom mirror at home. The words flowed right over me—I was too nervous to pay attention, but by keeping my eyes on Rob I knew exactly how to respond—what the audience craved from me—at every single moment. When one corner of his mouth turned up, I laughed, like everyone else did, at his joke. When he looked apologetically at me, I gave him a stern Alice Kramden look, which the crowd loved, and when his voice got louder, and his hands started waving in the air in the service of some over-the-top story, I simply put my hand to my face and shook my head in apparent mortification—and we brought down the house.

I thought it was over, but then Rob said, "Now, I know there's someone else who'd like to say a few words about Elizabeth." To my surprise, Meg came up to the microphone. I glanced over at Aurora, making an I-had-no-idea-this-was-happening face. She had to be feeling a little left out, but she gave me a game double thumbs-up. I could count on Aurora not to be petty.

"Rob is okay," Meg was saying. "But the fact that he picked Elizabeth makes him even cooler." Rob, still near the mike, patted himself on the shoulder.

Although Aurora knew me better, I had to concede that Rob was right to call on Meg. She gave the perfect speech for that event—short, charming, and not too personal. The audience was satisfied, and yet there was nothing that would sell to the tabloids and torment me for the next week. The dividing line between private and public had shifted. Aurora, my parents, my past—all were crowded into the ever-shrinking space reserved for the imperfect, authentic, and spontaneous.

At home after the party, I watched Rob lift his chin to undo his bow tie. I hadn't talked to him all night.

"Did you know that we get paid to wear some of our clothes?"

"I guess," he said.

"I mean, it's not just that we get them for free. They actually pay us thousands of dollars to wear them."

"Okay . . ." he said.

"Can we stop taking that money? It makes me feel like—"

"Sure," Rob said.

"You don't care why?"

"Not really," he said. "You don't like it; we don't do it." Rob put his jacket and tie on a chair and came over to me. "Now, about *this* dress . . ."

"I'm not getting paid to wear this one," I said.

"What I would give you to take it off," he said, and he reached his hands behind my back to unzip me. We kissed, but I wasn't quite done.

"One more thing," I said.

"Yes?" He sounded a little impatient, like a teenager who just wants to get back to his video game.

"Can you be the one to tell ACE?" I was a new client. I didn't want one of my first interactions with the agency to be telling them that I wanted us to earn *less* money.

"No problem," Rob said. My mind was still whirling. Would he remember to tell them? And could they be trusted? How could we know for sure that they weren't still earning a commission to send us clothes? Maybe they would just stop paying us and keep the money for themselves? I had always taken pride in handling my own finances, but Rob had a money manager, who was helping me now, too. Did Rob even see his income statements?

My dress was on the floor now. Rob's body against mine answered all the questions in my head. *Don't worry. You're safe. I'll take care of you. This is good.*

2

quickly learned why Rob had so many nice houses. He was stuck in them.

At first I had assumed the plotting and secrecy involved in our comings and goings was because we were keeping our relationship on the down-low. Then I thought it was because we were the latest breaking news. Now it finally dawned on me that this was it. This was how Rob always lived. He was stuck, and so was I. And it would be this way for the rest of our lives, or at least until Rob and I were so old and withered that the world lost interest. There was the L.A. where most people ate, exercised, worked, socialized, saw art and movies, walked on the beach, hit the Grove, or wandered from shop to shop in Beverly Hills. Then there was our L.A., made up of back entryways, private rooms, underground garages, and friends who lived like us, in walled-in estates and gated communities. I could never again pop out to get a spur-of-the-moment frozen yogurt.

The Studio in Beverly Hills became one of my favorite refuges. At first I had just gone there to meet Meg for lunch when Rob went to practice or had a meeting about the New York expansion. Now it felt more like a club where Rob and I were both members. I could go to meet friends for lunch or tea and then make calls and send e-mails out of Rob's office. There were always people around, industry acquaintances and my new reps from ACE. At the Studio nobody took my picture, asked for my signature, or stared at me like I had bird poop in my hair. Ironically, the most mysterious, exclusive building in L.A. was the only place where I could feel normal.

My earliest memories of the Studio are the afternoons I spent in its grassy courtyard that fall, planning my wedding with Meg. As soon as Rob and I got engaged, he'd brought in Bethamy, the Lotus event planner who'd spearheaded our engagement, my twenty-fifth birthday party, and every other small and large event in Rob's life, including his first wedding. Bethamy said our wedding would be a dream come true, not just for me but for the country, since America didn't have a royal family, unless you counted the Kennedys, and they would be attending anyway.

Bethamy could see that I was nervous, but that was perfectly normal, especially in cases like this, where the groom was so much more accomplished, but only because he was so much older, by which she meant distinguished, but her doctor would give me beta-blockers, actually she had some right here, which weren't so much blood pressure pills as they were like a spa treatment that you took internally. Bethamy understood that it was hard for me to process all the options and directions and concepts involved, but not to worry, she, Bethamy, was captain of this ship, and she was completely confident that my wedding day would be the best day of my entire life, but that was not including my wedding night, wink, wink. Bethamy had my back. All Bethamy required of me was that I relax and enjoy the ride. "Just show up, darling. And do your dieting in advance. My brides aren't allowed to faint."

"How's it working out with Bethamy?" Meg asked me. She had brought sushi for our lunch to the Studio from Yoshu, a chef on Wilshire who also did all the sushi we had at home. The Studio cafeteria was decent, but Yoshu was our favorite.

"Oh, she's cool. Rob's known her forever, and she really knows her stuff."

"And . . ."

"And I hate her," I said.

Meg burst out laughing. "Join the club. I didn't want to say anything . . . But why in the world is she the queen of your wedding?"

"Rob's always worked with her. I can't, like, fire her."

"Oh, sweetie, you clearly haven't started practicing here at the Studio."

"What does that have to do with it?"

"Let me try this," she said patiently. "What do you want from your wedding?"

"That's easy," I said. "I want to gather my family and closest friends. I want them to bear witness when Rob and I make a lifelong commitment."

"That sounds nice," said Meg. "What does Bethamy want?"

"She wants . . ." I slipped into Bethamy's run-on squeal. "A fairy tale—she's thinking Cinderella's night at the ball, where I arrive in a golden horse-drawn carriage in a con*fec*tion of a dress—can't you see it?—*stunning*, and Rob gallops in on horseback and the entire wedding is a grand ball and the colors are gold and white with a touch of royal scarlet and Rob and I are the most perfect, most beautiful, most unforgettable couple in the entire world." Back in my normal voice, I continued, "I don't want the spotlight. I mean, I know I'm the bride, but people already stare at me constantly. I just want to celebrate love."

"Does Bethamy know what you want?"

"Probably not."

"And who does Bethamy work for?"

"Me, I guess, but really Rob."

"Does Rob know what you want?"

"No." I could see where she was going with this. "I get it. I'm supposed to tell Bethamy and Rob what I want. But I . . ."

Meg interrupted me. "Let me guess. There are reasons you don't want to talk to them. You want to be a good girl. You want to follow the rules. You don't want to be seen as difficult. Your parents taught you to behave this way—it makes for polite and manageable kids—but if you leave your wedding in Bethamy's hands, you're going to pop out of your own wedding cake, and then you and Rob will parachute into a pool of champagne—"

"Full of color-activation crystals that will turn my gown from angelic white to gold lamé!" I chimed in.

"It's your wedding, Lizzie."

I got the subtext: I, Lizzie Pepper, was a total wimp. "You're like Rob," I said to Meg. "You know what you want and you just go for it."

"I wasn't born this way," she said, "and, believe it or not, neither was he. We learned to access our power."

"How?" I asked.

"Here." She gestured toward the buildings, where One Cell's Practice, lectures, and classes were held.

Meg touched a nerve. I had spent my whole childhood trying to please my father. I took on his expectations of perfection, so I got straight As; I practiced the cello, which I despised, for forty-five minutes every night; I played soccer (mediocrely, but I gave it my all). I didn't date. I made curfew. The first time a cigarette touched my lips, I reported it to my mother (though I hid thousands after that). And when I got the role of Lucy McAlister, and the show became a massive hit, I committed to stay on the cast for its entire six-year run—four years of which I'd always assumed I'd spend in college—because my father couldn't countenance quitting. But all of that rule following and achievement didn't give me half the confidence that Meg and Rob had.

I was suddenly profoundly curious. I jumped up, grabbed Meg's hand, and dragged her inside, to the hall that led to the Main Practice Room. I stopped in front of a big bulletin board wall, covered with notices and sign-up sheets.

"Where would I start?"

Meg moved her finger in circles as she scanned the wall. Then her index finger landed on a sheet. It read, "Introduction to the Whole Body Practice: Accessing the First Mind."

"Sounds like psychobabble," I said.

Meg smiled. "I actually met Rob in the Intro Practice. We went through it together. It was my sixth time and his first. It basically teaches you how to figure out what you really want. Seems obvious, but you do exercises to help you move past the obstacles that other people put in your way. So you can have the wedding that you want . . . and tell your fiancé if you can't deal with his staff! It's the first One Cell class most people do, and Rob always says it's the best."

I was signing my name to the form before she finished her sentence. Bethamy was driving me crazy, it was true, but it wasn't only my overbearing wedding planner that led me to the Studio. It was what Meg had just told me: "Rob always says . . ." She seemed to know my fiancé better than I did.

I wanted to connect to Rob. For a while now I'd been trying to go deeper with him, to get past his impossibly flawless exterior. Bethamy wanted to cast him as Prince Charming in our wedding, and I wanted the opposite. I wanted him to know that he could leave his work at the office. I didn't need him to be perfectly chivalrous every minute of our lives. And suddenly, One Cell seemed like it might be the way to reach him. Rob credited the Studio with his acting prowess, which I so envied, but for a long time I'd suspected that it went much deeper than that. The Practice was core to who he was. And Meg, who'd studied alongside him, seemed to know him as a *person*, not just the model fiancé he was for me. Spending time on the periphery wasn't working. Maybe getting closer to One Cell meant getting closer to Rob. I sure hoped so.

And thus began my journey into the world of the One Cell Studio. It was that easy. I'd felt like Rob was holding me at arm's length, and I'd been waiting for him to invite me, but all I had to do was step forward on my own. And, that, he told me later, was one of One Cell's tenets. Nobody was to be persuaded. Everyone was expected to find their own way to the Studio.

I bought it, hook, line, and sinker.

And suddenly there I was, on a path to an enlightenment I'd never known I lacked.

belly of the beast, I texted Aurora. *i'm all in.*

it was nice knowing you, pepper, she wrote back.

Introduction to the Whole Body Practice met at the Studio twice a week for two hours. The leader, Cece, had grown up with Meg. She was an elegant Brazilian woman who made the shapeless One Cell robes look like an effortless fashion statement.

There were about ten people at the first practice. (The second week, a guided meditation titled "Truth and Consequences," the room was maxed out at sixty people. When Meg met me afterward, she looked at the crowd flowing out of the room and said, "Well, Lizzie, you sure can fill the house." Apparently One Cell practitioners weren't completely immune to the lure of celebrity.)

We gathered in a large, airy room with clean white sand on its sunken floor. A simple wooden bench circumscribed the perimeter of the room. There were posters of Teddy and Luther Dillon, the cofounders of One Cell, surrounding us. Each poster had one of Teddy's aphorisms, like "The being is the mirror of the mind" or "Readiness doesn't wait for tomorrow." On the bench near me, someone had carved "The self is not limided." I smiled inwardly. At the verry least, the self is not limited by spelling rules.

For the first hour, we stood in a circle in the sand, barefoot, wearing our robes, in perfect silence. As the minutes passed without anyone saying a word, I grew uncomfortable, then impatient, then angry. But then something strange happened. A lightness came over me, and I stopped my restless shifting. The central issues in my life—joys, fears, hopes—floated in and around my head without demanding resolution. There they were, my little collection of unruly concerns, corralled for the first time like a motley petting zoo. I watched them from an unfamiliar remove.

Cece broke the spell, and then we sat on the bench while she led us in a meditation. To my surprise, people were alert, with eyes open, taking notes in black-and-white composition books. I rediscovered my notebook from that class recently, with phrases like "conquer the second self" and "getting to the radiance of self-fulfillment." I'd underlined the latter three times in bold black strokes. It would be too easy to say that I was caught up in something meaningless. The truth is that all my notebooks from high school look the same—full of nonsensical phrases that clearly meant something powerful to me at the time.

Finally, we began the series of poses. Odd, asymmetrical poses that looked like a parody of yoga. Now, I'd always found yoga painfully slow, and I never met a Shavasana (Corpse Pose) that didn't put me to sleep. But the Studio was on to something with their weird, airplane-crash poses. When the two-hour class was through I felt light and energized, though not remotely thinner. Alas, I'd have to keep the personal trainer.

That night I filled Aurora in on some of what I'd learned from Cece's talk. "She began by asking us to shout out rules of behavior we'd learned as kids. People yelled them out: 'Do your best.' 'Listen when others are speaking.' 'Do unto others as you would have them do unto you.' I added one of my father's favorites: 'Never give up.'"

"Your dad is a pit bull," Aurora conceded.

"Cece walked us through the values governing those rules. Love. Kindness. Forgiveness. Achievement. Then she said, 'These are important values, but life isn't about being a well-behaved child. You are a grown-up, a spouse, an employee, a boss, a friend to adult friends, a parent. Nobody ever teaches us how to play any of *these* roles. We're here to address the gap between what your parents taught you and the life you're leading today.'

"Think about it," I told Aurora. "My parents did a good job, no question about it. But I left home at seventeen and was instantly on *American Dream*. It was a great experience, but I missed out on a lot."

"Beer pong and midterms. Poor you," Aurora said.

"We float through our lives, following our parents' plans; believing what doctors tell us about our bodies. We're totally out of touch with our own selves. We need to take authority over our lives. I know it sounds silly, but the Practice is about being a grown-up."

"In that case, sign me up!" Aurora said.

The Whole Body Practice wasn't touchy-feely—it was pragmatic. We stripped down our life choices. Emotions, we learned, were obstacles. In class we practiced provoking our emotions, then distancing ourselves from them, observing them from afar. "Emotions are a chemical reaction," we chanted during the meditation. The poses enabled us to change our body chemistry. We would never again let our emotions control our lives. And I suddenly understood why Meg and Rob reminded me of each other, why they both seemed so clear and direct and easygoing. They lived the message of this practice every day. I was excited. This wasn't just a route to knowing Rob better. It might be the answer to all of life's challenges.

And so it was that I eventually called Bethamy and said, "I'm sorry if this disappoints you, but I'm changing the wedding. It's not going to be in

Malibu. It's going to be in Ireland, in the town where my grandparents were born. There won't be a theme. And I will be making the guest list myself."

"I'll have to talk to Rob about this. I always do his list—he doesn't even know who his own brand manager is!"

"I've already spoken to Rob," I said firmly. "It's up to me. You can confirm that with him if it's important to you. Also, the wedding's going to be intimate. No brand managers." I hung up, checked twice to make sure the phone was really, truly hung up, then turned to Meg and we did a little victory dance.

The Whole Body Practice did much more than free me to fire my wedding planner. I had hoped that it might bring me and Rob closer, and the results were immediate. At dinner the night after my first practice—weeks before I even fired Bethamy—I babbled in excitement.

"It makes so much sense," I said. "I've been playing the same role—class valedictorian—for way too long."

Rob nodded thoughtfully. "You're a high achiever. That's not a bad thing."

"But I've always worked to someone else's standards. My high school teachers, then Steve Romany and Alice Baer" (the showrunner of *American Dream* and its director), "and always my dad."

"All good people," Rob said. "But, as your fiancé, I have to say that I trust you with yourself more than I trust any of them. I can't wait to see what you find when you follow your own instincts."

"Take a look in the mirror," I said. "I already found you, all by myself." Rob smiled for what seemed like just a moment too long, then stood up and took my hand.

"Come with me. I want to show you something." Aha! I was breaking through to my hard-to-read fiancé. It was about to happen. He was finally going to take me to his private sanctum, into Bluebeard's chamber, to reveal whatever secrets he kept from the rest of the world. This must have been what he was waiting for—a sign from me that we were in alignment.

But no. Bluebeard's door, off in the gym, stayed shut tight, keeping its secrets for now. Instead he led me to our shared office and opened a PowerPoint slide show on his computer. The title slide read "Studio Manhattan, Construction Launch." Below that it read "Tomorrow, Manhattan. Next, the World."

I expected the slides that followed to show images of the new Studio I'd heard Rob and some of his One Cell associates talk about—a space in New York that would bring the Practice to a whole new population. But instead of marketing or architectural plans, Rob was showing me images of what looked to be the slums of the world. Families standing outside decrepit houses. Dirty children playing on the ground. Shots of Third World bathrooms. In the background, stretches of beautiful blue mountains.

"What is this?" I asked.

"The One Cell community is something of an island," Rob said. "Why should self-knowledge be the privilege of the rich? One Cell helps people realize their greatest dreams. Who can it better serve? We aren't going to feed them, Elizabeth. We're going to *teach them to fish*! Manhattan is just the beginning. Someday the Studio will be known as a place where people from all walks of life do the 100. A worldwide practice for self-actualization." His eyes were shining. So this was what my husband-to-be was planning, what all those meetings at the Studio were about.

Even then I thought his idealism was overblown, but it was sweet. I liked what it said about him. Also, to be honest, I wanted to believe that the practice I was learning at the Studio wasn't another rich person's dalliance, like Isle Goodwin's solo pilgrimages with her personal guru, which basically were excuses for her to take an annual trip to his ashram in India, or Minette Stone's monthly weekends at Malibu's Total Purity Cleansing Center, which billed itself as rehab from the toxins of daily life but which everyone knew was the best way to lose a quick fifteen pounds. Aside from needing ammunition against Aurora's mockery, I liked the idea that One Cell was trying to do good in the world.

"I want to help," I said. "This is something I could really see myself being a part of."

"Of course!" he said, and I could tell he was delighted—and maybe even a little relieved. "I'd love your help."

"You're a good man, Rob Mars."

"I try," he said.

But seriously, that locked door was killing me.

3

Man of Her Dreams was premiering at the Aspen Film Festival at the end of November. It would be the first time since Rob and I had met that I'd get to be the star while he played dutiful consort. At last, I would reclaim center stage. Much as I respected my fiancé's success, being cast as the young, innocent girl who'd been swept up in a fairy-tale romance by a powerful movie star was starting to get old. Here was my chance to remind Hollywood and the rest of the moviegoing public that I already had a respectable career, thank you very much.

We landed in Aspen and were met by Rob's local driver, Pete, who was straight out of a ski resort brochure, cut from the chair lift and pasted into the driver's seat of a Range Rover. He had a skier's tan: a reverse raccoon mask, the top half of his face pale where goggles had shielded his skin.

While Rob and Pete talked powder depth and texture in the front seat, I watched the snow-covered peaks go by. A magpie landed on a wooden fence. The world was black and white.

We drove up a winding country road to a huge wooden lodge. Its windows glowed. The mountain rose behind it. Even though it was nearly six o'clock and the sun had already dipped behind the mountain, the slopes were brightly lit for night skiing, and a chairlift was still running.

"That's Argus Lodge," Rob said. "We ski in, ski out from there."

"Why isn't there anyone on the chairlift?" I asked. At Chestnut Mountain, where I'd skied as a kid in Chicago, there was always a line for the chairlift, no matter how bitterly cold it was.

"It's a private mountain," Rob said. Sure. Our own private mountain. Why not? Rob went on, "You might encounter Hunter skiing the bumps, but otherwise it's very quiet." That would be Hunter Dix. *The* Hunter Dix.

About three minutes past the lodge we came upon a few rustic houses and stopped in front of one.

"This is my—our—cabin!" Rob said, and he popped out of the car to open my door. The front hall opened into a great room—it must have been forty feet tall, with a dramatic waterfall plunging down one wall, and floor-to-ceiling windows looking out at a perfectly framed snow-capped mountain. A fire roared in the massive stone fireplace. There was a long rustic table that probably sat twenty, and a chef's kitchen with windows all around. Multiple glass folding doors led to a deck, where the steam from the hot tub was red, tinted by colored landscape lights. Four fire pits lit the pool with orange flame.

I got out my phone. "I'm sending a picture of this *cabin* to Aurora," I told Rob, "so she can see that we know how to rough it."

The premiere was the following afternoon. Rob and I did our practiced red carpet routine, smiling and posing and waving, staying on message for the event. This time my refrain was "I can't wait to see *Man of Her Dreams*. I haven't seen it yet! But working with Olson Nelson was amazing." It was a lie. I had seen the movie at our screening room in Brentwood, with my agent, manager, and publicist, right before I fired all of them, and I was not a fan. The movie had started off as a light romantic comedy, but Olson had cut almost all the jokes, and the ones that were left felt lonely and flat. He had also cut what I thought was my best work of the film: the third-act monologue where I convince Luke, my dream date, that we belong together, even if it means stepping out of reality forever. Instead, in the final cut, my costar, Matt Wilson, has the last word, telling me that having each other in our dreams is enough. If you asked me, it made for a depressing ending. And my performance was reduced to the generic cute girl of every romantic comedy—offbeat, ready for love, with the winningly humble habit of hiding her hands in her sleeves. (Ironically, my best surviving scene was the one that we shot right before my ex-boyfriend Johnny executed his spectacular film/relationship bomb. I guess I'd been having a good day up until that moment.)

Also, Olson Nelson was *allegedly* (that's for the lawyers) having an affair with Sandra Beakley, which might explain why the camera spent such a disproportionate amount of time lingering on the minor character of my little sister.

So my stock statement was that it was great to work with the director, which everyone knows is industry code for *I don't like this movie, but you can't blame me for putting my faith in a director with a good track record and reputation. Now I am being professional out of respect for those who invested in this film and to demonstrate to future filmmakers that I would never sell them out.* The important thing was to be visible in the industry— to remind Hollywood that I was cast in this, and would be cast again.

Not that it mattered. I could have ratted out the director, panned the movie, and declared frozen peas the new celebrity weight-loss secret; apparently all anyone was ever going to write about until the end of time was the endlessly fascinating love story of Lizzie Pepper and Rob Mars.

When the photographers shouted questions at Rob (*"When's the wed-ding?" "How much was the ring?"*) his only response was "I'm here to see Elizabeth's movie. I'm excited and proud." It was actually true that Rob hadn't yet seen the movie. The fact of the matter was that he and I had never watched any of my movies together (or *American Dream*, for that matter). I had never seen him see me act. Now, as we settled into our seats for what I knew would be a cringe-inducing 110 minutes, I didn't worry about the audience. I was focused on Rob. What would he think of my acting? If he didn't think me a good actor, would he still love me?

In anticipation of this very moment, I had made sure to warn Rob about the sex scene. Ironic as it sounds, given what happened, I didn't want to blindside him. In the beginning of the second act, my character, Catherine, undresses and climbs into bed with Luke—the man she first met in her dreams. I was fine with doing nudity at the time. I'm not par-ticularly modest, and I'll pretty much do anything that feels true to my character if I believe in the movie—which I still did when we shot that scene. Now, however, I had my regrets. But I was also curious to see Rob's reaction to my naked, strategically waxed body on the twenty-foot-tall screen.

And so Rob watched the movie and I watched Rob. At the end of the first act, when Catherine realizes she's (basically) alone in the world, Rob put his hand on my knee. I took that as a sign that he didn't like to see me sad, which meant, in some way, that he bought my character's despair.

After that, Rob seemed intently focused on the screen, so I just sat there, trying to convince myself it was a sweet movie after all and noting that I was really skinny. (Lately Rob and I had been eating a little too well, and my hip bones were now covered by a layer of soft flesh. After the screening I would return to a carb- and dairy-free existence. Again.) My nude scene came . . . and went—with no perceivable reaction from Rob. I should have known. He was too professional to take such things personally.

But then it happened. Third act, just as my mind was turning to what questions I should anticipate from the press outside the theater. Suddenly, there I was, up on the screen, delivering the monologue that Olson had stripped from the film.

It was impossible! I had seen the "final" cut just one week earlier! Changes at this point were unheard of. Someone—someone very high up—must have liked my performance enough to demand that Olson reinstate it. I poked Rob and started to tell him, but he turned to me and smiled.

"Better, isn't it?" he whispered.

He knew! The one who'd been blindsided was me.

That night, after smiling through the party and posing with my costars and pretending it was perfectly fine when Celia Montbatten, who is a giraffe of a woman and has no business wearing five-inch spikes, nailed the top of my foot with her full body weight and then fake apologized by saying, "Oh, I didn't *see* you," as if I were short and insignificant, when really she didn't see me because she stepped *backward* onto me. After Olson Nelson gave me the stink eye all night; after noticing how Rob tacked on a whispered "And thank you" when he congratulated Olson; after all that, in the limo heading home, I finally asked Rob what he thought about the surprise edit.

"You did a spectacular job with that monologue and people deserved to see it."

"But did you have something to do with it? Did you ask them to do it?"

He put his arm around my shoulders and grinned proudly. "Elizabeth, I didn't ask them to do it. I *told* them to do it."

"But you can't do that! How did you do that?"

Rob chuckled. "Actors are powerless in this business. We make a movie, put our hearts into it, and have no control over how it turns out, how it's promoted, whether it gets distributed or goes straight to video. We're artists, yet we get treated like the paint on someone else's canvas. But that's not how I play the game anymore. And you don't have to, either. Haven't you learned this in the Practice? The self is not limited. We have the power. We *are* the power."

It wasn't hard to guess how it went down. Someone gave Olson the message that Rob wanted that scene. Olson didn't give a rat's ass what Rob wanted. Then Olson was encouraged to include the scene and strongly reminded that the distribution company, Radian, was owned by ACE, and that all purse strings led back to Rob Mars. Fait accompli.

Rob leaned back and crossed his arms, smiling a bit smugly. I was impressed. This was how I wanted to be. After so many years of following a script, listening to a director, and having my days arranged around call times and media appearances, a little power was very appealing. "But, hon, one thing?"

"Anything."

"No more surprises."

"Yes, ma'am."

I was still so naïve. It hadn't occurred to me that anyone would leak the change, or hold Rob accountable, but of course the piece on *Movieline* came out the next morning and the whole world saw my busybody fiancé leveraging his status to boost my comparatively lame career. Oh, the press loved me when I was standing next to Rob, a picture-perfect pair. They loved that we were engaged. They were so dying to hear about the wedding details that Lotus was getting offers for exclusives on the *planning sessions*. (Before I fired her, Bethamy was unabashedly angling for this, as she wanted to pitch her own wedding reality show.) But when it came to my work, I was perpetually relegated to Rob's shadow.

My father was not pleased. "Don't get me wrong," he said, "I think every minute you're onscreen is brilliant. But look at the press, Elizabeth. We have to think about how these things play. Rob should *know* that." It was always amazing to me how personally my father seemed to take these missteps. Like he was watching a bad play by a football team that he'd put a lot of money on.

My father was hung up on public opinion, but Rob was thinking bigger. He was showing me how to take charge of my work. Next to Rob, my father seemed out of touch and provincial.

When I got off the phone, Rob raised his eyebrows at me. "Everything okay?"

"Dad's not used to me having another man in my life," I said.

It didn't pass my notice that no one—not the press, not Rob, not my father—asked me how *I* felt about the edit. The fact of the matter was that I wished I'd been bold enough to fight for it myself. Rob had used his powers for what he thought was good, and I loved that about him. The Studio was teaching me to do the same. The press had decided that Rob was controlling me and my career at just the moment that I was convinced he, and his organization, were teaching me to stand up for myself. The truth, which might have saved me, was coming from the source I trusted least.

4

My engagement to Rob had put me in the spotlight, but professionally I needed to get out of his shadow. As expected, *Man of Her Dreams* tanked. My phone went silent, a sorry companion, like a little sick puppy whose tail never wagged. I refused to succumb to the post-movie blues— and yet I kept finding myself in the kitchen, wolfing down midnight snacks of garlic bread and salted caramel gelato.

My new agency, ACE, had yet to deliver on the big movie my father and Rob had planned for me. Cherry Simpson, my rep at ACE, said, "Honey, honey, we wanted the engagement first. Trust me, you'll get a better deal." Cherry was breezy and efficient. She looked like a lot of mid-fifties Beverly Hills fashionistas. She had the sinewy body and taut cheeks of a 100 percent green juice diet, blond extensions, and an upper lip that was borderline natural. The overall effect was of a very young corpse.

In our first meeting she'd told me I was prettier in person—a back-handed compliment—and that she thought I needed to go the action route, which was also not a ringing endorsement of my acting. "You have to be patient. I'm working on *Skye London: The Emerald Isle* for you. It's a franchise based on the Skye London video games. She's a rogue cop avenging her daughter's murder. You would be a perfect fit." Yeah, sure, the former Lucy McAlister, America's sweetheart, was a shoo-in as a rogue cop. Not to be paranoid, but I was pretty sure Cherry had been given a mandate: "Handle Mars's girl. Doesn't matter if she can act. Get her something big."

But so far the Mars power play had yielded nada, and all I could do was endure the waiting game that every actor knows too well. I got skin treatments: weekly facials; monthly photofacials; occasional lunchtime peels; a "baby Botox" treatment every six months (preventative); and a noninvasive nose job—just to refine the tip. In the mirror my face looked like it had been airbrushed. Since my practice at the Studio wasn't producing the big-screen skinny body I needed (and the late-night binges weren't helping), I took up a new exercise program called Infinite Space, which used suspended weights for three-dimensional movements, supposedly creating long, lean, dense muscles that burned a thousand extra calories a day. I supported Rob as he tended to his countless projects. I planned the wedding. I told myself to be patient, there was no rush.

And then something happened that changed the timeline entirely.

Cherry Simpson finally scored me the much-sought-after meeting with Danny McDaniels, who was directing *Skye London*, and as Cherry told me, again, "That's what you need. An action movie, a franchise." So I heard.

Danny McDaniels was in his fifties. The success that had launched him was *Ninjas Gone Wild*, which, legend had it, he made in film school on a budget of $200,000 that he earned selling cocaine. His unique anime/torture porn had since made billions of dollars in the video market. The movies were terrible, but they made him so rich that Hollywood was forced to treat him as legit.

Danny looked like a teenager who'd taken over his dad's office. The walls were lined with posters of his movies, showing men with enormous guns and women with enormous tits. He was facing the wall, playing a video game, and just as his assistant led me, Meg, and Cherry into the room, his avatar died, making a sad little wilting sound. Talk about entering on an inauspicious note.

"Motherfucker," he said. And hello to you too. Then he spun his chair around to face us. "Lizzie Pepper! I love you! Awesome, awesome."

Half an hour into the meeting, Danny McDaniels had yet to bring up *Skye London*. Then he had a lightbulb moment. "Hey!" he said, snapping his fingers. (Apparently there really are people in this world who snap their fingers when they have, or pretend to have, an idea, and Danny McDaniels was one of them.) "God, wouldn't it be great for you and Rob to work together? I bet you'd love that."

Okay, I'm slow, but it really took me until then to realize that I was going to witness that same flash of genius in every single meeting I ever had from now until forever. Sure, one day someone might want to work with me. But my fiancé was the Holy Fucking Grail.

I didn't have time to come up with a good response to Danny McDaniels's brilliant idea.

"Excuse me," I said, bolting out the door and into the ladies' room. Meg followed me. I ran into the nearest stall and retched until I could only dry heave. I finally emerged, apologizing. "I don't know what's wrong with me. It must be food poisoning."

"Or . . ." Meg said with a half-smile.

I looked at her blankly.

"Or you're pregnant, dummy."

Suddenly it was so obvious. The midnight garlic bread binges. The salted caramel gelato. I wasn't depressed about not having work. I was hormonal. I was pregnant. *Oh my God.*

I splashed cold water on my face. This was not the plan. Rob and I wanted kids one day . . . but now? Before the wedding?

"Do you think I have to go back into that stupid meeting?" I asked

Meg. She didn't respond. Instead she waited. As Meg knew full well, I'd completed the Introduction to the Whole Body Practice. When I asked Meg the question, my new mental reflexes sprang into action. I pushed the muddle of new emotions aside and zeroed in on my core truths. Did I want to finish the meeting? *No.* Did I care what Danny McDaniels thought of me? *No.* Was I my own being who made my own choices? *Yes.*

"I want a red velvet cupcake from Sprinkles," I said.

Meg grinned. "Sprinkles it is." Twenty minutes later we were in the backseat of the car, red velvet cupcakes in hand. Meg lifted hers in a toast, whispering, "To the best little secret in the world." We took huge bites and both broke into excited giggles.

I hadn't returned to the meeting, and it didn't matter. I guess Rob Mars's fiancée can bail on a meeting without explanation whenever she wants. I landed the part anyway. I was Skye London. And I was pregnant.

The next morning I called my gynecologist and asked to come in. Dr. Masler had been my doctor ever since I moved to L.A., but things had changed as soon as Rob and I went public. When I called to schedule my annual checkup, the nurse said, "What name do you want me to put down in the book?"

I said, "Lizzie Pepper."

She said, "No, I mean, I know who you are, but usually we put VIPs under a different name."

Oh. Right. Thinking fast, I said, "Aurora. Aurora Janevs." (This was before Aurora had been outed as my best friend. Later I went by Ella Mae.)

Meg had driven me to that appointment, and I'd been surprised when she parked in a back lot and took me up the service elevator to a private entrance I'd never seen.

"How did you know to do this?" I asked Meg.

"I call ahead everywhere we go," she said. Little by little, I was learning how hard Meg was working to protect me and help my life run smoothly. She anticipated my every need, and Rob's, too. I half expected her to write my wedding vows for me. Eventually I knew the drill. Any doctor or spa treatment would make room for me last minute. No matter when I arrived, I would be taken straight to an exam room—no waiting room for me—and no waiting. The doctor always saw me immediately. No wonder I'd spent so many hours in waiting rooms when I was only an IP instead of a VIP.

Dr. Masler confirmed the pregnancy. Although Rob and I had left the possibility open, I never imagined it would happen so quickly and easily. Rob and I had only known each other for nine months, and we'd been engaged for ten weeks. Ten weeks, it turned out, was exactly how pregnant I was. The baby was due June 8. I mechanically entered the date into my phone.

On our way out of the office, Meg said, "Time for a new obstetrician."

"What?" I said. "I can't leave Dr. Masler. He'll be hurt. I've known him forever."

Meg nodded. "I'm sure he's really good, but I'm afraid you're going to need someone who's used to handling high-profile clients—not just a top doctor, but one who can protect you."

"Protect me from what?"

"The press loves a pregnancy. We need to safeguard your records, any complications, and, assuming all goes well, your hospital visit for the delivery."

"I'm sure Dr. Masler can—"

"I totally saw Lizzie Pepper's vagina!"

Meg waited for me to give her a baffled look before she continued: "When you were seeing the doctor, I overheard one of the nurses say that to another nurse."

So I switched doctors.

A stew of mixed anxiety and excitement churned in my belly—or was that the baby? A little being that was part me and part Rob. This child would bind us together. Our love was already dividing and multiplying (with one critical extra division I had yet to know about). As with the rest of this relationship—it was everything I wanted, it was just that the pieces were falling together faster than I'd anticipated. I felt a little like I was always trying to catch up with myself. We're dating—wait, we just met. We're engaged—wait, we're just getting to know each other. You're pregnant—wait, we're not even married. I still hadn't shaken that strange feeling of both loving Rob and feeling like we were still in the very beginning of our relationship. But if anything would bring us closer, it was a baby. And if I was going to be a mother, I wanted to be a great one.

Had our roles been reversed, Rob would have found a big, romantic way to surprise me with the news. We'd take a boat to the middle of a lake and the pregnancy test would float down to us in its own tiny hot-air balloon. Now it was my turn to surprise him. But how?

Aurora was the first and only person (besides Meg) whom I called with the news.

"Pepper, this is huge. I am 100 percent happy for you slash 75 percent worried about you," Aurora said.

"I'm not sure that's how percentages work . . ."

"Oh, stop. You know math wasn't my subject."

"I'm fine! This is good news. The doctor says everything looks great."

"No, I'm not worried *that* way," Aurora said. "It's all just so fast—"

"I know, believe me."

"Have you guys even talked about—I don't know—whatever it is that people are supposed to talk about before they have children together?"

"Probably not. But does anybody actually have those conversations?"

"Well, what about the One Cell birth plan? Are you allowed to give birth in a hospital or does it happen at the Studio, on a bed of sand?" I was beginning to regret how much I'd told Aurora about the Practice.

"Oh, please. Even if that were a thing, which it isn't, I am a free person! Will you stop worrying and just be happy for me?"

"Fine." Aurora relented, and we tried to brainstorm ways I could break the news to Rob.

"I could cook him a dinner of just baby things: baby corn, baby carrots . . . ?"

"Veal?" Aurora suggested.

"Put a bun in the oven and have him check on it?"

"Don't you have a chef?"

Finally we decided that I'd put together a movie night for us. In the screening room I'd play a slide show of us together, and at the end would be a picture of the positive pregnancy test. It would require some help from a couple of trusted production friends, and it meant the news would have to wait until Rob came home from shooting a commercial in London, but he would love it.

A good enough plan, except that's not how it went down.

I guess I should have gone into hiding—it wouldn't have been a big stretch from my new normal. But *Skye London* was scheduled to start shooting in the summer—soon after the baby was born—and I was still operating under the delusion that I would have a post-baby career, so I thought it was important to stay visible.

Meg was my date for the premiere of Hunter Dix's new movie, *Lady Luck*, since Rob was in London. I wore a dress from Siri Jones's For Thieves Only line. I wasn't showing yet, and I was working out like a demon to counter the irrepressible midnight snacking. But I was a little bloated, so the flowy bohemian silk felt like the right call.

It started the minute I climbed out of the car. The photographers yelled, "Lizzie! Lizzie! Show us the bump! When are you due? Is it Rob's or Johnny's?" I was absolutely floored. I was only thirteen weeks along! How could they possibly know? Someone had to have leaked it, but who? Besides Dr. Masler's office, Meg and Aurora were the only people who knew. I ignored the shouted questions, but I knew it was hopeless. I would top *Rounder*'s "bump alert" list. So much for my plan to surprise Rob. The press had beaten me to even this incredibly personal news. If I hadn't been so disappointed, I would have been impressed.

As soon as we were safely seated in the theater, I turned to Meg and whispered, "What was that?"

"I have no idea," she said, and texted furiously throughout the screening.

By the time the movie let out, the mystery was solved, at least partly. The dress I was wearing was straight from the press release wherein Siri Jones had announced her *maternity* line. This very dress had been featured in *Glam* as a stylish option for women trying to hide that they were expecting. Wearing it was the equivalent to hanging a sign around my neck that read: "I'm pregnant."

But Siri had known to send me the dress, which meant someone had earned a pretty penny giving her the tip. So there was still a leak. Someone was making money off the most personal details of my life. Meg? Impossible. A nurse at the obstetrician's office? But we had a nondisclosure. Aurora? I couldn't help but remember all the questions Aurora had asked me. This wasn't the first time the question of discretion had come up between us. And she always needed money—not so much for herself as for her nonprofit. Would my best friend sell me out? It was an awful thought and so, for now, I chose to blame the nurse.

I called Rob that night, waking him up at the crack of dawn in London. "You're not going to believe the latest gossip."

"What is it now?"

"*Rounder* is saying I'm pregnant."

"Figures," he said. "At least they didn't find the wedding location."

"I *am* pregnant."

There was a silence. Then a joyful whoop. "Yes! I love you, baby." I couldn't see him, but I was pretty sure there was a fist pump happening on the other end of the line.

"I'm sorry I had to tell you like this. I had a plan—"

"This is the best news I've ever had in my entire life. I wouldn't have it any other way. You're making my dreams come true." He paused, knowing exactly what was coming.

"*My* dream is for you to stop saying I'm making your dreams come true."

"And if I make *that* dream come true?"

"Then I'll never admit it." I looked out the window. The moon glowed, and the landscape lights made the gardens look like a fairyland. I cradled the phone, listening to Rob's soothing voice. We were thousands of miles apart, but we were forever joined, and inside me a tiny, inaudible heart beat as fast and determined as a hummingbird.

5

My first Christmas with Rob was at Grace Island, an off-the-grid private island in the British Virgin Islands that belonged to his friend Roger, a Formula One driver. We had already spent a long weekend in Mustique at a villa owned by his friends the Spencers. It was the type of getaway that was starting to feel normal.

"It's a little extreme, isn't it?" my mother said when I told her why we wouldn't be coming to Chicago for the holidays.

"I know. But it's the easiest way for Rob—and now me—to have some privacy."

"How will you ever go back, though? How can you go on a normal vacation after borrowing a private island?"

"Mom, I am marrying Rob Mars. I won't ever go back to normal."

That gave her pause. Then she kind of snorted and said, "I'm trying, but I can't find anything wrong with that." We laughed.

private island: overrated, I texted Aurora, lounging poolside.

omg diva of the century

i know, but someone had to say it.

Here's the thing: I've heard it said that once one's basic needs are met—food, clothing, shelter—one's happiness or satisfaction with life finds a default level and stays there. Anyway, so it seemed to me. My struggles and anxieties and challenges and pleasures had all shifted when Rob and I got engaged, but I was no happier or sadder than I'd ever been. A private island sounds heavenly, and it *is*—in the same way that any fine beach in winter is a treat. But in our cases the *privacy*, which is what makes it sound so damn fancy, wasn't a sought-out luxury. It had become an expensive necessity. Rob seemed to love the utter seclusion, but what I truly longed for was a vacation from our everyday isolation, an impulsive stroll down a beachy strip, poking into souvenir shops and buying fudge. It was a freedom I hadn't felt for a single moment since that day in Cannes when Rob and I first went out in public together. I know, poor Lizzie.

Again: I fully recognize that Grace Island was paradise. But I reserve the right to say, without self-pity or any expectation of sympathy, that it was not for me.

One moment stands out in my memory of that Christmas. It was nothing, really. A gesture, a glance, a strange expression—these tiny moments happen all the time, catching our attention like a bird overhead, then flying past, nearly forgotten.

It began with Rob's brother, Scotty. His wife and baby were back in New York, where he was leading the effort to establish the Studio's new outpost, but his honey-haired assistant, Samantha, had come with him on this trip. Scotty immediately started disappearing with her every morning on a motorboat. There was clearly something going on between them, but nobody spoke of it and nobody seemed to mind.

"Did Scotty and his wife break up?" I asked Rob.

He shrugged. "I don't think so."

"What about this Samantha?"

Rob rubbed my head. "You and I know better than anyone the evils of gossip." If it had been anyone else, I would have said, "Give me a break." But Scotty was my fiancé's brother and a Core Leader at the Studio. The whole thing made me completely uncomfortable.

Scotty and Samantha's unexpected coupling, and our group's general indifference to it, sparked a brand-new worry in my mind. I lounged at the pool, feeling bloated and not quite sure of the bikini that showed off my growing belly, trying to concentrate on my book. I'd brought along a memoir called *Papillon*, which had been the basis for a Steve McQueen movie in the seventies. The book had been sent to Rob for a possible remake, but he passed it to me, knowing how much I love an adventure tale. This one was the true story of an infinitely resourceful Frenchman, nicknamed Papillon, who was convicted of murder in the 1930s (falsely, he claims). After multiple failed attempts, he finally escapes what was meant to be a lifelong prison sentence in the islands of then French Guiana. The dramatic saga of his numerous ingenious escape plans—he ultimately is the first person to ever escape a bleak place called Devil's Island by floating away on a bag of coconuts—lent a little drama to our otherwise relentlessly tranquil setting.

I was reading about the grotesque seven-inch biting centipedes that regularly dropped into one of Papillon's cells, when I looked up to see Meg and Rob down below on the beach. They'd been paddleboarding, and Rob was reapplying sunblock to the hard-to-reach part of Meg's back, just above her bikini strap. It occurred to me that—other than in his movies, of course—I had never actually seen Rob touch another woman. What I saw was nothing but chaste—a quick, clinical circling of fingertips and he was done—but a flash of doubt and dread crept along the back of my neck.

Were Meg and Rob lovers? Or had they once been? They'd practiced at the Studio together. She was woven into every part of our lives. And, as Aurora had pointed out, she was hot.

Rob and I had talked about our sexual pasts, but we'd never listed out our past lovers. What was the point? Either he'd had as many lovers as one might imagine, which I didn't need to hear, or he hadn't, which would raise the question: Why not? But Rob had certainly inventoried his sexual history during his 100. Most likely in Meg's presence. So she knew his past, where I didn't. Was she part of it? Rob, like his brother, was used to getting whatever he wanted. Why shouldn't he get tired of me one day? I was already turning into a pregnant cow. Anxiety churned in my gut.

In my Intro to the Whole Body Practice at the Studio, this feeling of panic was exactly what we had learned to address. *Emotions are chemical reactions*, I told myself, closed my eyes, and burrowed my toes into the sand beneath my chaise. I was trained for this. Fear wasn't truth. The present was what mattered. The facts of the present. Rob and I loved each other. We were engaged. I was pregnant with his baby. He had never been anything but loving to me. This fear came from inside me, from my past, from self-doubt, from weakness. *I am not my emotional self. I control my experience.* Then Rob and Meg climbed the sandy path toward me, open smiles on their faces, and the feeling fluttered off into the cloudless blue sky.

Christmas Day. For Rob I'd made a photo book in which I'd painstakingly paired our first texts with phone photos of our first year together. For me, there was a Tiffany-blue box, but instead of harboring the expected piece of jewelry, inside was nested a car key. He'd leased a white Ferrari, it turned out, which was waiting for me in Malibu, and which I would promptly exchange for a more practical black Range Rover.

"We miss you, honey," my mother said over the phone that morning.

"Your father put up a beautiful tree. I did it in all gold and white this year. And your stocking is hung next to ours."

"Save me some pecan pie, okay?" I said.

I remembered the Christmas mornings of my childhood: coming downstairs in new holiday pajamas to a fire in the hearth of our toasty living room; the pine scent of the Christmas tree; a ham out on the kitchen counter for us to pick at all day (in flagrant violation of health codes); and, in lucky years, a fresh frosting of snow on the windows. We always had neighbors over, the Guineys and the Pattersons, because otherwise it was just the three of us. Until we were too cool for it in high school, Ellie Patterson and I joined carolers in the neighborhood every Christmas afternoon. The "now bring us some figgy pudding" chorus of "We Wish You a Merry Christmas" was our unspoken cue to break off caroling and sprint back to my house for my mother's famous-for-this pecan pie. For me, Christmas would always be the traditions of my childhood. Even last year I had gone back to the mall to see the same animatronic reindeer moving their tired, balding heads back and forth, up and down. I loved my new life, but I couldn't help feeling nostalgic for holidays past.

Late Christmas morning, lounging by the pool in a post–carb fest stupor, I turned to Rob and said, "I love it here, I really do. But our baby has to have some snowy Christmases, okay?"

"And sit on Santa's lap at the mall while I stand by to make sure he doesn't do anything pervy?"

He got it. He understood what I needed for our child. "Exactly," I said.

We both knew that it wasn't going to happen. Not like that anyway. The mall would have to open after hours for us, and Rob would have to hire extras or something to make sure the place wasn't deserted and spooky. But we both wanted it, and for now that was all I needed.

6

I celebrated the new year by plowing through books and lists, determined to school myself on every aspect of pregnancy, childbirth, and after. But that sunny, secluded Christmas had stirred an extra concern: How would this innocent creature grow up in our rarified world? The luxury and isolation that was such an adventure for me—how did that work for a child? Back in Chicago, I had grown up playing with the neighborhood kids on our tree-lined street. Unsupervised, we made mud pies in the empty lot and roller-skated on the sidewalks until dinnertime. Baby Mars would enter a world of camera lenses and voices shouting our names.

My fears may have seemed like a new mother-to-be's paranoia, but when we finally officially announced my pregnancy, the world went truly mad. Just as they loved it when Rob and I got engaged, they were seemingly over the moon to hear that I was expecting. I couldn't get the tiniest bit of traction on my career, but the public gave a standing ovation to my casting as Rob's romantic interest. Unfortunately, our observers didn't know how to be a passive audience. The story wasn't locked; their actions had consequences, and Rob and I weren't protected by the safety screen of fiction.

Everyone knows this part of the story: In the beginning of February I had my first meeting for *Skye London*. I was twenty weeks pregnant, finally feeling like myself again. Lewis, the driver, was taking me and Meg to the lot in Burbank. We were aware that a car or two was following us, but when Lewis pulled up in the parking lot behind the producer's office it looked like the coast was clear. I stepped out of the car—Meg right behind me—and suddenly men with big cameras ran toward me from every direction. The door to the building, and safety, could only have been twenty feet from the car. I didn't have time to think. I lifted my Chloe satchel to hide my face and started to run. Then I'm not sure what happened. Paparazzi were right in front of me. Maybe I crashed into them. Or maybe in my mad dash I tripped over someone's foot. All I really know is that I went down. Hard.

I didn't catch my fall. Both my hands were up holding my bag in front of my face. I landed on the left side of my belly. I screamed, and there was a collective gasp as everyone realized what had happened and what it might mean. But the bulbs never stopped flashing.

Then Lewis was scooping me up and carrying me in.

In the lobby, cramps wracked my body. It wasn't a horrible pain, but the terror that accompanied it made my whole body shake. Was this what a miscarriage felt like? I took deep breaths, trying to calm myself, muttering expletives under my breath.

I'd run out of my introductory meeting with the director of *Skye London* to throw up in the bathroom. Now I was missing my first meeting with the producer to go to the hospital. In a minute the industry would forever label me high maintenance. I couldn't have cared less.

I was put on bed rest and anti-contraction meds for a week, during which Rob and I watched rumors of our baby's death circulate alongside horrible photos of the fall. The headlines were "Did Lizzie Lose the Baby?" and, for the shots of me in the arms of Lewis, who happens to be African American: "Lizzie's Baby—White?" Spare me.

After a week in bed Rob took me to the new doctor for a follow-up appointment. The doctor, Henri, didn't just give me an all-clear. He also surprised us with the report of *two* heartbeats, and *two* penises. We were having twin boys!

We came home to Brentwood relieved and happy. I just wanted to put the scare behind us. But then I saw our handyman and his crew leaving our suite. The smell of paint filled the room. I looked at Rob questioningly. He smiled and winked. "A little present for you."

Entering the bedroom, my eye was instantly drawn to the open door of Rob's dressing room, out of which came an unfamiliar light. I soon saw why. His shirts and suits were no longer hung from dark to light along the walls. The closet bars and hooks and shelves were gone, and the room had a fresh coat of white paint. Then, through the doorway, I saw the stirrups. At first I didn't realize what they were—so familiar, but so out of place in a home—an odd metal armature I thought might have been a sculpture. I had to step into the doorway to understand. Rob's closet had been converted to an examination room. Its centerpiece was one of those ob/gyn chairs with its undignified stirrups jutting out. It was lit from above by a ghastly fluorescent spotlight. Various monitors and medical supplies were neatly shelved on the far wall. It looked like a torture chamber.

"I can't give you a normal life, Elizabeth," Rob said. "And our children will have some of the same challenges. But they will be so loved—"

I interrupted his pronouncement by bursting into tears.

Rob's face went white. "I'm so sorry," he said. "I'm such an idiot! I shouldn't have surprised you." I'd never seen him so flustered. He put his arms around me. "We can dismantle it. Meg and I just thought it would help you feel safer to be examined here, whenever you want."

I knew they meant well, but I couldn't stop crying.

When I calmed down, I felt ashamed. "I know emotions are a chemical reaction . . ."

"No, love! Don't do that to yourself," Rob said. "Emotions don't govern us, but for Pete's sake, we still have them. It breaks my heart that I can't give you a simpler life, Elizabeth. And our children, too." He looked like he was going to cry.

"It's not your fault," I said. "Your success is a blessing. We have to take the bad with the good." He was the only person who loved the fluttering beings inside me as much as I did. They were a double miracle, a great treasure whose worth was only ours to appreciate. Our love for them was something we would share forever, no matter what. Rob held me for a long time as we mourned the childhoods that didn't yet, and would never, exist.

A few days later the tabloids gleefully reported news of my home examination room as yet another wild extravagance. What nobody knew was that for me it represented my first failure as a parent. We had everything money could buy, but we couldn't offer our future children the most fundamental gift: freedom.

For a while the door to that room stayed shut tight, a silent symbol of the privacy our unborn children would never know and Rob's futile efforts to compensate. Then, when enough time had passed, I had Meg donate the whole setup to a hospital.

7

The fetuses and I were physically fine, but after the fall something had changed in me. I didn't trust the outside world. My babies weren't safe. And keeping them safe trumped giving them a childhood like mine. I let go of that dream. The boundaries of my world tightened even further, to the people and places where Rob and I fit best. Even so, I wasn't myself. Every time I had to leave the house, I was anxious for the two days prior, and when Lewis brought me back home, I spent the first half hour sitting on the couch, staring straight ahead. Rob was so impossibly calm and understanding that finally one morning I confronted him about it.

"You think I'm crazy, don't you? I mean, I know I'm crazy. Do you think it will go away when the babies are born?"

Rob, who was in the middle of getting ready for a meeting, came out of his (now restored) dressing room and sat down on the bed next to me. He put a hand on my belly.

"I don't think you're crazy. In fact, I think this is a perfectly rational way to react to what happened to you. It was very scary and upsetting."

"But you would never do this. Nothing fazes you."

"Maybe that's true now—although I haven't ever been pregnant, so who can say—but you should have seen me after *The Son* came out." Rob lay down on his side, facing me, moving his hand in slow circles on my belly as he spoke. I knew, as everyone did, that in addition to the fans who had convinced themselves that he actually was the Son of God, others had protested the movie, citing various blasphemies, specifically the steamy moment with Mary Magdalene and, of course, the graphic castration scene (even I can't really believe they went with that). The fanatics and the protestors had set up opposing camps outside his house in the Hollywood Hills. "It happened overnight. And maybe I should have been grateful for the notoriety at that point in my career, but I couldn't handle it. People wanted something from me that I couldn't give. They asked for prayers. They begged me to heal them. They wanted my blessing. I had no idea how to live up to that. I could only fail those people."

"I so can't picture that. You! You're like a rock."

"I didn't leave my house—my little bungalow up in the hills—the street was so narrow it was like a one-way dead end. I didn't go outside for two solid months. Ordered food. Sent Lexy out for everything else. I literally didn't step out the door until Christmas, when I had to go home because my folks were expecting me."

"Christmas, huh? Sounds like the worst time to venture out in that crowd."

"You're telling me."

There was no doubt in my mind that he was telling the truth, but I couldn't reconcile the situation Rob was describing with the man in front of me. "But how . . . how did you change? You just got used to being seen as the Messiah?"

"Not at all," Rob said. "How do you get used to that? One Cell got me through. I did my 100."

And there it was again. The miraculous, life-changing 100 I'd been hearing so much—and yet so little—about. Every time I felt lost, or worried, or unsure of my place in Rob's world, the answer seemed to lie deeper in the Studio. I wanted Rob's strength. And I wanted to understand what lay below it. The 100 promised both.

I joined a Core Group, all twelve of us committing to take turns doing our 100-but-really-a-lot-more questions together. I was the seventh to take my turn. Over the first six sessions, I'd listened to each one go through what I was about to experience, and I knew what I was in for. Every secret I'd ever kept would be laid bare. I'd seen people lie, posture, perform. I'd seen them weep, give up, and plunge into darkness. And, unfailingly, I'd seen them pull themselves back together in an amazing exhibition of the human spirit. When I asked Rob about his 100, he couldn't articulate what it had been like for him. He shook his head and laughed, as if it was too amazing and complicated to even describe.

"You just have to experience it yourself. That's the whole point of it. I could never do justice to my experience. You'll see. You'll totally get it. God, you'll rock it, Elizabeth. You were made for the 100."

The Core Group met at the Studio, in a windowless practice room with a neatly swept dirt floor at the edge of which were white folding chairs. One could wear one of the Studio robes, or any loose, comfortable clothes. I came in sweats and a T-shirt, with no jewelry and no scented products. Frankly, it was my everyday maternity garb anyway. We started at noon. Most people's 100s ran at least twelve hours, past midnight.

In these sessions, the 100 took the place of the guided meditation. After our silent standing meditation, I stayed in the center of the room, while the rest of my group sat in folding chairs. I stood in the dirt in the grounded position I had learned to hold, though never for such a sustained period. The leader, Mary, always began with the same straightforward questions, only now they were directed toward me: *When was I born, where, to whom? What were my first memories of walking, talking, eating, playing? How was I educated? What teachers did I remember, what friends, what hobbies and interests?* The questions went on and on and got increasingly specific and personal. *What was my first job? What did I learn from it? Describe the circumstances. When did I have my first kiss? Who was it? Describe the circumstances. When did I lose my virginity? Did I have shame associated with sex? Describe the circumstances. Had I had oral sex, anal sex, homosexual sex or sexual fantasies, sex or sexual fantasies involving animals? Describe the circumstances.*

At first I was on edge, choosing my words as carefully as if this were an interview with *Glam*, but as the afternoon wore on, without food or drink, holding my position as best I could, I just responded as clearly as I could. The questions veered abruptly from stuff I would expect on a medical intake form to odd probing into my sex life. Knowing that everyone went through the same process, and I had nothing to be ashamed of, I answered honestly. Mary listened carefully, a kind, understanding expression fixed on her face.

Two lines of questioning caught me off guard. The first concerned Aurora. Mary had asked me a number of questions about my family and friends, and delved into whether and how they supported or interfered with my core goals. I had expected all of this.

Then she said, "Who is Buddy White?"

"I don't know a Buddy White," I said.

"Buddy White is Geoff's stepbrother. He has been in contact with your friend Aurora. Has he tried to meet with you?"

"No," I said.

"Buddy White is no friend to the Studio. Many of the lies in the press can be traced directly to Buddy White. Your friend—Aurora—she may not be aware of his intentions."

"I'm sure she isn't."

"Her association with Buddy White worries us. We want you to know the risks involved." Then Mary told me how this man fed lies about celebrity practitioners to the press in an effort to discredit the Studio. He was a privacy risk, and she wanted to make sure I knew not to meet with him. Also, she warned me, if Aurora believed what he said, I might want to distance myself from her.

Aurora had expressed concerns about the "cult." I could see her buying into this guy's lies, and if he convinced her that I was in danger, I could even see her being indiscreet. I made a mental note to set Aurora straight, as soon as possible.

That was an unexpected sidebar to the 100, but it was completely eclipsed by the personal revelation that awaited me.

I had no idea how much time had passed. There was no clock in the room and I wasn't wearing a watch, but my stomach was grumbling and more than anything I wanted to sit. I longed to sit. I paced and stretched, as I'd seen others in my group do. They shouted out encouragement, as if I were in the last leg of a marathon. It was probably around dinnertime when Mary asked a question I never anticipated.

"You told me you have no siblings, but you have a sister. Describe the circumstances."

I froze. This question had come from her list like all the rest, but nobody knew about my sister. Nobody. Not Aurora. Not even Rob. In fact, my sister's existence was the only secret I'd kept from my fiancé. A dark corner of my past that I didn't know how to explain. So how did Mary—how did One Cell—know? All my life I had consistently answered no to the question of whether I had siblings, in every interview and to every friend in every context since she'd left our family for good. I told myself it wasn't an out-and-out lie, since my parents had adopted Allison as a newborn, and she had left when I was still so young. But it was a lie, because her origins had never mattered to me. Allison was and always had been my sister.

Unsettled, I stammered, "How did you . . . ? I didn't—"

"Please focus on the question. We all have secrets. This is a safe space. You'll be amazed at how it feels to let it go."

I returned to the center of the room and stood completely still. I took a deep breath. The words came out as if I'd been chanting them in my head forever, and maybe I had. An unspoken secret pokes relentlessly at the conscience, demanding to be revealed. "I have an older sister, at least I did. Her name is Allison. I don't know where she is. She might be homeless. Or dead." There. I'd said it.

The faces of my Core Group didn't change. We had heard far worse— a man who admitted to beating his wife in an alcoholic rage, a girl who described the thrill of cutting herself in excruciating detail; this room had heard the greatest joys and sadness of all our lives.

Allison. At this point some of her story has already been in the press, but this is the truth from my perspective. I'm telling it the way I know it.

My older sister, Allison, had always been troubled. Born to parents who had their own personal struggles, my parents thought by giving her a good home and an education, they could break the cycle. But Allison needed something different, and my parents were utterly overwhelmed by the challenges she presented. School and Allison did not mix—she probably had undiagnosed ADHD—and she avoided it at all costs. She ran away from home many times, but she left for good when she was fifteen and I was four years old. I hadn't seen her since. My memories of her had broken into pieces, and I remembered them with an '80s Instagram filter. The corner of a patchwork quilt that resurfaced in my mind whenever I heard someone say the name "Allison." A flash of her angelic curls as she twisted her head to refuse a spoonful of medicine. Her hand, holding up a missing puzzle piece that she'd either taken from me or found for me. My sister, silhouetted in the doorway, her white-blond hair a wild mess, beautiful and scary. And then, this moment: my mother carrying me out of my bed in the middle of the night and putting me in the backseat of our car, wrapped in that same patchwork quilt. I fell asleep, and slept for what felt like hours until the car stopped. The engine was still running, but cold air came through the crack of the door and chilled my cheek. I opened my eyes.

"You stay here. I'll be right back," my mother said, probably thinking I would fall back asleep, and she went out into the cool night.

Curious, I watched her walk up the path to a cabin—my uncle's summer cabin, the windows of which were lit with a sour yellow light. The front door opened then closed behind her. Suddenly I felt very alone. I'd been told to stay in the car, and I always did what I was told, but I'd never been left alone in a cold car on a dark night before. I quietly opened the door and followed my mother.

Then—the blur of my mother pleading with my sister. A voice of desperation I'd never heard from my perky, unflappable mother. Allison's eyes, hooded and unfriendly, my mother imploring, giving up. My mother seeing me, scooping me up, and hurrying back to the car. And, finally, my mother driving us home—just the two of us—with tears silently streaming down the side of her face.

That was the last time I'd seen my sister.

Soon after that we moved from Lincoln Park to Highland Park. A different house, a different school, a neighborhood where nobody knew there was an older child. Nobody remembered the late nights with Allison pounding on the door, and the horrible night my parents called the police on her because the school psychiatrist had told them to try "scaring her straight." Ostensibly, the move was for my father's job, but to me it felt like it was our turn to run away.

After she was gone, my parents avoided talking about Allison's existence—or maybe they thought I was too young to handle it. But when I was a teenager I started asking questions. I wanted to know why they had given up on their daughter. My father said, "We never gave up on her. She gave up on us. At some point we had to protect ourselves. We had to protect you." The only time I brought it up with my mother, she burst into tears and fled the room. And then I became a star, and my parents devoted themselves to my success. And the more I succeeded, the smaller the shadow of sorrow in our house became, until it seemed like we'd buried it forever.

I never told a soul—and, amazingly, the press had never found her out. On *American Dream*, I never corrected the journalists who asked me about growing up an only child. In a very real way, I had. But by omitting her from my bio, I had unwittingly made Allison into an even bigger secret. If she were discovered now, the story wouldn't just be about why she had left and what had become of her. It would be about my lies and how I hid my own sister's existence.

Allison had been a secret for most of my life, but I had spent weeks listening to my fellow practitioners do their best to be honest about their mistakes, flaws, and darkest desires. I had just endured hours breaking down my own life for them, trying to explain who I was and why. My defenses were exhausted. The artifice was gone.

"If she's still alive, she is still my sister," I told them. "I love her, but I've hidden her existence because she's a question I can't answer."

I told them how conflicted I'd always been about Allison—missing her, wanting to somehow rescue her, but benefiting from her absence, flourishing as my parents' only, perfect child. I was the daughter who exceeded my parents' expectations, and yet my mother had never shown half the worry or any of the heartbreak I saw her devote to my sister. When Allison left, a fissure formed between my parents, and I stepped forward to fill the gap. I was trapped there, and if I pulled away, I feared what was left of our family would collapse.

I peeled back the layers: The guilt I felt for the success I enjoyed. The cowardice and compliance that made me follow my parents' lead. The fear that I would be discovered, and the shallow attachment to protecting my own image. The need to be perfect, always, because the family couldn't bear another failure. My sorry attempt to help others—but not my sister—by working with the rehab center LifeHeartTruth.

It was out. Tears ran down my cheeks, but I felt relief.

Then something happened that hadn't occurred in any of the other 100s. My Core Group started to clap. This applause was different from all the other applause I'd received in my life. It wasn't for a performance or an achievement. It was just for me being me.

My 100 was over. My Core Group joined me on the floor, and as we went through the poses, I felt light as air. I looked around the room. Any one of them might sell what I had revealed, but I didn't think they would. I trusted them, and that was a feeling I hadn't had in a very long time. But also—what if? What if the truth about my sister did come out for all the world to know? In that moment, for the first time, I felt brave and strong enough to face the consequences. This was the breakthrough I'd hoped for.

And yet I had no idea how soon this confession would come back to haunt me. And even if I'd known that, I couldn't begin to imagine how much damage it could do.

My 100 ended after midnight. Lewis drove me home. Rob had waited up for me, reading a pile of sky blue–bound ACE scripts in bed. He put his reading down when I came in.

"Well?" he said.

Then, at last, I told Rob about Allison. Out of nervousness, I busied myself with getting ready for bed as I talked, but I hadn't gotten far when Rob beckoned me to him.

"Come here." He was lying on the bed. I sat down next to him. "Whatever you tell me is okay. You can't scare me off now. I'm in. Whatever challenges are ahead, we'll face them together."

I needed to hear that. Tears rolled down my face as I told him, "My success eclipsed Allison entirely. She's alone in the world, and I've always felt like it was my fault."

Rob stroked my hair. "You were a young girl," he said. "You can make your own choices now."

Then a realization swept over me. "I don't want to act," I said, slowly and with certainty. As soon as I said it I realized it had been true for a very long time. Me and my stardom were my parents' redemption. My success came from guilt, not inspiration. In high school I had liked acting—it was my decision to put myself up for TV pilots—but then my friends were going off to college, and I hadn't wanted to miss out. I had wanted to quit *American Dream*. But my father wouldn't let me do it. He made me honor that commitment, and now acting was the only skill I had. But was I meant to be an actor? I'd never had a chance to try anything else.

I tried to explain it to Rob. "These babies are my chance to be something real. Not a made-up character. Not a superhero or a spy's girlfriend or a pioneer. Not bound to the career that I stumbled into at seventeen. It doesn't feel right anymore. I want to try being a wife and a mother. The best wife and mother I can be." I thought about how I'd been willing to sacrifice the part in *American Dream* to be at Granny's side when she was ill. This moment felt just as important.

"Come closer," Rob said, reaching toward me. I lay down next to him. He put his hands on my belly. "I would love for you to focus on the twins," he said. "To be honest, Meg and I were just talking about this. Meg was saying, and I agree with her, that a child needs his mother more than anything. It is the greatest role in the world."

"I'm quitting *Skye London*," I said.

Rob stroked my hair, and we were quiet for a bit.

"Okay, you said that out loud. How does it feel? Is it what you want? Are you happy?" he asked.

"Very," I said. And I was.

Now Rob knew all my secrets. What I didn't think about at the time was that he was still keeping at least one secret from me—the door to Blue-beard's chamber remained shut and locked, a reminder that even though I'd done my 100, no matter how close we were growing and how the twins would bond us, there was still a piece of him that might never be mine.

My parents found out that I'd quit *Skye London* by reading it in the press. My father was livid.

"How could you do this without speaking to me? It's a terrible mistake. But don't worry, we can probably get you back in. I have a call in to Cherry Simpson—"

"No, Dad. I don't want to do it. I'm really not sure I want to stick with acting."

"This is what we've worked for, Elizabeth. All these years of training and you quit the Olympics. You want to reconsider your career, fine. Do it after *Skye London*."

"I'm not sure you heard me—"

"I heard you, dammit. I just can't believe it. What does Rob say?"

"He supports me, Dad. He knows I am capable of making my own decisions. Acting doesn't define me."

"Elizabeth, this is nonsense. Is this what they're teaching you at that fake Hollywood commune?"

"Okay, Dad, this conversation is over."

"No, Elizabeth, it isn't. I'm not going to stand by and watch you throw everything away."

I hung up. My father had to have the last word, but I didn't have to listen to it. Afterward, I felt giddy. This is what it felt like to take control of my own life. I was going to be a mother. It was about time.

A week later, on our way home from a One Cell dinner, Rob asked if I was ready to commit to the Practice.

"What does that mean, exactly?"

"It's a formality, really," he said. "Your Core Group gathers, and anyone else you want to support you—I hope that would include your loving fiancé—"

"It might," I said.

"And there's a simple ceremony. Each supporter offers a truth that he or she respects about you. They're not always compliments. If I remember correctly, Meg commended my 'perpetual control'—that one hit a little close to home. But it's kind of nice to feel . . . understood. Then you state your life goals—they don't have to stay the same, of course they're always evolving—but it's meant as an acknowledgment that at any point in time we should be able to articulate our goals. At the end, you make a statement, committing yourself to making the Practice an integral part of your life, and raising our children to learn the Whole Body Principles, and you get one of these." He twiddled his Truth necklace, the one he never took off.

"It may sound like a big commitment, but actually you're already doing it. If you're comfortable with the involvement you have right now, you'll be fine." He pulled into our drive, rolled down his window, and said hi to the guards as they raised the gate. "Also," Rob said, "it would mean a lot to me."

Rob's twin sons were in my belly. We would soon be married. I was still getting to know this man, who had so quickly become my world, but I believed in him and in us. All my life I had followed my parents' plan for me, their edicts, their ambitions, their secrets. I judged myself on my ever-seesawing public image. Now I wanted to let all of that go. With Rob's strength to guide me, I was separating from them, choosing my own way. Even Aurora was less a part of my decisions than she'd been for many years. My 100 had been my confession, and after that I felt a new sort of intimacy with the Studio. I was known, understood. I saw me and Rob raising our children in that community. It would be the philosophical, social, and moral center of the life we built together.

And, although I couldn't have put it into words at the time, I would have done anything to deepen my connection to this too-perfect man.

The next day, in front of Rob, Liesl, his mother, Scotty, Meg, Mary, and most of my Core Group, I stood up and committed myself to the Studio. Mary handed me a thin string, and led me to a table with bowls of beads. I was to put as many beads as I wanted on my Truth necklace, to represent whatever elements of strength I chose. I selected three beads: one for independence, one for strength of spirit, and one for love. My father had always said, "The Peppers aren't joiners," but that was kind of the point. I didn't obey my father. I was a grown-up now.

8

Aurora, my mother, and Rob's mother cohosted my baby shower. Before Aurora could even worry about the cost, I told her I would send her the money for her share, and it would be between us. As soon as she received the check, I got the call I knew was coming.

"Ninety thousand dollars for a baby shower! You could feed a Third World country for that."

This was my life. It was hard enough to get used to it on my own.

"Actually, Rob *has* adopted a Third World country." That shut her up.

It was an exaggeration, but he did send a lot of money to Burundi and had built six schools and a hospital there. One of our bathrooms in Brentwood was done in Burundian copper, and Rob had gotten it photographed for *Celebrity Homes* in an attempt to start a trend. It's the little things . . .

The day before the shower, Aurora and my parents took me out to lunch at Duke's, which I knew my father would love, but I don't know if he ate a bite of his cheeseburger.

"Everything is moving so quickly, Lizzie," my mother said. "Your father wants to make sure this is what you want."

When my mother spoke for my father, it meant she knew a storm was coming and was doing everything in her power to temper it. Doug Pepper was not happy.

I smiled and patted my belly. "There's no turning back now."

Dad wasn't one to pussyfoot. "Elizabeth, you pulled out of *Skye London*. Your connection to Rob was supposed to help your career, not stall it. And now I'm hearing rumors that you've become part of that . . . organization." He shook his head. "You really have to be more careful."

"Um, Dad? Maybe you didn't notice that I'm pregnant? Even if I do decide to go back to acting, I'm allowed to take a break."

"Elizabeth, you weren't meant to be a star's wife. *You're* a star."

Aurora joined in. "The thing that's freaking me out is this One Cell Studio. Lizzie, have you googled it? There is some crazy shit going on there. Seriously. They say it's a cult. Once you're in, it's hard to get out. It's supposed to be a nonprofit, but people pay to practice there. The group leaders and lecturers don't get paid. And that town where it started, Fernhills—people who live there have no contact with people on the outside."

A baby shower is supposed to be a sweet, joyful event. Babies! What could be more pure and innocent? But instead of being celebrated I was being ambushed. "Whoa," I said "everybody just calm down. Yes, my life has changed very quickly. But you need to trust me. I'm an adult. I make my own choices. This is what I want. And that's all that should matter to you."

My father pounded his fist on the table. "No, Elizabeth. Let me tell you what we're going to do—"

A rage that I'd never known hit me. He was *still* doing it. Telling me what *we* were going to do. I focused on the Whole Body Principles: observing my rage, defining it, and discarding it. When I spoke, I was perfectly calm.

"Maybe I didn't make myself clear. I'm making my own decisions now. I'm happier than I've ever been. I don't need you to tell me what to do."

It was the first time I'd crossed my father, and it didn't go well. "You are out of your league, Elizabeth. Who do you think made all of this happen for you? You think you met Rob because he wanted to hire you for some movie? I have worked extremely hard to give you this life, to give you every opportunity in the world, and you are squandering it!" He rose and stormed out of the restaurant.

I was accustomed to my father taking credit for my success, but this was the first time I'd heard him take credit for my relationship with Rob. What the hell? West Bengal was three generations away and nearly erased by American crossbreeding. My father couldn't have thought he had any right to a hand in my romantic choices.

My mother stood up and patted my hand before hurrying after him. She always stood by her man. I knew the parting glance she gave me well. It said, "Don't worry, dear, he'll cool down."

"Wow," Aurora said. "You grew balls." We laughed.

And then my phone buzzed. It was Lewis calling from the parking lot of Duke's to ask if it was okay for him to take my parents back to the house without us. Oh, it must have killed my father that Lewis didn't follow his orders without my sign-off.

Aurora, however, was still in this. "I'm not trying to tell you what to do, but there's a guy I want you to meet. He used to be part of One Cell and now he helps people extricate themselves from the Practice. I'm not saying he's right. But it can't hurt to talk to him—just to get a perspective. Buddy White is—"

Buddy. The name hit me instantly. Buddy White was the man whose name had come up in my 100. I'd been warned about this, and now it was happening.

"Aurora, Buddy White is the disturbed stepbrother of Rob's friend

Geoff. You can't trust him. I don't trust him. Please don't tell him any-thing about me!"

Aurora looked thrown. "No, Lizzie . . . I don't think—I mean, are you sure? I've met him. He's totally down-to-earth. I can't see why he'd want to hurt you."

She was so naïve. I prayed she hadn't already somehow exposed me. "Just promise you won't talk to him about me? You have to promise."

"Okay, Lizzie, I promise."

When I came home, Rob was at the kitchen counter, reading the paper.

"I have a question for you." I chose my words carefully. "When we first met, you were much more interested in dating me than in hiring me for a movie, weren't you?"

"Definitely," he said, moving the paper to smile at me.

"The gossip mags have always said that it was an arranged meeting . . . was it?"

"Every meeting is an arranged meeting," he said.

"But was it a setup?"

"Yeah, my agents set it up with your dad." His face was open and un-concerned. It was as if he had just told me there was leftover pasta on the stove. He clearly wasn't hiding anything.

"Tell me more."

Rob looked a little confused. "I'm not sure what you're asking. My agents put the word out that I was single. I can't exactly go to 7-Eleven and ask out the checkout girl. I can't even say hi to a woman on a movie set without rumors flying. So that's the way we've done it ever since Lexy and I broke up."

"And my dad contacted you?"

"Actually, if I remember correctly, we reached out to him. I thought you were cute, and someone—maybe Bethamy?—knew that you grew up with that poster of me on your door. I didn't know how I would feel about you. But it couldn't hurt to meet you."

No wonder he called me Elizabeth. He'd picked it up from my father before we'd ever met. Rob stood up and wrapped his arms around me. "What's this about?"

I explained to him that my father was still upset that I'd turned down *Skye London.*

"Ah," he said. "He's probably thinking I haven't fulfilled my end of the bargain."

"What do you mean?"

"Before you and I met, I promised your dad I'd help you get a franchise." *Oh, and there's tomato sauce in the skillet. It might need salt.* Rob saw my face. "I thought you knew."

I shook my head. No, I didn't know.

"Being with me changes your life. It puts you in the spotlight. It restricts your freedoms. Your father was just looking out for you." He kissed me and held my cheeks in his hands. "Okay?" he said.

From the start, my father had seemed overly focused on what my relationship with Rob could do for my career. Now it was clear why. The two men in my life had planned my future like I was one of my father's investments. They'd negotiated our potential relationship long before I introduced them for what I thought was the first time in Chicago. I didn't blame Rob. This was how the world worked for him, even when it came to love. And he'd been nothing but forthcoming and honest about it when I'd asked.

I left my latte on the warming tray and walked across the house to the wing where my parents were staying. I entered without knocking. They were already in bed: my father reading the paper, my mother on her laptop.

I walked calmly up to my father and stopped. My voice was cold and steely. "You set me up with Rob. For my *career*. I'm not part of your portfolio, Dad."

"Now just a minute, Elizabeth. Everything I did, I did for you," he said.

"I want you to leave. First thing in the morning."

"Calm down, sweetheart," my mother said. "Your father was just trying to help you."

"I am calm. I want you to leave. Both of you. I'm done."

"This is ridiculous, Elizabeth. You'll see."

It was impossible to fight him because he only ever won. Doug "Pitbull" Pepper never backed down. But I could fight back in my own way.

It was the last time we would speak for a very long time.

The next day was the baby shower at the Polo Lounge. Bethamy would have insisted on a theme: two peas in a pod or Thing 1 and Thing 2 from the *Cat in the Hat*. Instead, Meg and I planned a simple shower in nautical colors: navy and white with pops of canary yellow. The pile of presents that came in was tall and all of them were professionally wrapped, embellished by little wooden rattles, organic mini cuddle blankets, and a slew of little Truth bracelets for the babies (who could wear them until they broke because newborns were "unsullied"). All the gifts were in doubles, most of them baby blue. I opened matching cashmere onesies and other tiny designer clothes, most of which I would later find had unfinished zippers that scratched the babies or tiny buttons that drove the mother crazy. There were two real fur jackets, size six months, and at least twenty silver spoons (ha, ha). Everything I'd read said that the parents of twins should treat them as individuals. No rhyming names; no matching outfits; separate birthday cakes. Already I could see that the world wasn't on board with that approach. Two matching babies was what they wanted from me. Later I would give away exactly half of each gift.

At the very bottom of the heap was Aurora's present, hand wrapped. There were two woolen baby hats, one striped and one solid. With them was a scarf in the same autumnal colors that was clearly meant for me— it was a set, to be sure, but a subtle one. Each had a silky tag that read "Knit with love by Aurora." I loved the gift, and I told her so, but I would never be able to wear a scarf like that in public.

My parents didn't attend the shower, having flown home in a huff that morning, but I barely noticed. The room was a sea of well-wishers. Everywhere I turned, I was congratulated and praised. And much as I knew that people pandered to Rob, I had never experienced it myself. I believed them. My new life, the one I had made for myself, felt great.

The next day, in *Glam*, the infamous Buddy White was quoted as saying that my parents had staged an intervention to get me out of the Studio. Is that what lunch had been? An *intervention*? Aurora texted immediately, insisting she hadn't said anything, but my Studio contacts confirmed that she was the informer. And so, with great regret, I had to shut out Aurora, too.

After that, I had a different view of the rumors that practicing with the Studio meant leaving your family and friends behind. Nobody had urged me to sever ties. On the contrary, I was finally listening to my own instincts. The Studio was teaching me how.

9

I was supposed to have an "elective" Cesarean, which meant that I had chosen it, even though I hadn't. I wanted natural childbirth—I wasn't against drugs, but I wanted at least to give it a try. But my doctor, Henri, said it wasn't an option for "someone like me." Aside from the fact that any twin pregnancy was automatically categorized as high risk, Henri said that if I wanted to guarantee my privacy, while in labor and while giving birth, he absolutely had to book an operating room in advance. The risk that someone would get a shot of me indisposed was just too high. This was how "everyone" did it—Jessica Rand, Chantelle, Isle Goodwin.

On the night of May 14, with my Cesarean only a week away, Rob was receiving an award for humanitarian service at the Studio. There was a whole fund-raising event around it to support Studio Manhattan, the New York project, and Rob was giving a speech. At eight months' pregnant, I wasn't going anywhere, so I sent Meg as my stand-in. She had nothing of her own that was suitable to wear, so Genna pulled some dresses out of my closet. Meg selected a simple black crepe gown by Lanvin. Joaquim did her hair in an updo. As she was on her way out, I realized that something was missing. Jewelry. It couldn't be too showy—as a longtime One Cell practitioner she lived modestly—so I added a vintage cameo on a black choker. She looked stunning.

Rob and Meg left, and I spent the evening on the couch, nibbling on sesame sticks.

I dozed off in the den, but woke up sometime after midnight when I heard the voice of the house alarm say "A door is open." Bleary, I lumbered down the dark hall. There were murmured voices and giggles, a "shhh." I reached the dimly lit entryway just as Rob caught Meg in his arms. She laughed and leaned in to him, her eyes shiny and unfocused.

"I can't hide it anymore," Meg drawled. "No more secrets."

"Hi," I said.

Both of them started at the sound of my voice, but Rob didn't let go of Meg. Indeed, if he had, she certainly would have slid to the floor. We stood frozen in that awkward tableau until Rob finally broke the silence.

"I'd better get this one to bed. Be right back, love." He started to walk Meg to her room.

"Hurry, please," I said. "Because we need to go to the hospital."

Rob spun around so fast he almost dropped Meg. "What's happening? Are you okay?"

I said the words at the same time as I understood what was happening to me. "My water just broke."

Lewis drove us to Cedars. Henri met the car with a wheelchair. In between contractions I put on a hat and wrapped the scarf Aurora made for me around my neck up to my nose. (It was the one time I *could* wear it—when I was trying not to look like myself.) They took me up in the service elevator to a three-room suite on the maternity floor. I would find out later that Meg had booked this suite for the entire two-month block leading up to my scheduled Cesarean, just in case there were complications. At $4,000 a night it was less than our travel per diem.

Now Henri conceded that I could skip the Cesarean after all. I labored in my suite for almost ten hours. Lewis was stationed right at the door, taking IDs and making sure everyone who entered, including all medical personnel, signed a confidentiality agreement. The hospital and any employee who signed the agreement were each liable for damages of $1 million, minimum, if a single photo was leaked. It was a fair price, since $1 million was exactly what *Rounder* was paying for the exclusive first shot of the babies.

Let me set the record straight, for once and for all. The Studio has no birth rites that I know of. I did not pick the original Cesarean date because it was Teddy Dillon's birthday, and I wasn't disappointed that the boys had other plans for their arrival (though maybe, in hindsight, it was a sign). A "high priest" did not deliver the twins, unless Henri leads a secret double life. Rob did not put sand on the floor of the hospital room. The babies do not have secret One Cell names. I did not have an affair with Henri. I was not vajazzled and did not know that word or concept existed until I saw it in reference to myself on *Sheigh Moi*. And, no, I was not blindfolded. Good one, though.

And there you have it, sorry to disappoint. I hate that I have to defend the most private moment in a woman's life, but one gets tired of being thought a freak. We led a rarified and even weird life, to be sure, but birth and death still play out as they will.

When the contractions grew unbearably intense, Rob's voice rose over my distress. He quietly whispered how grateful he was to me, how proud he was to be my intended, how excited he was to meet our children. Everything was going to be fine. If the Whole Body Principles had prepared Rob for anything, it was childbirth. Even if he was just playing the role of supportive father, saying the requisite lines, what difference did it make? He was calm, focused, and deeply present.

At some point, when I couldn't take it anymore, the epidural kicked in and worked way better than I could have imagined. Then I pushed, and our boys, first Casper, then Leo, were born at 8:15 and 8:46, respectively, on the morning of May 15. Their tiny wails came in stereo from somewhere behind me, one clearly more pissed off than the other (that had to have been Leo). It was the sweetest sound I'd ever heard.

As soon as the babies had been weighed and assessed, Henri put them on my chest. Slick wisps of dark hair peeked out from under the little cap that hid Casper's cone head. Two round bundles, their faces a bit spotty from the delivery. It was hard to imagine that they would grow into people, with talents and moods and preferences. Right now they were unformed and perfect. We would feed them, help them sleep, and keep them safe. Together Rob and I would watch their lives branch in more and more directions as they learned to walk, swim, jump, read, make friends, and imagine. The scope of it, of nurturing and protecting these helpless beings, was daunting. Their lives were so simple now, but the responsibility that lay ahead was unfathomable. Along the way we, their parents, could only make them less perfect. I desperately wanted us to make the right decisions for them, though I had no idea how.

I felt two heartbeats, quick against my own, and prayed that those little hearts would know more joy than pain. I knew I would love any child, but Cap and Leo were mine, and I forgot about everything else.

Though my feelings about this are clouded by later events, I will never forget seeing Rob with his new children. Nurses still bustled around us, cleaning up, but sneaking glances at us to confirm, I suppose, that celebrities act just as lost and in love as any other new parents. Rob knelt down next to the bed and nestled his head against me, his arm reaching around both boys. The four of us were a nest of love. Our family was complete. I felt like the luckiest woman in the world.

10

In the last days of planning the wedding, Meg brought me lists of questions, but I ceded all the last-minute decisions to Bethamy, the wedding planner I couldn't stand but had rehired in postpartum panic. Oh well. So much for making my wedding my own. Now that I had the twins to juggle, I decided it didn't matter.

Arrangements were made. People prepared what I would wear and where I would go. There was only one path in front of me. All I had to do was keep walking forward. If that makes me sound like a cow plodding stupidly to the slaughter, well, all I can say is that the cow is mercifully unaware of her impending doom.

Also, Henri gave me a little pink pill to take every morning. Beta-blockers. Henri promised they were perfectly safe for breast-feeding. I'd refused them before, when Bethamy thought I had too many opinions about my own wedding, but now I took one every day, and I felt like a million bucks.

In the end, the primary goal of wedding planning wasn't how to represent our love in a ceremony that bound us for life before all of our loved ones. Rather, the central focus was keeping the date and location secret. Our jet first made a quick stop on the Isle of Man. We got off the plane long enough to take some "vacation" photos on the beach nearest the tarmac. Then, as soon as it was getting dark, we stole off in a yacht to Dublin. Immediately before the wedding, we e-mailed our *Rounder* contact decoy photos of the four of us—me, Rob, and the babies—relaxing on our island vacation. By the time they hit the newsstands six days later we'd be married and off on our honeymoon in Australia. That was the plan, anyway.

The boys were two months old and still exclusively breast-feeding, one after the other, every four hours when we arrived at Ballybridge Castle, the thirteenth-century stronghold Bethamy had picked because she seemed to have such strong opinions about the pros and cons of various European castles. I still wasn't speaking to my parents—or Aurora, for that matter. Our falling-out had persisted through the twins' birth, which felt even bigger to me than the wedding. I had moved on, and the wedding represented my new, adult life. Most of the guests would be Rob's family; friends from the Studio; actors, producers, and directors we'd worked with over the years; and a number of people who had traveled with us to help with the wedding, though Genna, Talia, Joaquim, and Rob's stylist really counted as friends.

At least there was Meg. Soon after the boys and I came home from the hospital, Meg had tried to apologize for her condition the night I'd gone into labor. Oh, right. I'd nearly forgotten about seeing her drunk and whispering about secrets in my fiancé's arms.

"The way I grew up—it was really insular. In Fernhills I was immersed in the Practice. I'm kind of—realizing some stuff. I mean, coming to work for you was the first time I've really seen the real world—"

"This isn't exactly the real world—" I reminded her.

"That night was the first time I had alcohol."

I stopped her. "Please. I think you're allowed to have a few drinks on a Friday night." I thought of Meg as a close friend, but she'd never before mentioned any personal issues. Under ordinary circumstances I like to think I would have paid more attention to what she was trying to tell me. A good friend would have asked about what she was going through, but the boys were only a week old. All I cared about was getting them on the same sleep schedule.

Without family at the wedding, I was grateful for Meg's familiar presence. Of all the new people in my life, she was the one who knew me best. She could laugh with me about Bethamy, who was in high form, following me around with her iPad and asking questions like "Which font do you prefer the calligrapher use for the menus? I suggest the serif. Her sans serif is rather plain." ("Ask Rob.") "Do you want the foyer lit for photography during the ceremony? The photos will be worth much more." ("Yes.") "Who will you dance with when Rob dances with his mother? I understand your father isn't here, it's too bad, darling, and I wish you'd told me sooner since I did floral for both your parents and the seating is a nightmare." ("Rob and his mother can dance alone. I'll watch.") And "Where do you want the babies in the photos? We can make sure no photos are taken if you're working on a birth date revision. It's always the best way to go with twins since they tend to be small. Nobody's paying attention. You'll make the official birth date a few months later and they'll do better at sports." ("Rob and I will hold the boys in our arms!")

The morning of the rehearsal dinner, Rob had a surprise for me. He led me outside the castle to the blissful paparazzi-free front entrance. We got in the back of a beat-up, nondescript car, and were soon chugging along, surrounded by green meadows dotted with houses and sheep, crossing a bridge to Achill Island. Now the narrow road led us down the rough, rocky coast, where the Atlantic pounded against the land. Sun pushed through gaps in the omnipresent clouds.

We got out of the car at a deserted village, crumbling stone structures left over from the famine. The wind whipped my extensions back and forth (Joaquim was going to have a heart attack), and Rob seemed to know exactly where he was going as we clambered down a steep path to Annagh Strand. Now, truly, we were in the middle of nowhere. There was not a soul in sight, and it seemed like no one had ever been here before, and no one would come after. Rob loved places like this. When he talked about traveling "beyond the beyond," he reminded me of my beloved explorers.

Rob led me across the grass; spread out a blanket; opened a bottle of Guinness; and unpacked some cheese, crackers, rhubarb bread, and nuts. He had every detail planned out (and when I say "he," I'm sure I mean Bethamy).

I'd barely had a sip of anything since the boys were born, and the stout went straight to my head. I was Lizzie Pepper, the quiet, serious girl from Chicago, Illinois, and I had traveled a long way to get here. I'd worked hard, from such a young age, and this incredible life was the payoff. I sat cross-legged and looked at my soon-to-be husband.

"I love you," he said.

"I love you too," I said.

"I love you the most."

The moment was too perfect. It deserved total joy, but that forced me to confront the hole in my heart. Rob's tenderness broke me, and l fell into his arms, crying. "It isn't right. My parents are missing my wedding. My mother's family is from this county and she isn't even here! Aurora has wanted to be my maid of honor for years. I have nobody except you."

He held me in his arms. "I want to give you everything, and somehow you've lost the most important people." He turned my face toward him and I saw tears in his eyes. "We'll fix it, love. I know we can. If tomorrow isn't perfect, we'll get married again. I'll marry you a hundred times."

Even up until that day I'd had my doubts about my husband-to-be. His polish was so impenetrable. But time after time, just when I felt completely alone, Rob showed his true colors. He wasn't just loving, he understood me. And in that moment, I saw it. All my sacrifices had been for something amazing. True love.

"Aren't we a sight?" I said.

I lay down on the blanket next to Rob. Here, away from Hollywood and the Studio and our mansions, Rob and I were just a man and a woman whose hearts and bodies were meant for each other. Tomorrow's ceremony, though I knew it would be beautiful, felt like a role I had to play. But in that precious handful of time, beside the glorious ocean, with my gorgeous husband-to-be lying next to me, I felt deeply in love. I didn't want to go back down to the off-balance guest list, the secrecy, the eventness of it all. We lingered until Rob's phone started buzzing. We were already late to hair and makeup for our rehearsal dinner.

The wedding was the following day. The pictures of me in the wedding dress "of my own creation" were my big fashion moment, I guess. But I've never told the real story of how that dress came about, which also happens to be the story of how I almost ruined my own wedding.

Rob had been banished from our room, and my team was getting me dressed. I sat in front of the mirror, idly watching Joaquim do my hair, when there was a strong rap at the door. It was Rob's lawyer, Keith, holding a thick leather binder.

"I tried to get this to you yesterday, but you two were MIA," he said. "You need to sign this before the wedding." He handed me the binder.

In it was a two-hundred-page prenup, flagged with "Sign here" tabs. On top was a note in my father's familiar handwriting. "Elizabeth, please execute. D." Classic Doug Pepper. Every major life event deserved a contract.

"I can't read this!" I said to Meg. "The wedding's in . . ." I had no idea what time it was.

"An hour," she said.

"The wedding's in an hour!"

"Leave it," Meg said. And I did.

A half hour later, I was ready. The one-of-a-kind dress by Michael One had a tight, structured bodice, and a voluminous silk taffeta skirt embellished with tiny pearls. My hair was up in a side bun, which made me feel like a drunk Princess Leia. I already knew I'd regret it one day. When they added the weighty diamond-and-sapphire headpiece that Rob had presented to me the night before—my something new, blue, and borrowed—it gave me an instant hangover. I didn't have anything old, but I figured the thirteenth-century castle would do the trick. Meg asked me if I was ready to go down, and I was about to reply when a text came from the twin's nanny, Lala.

So sorry to bother you, it read. *But can I pick up bottles to use during the wedding?*

Lala wanted milk for Cap and Leo. I'd been pumping double-time for just this purpose. She should have had several extra bottles in the mini fridge of the room down the hall that she was sharing with the boys.

I texted back. *It's in the mini fridge?*

Sorry Miss Elizabeth, but we used it yesterday ☺

My heart sank. I should have realized it was gone. While Rob and I were off on our romantic excursion, my baby bears had drunk all of the extra milk I'd pumped so industriously. There was nothing left to use when they got hungry during the ceremony. Greedy children.

Okay, pumping now, I wrote back. I looked up at the staff. "I need twenty," I said.

"Everyone out," Meg said. When they left, she asked, "Is everything okay, sweetie?" She clearly thought I had cold feet.

"Everything's fine," I said. "It's just that I have to pump."

She looked relieved. After undoing the hundred or so velvet buttons on the back of my dress, she retreated to the bedroom to give me privacy.

I carefully rolled down the heavy bodice of the dress, put on the nursing bra that held the cones of the pump in place, and hooked myself up. The pump made a wheezing sound as it went about its undignified task. Usually it sounded like it was saying, "Whack-a-Mole, Whack-a-Mole," but today, for some reason, it whispered, "What the fuck, what the fuck." I rolled my chair closer to the desk and, for lack of anything else to read, started to flip through the prenup as I pumped.

It was a riveting document. I had no idea, for instance, that if my marriage to Rob ended in less than one year, then my corporation, Pepper Mills, would receive $2 million. If we got divorced after the first year, I would be awarded $3 million for every year we were married. If we stayed together for ten years or more, I would be entitled to half of our "community" property or $30 million, whichever was more. It was a little horrifying to see that I would have only one week to vacate all properties and to claim all clothing and personal effects. The furniture and vehicles would be Rob's, unless in the course of the marriage he chose to designate me as the owner. It was understood that each of us would have the right to withdraw from any joint projects without damages from the other. In the event of divorce, I acknowledged that Rob and I would have different standards of living thereafter, and Cap, Leo, and any subsequent children (as if!) might be exposed to this discrepancy.

I found what I read entertaining, but I didn't take it seriously. Rob and I were committed for life. As far as I was concerned, signing the prenup just confirmed to Rob, his staff, and anyone else who knew about it (because it would inevitably leak to the public sooner or later) that I wasn't a gold digger.

I was halfway through the document when I felt a dampness soak through the silk taffeta of my dress. I looked down and saw a dark, wet stain spreading across my lap. I had forgotten to attach the bottles to the tubes of the breast pump. Oblivious, I'd pumped an entire feeding out onto my dress.

The yeasty smell of milk rose up, and I began to cry. This milk that soaked me was gold, the only ticket I had to making it through the ceremony without worrying that my babies would fuss. Also? My wedding dress was destroyed.

Meg found me sitting in the desk chair, naked from the waist up except for the nursing bra and those horrible plastic cones it held over my poor, abused breasts.

"I ruined the dress!" I cried. "And there's no milk for the boys."

Meg stared at me, taking it all in. "I really want to Instagram this moment."

I couldn't help laughing. "You do it, you die."

"You're no fun." Coming up next to me, she fluffed the skirt of the gown. "There's so much of this dress. Can't we make it work?"

I sniffled. "Maybe."

Using the nail scissors from my cosmetic kit, I carefully cut the taffeta away at the seams until all that was left was the silk underslip. I put it on. It fit me nicely, but it looked cheap and see-through. I cut the tulle petticoat in one long spiral, and draped it over and around myself, twisting it strategically into what the fashion world would call a reinvented toga. Meg helped me fasten it in place with the headpiece. My headache disappeared, and I had an excuse to pull out that horrible side bun. My hair fell down into natural, loose curls that complemented the bohemian toga. Looking in the mirror, I smiled. The perfect princess was gone, and in her place was . . . me. Together the two of us stared at my reflection.

"You know what's crazy?" said Meg. "I like it better."

"*Now* you can take the picture," I told Meg, handing her my phone. "For reference. I'll need to retie it next time I nurse." Nursing, by the way, was how I would spend a good half of the ceremony. Not that anyone noticed.

And that is how Michael One's creation suffered death by breast milk and why he later sued me for intellectual property theft. I thought I was doing him a favor by not associating him with my last-minute ensemble, but my refashioned dress brought several top design houses knocking at Lotus's door, asking for me to wear their creations. Before I'd been merely a stylish celebrity. Now I'd been promoted to fashion icon.

Oh, and I never bothered to finish reading the prenup. I'd bought houses and made movies and opened bank accounts and paid taxes without reading any of the fine print. Why start now?

The media found us after all. Nobody was surprised except Bethamy, who ran around for fifteen minutes pretending that someone's head would roll. I began to suspect Bethamy was the one getting the kickback for leaking our location.

We were supposed to eat dinner in the garden behind the castle, but the helicopters were circling overhead as if there was a murderer on the loose. Good old Bethamy had planned for this: A stand-by crew arrived to tent the back so we could at least have cocktails out there before coming inside, where it was quieter for the feast.

I peeked out the window of my room to get a look at the arriving guests. There were Rob's parents—Liesl, whom Rob treated with more respect than love, and Alan, whose sad smile went forever unexplained. There was his brother, Scotty, with his girlfriend, Samantha (wearing white!), on his arm. Soon after Christmas there had been a swift and silent divorce.

Geoff arrived alone. His girlfriend, Patricia, was nowhere in sight. The official word was that Patricia was in Indonesia, on a mission, but there were also whispers that she had broken from Geoff and the Studio, and that one night she had disappeared and nobody had seen her since. But I didn't have time to worry about Patricia today.

The scene was a little too familiar: a sea of camera flashes and celebrities and agents. I had to remind myself that this wasn't a premiere, it was my wedding. Where for some reason everyone, even Celia Montbatten (God knows how she'd scored an invitation), was being subjected to a wholly undignified security check.

The day before, I'd been upset that my family and my oldest friends weren't present, but that feeling had faded. I looked out at my new friends—*our* friends—and felt nothing but excitement for the life we would build together. Rob and I had first met a little more than a year earlier, but I had no fear about how quickly my children, my husband, and this marriage had come about. My closest family and friends had joined the press in deciding I was losing my own identity, becoming just another appendage of Rob's. But the way I saw it, I wasn't Daddy's little girl anymore. This was the new me, the grown-up me. I was my own woman.

The crowd below saw me emerging and burst into applause. I posed for photos at the top of the double stairway leading down to the main hall. Rob joined me for more photos, and then he and I walked separately down the two staircases, joining where they met and continuing down the aisle together. More photos. And then, it was time.

It was "The Wedding of the Year," as *Rounder* would dub it in a six-page spread the following week. Another overly choreographed pageant. Another tabloid grand slam, with us on the cover of all three big magazines. Lotus was thrilled.

The man at my side was the quintessential leading man. I myself had already gotten married onscreen three times. I could play this part in my sleep. So at first, by habit, that's what I did. I acted. Calm. Blushing. In love. When the priest spoke, I let an expression of somber piety settle on my face. Even when we kissed, I knew how to make it look cinematic and so did Rob.

But mid-kiss, something happened. Rob paused, holding me close, and I heard a small gasp. It came from me. For all the fanfare and cameras, the breast milk fiasco and guest list drama, I believed in this romance. He was my life, my love. We kissed again, through both of our tears and laughter, and, at last, we were a completely unstaged mess of love.

PART THREE

ILLUMINATION

1

This is what it meant to take the twins on a walk around our gated neighborhood in Brentwood. In the kitchen, Elsie, the cook, would hand me a sack of snacks. Down the hall, Meg would confirm that I'd be back within an hour for a phone call with earthCosmetics (or whomever). At the doorway, as Lala wriggled Leo's pudgy arms into a sweater, Lewis would ask if we needed a ride. And, always, a security guard would trail us, promising to stay so far back that I'd never know he was there.

I knew.

I rarely socialized anymore, not with Rob traveling so much, but I was never alone. Everywhere I went, everything I did, was aided, managed, and observed by our staff. I started to feel more watched than protected.

During the twins' first couple of years, Rob made three movies in a row. Spain, then Iceland, then London. Their first solid foods came from craft services. They learned to manage steps by climbing in and out of his trailer in Reykjavik. But when Leo started trying to eat pennies and pebbles off the soundstage floor and Cap began ritually throwing up on every plane ride, we retreated to Malibu, where we stayed until I got tired of pulling Leo's sand-filled fist away from his mouth, and decamped to Brentwood.

Today Rob was in Uzbekistan, working on a stunt where he engaged an enemy on top of a moving plane at ten thousand feet. Being Rob, he was performing the stunt himself, on top of a moving plane at ten thousand feet.

Meanwhile, I was in childproofed Brentwood, playing hide-and-seek with Cap and Leo in the backyard. Leo had very specific rules he wanted me to follow. He was the only one who got to hide, and he always hid behind the same skinny jacaranda tree trunk. I'd pretend not to be able to find him, and after about thirty seconds he would come running out, yelling, "I'm *right here*, Mama!" Then he'd run right back to the same tree and yell, "Mama, find Leo *again*!" He really must have had a poor opinion of my intelligence back then. Meanwhile, Cap was going through an attachment phase. He clung to my leg the entire time, and then when Leo came running out, Cap would echo everything he said. "Mama, find Cap *again*!"

When we got tired of hide-and-seek, we made three-letter words out of alphabet blocks on the patio under the shade of the pergola.

I knew every one of the babies' board books by heart. I've always been able to look at a page of a script and memorize it on sight. It's a skill I picked up on *American Dream*. Now this ability felt like a curse, the singsong pages of *Mr. Brown Can Moo! Can You?* and *But Not the Hippopotamus* echoing in my head all day long. I was so immersed in babyland that once, when talking to Meg, I interrupted myself. "Plane!" I said, pointing excitedly to one flying overhead. As if Meg were a two-year-old to whom a passing plane was breaking news.

By my own choosing, my career was unofficially on hold. When I had bowed out of *Skye London*, my agent, Cherry, simply stopped calling. There was never an open discussion about what the long-term plan was or whether she was still my representative. This was how it went in Hollywood, the unspoken play of ACE and other agencies. They either called you or they didn't. But—just in case you became hot again—they never dropped you.

The Studio, where I'd been spending so much time before the boys were born, wasn't the refuge I'd hoped for. There were no other babies around—sessions for children began at age six. Twice a week I slipped out of the house to practice, but my days of brunches in the courtyard and lingering after a practice to catch an interesting lecture were over.

I thought I could get involved in Rob's project for One Cell, the New York Studio. I've always loved New York, and helping with the interior design of a studio that had a New York vibe sounded like it wouldn't place inordinate demands on my already taxed attention span. One morning after Practice, I saw Rob talking with Angus Murphy, the project manager for New York. I left the boys playing on the lawn and went up to them.

"Rob has told me so much about the New York Studio," I said.

Angus raised an eyebrow and glanced at Rob. "You don't say?" Something passed between the two of them, an odd little nod of reassurance from Rob, as if to confirm that we had indeed talked about the project.

"I'd love to get involved, if there's a way. I mean, I don't know much about architecture and building, but I do like design, and there's really nothing for me to do at Rob's houses. They're completely done already."

"How wonderful," Angus said. "We'd love your help when we get closer to that stage, right, Rob?"

"Definitely," Rob said. "I was going to suggest it myself."

But when would that time come? I couldn't seem to pin them down.

There was no way I was going to keep my parents out of their grandsons' lives for good. They had come to meet the boys on their first birthday, but my father and I kept our distance. He'd hold a baby in his arms, singing "Red River Valley" or "Shenandoah," the songs he'd used as my lullabies.

But when his eyes caught mine, the warmth left his face and he quickly looked away. This had been our first fight—my first rebellion, really—and we were both too proud to let it go. I needed him to apologize for arranging my meeting with Rob without telling me. And my father was still outraged that I'd turned down *Skye London*, throwing away my career. My mother tried to sweep it all under the rug. "The Pattersons made the assumption that I was at your wedding," she said in a private moment, "and I would prefer if you let them go on thinking that." It killed her, missing the wedding, though I'd made it clear that she was welcome to attend . . . without my father.

For now, Cap and Leo were oblivious to the privilege into which they'd been born, though they did love the boxes of clothes and toys that arrived in the mail every day. Whatever was in a box, Leo put it to use right away, modeling designer kidwear or attaching himself to the newest toy and keeping it tucked under his arm all day and night. As for Cap, well, he mostly went for the boxes themselves and whatever packing material came in them. They say that siblings find ways not to compete, and my sweet Cap's approach was to let Leo have everything. I was keeping a close eye on this dynamic.

I didn't want my sons to walk around wearing or carrying promotional items—they weren't billboards. Originally, I had planned to triage the onslaught of gifts before the kids saw them, separating the gifts into giveaway piles, birthday presents for friends, and special occasion treats for the boys. But it became impossible for even Meg to sort and manage the relentless tide, and the boys quickly learned to listen for the telltale thumps as the security guards delivered that day's booty at the side door. So in the end it was a free-for-all. I worried that this was a slippery slope, the combination of circumstance and laziness that at first spoiled celebrity kids and eventually brought them to ruin. Some moms worry about whether their kids are hitting appropriate milestones, how to make them eat their vegetables, and what brand of diapers is most absorbent. Me, I feared that the mini biker jackets and designer snack bags were gateway indulgences that would lead Cap and Leo to spending their waking hours staring at the latest high-tech devices, to demanding luxury sports cars from their father (who wouldn't think twice about providing them), and to frequenting the nightclubs of Sunset Strip, ordering bottle service and doing God knows what else kids did today.

Also, I had nanny issues. When the twins were born, Lala had been sent over by Lotus's domestic-staffing division, and she was unquestionably qualified. She kept them on a firm schedule. Her voice was always calm and direct. With Lala, even Cap always went right down for his nap while it took me a half hour of peeling his arms from around my neck. The problem was that I was convinced Lala hated me. It wasn't anything she said or did. It was the look she gave me when I asked her not to use the TV in the twins' room. It was the way she told them to "go to your mama" when I came in the room, as if greeting me were an obligation my children should endure in the name of propriety. Maybe the bad vibe was grounds enough to dismiss a nanny. After all, she was there to help me. The Practice was supposed to have given me the confidence to take charge of my own life. It should have helped me decide what to do. But I wasn't upholding my A-student record—the minute I'd become a mother I'd slacked off my practice of the Whole Body Principles. Just like I'd slacked off working out. And maintaining my skin and hair. And having a life. At any rate, I couldn't bring myself to let Lala go. First of all, the children loved her. And second, well, look at me. Look at the way I lived. I was the Lady of the Manor, and Lala saw firsthand what a ridiculously luxurious life I led. If I were a nanny, I'd hate me, too. I kind of respected her for it.

I was a stay-at-home mom, except that I couldn't do any of the things normal moms do: go to the park, meet other moms for coffee, have playdates, take music classes for tots. I *really* had to stay at home. We'd been sent a fleet of free strollers, every double stroller on the market, most of which I donated to a women's shelter, but I never used the ones I kept. The boys and I couldn't stroll anywhere outside our gated enclave. The tiny distance between the car and a store or appointment was hard enough to navigate. When photographers jumped out at us, Leo stared at them and growled like a bear. Cap buried his face in my shirt and whimpered.

I'd bought into this life. As everyone knows, being rich and famous has come to mean that your candid photograph is worth money, and anyone is free to take one at any time, so long as you are on public property. It's the price you pay. I get it. You can't exactly say that I was fully informed of this when I accepted the role on *American Dream*. I was seventeen; I wanted to be an actor; I took the first part that came along. And yet, if at the time or any day since someone had given me the choice, I would have taken it all—the career and anything that came with it—in a flash, without a second thought. It was the same when I married Rob. I knew I was catapulting to a new level of exposure, and I didn't just accept it. I embraced it, the whole deal, whatever it might include.

But I, like any young aspiring actor, never considered what my choices would mean for the children I might have in the unimaginable future. In the ideal bubble that any parent tries to create around a toddler, fear and anxiety don't exist—maybe there's a page in *Goodnight Moon* the child doesn't like, or a door slams unexpectedly, but in general I think we can all agree that little children shouldn't be surrounded by aggressive men holding big cameras and shouting names they recognize and words they don't understand. I didn't think of that until I was already pregnant and it was too late. Now I saw my recent fears becoming reality: The cameras' bright beams of judgment would follow Cap and Leo for their entire shared childhood. The shadowy crowd of figures holding those cameras would obscure the streets and trees and people from view, blocking sidewalks and doorways and windows. The photographers, blasted by their own lights into silhouette, would be the constant foreground of my children's view, blotting out reality, forming a horizon behind which the sun always set. Our children wouldn't skip ahead of us to investigate a flower or push down a protruding sprinkler head. They could never, ever, ever play hide-and-seek in a park. If they learned to roller-skate or bike, it would happen in the great rooms and long halls of our houses or in rinks that we rented after hours.

Only Pops, my old paparazzo nemesis, adjusted his behavior when the twins were born. He now kept a respectful distance, and would chastise the other paparazzi: "Back up, guys. Let them walk. You're frightening the babies." I wasn't naïve—I knew it was most likely his new strategy to curry favor—but, even when it got him nowhere, he stayed faithful to his new approach. It was a little eddy of humanity in a river of intrusion. As for the rest of them, I wanted to hand out T-shirts reading "I scared a toddler today." Fine, earn a living. But own the truth of what you do.

Now the boys were nearly two, and I wanted them to meet other kids. The books said that was important so that they didn't define themselves by each other. Ignoring the warnings of everyone around me (actually, just Lala and her furrowed brow), I asked Meg to research activities for them, and we signed up for a class called Double the Fun in Brentwood, at Little Hands.

On the drive to our first class, I examined the strange knot of unease in my gut that had tightened when I fell during my pregnancy. I had never thought of myself as shy. Quiet, maybe, but never shy. But it had been such a long time since I'd had normal interactions with normal people. I summoned my rusty One Cell training. *Emotions are a chemical reaction*, I thought, climbing out of the car. No matter what happened, I would walk steadily. I would be another one of the moms. I would offer my boys the opportunities they deserved. I could do this. It was just another role to play. The Studio helped actors gain control—and it had prepared me for this odd version of parenting.

Since pairing up with Rob, I had learned to avoid making eye contact in public. It kept people at arm's length. But when we entered the parenting class I couldn't help glancing up furtively to scan the small, colorful room. My gaze swept across a cascade of averted eyes, every last mom pretending not to recognize me, pretending they hadn't been staring. Not the finest bunch of actors I'd ever met. I half appreciated their effort and half wished they would just stare until they got it out of their systems. The sets of twins, many of them in matching outfits (Really? People still did that?), were mercifully oblivious, so I focused on them and plastered a mild, noncommittal smile on my face.

There were about ten moms in the class, including me. We sat in a circle, each of us trying to keep both of our kids in our laps for the entirety of a chipper hello song. There was one mom who had brought her triplets. She looked perfect, every hair in place and a beatific smile on her face and I couldn't help assuming she'd hit some psychopharmaceutical jackpot. After an absurd attempt at mother-child Pilates ("Pick one of your children—the 'good' twin. Ha, ha."), we let them run around knocking over a herd of inflatable plastic horsies. (Or, rather, most of the children, including Leo, knocked them over. Cap waddled around carefully standing them back up. *That's my boy*, I thought.)

Because it was the first week, the teacher, Jamie, asked us to go around the circle introducing ourselves and saying what was going on with us and our children. The first few moms mentioned sleep issues; one baby liked to throw her food to the floor when she was done eating; one mom burst into tears because she still wasn't back to a size zero, and her husband had only ever known her as a zero, and breast-feeding made her so hungry she'd eaten a *whole bagel* (gasps of horror from the assembled), and this new, size-four body felt *huge* and *clumsy*.

My turn was approaching. I had a hundred concerns: My husband is always traveling; the children and I are prisoners in our own home; my nanny hates me; I've lost my closest family and friends; my sons can't possibly have a normal childhood. I wanted advice—for the boys' sake more than my own—but I couldn't trust these women. Or anyone. Instead, I positioned myself, just like I did in every magazine profile: Lizzie Pepper, Girl Next Door. Experience told me to pick a problem that made me come across as a responsible mom who had authentic, relatable concerns, but was too boring to be tabloid fodder.

I said, "Does anyone know which plastics are safe? And whether it's okay to put them in the dishwasher?"

After class, one of the moms came up to me as we were leaving.

"Your sons are adorable," she said. "What are their names?"

Cap and I were waiting on the sidewalk as Lala buckled Leo into the car. "That one's Leo, and this one is Cap."

Her daughter, Olive, grabbed a hunk of Cap's hair and pulled it toward her mouth. Cap watched with a look of detached curiosity, as if he were conducting a study of the behavior of young human children.

The mom knelt down next to her daughter and cooed, "Olive, Mama understands that you want to eat that little boy's hair, don't you, clever girl? If you are hungry you can have an organic apple wedge. Right now you're hurting the little boy's body. Mama is going to help you stop hurting the little boy's body."

She put her hand on Olive's hand and tried to pry her little fist open. "May I have permission to touch your body? Mama is opening your hand now."

Olive looked at her mother placidly, then opened her mouth and screamed at the top of her lungs, "Noooooooo!" She held tight to Cap's hair.

Now Cap was alarmed. The mother was on one side of him and Olive on the other. He held his hands straight out to me and whimpered, "Mama!"

The mother pried, Olive screamed, and Cap's bottom lip began to tremble. I knelt down in front of him and said, "Just a minute, honey. It's going to be okay." Thinking fast, I took a breath mint out of my purse and said, "Here, Olive. Want a candy?"

Olive's eyes lit up. She instantly released Cap and smiled. "Yummy!"

I picked up Cap and turned to the mother with a smile of shared sympathy so that she knew I wasn't judging her child. They all had their moments. But to my surprise the mother was staring at me, horrified.

"You bribed Olive!" she exclaimed. "And we don't do processed sugar." She swept Olive up and stormed away. That was my first and last Double the Fun class.

Next I hired a music teacher to come to our house. I asked Meg to invite the children of a few other actor moms. We had a little class of five. The music teacher, Bliss, always said they were her best-dressed class. Then Bliss sold pictures to *Rounder* and moved to Tulum, and that was the end of that.

The life I once lived, and the new life I'd imagined, seemed farther and farther away.

2

For the boys' second birthday, Lala and I took them to Prague to visit Rob on location for *The Search for Helen Grant*. The production had given Rob the top two floors of the Hotel International, but he was using only the presidential suite and the service elevator, which the hotel seemed to have hastily draped in cheap velvet in his honor. They'd cut a rectangle out of the fabric for access to the elevator buttons.

As soon as Lala left to put the boys to sleep in their suite, Rob threw me to the bed.

"I need you," he said, covering me in kisses, dispelling in an instant the loneliness of his absence. I needed him, too. My vision of our marriage, our family, our future included a partner. A grown-up to share my worries and stories and bed. Our relationship was turning out to be far more long-distance than I'd anticipated. But what choice did we have? He was my adventurer, my expedition-bound husband whose travels pulled us apart but were inextricable from who he was.

"Wait, wait! I brought you a present," I said. It was a small pencil-and-ink canvas, a nude reclining on a bed with a cloud of blue hair. (I'm telling you—it isn't easy to get presents for Rob Mars.) I'd carried it carefully on the plane, mummified in bubble wrap. Now I took a nail clipper and struggled to cut through the stubborn plastic cord that the gallery had used to secure the package.

"Here, let me—" Rob said. Just as he leaned forward, the cord snapped free, catching him right in the eye. "Holy bejeezus!" he yelped, falling backward on the bed with his hand clenched to his eye.

"Oh my God, are you okay?"

Eye squeezed shut, he said, "I am totally fine. Did not need that eye for the major motion picture I am shooting tomorrow."

"I am so sorry," I said.

"Just come here already." He pulled me down on the bed next to him. "If I can't see you, feeling you will do."

I laughed. "Did you actually get hit in the eye or are you faking it to get me in bed?"

He rolled on top of me. "I'll never tell."

Our reunions were always passionate—it's something I never want to forget, for our sake and the boys'.

Afterward, he gazed at me (for the record, his eye: completely unin-jured) and said, "Now, about that present . . ."

I shrugged. "It's a Picasso. Whatever."

Rob's call time the next day was at six a.m., Eastern Bloc Time. The boys were insane with jet lag. Leo was wired and pulling Lala in all directions, while I carried Cap, a grumpy two-year-old lump, to the set.

I had always loved being on location—the camaraderie, the intensity, the lifetime supply of M&Ms—although I didn't exactly pick the best day for my return. Today they were shooting the scene where Rob first teams up with a female scientist to look for Helen Grant, a dying woman whose singular cancer genome holds a possible cure for leukemia. Par for the course, "teaming up" meant hooking up. This female scientist just happened to be played by Wendy Jones, who famously ditched her squeaky-clean Disney image by guest-starring on *American Dream* as the vixen to my good girl. The PR machines had cast Wendy as one of my dearest friends, but she was not—not since the end of season three, when she'd attempted to seduce my real-life boyfriend, then casually apologized and commended his honor, saying "Very impressive. Justin wouldn't cheat. He said he wouldn't trade quality for sexy." (It went without question that I was the Madonna in that equation and therefore the antithesis of sexy.) Wendy, who had once been tied to Rob in the tabloids, was cast as his love interest in this movie. Awesome.

The scene currently being shot had them walking down the street, arguing about whether Wendy's character could have her turn to drive the car. (He thinks he's a better driver because, you know, she is a *woman*. Just because Rob had his pick of films didn't mean he could or cared to avoid the sexist clichés.) Finally, she says, "How do you plan to drive without the keys?"

Rob pats his pockets, confused. *Where did those damn keys go?*

Wendy dangles them in front of his nose. "Looking for these?"

Having outwitted him, she'll get to drive. Cue the hot public makeout that will cut to them in bed together.

I watched several takes of this riveting scene, by which point Cap desperately needed a nap. While Lala entertained Leo, I spent two miserable hours in Rob's trailer failing to get Cap to sleep. Eventually, he crashed on my shoulder as I walked around the parking lot. Afraid to put him down, I returned to the set, where I stood bouncing gently, rocking from hip to hip. I tried to think of it as my workout for the day.

They broke to relight the scene, and Rob brought people over to meet me. I jiggled Cap as Rob introduced me to the director and the producer, and I was still jiggling him when I said hi to Wendy, her perfect body sheathed in a tight red Bond girl–worthy dress.

"This must be your son. Adorable," Wendy said.

"Thank you," I said.

"And you look amazing! I can't even tell you had a baby." (Two babies, but who was counting?) It didn't matter what Wendy said—we both knew the truth. Unlike me, Wendy had successfully made the transition from teen TV ingénue to leading lady. A movie star. Her eyelash extensions were freshly done; she had the glowing skin of a woman who does all the maintenance I'd dropped when the twins were born; the whites of her eyes were flawless—evidence of a recent Master Cleanse. Meanwhile, the shadows under my eyes had aged me ten years, and Cap, sleeping on my shoulder, had dragged my shirt down my shoulder to reveal the wide strap of a graying nursing bra. It was my least favorite part of being a female actor: that eternal youth, beauty, and style were critical to the job. Another downside of picking a career as a teenager. I never thought about how I would age into it, and even if I had, I was too young to care. My parents might have considered it, but they had other goals in mind. One benefit to having boys was knowing they were less likely to be judged for their appearance. My sons would choose their own careers, and they would almost certainly find themselves in professions that required brains, not beauty.

I boosted Cap in my arms, pulled my shoulders back, straightened my posture, and tried to fix my shirt. Wendy Jones felt sorry for me. And for once I agreed with her. I had never been more famous, more talked about . . . and more alone. The movie set on which we stood was an illusion: The leaves on the trees were paper; the getaway car drove itself, fixed on a track. My husband wasn't a con man; Wendy wasn't his lover (as far as I knew); her real eyelashes weren't three inches long. But everything here was scheduled and scripted. There was a beginning, a middle, and an end. There were no plot holes or loose ends. Meanwhile I was isolated and lost, and for the first time I started to think that the set—a place where I was a central player—was, for all its smoke and mirrors, a reality I wanted back in my life.

Something was missing. Whether it was being an actor, being with my husband, or being Lizzie, not Elizabeth—all the pieces of my life had been shaken up and had then resettled such that I no longer recognized myself. My identity—the child who'd made snow angels in her backyard; the girl who'd explored the outskirts of Memphis; the hardworking actor who wasn't sick once in six seasons; the young woman who'd fearlessly teased Rob Mars; and everything else that made me the person I'd thought I was—it had all collapsed into a shadow. I finally acknowledged the feeling that had been growing over the past two years. I was a movie star's wife and a mother, and nothing more. My role was to circle the widow's walk, waiting and hoping for my long-lost shipman to return to port. Reuniting with Rob reminded me that I had a husband, and a very handsome, loving one at that—but it wasn't enough.

That night Rob and I walked across Charles Bridge. The cobblestone span was lined with baroque statues, in front of them vendors hawking souvenirs. Reflected light darted restlessly on the river below as if searching for anchor.

"It's not working. Being with the boys full-time," I blurted out. "I think I miss acting."

"Oh! I thought you decided to take a break from acting," Rob said.

"That was almost three years ago. Now . . . I don't know."

Rob stopped to buy the boys two marionettes. They cost Kč375 each—about twenty dollars—but Rob gave the seller a Kč1,000 bill, refusing change. The vendor ran after us holding out a third marionette. I couldn't tell if he was trying to sell us another or give it to us since we'd paid extra. The other vendors took notice. Now that we'd made a purchase, they converged with various souvenirs in their hands.

"No, thank you," Rob said, and made a mistake: He smiled.

Someone yelled "Rob Mars! Rob Mars!" Faces turned toward us and began to converge.

Being Rob Mars. That was it, the pinnacle of success as an actor. I somehow thought that being his wife, joining his organization, having his children, would put me right up there next to him, but, close as I was to him, he still had something that I wanted.

"We'd better turn around," Rob said. But the crowd was now thick with people holding out scraps of paper and squeezing next to us so their friends could take pictures. There was no escaping—Rob stood a full head above the crowd. We stopped, spent fifteen minutes posing and giving out autographs, then made our way to the hotel as quickly as we could.

Safely back in our room, Rob said, "I think it's wonderful that you're spending so much time with our sons. My job—it pays the rent. Big deal. What you're doing is much more important."

"Oh yeah? Wanna trade?"

"We can talk about that."

I gave him a skeptical look.

"I'm serious!" he said. "It's really important for kids to be raised by their parents. I always went to my mom's office after school, then home with her for dinner. It was great."

He and his mother were close, allegedly, though I had yet to see evidence of it. Rob shared few stories from his childhood, and they all ended with the same blanket summary. "It was great." But was it? It seemed to me that the greatest memories defied generalizations. Mine were household traditions—like helping my father reshingle the garage roof or washing the window screens together every spring. They were awkward or embarrassing moments—like throwing up in a houseplant as a sophomore at a party full of seniors or playing truth-or-dare on the beach or dancing to "Paradise by the Dashboard Light" on the tables of a Tennessee bar. Rob's stories, whatever they were, had been white-washed into oblivion by too many years of interviews and sound bites. And now, when it came to raising our sons, I found I had no idea what his childhood was really like, or whether it was remotely useful as a model for our children's.

"I want to be at home with them, I do, but I left so much behind . . ."

"So move forward with a movie. Or stay with the boys. Or commit to investigating other options." I don't know which came first—the One Cell Practice or his decisive mind—but they fused into a resolute, unflappable wall. I felt cornered. I didn't want to be in this discussion, where I was supposed to choose between acting and mothering, right at this very moment. Seeing my expression, Rob softened. "That sounded cold. I just mean that the world is your oyster. Whatever you want, we can make it happen."

The boys were playing with the marionettes on the hotel floor, the strings that controlled them already hopelessly knotted. Cap's was a peasant girl with short, yellow braids. Her arm was twisted up and above her shoulder.

"Fix!" he wailed, throwing her into my lap. While I worked to free her, and Rob and I talked, Cap kept pleading "Fix! Fix!" with increasing desperation.

"I know I have infinite options. That's part of the problem. I'm just not sure . . ."

"Okay, so we'll think about it. There's no rush." Rob's voice was soft and comforting, but I saw his neck tighten. He couldn't stand dithering. For some reason Lexy Hartfield, Rob's ex-wife, popped into my head. After their marriage she had vanished from the industry. Lexy, the great beauty and widely respected actor, gave it all up, never to return, not even after the divorce. But why? She had no children to occupy her, no new career to my knowledge. I remembered the note she'd sent me when Rob and I got engaged. "This above all: to thine own self be true." Had she quit acting in order to be true to herself? Or was it the other way around? Was she warning me not to follow her path?

Now, without a word, Rob took the tangled marionette away from me. He pulled out a nail clipper and, with one swift gesture, severed all the strings. He handed the incapacitated toy back to Cap, whose stunned silence made me realize how very loud and constant his wails had been.

"I don't want to change anything," I said. "Only—I guess it's that I'm lonely. I wish you didn't have to travel so much."

"I miss you too, Elizabeth," Rob said, and he held me.

But I didn't miss him. Not exactly. Along with my shaken identity, I felt a hollowness. His absence, yes, but I wasn't sure it had anything to do with his travel. What I longed for was the feeling I'd had in those first few months, when we were discovering each other and falling in love. Now we had been married for almost two years, and it still felt like the beginning, but in the wrong way.

I thought of Rob on the beach in Malibu, his shirt soaked from his run and hair sticking out in short points from his forehead. Rob in the middle of the night, his arm, heavy with sleep, wrapped around my waist. His boyish grin as he spun me into a kiss. In that first year of our relationship, Rob was always at my side. Thousands of pictures were taken of us together, and in all of them we both look radiant. We were eager and giddy. We wanted to please each other. We were in love. Our conversation overflowed with stories from the past, recounting the day in process, and planning how we would live together this week, this year, forever. Life was full and felt full.

But our love hadn't matured. It was still smooth, like a baby's skin, and when something is smooth, it has less surface area. There are no wrinkles, no scars, no accidents, no cracks and crevices for the character of life, no mud slides or earthquakes to generate the silt to preserve the fossils and save precious moments of time for future examination. We never fought, not even a middle-of-the-night squabble over the covers. A tentative, hopeful unfamiliarity hung over us. We were still polite.

Where was Rob? Where was the person who wakes up in a bad mood for no reason at all? Where was the man who leaves his jeans on a chair, just once, instead of hanging them over his valet stand without a wrinkle? And what about my part in this? Why didn't I tell him that I used to love to sleep in on Sundays, or read the paper in bed with a coffee until noon? Why didn't I tease him for the neck twitch that told me he was against something even when he refused to admit it? Why did Meg still seem to know him better than I did? Why didn't I tell him how much I wanted to know what was behind Bluebeard's door?

Our love was an absence, a clean white room with fresh paint and hospital corners and hinges that open without the slightest noise. Our love was, in Rob's words, "great."

I didn't fault Rob. Never once had he tried to make me into someone I was not. If I'd said, "Today I want to dress in a clown costume and ride a double-decker bus around the city," his eyes would have crinkled with pleasure. He would have made it happen. Rob wanted me, us, everyone, to embrace their wacky, unique selves. He wanted me to have a dream and act on it. He unrolled the world like a carpet at my feet, but I didn't know which shoes I wanted to wear. I started to feel lost, as if the longer I lived in that over-accommodating world, the more I became a doll—a placid Stepford doll with no complaints, no desires unfulfilled, and nothing to say. Being a wife and mother should have been enough. It could have been, if Rob and I were in it together, if our relationship had been what I expected (and what, for that matter, the public wanted it to be). I didn't want to admit it; I couldn't after taking such a stand. But maybe my father was right. I had sacrificed my career, and for what?

I had the world at my fingertips. I had a beautiful family. I could buy a house and live anywhere on Earth. But it was all on the surface. I had no idea how to find or fix what lay beneath.

3

Something had to change. I knew that at the back of my mind, but it huddled there like the rest of the to-dos I never seemed to check off my list. The children's day-to-day needs and milestones constantly stole my attention, and time passed, slow days that transformed quickly to months.

The year Cap and Leo turned three, we had the Christmas party at which Rob, late returning to L.A., famously arrived by helicopter, landing in the middle of our lawn in Brentwood, surprising us all, and decapitating the piñata. When Rob left, we returned to Malibu, where the house had settled back into its regular mode: quiet, empty, waiting for its lord and master to return, the sense of unmet expectations broken only by the sound of two pairs of feet trotting up and down the stairs, never going in the same direction.

I'd taken to running every day, two miles down and back on the narrow ridge of dunes in front of our house. But that January morning it was cold and foggy so, for the first time in a long time, I dragged myself to the gym for a run on the treadmill.

I walked in the door and couldn't believe my eyes. There was Meg, exiting Bluebeard's chamber as if she did it every day. She started when she saw me, and I watched, dumbstruck, as she hurriedly locked the door behind her.

"What . . . what the fuck?" I sputtered. Meg was my friend.

"I—I'm sorry," Meg said. Then she was silent. We stared at each other.

"What were you doing in there?" I asked. My first assumption was that she'd gone in without permission. What else would I think? The locked door was a frustration she was supposed to share with me. In fact, she and I had often joked about what Rob might be keeping in there. I specifically remembered her hypothesizing that it was chock-full of his taxidermy collection, a secret sexual fetish he hid from the world.

"It's something Rob asked me to do. Nothing important. Paperwork." Meg was a terrible liar.

"You have got to be kidding me! Tell me right now what you were doing. I insist."

Meg's cheeks were red. I'd never seen her so flustered. "Please believe me—I'm just following Rob's instructions—"

"And now I'd like you to follow my instructions. *Tell me exactly what you were doing in that room.*" I'd never before spoken harshly to her.

"You're putting me in a difficult position," Meg stammered. "It's . . . it's complicated."

We were at an impasse, and an image flashed in my mind—a photograph I'd seen just weeks earlier.

Leo had come trotting up to me with that week's issue of *Starlight*. "Mama, I see you, Mama," he said, and pointed at a picture. But the woman in the picture wasn't me—it was Meg. I understood Leo's confusion. The photo showed Meg standing next to Rob, both of them dressed for a black-tie affair. They were in London, on a trip they had taken six months earlier. The headline read "Lizzie in the Lurch?" And below that: "Rob Runs Around with Lizzie's One Cell Bodyguard." I'd sighed. This was to be expected. Every movie Rob did generated new press. Rumors flew about him and Wendy Jones on the set, then him and Siena Wolf on the set, then him and Katie Mulligan on the set, but I didn't believe them or care. This time, I'd not only been aware that Rob was taking Meg to the Directors' Gala—it was my idea! I'd thought it would be fun for her and nice for him to have company other than his Lotus rep, who had the personality of a goldfish.

"That's not Mommy," I said brightly. "That's Mommy's friend Meg. You know Meg. The one who chases you around the dining table."

But when I looked closely at the picture, I saw that Rob was laughing, clearly in response to something Meg had just said. He was laughing so hard that his eyes squinted into horizontal crescents, his nose wrinkled, and his mouth contorted. His face looked almost ugly, or as close to not handsome as Rob Mars could get.

I couldn't remember the last time he'd laughed that hard with me.

Then I thought of Meg, who had seen Rob through his 100 and had watched his transformation at the Studio; Meg and Rob, together on the beach that Christmas I was pregnant; Meg tipsy and hanging on Rob's arm the night I went into labor. Meg in *Starlight*, making my husband laugh, somehow closer to him than I was after three years of marriage. And now it turned out that she had access to my husband's private room, the single room he wouldn't let me, his wife, enter.

At this point, Meg was my closest confidante. She'd introduced me to the Studio. She'd helped me plan my wedding. She'd watched me nurse my sons. She knew every doubt or hope I'd had. I had been so eager for a friend, so eager to trust her. Meg had guided me, influenced me, maybe even manipulated me. The whole time I was opening up to her, she'd been keeping the secret of Bluebeard's chamber from me.

All of these people, all working for us and acting like our friends.

I found new respect for Lala, who didn't disguise her distaste for me in the least.

Meg and I stood staring at each other in the gym, neither side willing to back down, the locked door next to her at once ordinary and throbbing with mystery. Then I noticed her neck. On it was the Truth necklace she'd been wearing since I met her, but only now did I notice that it had four beads—one tiger's eye, two peridot, one black as charcoal. They were the exact same beads that Rob wore. I'd been wrong to trust her. "It's complicated, is it?" I said to her. "Let me simplify it for you. You're fired."

"Lizzie, no. Please don't do this. I'm your friend." Meg's face was white.

"No, you're my *bodyguard*."

"I—I haven't been perfect, I'll admit that. I can't explain right now, but I would never do anything to hurt you. You have to believe me."

But I couldn't and didn't. "Leave," I said.

"Please trust me. I'll prove it to you. I'll find a way," Meg said. But the next morning she was gone, and that was my answer.

Firing Meg felt surprisingly empowering. So the next day I fired Lala. That witch.

After the domestic bloodbath, I decided to confront Rob about Bluebeard's chamber. He'd told me it was his private office, and I'd accepted that, but now that I knew he'd given Meg access, I was justifiably angry. I would insist that he unlock the door for me, too. I left a message on his cell: "Please call me as soon as you can. There's something we need to discuss."

Rob and I had never had a disagreement, not really. I couldn't even imagine him losing his temper. He was so cool and logical. So I would be the same. Respectful, but firm. Before he called back, I played out the conversation in my mind. First, I would acknowledge his need for privacy.

Next, I would tell him it was inappropriate for the staff to have access to parts of our house when I didn't. That seemed right. Fair. Indisputable.

But then I realized where I'd gone wrong. In the best-case scenario, Rob would concede that I was right. It would go something like this: He'd say, "Sure, I didn't know it was such a big deal to you. Go ahead and look. There's nothing there."

I would respond, "Thank you. Where's the key?"

And he would say, "Meg can let you in."

Then I would have no choice but to admit that I'd rashly fired Meg, one of his oldest friends, the woman who made him laugh so heartily, because I saw her coming out of that room. And when I told him that, Rob would see me for the petty, jealous housewife I'd become.

I absolutely had to tell Rob that I'd let Meg go. There was no way around that. But I wasn't going to embarrass myself by revealing the real reason. Bluebeard's chamber would have to wait.

"It was impulsive," I told him when he called back. "I'm just not used to all this staff. Besides, I can take care of myself!"

"Whatever works for you is fine with me," Rob said. "The whole point is to make your life easier. You and the boys are all I need." But I couldn't let go of the thought that he needed us . . . *and* whatever was in his lair.

★

I don't know how much time went by after that. Weeks, maybe months, before the package arrived.

It didn't come with the regular mail. It was FedExed—a box from Neiman Marcus. I hadn't actually ordered anything from Neiman Marcus, but I did so frequently enough that nobody, including me, thought twice when the box came in along with some others.

Jake, Rob's assistant, had been helping me out with administrative tasks ever since Meg left. As usual, he had sliced open the box, but left the contents, obscured by tissue, undisturbed. Inside, below a hideous purple T-shirt that was exactly not my color, were a note and a key. I unfolded the note. All it said was "I promised you proof."

Meg. I fingered the key. It could open only one door: Bluebeard's chamber.

The key presented a quandary. If it fit, it promised to reveal Rob's secrets, whatever they might be. Meg, in sending it to me, was betraying Rob's confidence and, perhaps, proving her loyalty to me.

Or was it a trick? Was she tempting me to invade Rob's privacy? Was it a test of my loyalty to my husband? To use the key meant trusting Meg over Rob. It meant breaking my promise to my husband. It meant letting my curiosity trump my principles. To use the key was wrong. I went into my closet and slipped it into a secret pocket in the front flap of one of my Chanel chain bags. (Oh, Coco, you knew the secrets a lady must keep, didn't you?)

But to not open that door! Why should my husband have secrets from me? Why should my now-former assistant have access to a room that I myself had never entered? What was inside? I deserved the answers to these questions.

I lasted all of forty-eight hours. Then I decided to use the key.

4

I waited until three in the morning. Even without Meg and Lala we still had at least five staff living in the house—I wasn't entirely sure of the numbers. And out in the security booth there was twenty-four-hour monitoring. All night a guy watched a rotating scan of the halls, entrances, and exits. It was my house—the absurdity of hiding from the security staff wasn't lost on me. Nonetheless, I calculated how to get to the gym without being caught by the cameras. I put on workout clothes just in case I was busted. I had a right to work out at any time of the night I wanted. Again: *my* house.

I took a long route to the gym, avoiding the cameras trained on the front door by going up to the second floor, peeking in on the boys, then coming down the back stairs. Once in the gym, I took some jabs at the punching bag. Hitting the bag gave me an unexpected surge of confidence, so I went at it some more, until I hurt my hand. Leave it to me to overdo it in the gym in the middle of the night when trying to expose my husband's secrets.

Finally, when it was clear that nobody cared what I was doing, I put the key in the doorknob lock of Bluebeard's chamber. It slid in easily. I turned the knob, and the door opened. With a furtive (and useless) glance behind me, I crept into the room, feeling silly for sneaking around my own house like a thief, and turned on the lights.

The room was an office. Just an office. Unglamorous, with a slightly stale smell. Unlike our proper offices in the house, which had been done by a designer, this one looked like an out-of-date Staples showroom, with several metal file cabinets and a simple desk with a clunky cordless phone on it. A fax machine dominated half the desk. In a way the spartan room was reassuring. There were no skeletons; it was clearly no love den; and it was utterly impossible to imagine Rob spending any real amount of time here. My husband definitely wasn't hosting drum-banging male re-wilding sessions in the small, unappealing room off our gym. (Oh yeah, there was *that* rumor about One Cell, too—sorry, no dice.)

What caught my eye was a poster-size photo that was mounted on foam board and hanging, unframed, on the wall above the desk. It was an image of two young boys standing in the middle of a road. They faced away from the camera, holding hands, looking toward an orange sunset.

I took the picture down to get a closer look. Though it was taken straight into the sun, and the figures were only silhouettes, I could tell it was Cap and Leo. The image was expertly lit, the boys perfectly haloed. It had obviously been professionally done. Across the top of the poster, in cursive, read, "A world of opportunity lies ahead . . ."

The photo was obviously a present for me. For all the jewels and cars and trips, this time Rob had hit it out of the park. He knew exactly what I wanted, what was most important to both of us. I bit my lip, feeling bad for having doubted him. My unchecked suspicion, this midnight sleuthing expedition, a key from a supposed rival, and all that was behind the mystery door was a mundane office where my husband was hiding nothing but his love for our family. This must have been what Meg wanted me to see—that whatever secrets Rob kept from me were completely innocent. As was she. Clearly I'd been watching too many crime shows on cable.

Hard as it was to feel truly close to Rob these days, when I looked at his gestures, his words, the way he'd acted with me from the very beginning, I knew that deep down we loved each other and could make it work.

Feeling ashamed, I went to hang the picture back on the wall. It slid down, missing the hook. I tried again, no luck. I turned it over to see where the wire was. On the back of the picture was a phone number. Mommy Brain hadn't taken my memorization skills away from me. As soon as I registered the number, I knew it by heart. I hooked the photo back up on the wall.

My years of anguish about this room had been for nothing. I had blamed my lack of direction, the disruption of my career, on my children. I'd blamed my loneliness on Rob, for traveling so much. I'd blamed my insecurity on Meg, for having more access to my husband than I did. I'd blamed my discontent on Lala, for . . . well, just for being surly. And, in some way, I'd blamed all of it on this room, for holding secrets that kept me from knowing my husband. Hadn't I learned anything in all my sessions at the Studio over the past four years? No person or room was the root of my troubles. I had to stop blaming everyone but myself. I saw, at last, that the problem was me. And I knew exactly how to fix it.

"You did the right thing, coming to me," Geoff said. I thanked him for seeing me on such short notice. If there were any answers to be found, they were here, inside these tall green walls.

Geoff's mismatched eyes flickered and he looked directly at me. "It's tough having Rob away, isn't it?" he said. "You must be lonely."

There it was, the intensity that made him oddly compelling. Hearing the word "lonely" out loud made tears well in my eyes.

"You let Lala go, didn't you?"

"Yes, and Meg," I admitted with some trepidation. He probably already knew, and I hoped he wasn't angry.

Geoff shrugged. "Your staff is your business. Let's focus on you—what's the underlying issue?" Geoff, like Rob, didn't mince words.

Some people would have said that I was depressed, but in the One Cell Practice, a fluctuation like this always originated in self-doubt.

"I'm having trouble moving past my emotions," I told Geoff.

Geoff's office, right next to Teddy Dillon's suite, reflected his high-up position in the organization. The room was large and well lit, with a westerly view of Beverly Hills. An abstract painting covered one of the interior walls. The blinds were half down against the direct sun, which painted lateral stripes behind his head.

Geoff nodded. "Your emotions are getting in your way. What are you trying to achieve?"

I looked down. "I have everything a person could want. I know that, and I'm grateful."

"No apologies necessary here. Remember the continuum: emotions, desires, actions. We always want to move like the Practice: from stillness through the mind to action."

"I'm isolated. Rob travels all the time. It's hard to connect with people. I feel kind of trapped. I've felt this way for a while—I just wasn't admitting it to myself."

Geoff leaned back in his chair and rolled a mint in his mouth. "Let's talk about the children."

"The boys are fine, thank you. What I'm struggling with is—"

"Are you avoiding the question?"

"No! But that's not why I'm here."

"Elizabeth, I think you're forgetting how this works. Let me guide you. Are you providing an ideal growth environment for Cap and Leo?"

I sighed. "The best I can. But I wish they could have a childhood like mine." My mouth quivered as I tried to hold back tears.

"Elizabeth. I can see that when I mention your children you have Inner Conflict."

In the Practice, Inner Conflict stood in the way of happiness, success, and fulfillment of human destiny. It meant that my emotions and actions were at odds, and that I'd failed to follow the Whole Body Principles. Geoff told me that the way out was simple. All I had to do was to follow practical steps, one by one, toward my goal. When the exterior was in balance, the interior would follow.

Geoff went on, "You are in crisis. This isn't good for you or your family. But it's going to be okay. We can help you through this. Your nanny is gone and you're overwhelmed. The first thing I suggest for you is some help with your sons."

"No, I really want them to be with me. Rob and I both—we want them to be raised by family."

Geoff smiled. His teeth were pale yellow, and I couldn't help thinking those Altoids weren't doing him any favors. He said, "I have some good news for you. We are starting up a new daycare program right here at the Studio, which is as good as family, isn't it? Your sons will be able to socialize with their peers, and you'll get some time to yourself. You should give it a try."

I had to hand it to Geoff—Cap and Leo did need some other kids to play with, and I needed a break. Daycare at the Studio might not be such a bad idea.

"And another suggestion—" Geoff said. "Call your agent. I think you'll be amazed to find what opportunities are within your reach."

The very next day I brought Cap and Leo to the Studio at nine a.m. The teacher, Jana, met us at the classroom door.

"The transition is smoother if you don't come in," she said. I peeked over her shoulder and saw a clean, bright roomful of educational toys—a dress-up area, a corner full of blocks, a door to an enclosed backyard with a climbing structure and sand tables. I'd never seen this space before—perhaps because I hadn't been at the Studio much lately—but even so, everything looked new, as if it had been set up this morning just in time for my arrival. And perhaps it had. There were only two other mothers dropping off their children, and both of them introduced their offspring to "Teacher Jana" as if they'd never met before. Leo dashed over to the block area, and even Cap soon let go of my hand and ran straight to the miniature kitchen.

I was the one with separation anxiety. Out in the courtyard I read the paper, checking my watch every few minutes. I lasted all of half an hour. Hurrying back to the classroom, I peeked through the window. Leo was wearing a tutu and calmly hammering wooden nails at a play workbench. Cap was taking turns with two little girls sending marbles down a complex run. My doubts about leaving them didn't really matter. For once my boys looked like normal kids, leading a normal life.

Following Geoff's advice had instantaneous results. After dropping the twins off that first day, I went home and immediately called Cherry Simpson at ACE. Aside from social functions, I hadn't talked to a soul at ACE since the wedding endorsements had died down. It had been more than four years, and I figured it would take a couple of days for Cherry to return my call, but to my surprise her assistant put me through right away.

I started tentatively. "Cherry, I might be ready to work again. I was wondering if you—"

"Okay, honey, I have a great one for you. Parker O. Witt wants you to take the female lead in his new movie. It's shooting now in Mississippi."

It was as if she'd known I was going to call, and it occurred to me that someone (Geoff? Rob?) had given her a heads-up.

Actors of the world will hate me for this. I am fully aware that it's not every day a part in a Parker O. Witt film falls into your lap. But that was the reality of being Rob Mars's wife, and part of why I didn't feel like I had a right to be unsatisfied. I was incredibly fortunate—I just had to find my way. *Emotions are a chemical reaction,* I told myself. *Happiness is a choice.*

5

The movie was called *The Safe House*. My part was Abigail Warren, wife of a Mississippi cotton plantation owner in the mid-1800s. I secretly fall in love with a slave, Billy. My good-for-nothing husband, who has three children with Billy's wife, beats my lover to near death, and I engineer his escape. Billy returns—not for love as my naïve character fantasizes—but to convince me to let our barn serve as a station on the Underground Railroad. Conflicted though I am—my brother has just died fighting for the South—I let Billy do it, if only because it's a way to keep my love close. But then, when Billy dies from the injuries my husband has inflicted, I'm forced to decide if I will continue his work, shepherding escaped slaves through our barn. And (of course) I'm secretly pregnant with his child. It was an Oscar-worthy role if ever there was one.

The doubts that I had in my marriage—my loneliness, Rob's distance, the impossibility of giving our children a normal childhood—all flew out the window when Cherry told me about the offer. Actors wait years for parts like this, in the hands of the right director, to come along. This was what I had worked for all my life. I wanted it.

I despised my father's blatant opportunism on my behalf, bartering my love life for my career. And I was equally indignant at the media's claims that I'd married Rob to boost my status. When I decided to give up *Skye London* and stay home with the babies, a tiny part of me had done it to show that I wasn't in this for my career. I wanted to prove them all wrong. And yet, for several years now I'd been ashamed to acknowledge the creeping realization that my dream life as Mrs. Mars wasn't enough.

But with one brief phone call, everything changed. I felt like a cartoon of a withered flower that, when watered, springs back into bloom. My breath, shallow and restrained for so long, now filled my chest with air. I was buoyant and alive.

When I put down the phone after speaking with Cherry, I walked out to the backyard. The stone terrace was pleasantly furnished with comfortable seating areas. The pool shimmered, and beyond it was a view that stretched across the city. On a clear day you could see all the way to the ocean. Except for watching Cap and Leo's swim lessons, I barely ever made it out here. Now I stood looking out at West L.A., reveling in all that was mine.

Was it possible that my father knew me better than I knew myself? He had set me up with Rob to propel me to the heights of fame, and however noble I thought I was, maybe that was what I wanted after all. I had tried being a wife and a mother, and it wasn't enough. I had been reared to fulfill my father's dream, and, much as I resisted that notion, Hollywood was what I knew, what I did best, where I would find fulfillment.

I was thrilled that all I had to do was pick up the phone to land the part of a lifetime. And if that was so, then wasn't my father right about all of it? Didn't I love that my husband was a world-class movie star? Wasn't I attracted to his screen-perfect image, his fame, his power?

I finally admitted the truth to myself. This was it. This was exactly what I wanted from my marriage to Rob, from One Cell, from Hollywood, from the world. I wanted to be a star. A famous, glowing, trophy-flaunting movie star. And I was willing to accept any shortcomings in my marriage to get there. Shallow and selfish though it might be, this was who I was. Denying it was no use.

Being offered the part of Abigail Warren helped me envision a new future. The movie would come out, and the world would see that I wasn't just Rob's wife. My parents, Aurora, the press, even I myself wanted to find fault in a life that seemed too good to be true. But look at me now! This was the missing piece. I had a perfect life, and making the most of it might help me appreciate it.

Rob did the impossible and rearranged the schedule for the movie he was finishing up in Sweden—*The Life of Digby Dane*—so that he could be home with Cap and Leo for most of the month that I'd be on location in Mississippi. The rest of *The Safe House* would be shot on a soundstage in L.A. I'd grown up expecting whomever I married to support my work. Then I'd married a man whose career was so much bigger than mine it simply wasn't practical. But Rob understood what I was trying to do— trying to find the balance in my unexpected life—and he couldn't have been more respectful. Knowing Rob, he'd personally reimbursed his co-producers on *Digby Dane* for the toll the schedule change took on that movie's budget. Whatever the cost, it was certainly more than I'd earn for *The Safe House*, effectively making it a vanity project, but we knew without saying that it didn't matter.

Only three months had passed since Rob had been home for Christmas, but in that time a lot had changed: I had fired Meg, ventured into Bluebeard's chamber, put the boys in daycare, and decided to take a movie. All this to mitigate the loneliness of Rob's absence. And now, because I'd followed Geoff's instructions and pursued my goals, he was home.

Before I left for Mississippi, Rob and I overlapped in Malibu for only a day and a half, but I remember that time very clearly. It was a warm reunion (in part because of the big, bushy beard he'd grown for the second act of *Digby Dane*).

The night Rob got home, we both put the boys to bed—something we rarely had a chance to do together. Every night was a juggling act. From the minute I got them into the bath, which itself took a certain amount of creativity and/or bribing ("While you're in the bath I'll tell you all about the fantastic subway trains of New York City"), the boys became two slippery fish constantly wriggling out of my grasp. As soon as I had the second one clean and dried, the first was back in the tub. And that was the best-case scenario. Just as likely one or the other was experimenting with Daddy's shaving cream. Nonetheless, I'd gotten it down to a strict routine: bath, pajamas, read three books, talk about the day, sing "Shenandoah." But when Daddy was home, as daddies are wont to do, he brought his own excite-the-child-right-before-bedtime rituals. Dripping wet, the boys ran in reckless circles around the upstairs, and each time one of them reached Rob, he'd say, "Do you have a twin brother? There was a boy who looked *just like you*. He went that way." Cap and Leo would chase each other until they crashed into a pile of giggles that turned to tears at the slightest provocation. At last, a half hour after their bedtime, when I was gritting my teeth, Cap would practically beg to go to sleep. Then we each lay down with one of them (okay, it was always Cap with me and Leo with Rob, but I was in denial about it) and Rob read to them (tonight it was *Charlie and the Chocolate Factory*) until Cap was out and Leo could barely keep his eyes open. Rob and I smiled at each over their heads, and our smiles said, *We love them more than anything. This is what life's about. The four of us.* Everything looked brighter when Rob was home.

In Mississippi, my first day on the set of *The Safe House* was a harsh awakening. To the cast and crew I wasn't the quirky indie actor Lizzie Pepper. They could only see me as the famous actor Rob Mars's wife. And, if they'd seen my trailer, who could blame them? ACE had clearly sent over Rob's set rider as mine. I knew the minute I walked in because next to the door was a basket with a sign reading "Shoes Please." Definitely a Rob Mars touch. The trailer was completely tricked-out. There were marble floors and a full kitchen. The refrigerator was entirely packed with just three items: bottles of FIJI water, Rob's go-to protein powder, and single-use packets of the soymilk he used in his coffee. For privacy, all the windows had been replaced with LCD screens encased in Plexiglas. Cameras mounted outside the trailer projected onto the screens, so you could see what was going on outside without risking actual windows that someone might spy through. On one side of the trailer, all the screens showed a gray concrete wall. On the other, three of them showed the asphalt parking lot, with an occasional person walking past, oblivious to the cameras. The fourth screen on the parking-lot side of the trailer was on the fritz, filled with fuzzy snow. It was a rather jarring sight, but I couldn't figure out how to turn it off or unplug it. In addition to my bedroom and the living room/kitchen, there was a playroom just in case the boys visited, already stocked with coloring books, puzzles, and a huge plush turtle. Evidently someone had been told that Cap was inexplicably obsessed with turtles. Apparently there was a pop-up second floor, but I didn't bother to open it since it sounded structurally questionable.

After I got settled, Parker O. Witt's assistant walked me from my trailer to the set. We were shooting on the wraparound porch that day—mostly preparations surrounding a Christmas feast on the plantation.

When I arrived, my scene was already lit. Parker introduced me to the rest of the cast and told me we would start when I was ready.

Ordinarily, there would be run-throughs, staging, and rehearsals, but Cherry had told me that they would do all of that without me. "It's not part of your contract anymore. You're past all that. From now on, you fly in, shoot, leave."

I had protested, saying that I didn't want to be a diva. Part of what I liked about being on the set was the camaraderie. But Cherry cut me off. "Don't be nervous, sweetie. I'm sure you'll hit the ground running."

I knew my lines, of course. I'd learned them effortlessly on the plane the night before. But I barely knew my blocking or who my fellow players were before I was on and cameras were rolling. Tony Solo, who played my lover, pointed to a wicker rocker.

"You're there," he whispered, but he didn't return my smile of thanks.

That day it was all business on the set. They had already done a week of shooting, so I expected to feel a little like an outsider, but this was different. Actors aren't usually so cold.

At the end of the day, I sent Joaquim on a mission. He's kind of a party boy, and he already knew where the crew would be drinking that night. So I told him to do reconnaissance. Was everyone genuinely weird and stiff, or did they hate me? Also, I had Talia find the best local source and order chocolate chip cookies for the whole cast and crew. It was kind of buying their love, but it was also an old-fashioned gesture to say that I wasn't a snot.

The next morning when Joaquim showed up to do my makeup, he was very hungover.

"I did it for you, sweetie. It was a self-sacrifice," he moaned.

I asked a PA to bring him a water, and waited while he hydrated. Finally, he took a deep breath.

"The problem isn't you. It's Ellia Lopez."

Ellia Lopez had originated the part of Abigail Warren on Broadway. "They wanted her for the part?" That made sense. Most of the film cast had come from the play.

"It's worse than that. She was *here* until yesterday. She got booted."

No wonder everyone hated me. I'd replaced their friend. "Why? What did she do?"

"That's the problem. She didn't do anything. Parker told them 'No Lizzie, no movie.' It came from ACE."

"Oh my God." My agent, who had ignored me for three years, had forced Parker O. Witt's hand. And Parker O. Witt had a pretty strong hand. This was the true power of Rob, and it wasn't pretty. He'd traded something for this favor. An appearance at an event or in a movie. Money. Maybe just his goodwill. I had no idea what the role was worth, but whatever it was, Rob could afford it.

So much had changed. I thought about the day I arrived on the set of *American Dream*. The whole cast knew that Steve Romany had given me the part without an audition and they knew why—I hadn't been willing to leave my ill grandmother's side. When I walked into my *American Dream* trailer for the first time, there was a huge flower arrangement with a note that read, "For Lizzie, who knows what's important. We're so glad to have you on the team. Love, Your New Cast Mates."

Gone were the days when I had carved my own way. I wasn't a true artist, winning parts through sheer determination, and winning friends through loyalty and integrity. Now I was on the other side, part of the Hollywood powerhouse, where connections and status trumped talent. And trailer sizes matched egos. No wonder my fellow actors couldn't look me in the eye. But this was the deal I had made. My father had pitched me to Rob. I'd fallen for my husband in large part for his status. And Rob was buying my happiness. When you added it all up, this was one very expensive movie role, and I was damn well going to make the most of it.

The next day we shot the scene where Billy, on his deathbed, tells Abigail that there are two escaped slaves who need to be picked up at the train station. He asks her to get them because he can't. This is her moment of decision. She decides to do it, risking everything.

This was an intense scene, and I wasn't thrilled that it was shooting so early in the schedule. I'd had no time to sink into character, much less connect with Tony, as my lover, Billy. But it had to be done.

Billy lay on a hay bale. A makeup assistant spritzed his face to make it gleam with perspiration. He grimaced with the pain of whatever ailment was supposed to be killing him. Fake sweat ran down the side of his dirt-encrusted face, creating little dusty rivers.

Emotions are a chemical reaction. I thought of my sister, Allison, how much I loved her, worried about her, and yet had let her go. Where was she? Was she hungry, alone? Lost, lost? I drank in the emotions connected to those thoughts—the emotions I'd spent so much time in One Cell isolating and observing. And I thought of my own fears. The fear of doing something my parents didn't want me to do, of breaking the rules, of taking a risk, of upsetting expectations.

I knelt next to Billy and looked into his eyes, shining with fever or the shot of bourbon I'd seen Tony down right before the cameras rolled. This was about more than the love between two people. Abigail had a choice: to continue her life of luxury or to risk everything for justice.

"Seems to me there's an easy road and a hard road," I said. "A wrong road and a right one. My heart knows what is right." I kissed Billy's forehead, lingering in that moment, knowing that it might be the last time I saw him. Then I stood up and walked toward the barn door. Before I left, I turned around for one last look at my dying lover.

Billy's voice was weak. "Thank you, Mistress."

I imagined my sister, wasted and suffering, and let the shame and despair wash over me. "It's the world we were handed, Billy, each of us. And it's ours to change," I said, and opened the door.

Parker yelled "Cut" and the cast burst into applause. I had done it. I found exactly what I needed to expose Abigail's pain and love and final resolution to the camera. It felt right to me, and I could see from the faces around me that when it came down to it, we all cared most about the same thing—nailing the character. I was Abigail.

6

For the rest of the time on the set of *The Safe House*, I buckled down. I made myself visible on the set. After my scenes finished shooting, I'd hang around, watching the performances and gorging myself on the ubiquitous glazed doughnut holes. Eventually, the cast started to come around to me. They saw that, though I may have rode in on my husband's coattails, I wasn't lingering on them. It was clear that I wanted to be there, that my whole heart was in the film, that I *needed* it, as much as they did.

ACE had gotten me the part, and they had done it as a favor to Rob. I didn't care. (Except I did feel bad about Ellia Lopez. I called ACE and demanded that they get her a lead in a feature. Which they did. Even though she wasn't a client. She can thank Rob Mars for that one.) Once on set, I had proved myself worthy. But in the course of making *The Safe House* there was another change, a bigger one—and that was me.

I came to *The Safe House* at a personal low, having resigned myself to the notion that I would sell my soul for the right part. In a way, I already had. When it was handed to me on a silver platter, nothing could have stopped me.

But living that dream transformed it.

On the set of *The Safe House*, I discovered that it wasn't *being a star* that mattered. What I really cared about was *acting*, immersing myself in a character and telling a story, and, dammit, I was good at it. For the first time in a long time, I felt . . . confidence. To everyone else it may have been a subtle change, but to me it was huge. My father and I wanted the same thing, but for different reasons. He thought I was destined for stardom, but the truth was that I was satisfied with a fragment of that picture. Just the acting. That eclipsed everything else. Taking on a character, losing myself in her, and learning from her. The truths we find in art. The rest—the fame and fortune—I didn't care about it. Rob's power had gotten me this gig, but I was willing to fight and claw my way up to the next one.

This epiphany was tied to another realization. It was so inevitable that all it took was a life-size puppet of a big yellow bird to snap me to my senses. It came about three weeks into the production, when Rob had returned to Scandinavia and Teacher Jana's daughter, Jordan, who had started occasionally babysitting and working as my assistant, brought Cap and Leo to visit me for the last week of production.

I was in my trailer, showing the boys bits of *Sesame Street* on You-Tube. I wanted them to hear one of my old favorites, "What's the Name of That Song?" I had just found the link when Jordan came to get them.

"It's your call time. Come, Cap, Leo, we'll go to the playground," she said.

"Hold on a second, I just want them to hear this song," I said.

Jordan stood in the doorway, waiting patiently. When the song ended, she said, "Come, boys." Leo obediently hopped off the couch and Jordan took his hand. Cap resisted momentarily—he never liked to leave me—but Jordan reminded him that there would be swings, and that was enough to persuade him.

"Good-bye, sweeties," I said, but they had already disappeared out the door and across the parking lot.

I looked back at the screen. There was a related link on the sidebar: "Big Bird Learns About Death." I clicked on it. It was an old episode of *Sesame Street* that I had never seen. In it Mr. Hooper, the grocer, has died. The blurb below the video told me that the episode was written when Will Lee, who played Mr. Hooper, died in real life. The Children's Television Workshop producers took the opportunity to give children viewers a gentle perspective on death.

I watched the actors explain to Big Bird why Mr. Hooper wasn't there with the rest of them. Big Bird has trouble understanding. His *Sesame Street* family tries to explain, and you can see on the actors' faces how brokenhearted they truly are.

Watching those actors struggle on camera with the death of their colleague moved me, and tears rolled down my cheeks. Then I was crying harder, and it was about more than poor old Mr. Hooper. An aging actor died, and his colleagues loved him, and they wanted children to know the truth about life and death and joy and regret, and so all over America, schoolchildren absorbed pieces of their grief, transforming it into something brave and true.

I wanted my sons to learn hard lessons in unexpected ways. My childhood hadn't been careful or calculated. It was spontaneous games of hide-and-seek with neighborhood kids, and TV shows my parents didn't filter, and raw emotions that came and went as I grew. I didn't even care that much about Mr. Hooper when I was a kid, but in that moment his death was everything to me, and it felt good to weep for him, and for his fellow actors, and for the child I once was, exploring the world. I missed my parents. And it felt good to mourn life and love. It felt good to *feel*.

My husband, the Studio, the invasive press. All of them told me not to indulge my emotions. I could simply decide to move past them. But was it really possible? For how long could I ignore or manipulate my own feelings? Weren't they what made me *me*?

I had always thought of myself as someone who knew what was right for me and for those around me, and followed that instinct. But I'd gotten distracted by Rob's prestige and money and power, sucked into another role. Somewhere along the way, I had stopped being the girl who blew off a major audition for a network drama to be at Granny's side.

The Whole Body Principles made life black and white. They instructed us to set goals and work toward them without regard for the obstacles that emerged. But those obstacles are important. Mr. Hooper's death stopped *Sesame Street* in its tracks. Abigail risked her life of affluence for what was right and true. The Studio had taught me much; it had certainly helped my acting, but maybe it wasn't the only answer. Like Abigail, I knew in my heart what was right. I started to think that emotions weren't just scientific equations to be studied and used at will. They weren't a distraction to be ignored. They were spontaneous and sprawling and undefined. They were everything.

I hired a private detective. It was time to find my sister.

Starting that summer, Rob had an unprecedented six months off—it was the longest sustained time we'd had together since we were married. There were premieres, fund-raisers, and events at the Studio. The detective, Mike, tried to track down my sister, a task made more challenging by the critical need to keep it from the press. Meanwhile, Cap and Leo started to grow into their own people. Cap was serious, a rule follower, and still obsessed with turtles. Leo was a daredevil, climbing the stairs from the wrong side of the banister; jumping into the pool unsupervised; wanting nothing more than to be chased around the house, caught, and "tickle tortured."

Our assistant, Jake, seemed constantly overwhelmed, maybe because now he was handling my affairs as well as Rob's, but perhaps because he regarded all tasks—be they drugstore runs, RSVPs, or business meetings—as equally dire. Every day he presented me with a list of issues, and I made choices. Which watches would Rob like to keep? Where would we stay in Gstaad? Which car did I want now that my lease was up? Agitated and humorless, Jake would tap his pencil nervously on the table while he waited for my answers.

"Is the house on fire?" I'd tease him.

"Not that I know of," he'd say, without any acknowledgment that I was joking.

"Do follow up on that," I'd say.

After *The Safe House* wrapped, I was determined to build on it. I wanted my next part to be a big one. Not Skye London. Not an action hero. A part that mattered to me, if no one else.

Every afternoon the mail arrived by two. I hurried to Jake's office to see what had come in. He would hand me a script, if there was one, ask if there was anything else, and turn right back to his computer. Scripts trickled in, and I pored over each one, considering not just the parts that Cherry liked for me, but the smaller roles, the offbeat sidekicks and spurned lovers. Meanwhile, every day at least ten scripts came in for Rob. They sat in their sky blue ACE envelopes, stacked on Jake's desk, waiting to be unwrapped and moved to Rob's office.

Rob wasn't reading scripts these days. His film schedule was already booked four years out. He was taking a well-deserved break. Every morning he dragged his sea kayak down to the water and paddled straight away from land. At this point there were so many photos out there of him as a boatman hybrid that the paparazzi practically yawned when they saw him in his wet suit. He loved the isolation and timelessness of the open sea. My explorer husband. After his morning paddle, he'd swim for a long time, heading straight west. That was followed by a ninety-minute massage from Joseph, then a nap. All this before lunch.

Rob's homecomings had always been a welcome treat, but having Rob around for a long stretch upset the household dynamic. This became uncomfortably clear on the night of a benefit for the Motion Picture & Television Fund. Rob and I were all dressed up, hair and makeup done, saying what was meant to be a quick good night to the boys before we left. It was bedtime, but, in classic Rob fashion, he riled them up by giving them airplane rides, swinging them in circles holding one hand and one foot. Leo loved it, squealing with glee, begging for more. Cap, always more cautious, solemnly said, "Daddy, can I have a turn, too, but not as fast?" Spinning, Cap seemed to be laughing at first, but then the pitch of his laughter changed.

"Wait," I said. But Rob kept going. "Stop, Rob, stop! Put him down!"

"What?" Rob slowed, and when he finally understood that Cap was crying, Rob landed him gently and knelt down. "What's wrong, buddy?" he asked.

"Does your arm hurt, Cap?" I said, squatting next to Rob.

"Daddy hurt arm," he wept.

"I'm sorry, bud," Rob said. "It'll feel better soon. Come, let's brush your teeth." Cap, so full of trust, quieted down as Rob led him into the bathroom. I watched as he brushed his teeth. He held his toothbrush with his left hand, which I'd never seen him do, his right arm bent protectively against his stomach. Cap's face was utterly serious. He was trying to be brave for his daddy.

Rob brought him back into the room and tucked him in bed. "Night-night, little man," he said. He kissed both boys and stood up. "Ready to go?" he asked me.

I bent and kissed Leo good night. Then I turned to Cap. "Does your arm still hurt?" I asked. He nodded silently. I turned to Rob. "I'm worried about that elbow."

"Don't be," Rob said. "He's fine. He's not even crying anymore."

"He said it still hurts."

"Okay," Rob said. The muscles in his neck tightened. "What do you want to do?"

"He needs to see a doctor," I said.

"Right now?" Rob said. He looked at his watch. "My speech is in forty-five minutes. Can it wait until morning?" Matthew Brau, his agent and the head of ACE, was the chairman of the charity's board.

"I read that you're not supposed to swing them that way," I said.

"So now this is my fault?" Rob said.

"I didn't say that."

"Okay," Rob said. "We'll do whatever you want to do. You want to go to the ER? Let's go." He started to walk toward Cap.

"Wait." I grabbed Rob's shoulder. "Is it okay, with the paparazzi and everything? Should we have a doctor come here?" Neither of the boys had been to a hospital since they were born. I knew what a normal ER trip involved, but I had no idea how to handle an ER trip with one of Rob Mars's sons.

Rob stared at me as if I were daft. "If he's hurt—and you think he is—we go to the ER, like everyone else. Lewis will know the closest one."

I was so accustomed to factoring in our fame, and the media's response, that I didn't know when to let it go. When did the real world eclipse privacy, optics, and controlling the story? Not when we were dating and I needed a tampon, and not when I was in labor and took the time to put on a disguise. But now, at eight p.m., with an injury my husband wouldn't fully acknowledge, now we went full steam ahead.

Rob scooped up Cap. "Come on, Cap, Mama wants you to see a doctor."

"Noooo," Cap wailed. He was thinking shots.

"Noooo," Leo wailed. "I want to come with you. See the ambulance!"

Cap wailed through the car ride, and through our arrival at the emergency room. I was vaguely aware that we drove to a side door, and Lewis went in first—apparently, even in an emergency, there were still measures to be taken—and we were immediately led to a back room.

We sat there for a half hour, Cap finally sleeping on my shoulder, and Rob growing increasingly impatient. At last, a nurse stuck her head in and said, "It's going to be a while. There was a multi-motorcycle accident on the PCH. We're really busy."

I could tell Rob wanted to leave. He thought Cap was fine, and he wanted to honor his commitment. "You go ahead," I said. "I can take care of this."

"Are you sure?" he said. After some back-and-forth, I convinced him to leave. Four long hours later, the doctor came in, diagnosed Cap with "nursemaid's elbow" (putting the blame squarely on the "nursemaid," who in this case was Rob), and gently slipped the ligament back into place. Rob had never said out loud that he thought I was overreacting, but I felt slightly vindicated.

Rob was already asleep when we got home. He woke when I came in, and after he checked on Cap, I told him that the doctor had said that he shouldn't spin the boys around that way again, especially Cap, whose elbow was now vulnerable to reinjury.

"You told the doctor how it happened? That I was the one spinning him?"

I nodded.

Rob looked irritated. "You just gotta be more careful with that stuff, Elizabeth."

I had to be more careful.

Having Rob spend more time at home was all I wanted, but his presence felt like a disruption. We hadn't established a rhythm as parents, and now he felt like an extra in my life with the boys.

We finished all our summer travels and the boys started daycare again. One night that fall, Rob looked across at me in bed. I was reading a pile of crappy screenplays, discarding most of them after ten pages. He said, "Maybe you should look at some of my scripts? I've got hundreds piled up. You never know."

One wall of Rob's office was a built-in bookshelf stacked with scripts sorted by categories: action, drama, rom-com, director, other. Over the next few weeks I went through the dramas systematically, pulling out stacks of fifty at a time, sorting out any that were already in production or looked dreadful. I read the first act of each, reading further only if I was interested.

It was just after Thanksgiving—right before Rob was due to leave for a five-month shoot in Turkey—when I decided to take a break from the dramas (How many corrupt-major-institution-overturned-by-wily-male-hero scripts can one woman endure?) and started to flip through the most intriguing category—"other." Other. It was what I wanted. Something that defied category. Something I'd never seen before. Something weird, challenging, crazy.

As they say, be careful what you wish for.

7

It didn't have a sky blue cover, but it was in script form. There were six or seven binder clips of pages, and they were all held together by a rubber band. The cover page read "First Dates." It sounded like a romantic comedy—not what I was looking for, but the opening lines caught my eye.

EXT. OUTSIDE HER HOME—DAY

He rings her doorbell, transportation at the ready.

              RM
It's me.

              W
What are you doing here?

              RM
Can I steal you away?

```
              W
     Where are we going?


              RM
     Let me surprise you. Come
     downstairs. Your chariot
     awaits.


              W
     But I have plans! I'm sup-
     posed to get a manicure!


              RM
     Cancel. I'll wait.
```

Okay, this was weird. It sounded strangely similar to my first date with Rob. Maybe, I thought cynically, every first date where a man surprised a woman with a trip to a mysterious island started exactly the same way. Or maybe this script had given Rob the idea for our first date. But wasn't that *exactly* what he'd said to me? I remembered him calling the limo a *chariot*. (Who could forget that?) Had he hired someone to turn our romance into a script?

I flipped the page. Above the lines of dialogue there was a handwritten sticky note: *As requested, the following are potential scenarios to initiate an overnight visit. I hope they're effective!—Emil*

```
At sunset, he takes her hands in his.


              RM
     I'm having an amazing time.
```

I can take you home when-
ever you want. But I want
to ask you if you're willing to stay here with me
tonight.

OPTION 1

W

I would love that/Maybe.

He kisses her.

OPTION 2

W

I'm not that kind of girl/
Too presumptuous.

RM

Don't worry, you'll have
your own room. We're not
there yet. I'm very at-
tracted to you, but I re-
spect you too much to
proceed with anything but
caution.

W is impressed. She can't believe he's such a
gentleman.

```
                  RM
            You want to know what I'm
            really thinking?
He kisses her.
```

Now I was spooked. This was not a regular script. These were the *exact* lines Rob had delivered to me on our first date, and maybe to every other woman he'd dated. RM, the male lead character, was clearly Rob Mars. And W stood for "woman." Unless it stood for my former costar Wendy Jones. Or "wacko." What had I stumbled upon? Who was this Emil? Why was he scripting Rob's life? My God, was speaking his own thoughts really so hard for Rob? Was it possible that my love affair with Rob Mars was all an act?

I read on. More scenarios played out on the pages, some that hadn't ever come to fruition: The writer was not unreasonably confident that Rob Mars would score on the first date, so I learned that the morning after theoretically amazing sex, he was to say: "Whoa. I didn't expect this to happen tonight. But, boy, am I glad it did. You look radiant. No, don't change anything. I want to remember you exactly like this."

I also learned that if for any reason Rob wanted to land a difficult fish (that would be me), he was to say, "I know a place where we can truly be alone. Well, except for one person. The pilot of my plane—and he'll be otherwise occupied. When you're up there, the city is transformed. All of us, our houses and cars, shrinking down into nothing, and what's left, what's really visible, is the natural beauty and man's impact, great and destructive. It, well, it puts life in perspective."

That I'd heard. That was the Rob I'd fallen in love with.

And after sex on the plane, which the writer didn't even bother to pose as a hypothetical, Rob was to deliver the clincher, sweet and vulnerable.

"You know, I've looked down at the world from this plane hundreds of times, and every time it clears my head. But you've gone and made it foggy again."

Yes, I remembered. There had been tears in his eyes. He had laughed at himself as he wiped them away. Rob deserved an Oscar for that one.

My cell phone chimed. It was lunchtime. In the butler's pantry, Rob was making a smoothie. I had no idea how to look at him. What to say? I was in shock. I sat down in the breakfast room, and our regular chef, Elsie, put fig and goat cheese salads on the table for me and Rob. He came in with two mango-colored smoothies and handed one to me. "It has chia seeds," he said. "For omega-3."

"Thank you," I said, and faked a smile. I ate as quickly as I could. I had to get out of there.

"Everything okay, Elizabeth?" Rob said. "You seem distracted."

"No . . . I mean, yes, everything's okay. I'm in the middle of a script . . ."

"A good one?" Rob asked.

Good? No, that wasn't the word . . . How could he do this to me? "They're all the same, aren't they? A bunch of words that some writer spewed on a page. It's all bullshit." I'd gone too far, but my mind was reeling with confusion and rage.

"Well, well, well." Rob chuckled. "Someone's turning into quite the film snob."

I read the rest of the document with increasing dismay. Here was how Rob was to make conversation over dinner, and here was the joke he was supposed to interject if conversation ran dry. Here was an observation he could have about the texture of the walls at the restaurant we'd gone to once. Nuggets of charm he could offer upon meeting W's parents. Even suggestions for events still in the future, like a night spent reminiscing about our first Valentine's Day together ("Your eyes were sparkling just like they are tonight." Really? Had I fallen for crap like that? Gag.)

The very last lines were the hardest to read. Again, there was a sticky note from MAK, the apparent screenwriter: *Notes for if she has cold feet at wedding—Best wishes! Emil*

```
          RM
We'll fix it, love. I know
we can. If today isn't per-
fect, we'll get married
again. I'll marry you a
hundred times.
```

Those were the words Rob had said to me on the day before our wedding, on that isolated stand on Achill Island, when I'd been so upset that my parents and Aurora weren't at the wedding. They were the words that reassured me that I was safe and loved. The words that convinced me I was doing the right thing. The words that made every other worry and doubt fade. That was one of the most important moments in our relationship—the cornerstone—and it had been a lie.

Whenever I had doubted that I really knew my husband, I had come back to his words, the corny but heartfelt declarations of love that fell so effortlessly from his lips. They reminded me that he loved me deeply, and gave me confidence that we could weather anything. But none of it was real. I was horrified, absolutely horrified. But overshadowing the deceit and betrayal, darker and more devastating than the heartbreak, was how immeasurably sorry I felt for Rob. Was this how he always operated? On every date? In his last marriage? Was this what Lexy had been trying to warn me about in her cryptic note? What was it all for? Maybe he did love me, in his own way, but whoever he truly was had been completely over-shadowed by the heroes he played onscreen and the PR image he'd fabri-cated off-screen. If I gave him the benefit of the doubt, I would say that he didn't know who he was anymore and was too scared to find out.

I had married a blank slate, a hollow man. Our love was an invention scripted by a stranger, the elusive Emil. And yet Rob was exactly who he seemed to be: the best actor in the world. In a way I understood him bet-ter than I ever had. But I didn't love him. Not anymore. Not after this.

Worst of all, in this phony romance, I had played my part, and it was a doozy. I was the clichéd princess, swept off my feet, willing and eager to accept this faux Prince Charming at face value. I could have seen. I should have known. Rob may have commissioned this false romance, but I was complicit.

There were two days remaining before Rob left for Turkey. I'd had six months with the husband I longed to know better. Now I couldn't bear to look at him. I climbed into bed and pretended to have a migraine until he was gone.

8

On Tuesdays and Thursdays breakfast for the boys was always oatmeal, prepared by me. Leo scarfed down whatever was in front of him, but Cap was particular about his oatmeal. Pancakes? French toast? A stranger could walk through the front door, serve him anything with maple syrup, and Cap would eat it up. But his oatmeal had to be all me. If Elsie so much as dared place the spoon in the bowl, Cap's mouth shut in a straight line, and he shook his head slowly and mournfully, as if in apology for his own four-year-old irrationality. Or possibly in profound disappointment at his caregivers' collective stupidity.

And so, on the Tuesday morning after Rob finally left, I set about making breakfast. As usual, Elsie had everything prepped. The oatmeal was in a bowl in the refrigerator, a shield of plastic wrap stretched wrinkle-free across its mouth. Beside it was a measuring cup with exactly the right amount of milk, and three small white bowls containing brown sugar, chopped walnuts, and dried cranberries, each similarly sheathed. I poured the ingredients into the small pot Elsie had left on the stove, while Elsie busied herself disposing of the discarded plastic wrap and washing the bowls as soon as I emptied them. It was an absurd charade.

"Daddy went on a plane," Leo announced.

"That's right, sweetie. Daddy went on a trip."

"Is Daddy home?" he said. "Daddy's *not* home. Daddy's on a trip."

"Daddy went on a long plane ride to a place called Turkey," I said. "He'll call you on the computer tomorrow morning."

"Daddy is my only and my best," Leo said, his lips quivering. Leo was his daddy's boy, and Rob's trips were hardest on him.

"Daddy always comes back," Cap said, parroting what Rob and I always said when the boys asked about their father's frequent absences.

"That's right, sweetie. Mommy is here, and Daddy always comes back." Cap always liked to know exactly what the plan was. He'd accept any new adventure—a plane trip, a boat ride, a museum visit—whatever it was, he was game, so long as he knew what to expect. His world was still so simple. Every question had an answer.

A sob threatened to roll over me, the storm of emotion I was using all my power to hold at bay. Leo needed his father. Cap did not like change or surprises. *Daddy always comes back.*

I couldn't leave Rob. I couldn't even begin to think about what leaving Rob would do to my sons.

I knew what it meant to me. If I lost Rob, I lost everything. No friends, no career, and a worldwide reputation as a great man's leavings.

I was reared to believe in lifelong commitment, and my father had ingrained in me that we were people who *did not fail*. To end my marriage would be humiliating—the most public failure I could imagine.

But all that I could stand, if it weren't for our children.

Throughout high school, I saw my friends' families crash and burn, and I saw what it did to the kids. Aurora's parents had split up when we were in eleventh grade, and I watched the ground split open beneath her. My shiny, bold friend disappeared overnight, as if the electricity had gone out. For months, instead of dragging me to parties, all she could do was let me come to her house to sit in silence while we listened to her mother keening in the next room. Slowly, over the years, the old Aurora had come back, but her relationships were brief and fraught. She didn't trust men, and—somewhere deep inside—she didn't believe anyone would love her.

I knew what Aurora would tell me to do. *Stay with Rob. Stay with him until the twins are grown.* But I needed to hear her say it.

Aurora. We hadn't spoken since the baby shower, and with good reason. She had been leaking information about me to the press. When I'd stopped talking to her, the leaks—the verbatim quotes—had immediately ceased. She had reached out to me many times, trying to restore our friendship. And I had always intended to make peace with her one day. Aurora, for better or worse, would be my friend forever.

I still didn't understand why Aurora had sold those stories about me. She'd never copped to it, and it was out of character. But surely it had something to do with envy, and at this moment my life was hardly enviable. Now, when her discretion was more important than ever, I was willing to risk it. I would swear Aurora to secrecy, and I felt sure she wouldn't betray me again. Because when it came down to it, Aurora was the person who knew me best in the world.

That Tuesday I went through the motions of my day as if my world hadn't been rocked. The boys and I ate oatmeal. I pretended to read the newspaper while Cap pretended to read books about a puppy named Biscuit and Leo built cars out of LEGOs. Then I helped them change into their bathing suits and we walked out to the pool for their swim lesson. Cap and I sat at the steps, playing with squirt toys while Dom, the swim teacher, supported Leo's belly, chanting, "Paddle, paddle, paddle, kick, kick, kick." He was a nursing student slash wannabe actor, and he looked like a Roman statue come to life.

The water flickered in the afternoon light. Leo floated on his back, arms and legs straight out like a starfish. He was still fearless.

That night, after Cap and Leo went to bed, I called Aurora. I didn't plan what I would say, and I didn't need to. Aurora was a gushing font of apologies and forgiveness.

"I get it, Lizzie. I mean, I can't believe I missed your wedding, holy crap, you were supposed to *hand* me the bouquet, but I totally get it. You're, like, on a different planet. (Get it: planet Mars?) And I'm a god-damned blister. But I'll try, okay? I've been trying to tell you that. But you needed space, I know. And you have *twins*. I'm supposed to be, like, their godmother and I've never even—"

"Oh my God, Aurora, give me a chance to say I'm sorry!" I said. "I'd love for you to meet Cap and Leo. But first I want to just catch up."

I knew Aurora wasn't sucking up to me. I assumed that she, like me, wanted our old friendship back. But I had no idea that she, like me, had a more specific agenda for our reunion.

Three days later, when I walked into the Polo Lounge expecting to pour out my heart to Aurora, I didn't find her alone. She had a stranger with her, a guy who looked like a former football player, with colorless hair, ruddy cheeks, and kind-looking blue eyes. At first I thought she was going to introduce him as her fiancé. Why else would she bring a stranger to our lunch?

"You don't have to say anything, Lizzie, just listen," she said.

Then the man introduced himself. "My name is Buddy White," he said. The name was familiar, but at first I couldn't place it. "I used to be part of One Cell's leadership. I believe you know my stepbrother, Geoff."

That Buddy White. The one I'd been warned about.

"The Studio isn't what it seems," he said. "They are watching you, and your life isn't your own."

"You've got to be kidding me." I turned to Aurora. "I wanted us to talk."

"Wait, Lizzie. Please. This is important," Aurora said.

"Let me just tell you what my experience was," Buddy said. "I joined the Studio when I was at my lowest low. Broke, strung-out, another lost bum. A One Cell practitioner, Liz Forsyth, walked up to me on a street corner, and the rest is history. I used to say, 'I came for the free coffee and stayed for the direct path to self-knowledge.' One Cell saved my life, and I'll always be grateful for that.

"It was the first time I'd been drug-free in twenty years, and I was ready to make something of myself. I became a Core Leader, and I introduced Geoff to the Studio. My goofy stepbrother took to the Studio like a fish to water. He started working right alongside Teddy Dillon. But before long, Teddy lost control to Geoff. Her vision—the Practice I'd so respected—became the hook. Behind the scenes, Geoff started leading the Studio in the wrong direction. The push to raise money—and attract celebrities—was more important than the Practice. Volunteers worked long hours and then were going into debt for the classes they took.

"My wife, Eva—we met at the Studio. She was a Core Leader like me. She was the best of the best, Geoff's darling. All the celebrities flocked to her sessions. We were doing okay, a happy couple, until we decided we wanted a baby. Eva was having trouble getting pregnant. We wanted to try IVF, but we had no medical insurance and no savings. The Studio wouldn't help, so Eva decided she would branch out, open her own Studio, so she could get paid for her work.

"I thought the Studio was trying to help. Eva was sent to Fernhills for a sixty-day silent retreat, and we were told that after she finished, they would help us get on our feet, start an independent business. Well, I wasn't supposed to contact Eva while she was at Fernhills. And then, when the sixty days were up, I was told she wanted nothing to do with me."

Buddy glanced over his shoulder as if worried that someone was listening. "It wasn't until I myself left the Practice that I found out Eva had been trying to reach me. For years. What happened to her at Fernhills—and she's not the only one—I could tell you stories."

"It sounds like you've had a very hard life," I said. "But Rob has been involved with the Studio for a very long time. My husband is a good man." I believed this. No matter how Rob had failed me—his intentions were good. I didn't have time for this anti–One Cell crap. I had bigger problems. "Rob wants to help people, the way One Cell helped him. I know, I'm 100 percent certain, that if he saw anyone being mistreated, he'd put a stop to it."

"Your husband— But before I tell you more I should warn you. If Geoff finds out we've spoken, you'll put yourself—and your children—in real danger."

This guy said "danger" and "your children" in the same sentence. I'd heard enough. Buddy White, whatever his beef, wanted a high-profile supporter. It wasn't going to be me.

I turned to Aurora. "You're being used. It's too bad. I really needed a friend right now." I walked out of the restaurant, holding back angry tears.

I was so freaked out and devastated by the discovery of my professionally scripted marriage that Buddy White's story barely penetrated the fog. Ironically, what shifted my attention to it was the one person who wanted the opposite: Geoff Anciak.

The morning after my lunch with Aurora (and her unwelcome friend), I woke up at six, unusually early for me. I walked into the breakfast room to find Geoff himself sitting at the table, already halfway through an espresso.

I greeted him warmly, as if his intrusion was perfectly normal.

"Promised your man I'd check on you." He smiled, but there was nothing friendly about it. I smelled peppermint, and it made me faintly queasy. Geoff waited, as if I was the one who'd invited him. His narrow snake eyes were fixed on me.

Still ignorant of the reason for his visit, I offered him some breakfast—there was a plate of fresh almond croissants and jelly rolls that probably contained more simple carbs than I'd eaten in the past four years. But Geoff was all business. He took a large yellow envelope out of his briefcase. From it he withdrew a photo and laid it on the table in front of me.

"You've been busy, haven't you, Elizabeth?"

"What's this?" I looked down at the picture. It showed me, Aurora, and Buddy at the Polo Lounge. Yesterday.

"You tell me," Geoff said. "Buddy White is no friend to the Studio."

I had no idea what I was up against. "Where did you get this picture?"

"Your friend sold it to us."

Why would Aurora do that? She knew I had cut her off for leaking stories and that I'd do it again. She wanted my friendship back. I didn't buy it for a minute.

Geoff went on. "Better she came to us than the press. This man is toxic. He's been trying to extort the Studio for years, but we won't let him bully us."

"I don't know him. My friend tried to introduce us, but I left."

"Good," Geoff said. "Don't talk to him again. Remember, we're on your side. We're here to help you, to protect you."

Did Rapunzel need protection?

On top of all I was processing, this man had walked into my kitchen, with his Altoids and his photos of my personal lunch. Accusing my old friend, violating my privacy, and trying to control me. His warning, his *protection*, sounded much more like a threat.

My husband was utterly entwined with this organization, which taught us to put our emotions to the side. It was One Cell that pushed Rob relentlessly toward his goals, regardless of the path. I now saw the connection between Rob's philosophy and his deception of me. A man who believed emotions were a chemical reaction could mix the language of love in a laboratory and feed it to me like a pill. It made perfect sense.

What, exactly, was Geoff trying to protect me from? My emotions? The truth?

"Thank you, but I can take care of myself." In a bright, perky voice I added, "And please don't worry about who I talk to. I'm a grown-up! I can decide for myself who to trust! Can I get you another cup of coffee?"

Geoff smiled, his pale lips stretched in a soulless grimace. "No, thank you, Elizabeth. I've said my piece."

That night, I walked into my bedroom to find a single red rose, its stem snapped in two, lying on my bed. Just like the rose I had broken as a test on that first date with Rob so long ago. Nobody could tell me where it had come from, not even the security guards, but I got the message. Like it or not, I was being "protected."

9

Later, there would be speculation that Lexy, Rob's ex-wife, was the one who warned me about the Studio, or "saved" me from it, or "deprogrammed" me, but none of it is true. I'm the one who reached out to Lexy, and I did it because I had to talk to somebody, and there was literally no one else.

I knew and respected her work—of course I didn't relish the memory of her onscreen/off-screen love affair with my husband, but her performance in *Believers* was unforgettable, one of the reasons I wanted to become an actress. Post-Rob, however, her career had completely fizzled. Note to self. Now all I knew was that she led a quiet life in a northwestern town with a funny name, and I kept thinking about the mystifying note she'd sent me when Rob and I got engaged.

After Geoff's unexpected visit, I found Lexy's number in the synched address book Rob and I shared. I meant to leave just a simple message—"I know it's a little strange to hear from me, but I'd love to chat sometime"— but before I hung up, a flood of other words escaped my mouth. I said I needed help. I had to know why she had left Rob, and One Cell, and whether there was any truth to Buddy White's claim that my children and I were in danger.

No sooner had I put my phone down than Jordan came in. She was now officially working for us, taking my to-do list off Jake's plate, which was a relief. That guy was such a buzz kill. So Jordan walked in, and at the same moment my phone rang. I saw that it was Lexy, returning my call. Usually, when I got an incoming call, Jordan paused to ask if I wanted to take it, but this time she steamrolled forward, so I let the call go to voice mail. I needed privacy for my conversation with Lexy.

Jordan reviewed the day's items. What did I want for lunch? *A kale smoothie.* Did I agree to be listed in *Glam*'s Most Beautiful Women issue? They had offered me number twenty, but Lotus had negotiated me up to number five and thought I should move forward with the feature. *Okay.* Did I want to hire a school consultant for the boys? *Yes.* I was due for a roots touch-up—how was this afternoon after my training session? *Fine.*

When Jordan finally left, I listened to Lexy's message. Her voice was low and sexy, familiar from her movies but out of place on my voice mail. She said, "I've been waiting for your call. I need to talk to you. It's important." As soon as her message ended, I tapped "Return call." Instead of ringing as it had ten minutes earlier, the call now went to a recording. The number was no longer in service. It had to be a glitch. I tried twice more, then tried inputting the number by hand, then tried one last time from the landline. How could her number be out of service? She had *just* called me!

Two days later I was scrolling through the press alerts when something stopped me in my tracks. Lexy Hartfield (who popped up on my alerts because she was always described as "ex-wife of Rob Mars") was in Mustique.

Mustique. The private island where Rob's friends the Spencers had a villa.

The sequence of events was disconcerting. The *moment* I'd reached out to her, Lexy's phone had gone out of order. Now I learned that she was far, far away with Rob's closest friends. Was it coincidence, or was there a calculated effort to stop my probing?

I didn't know where else to turn. I had no one to confide in about Rob and the scripts I'd found or the Studio and the mysterious conflict between Geoff and Buddy. For the moment, I decided, there was nothing to be done. Rob and I were married, and we had children. What existed between us wasn't, had never been, and could never be love. Not my definition of love. The tabloids, ironically, had called it from the beginning: It was a sham. But, for the children's sakes, I wasn't going to bolt.

And, because I did nothing, for months nothing changed. Rob traveled and visited, we went to events, we made love, we doted on our sons, and I tried to convince myself that acting like a loving wife was not terribly different from being a loving wife.

We might have gone on like that, but I'd made a critical mistake: assuming my husband had only *one* secret.

In February, Leo and Jordan were in the kitchen, making guacamole. When Cap and I came into the room, Leo was perched on a bar chair in front of the counter, staring at his finger, which was bleeding.

"Leo, what happened? Are you okay?" I said.

Jordan, realizing what had happened, gasped. "Oh, no! I didn't see!"

But Leo looked up at me and smiled. "It hurts, but I'm strong." Then, as if he were singing a song from *Mary Poppins*, he added, "Emotions are a chemical reaction."

Those were big words coming out of his four-year-old mouth. "What does that mean?" I asked him.

"This is what it means," Leo said. "I'm strong. I'm going to help people be strong like me. Teacher Jana!"

He stood up, turned to the window, and closed his eyes. Then he slowly twisted his legs into a knot, the first pose of the Practice.

I looked at Jordan, who had gone back to mincing garlic. Intently. "Jordan, do you know what he's talking about?"

Jordan shrugged without looking up. "Sounds like a game to me." It was a lie. She knew that pose as well as I did.

"Come here, Leo, I want to talk to you," I said.

Leo had untied himself and gone back to the guacamole.

"Actually, I'm busy right now. I'm mashing."

I took a deep breath. "Let's put a Band-Aid on that finger," I said, and led him down the hall to my bathroom. When I glanced back toward the kitchen, I saw Jordan watching us, a thoughtful look on her face.

Leo insisted on opening several Band-Aids in a row, getting them stuck to themselves, then to his fingers, as he tried to throw them in the trash.

"What do you and Cap do with Teacher Jana?"

"First we do songs. After songs we do thinking. After thinking we learn how to be strong. I'm better than Cap. He cries during poses, and that's because he needs to learn how. I'm going to be just like Daddy," Leo said matter-of-factly.

I closed my eyes. For the first four, nearly five, years of their lives, I'd had complete understanding of my sons' brains. Every animal Cap identified—I knew where he'd learned it. Every food Leo liked—I knew when he'd first tasted it. Every word they used came from me or a book we'd read together. Even as they started to have their own thoughts and ideas—"I'm a doggie, and you're the mommy doggie, and we're going to fall in the mud"—I could source the books and experiences they were mixing and matching. But now it was clear that the daycare at the Studio had introduced Cap and Leo to the Whole Body Principles. I thought about when Cap had had nursemaid's elbow. There had been no sign of

One Cell's influence then. It must have started—or escalated—in the fall. Children weren't supposed to start practicing at the Studio until age six!

Perhaps I shouldn't have been surprised. What did I think the boys did at daycare every morning? Plenty of children grow up exposed to their parents' values, beliefs, rituals, and religions. It wasn't out of line that the Studio's daycare included a bit of their teachings.

But the first cracks in my commitment to the Studio had started to appear. I was thrown by Geoff's aggressive reaction to my meeting with Buddy White. And then there was that broken red rose, which seemed to be an admonition to play by his rules. Now my sons were being secretly introduced to the Practice. My children were involved and Geoff didn't want me to question One Cell? That, to me, was exactly why I should.

My whole life I had followed rules. I was about to find out what breaking them meant.

10

Tracking down Lexy wasn't as hard as I thought it would be. When I googled "Where does Lexy Hartfield live?" the top result was www.starstalker.net, a horrifying website where one can search or browse the home addresses of anyone who has ever appeared in the pages of *Glam*. All of our current and previous addresses were there, including those of our parents. And there was Lexy, inconveniently located in Bend, Oregon.

With her phone out of service, I could have reached her through ACE, but the risk of a press leak was too high. Instead, I took a day trip in our plane. A mistake, though I didn't know it at the time.

The house was a neat Craftsman bungalow surrounded by pine trees. Lexy herself answered the door. There's a funny moment when you see someone whose face is bigger-than-life familiar from the big screen. I've experienced it hundreds of times by now, but it still passes in a wave, like déjà vu or nostalgia. I know you and I don't know you. You look exactly like yourself, and you look different. That strange recognition prompts many fans to comment on it: You look smaller/taller/fatter/thinner/prettier in person. But Lexy was different. Even without makeup, she looked as if she'd stepped right off the screen. Her features sculpted and perfect, her skin perfectly even in tone (even here in the country, where there couldn't be laser treatments to be had for miles). She did not look happy to see me.

"I'm sorry to drop in like this—"

"Do they know you're here?" She looked over my shoulder and winced when she saw the town car waiting for me on the street. "They know." She sighed. "What can you do?" She led me to a pleasant sitting room with what I would guess was local art on the walls. "Sit," she said, and disappeared.

Moments later, she was back with tea. She poured us cups and raised hers to mine. "To life on Mars."

I didn't know where to begin. "I left you a message . . . but then you were in Mustique and I—"

"Timid, aren't you? They must be eating you alive. Listen, let me tell you how it is." Lexy then proceeded to describe my life to me with more detail than I myself knew. The initial appeal of the Studio; the gradual realization of its far-reaching tentacles; the seduction of Rob's charm; the wane of my career. When she was done, I wanted to cry.

"I'm sorry if you came here for answers. I don't have any," Lexy said.

"I . . . I had no idea what I was getting into," I said.

"Look, all I can say is to be very careful. I can't tell you the Studio had anything to do with it, but there was a period of my life when my mailbox was tipped over every night for a month. And I have no proof that they planted the stories that I have an uninsurable medical condition. And maybe it was the stress, but I started feeling like there were people following me wherever I went. Not just the regular paparazzi. Men with hidden cameras in their sunglasses."

It was hard to imagine the calm woman in front of me being scared or stressed by anything. But as she talked, a shadow came into her eyes.

"As soon as I mentioned to Rob that I wanted to leave him, my life went to pieces. And ever since, every time I've tried to do a movie, or even to go out in public, something happens to warn me. The anxiety attacks return and I have to flee. So I live here in this very nice town. I behave myself. It's not bad. I cross-country ski every morning." *And sometimes,* I thought to myself, *you go on luxury vacations.*

I had more questions for her. What should I do now? How was I supposed to stay true to myself? She hadn't been able to, had she? But that was all Lexy was going to say. She changed the topic, and we shared industry gossip over tea, as if she hadn't just warned me about what might happen if I so much as hinted to my husband that I was unhappy. I glanced out the window. All I could see were trees. The air, inside and out, felt clean and clear. Bend, Oregon. It wasn't a bad place to escape to. But after coming all this way, what had I learned? One message, one that made all the difference: I resolved to keep my doubts to myself.

Before I left, Lexy said, "Wait." She ran out of the room and returned carrying a very tall and skinny glass vase, delicately twisted at the top of its long milky neck. She thrust it into my arms so forcefully I nearly dropped it. "Take this," she said. "Make something up. Tell them you heard I had taken up glassblowing, and you had to have one of my works. Or whatever. Just don't let it be photographed—the guy who made this is my next-door neighbor. He'll bust my chops. But do it. Don't forget."

"I don't think it's necessary. Nobody even knows I'm here!"

"Just do it. Make sure you tell the driver and the pilot. Trust me."

Back in Brentwood, when I came to breakfast the next day, Jordan had a concerned expression on her face. She said, "I don't know how to say this, but I think you should look at Rounder.com."

I turned on my phone. Usually when there was a news item I got ten texts from various reps and acquaintances, but this time my phone was completely silent. As soon as I went to Rounder.com I saw why.

Allison. There were images of her, holding up pictures of me. "Lizzie's Abandoned Sister." "Lizzie's Secret Sister Tells All."

These were the first pictures I'd seen of Allison in twenty-two years, but the images told the story of the gap that can emerge between two lives. The woman in the photographs looked strung-out, wrecked by her life, prematurely aged. But also, under the toll, I saw that in her own way she was prettier than I, her coloring so pale and delicate, her bones finer, her eyes wider and more symmetrical. I couldn't stop looking at her and examining the dim details of the room she was in. The faint outline of a brown sofa, a shelf with empty china pitchers. Did she have a job? Hobbies? A family to replace us? It was impossible to tell.

My father called. I knew he would. I expected him to suggest that she'd done the photo shoot for drug money, because that had been her sole motivation for so long, but what he said completely threw me.

"Is everything okay with you and Rob?"

"Of course it is, Dad." It wasn't. But Rob didn't know that. And my father certainly didn't need to know it. And Allison had nothing to do with me and Rob, or so I thought.

Before I could stop him, my father continued, "Make no mistake. The person who did this isn't interested in Allison. This is about you, and it won't be the end."

With my father, it was always about me. My image. My reputation. My career. What about my sister, who needed us? How long could he deny her existence? But still, after years of alienation, he was certain he knew better.

"Shouldn't we be worrying about Allison right now?" I said. "Maybe this is a cry for help."

"Listen to me, Elizabeth. Here is what comes next. They're going to say, if you lied about this, what else might you have lied about? If you abandoned your sister, are you immoral? Your enemies can use this story to challenge your character."

Did Geoff know I'd visited Lexy? It was possible, and he wouldn't like it, but it was a stretch to believe there was any connection to the exposure of Allison.

"Dad, I don't have enemies. This is just part of celebrity. There are no secrets. I'm used to it. I guess it was silly of me to think you might be calling so we could talk about actually finding Allison and getting her help. I shouldn't have taken your call."

"Elizabeth, I'm just trying to protect you."

There it was again! Why did everyone think I was so helpless? Or in so much danger?

"Still not looking for protection, Dad. This conversation is over."

My parents had their own experience with my sister, the layers of love, loss, resentment, hope, disappointment, and betrayal. But I was an adult, with infinite resources, and without the history that made it so hard for my parents. I wanted to know my sister. Not quite able to process my visit with Lexy, I focused on Allison. If *Rounder* could find her, why hadn't my P.I.? He'd been scouring Chicago, looking in shelters, at hospitals, and on the streets. I was on the verge of offering *Rounder* an exclusive on my husband's exercise regimen when, studying the *Rounder* photos of Allison for the millionth time, it hit me. I grabbed my phone and called the private detective.

"Mike," I said, "I know where Allison is."

A few hours later Cap and I were on a plane to Kalamazoo, Michigan. Leo refused to come with us. Rob was touching down in Malibu before going to New York for the East Coast premiere of *The Search for Helen Grant* at the Ziegfeld. Leo had been asking every day when his daddy would get home, counting down to *Wednesday* as if it were Christmas. Now it was Tuesday, and Leo was dead set on staying home. So we decided Leo would stay in Malibu with Jordan, then fly with Rob to meet us in New York.

Jordan hadn't been able to find me a properly credentialed local driver, so one came up from Chicago to meet us. It drove home how close to my parents I was, and how easily Cap and I could have gone to see them. But if my father found out the reason for our visit, he would take it badly. He wouldn't be able to see my efforts as anything but a condemnation of his treatment of Allison.

The lake cabin that had once belonged to my uncle was in Harbor Country, on Lake Michigan. By the time we landed, snow was starting to fall. A storm, the driver told us. They were expecting five inches in Chicago. We drove to Michiana, a little town on the eastern shore of the lake, a popular vacation destination that was nearly deserted in winter. Out my window, the trees were barren of leaves, their hungry limbs striving skyward. Skids of snow collected briefly on the steep slopes of the branches, then slid off. Cap was bouncing with excitement. "Snow!" He wanted to feel it, play with it, eat it, was dying to open the door and run in it. "Are we in Aspen?"

I whispered with him, hoping against hope that he didn't inadvertently disclose our identities to the driver (who was, at least, pretending he didn't recognize us).

We pulled up in front of Uncle Nick's old cabin. As far as I knew, he'd sold it years before. From the outside it looked abandoned. Afraid of what I might find, I didn't want Cap to come in with me, but I could hardly leave him out in the cold night with a strange man.

"Here's what's going to happen," I said, reaching over to unbuckle his car seat. Cap turned to me, his eyes two dark circles—total focus. I continued, "We're going to see some people. They're doing a show, like Daddy's movies. So don't worry if they look or act funny. They're just pretending."

"I'm going to wear this coat," Cap said cheerfully. "I'm buttoning it myself." I'd brought wool coats for both of us, but, being L.A. wimps, we had already wrapped them around ourselves in the heated car. Cap got to work on the big job of fastening the four toggles that ran down the front of his. I waited until he said "Done!" and looked up proudly. I took off my scarf and wrapped it around and around Cap's head and shoulders, bundling him until he could barely move. There were at least two inches already frosting the walk. Cap was wearing Crocs—he'd insisted that they were excellent in snow—so I picked him up and carried him to the door.

In truth, I had no idea what to expect. Maybe I was completely wrong and this was all a wild-goose chase. Maybe, after all these years, Allison would turn me away. Maybe she hated me. I was a little scared, and not just because I didn't know the company Allison kept, but because Cap and I were—there's no other way to say it—we were commodities. Our photographs, our words, our *beings* had value, and drug addicts will do anything for money. I steeled myself, channeling my heroes, the explorers who braved the worst nature had to offer, determined to conquer the unknown. Compared to them, my situation was a joke. If Shackleton could cross the infamously treacherous Drake Passage in an open boat, I could damn well knock on this door.

When I knocked, Allison opened the door. I was stunned, especially by the ease of it. My long-lost sister was a three-dimensional person who walked and talked and opened doors when people knocked on them. For all these years, she'd been accessible, here, somewhere, waiting, if I'd only had the wherewithal to look.

On the shelf behind her were the empty pitchers I'd seen in the photos. They'd always been here, and always lodged in my memory.

This had been my uncle Nick's hunting cabin, the last place I'd seen Allison. We hadn't spent much time with my uncle Nick when I was a child, and when we did, he usually came to us. My mother tended to develop shortcut descriptions of everyone she met (my father was "a tough cookie but a straight shooter"; her friend Eloise Van, who had kicked her husband out decades ago but refused to divorce him, had "a wall around her heart"). Of my uncle Nick—the younger brother who'd never settled down, had a fondness for hunting and survival gear, played a mean banjo, and was prone to raving about "the Man"—my mother would say, "He's too smart for his own good."

But the few times we'd visited Uncle Nick at this cabin, he'd always done the same thing. He'd say to my parents, "Can I borrow the girl?" Then he'd follow me out into the woods and let me explore. If I wanted to build a fort, he was my willing assistant. If I was on a fairy hunt, he discovered glittery necklaces in hollow trees and under tangles of root. If I came close to falling in the stream, he never let out a word of warning. If anyone made me feel like I could one day be an explorer, it was Uncle Nick.

One summer there had been a girlfriend, Gracie, who filled the empty kitchen shelves with dishes and the bread box with fresh-baked muffins. She scattered wildflower seeds across the front lawn, and filled pitchers with the flowers that sprung up: blue and yellow violets, buttercups, larkspur, and bluebells. But by winter Gracie had gone (my mother always said, "Your uncle Nick missed the boat on that one"), and apparently since then the pitchers had sat empty on the wooden shelves, their various pastel colors seeming to fade into the same pale green.

Now Allison stood before that wall of lost opportunity, still in place despite the cabin's disrepair. I would have recognized her even if I'd never seen the pictures. In person, she looked like she had as a teenager, but even thinner in an unseasonable summer dress. An evil Hollywood voice in my head whispered that skinnier was always better, even if it was drug induced. But now, at least, her eyes were calm and sad. I was pretty sure she wasn't high.

"I missed you," I said, gulping down emotion.

She knew me right away. Unless she'd been under a log all these years, of course she knew that she had a famous, rich sister. Yet she'd never come to me for money or help.

"Baby girl," Allison said. She took a step back and smiled. "You look just like the magazines."

I rolled my eyes. "Crazy, isn't it?" I hadn't planned this far ahead. Should I hug her? Apologize for abandoning her? Was I going to help her? How? "I'm so glad I found you," I said.

"I didn't know I was lost."

"No, I'm sorry—what I meant—" I was at a loss. Cap bounced at my side like a golden retriever tugging on its leash, alive with innocence. "This is your auntie," I said. "Allison, this is Cap."

"You have your mama's eyes," Allison said, kneeling down to Cap's level. "Would you like some hot chocolate?"

"I'm four years old plus nine months old," Cap said. "Actually, my eyes are the same color as Daddy's. And I have really, really been asking for hot chocolate every day so far."

After he guzzled her hot chocolate, Cap got up to walk his favorite toy turtle, a small hard one that fit in his fist, along the wooden shelves. I sat at the kitchen table while Allison put on hot water, chatting emptily about the snowstorm, telling Cap about a deer that liked to come right up to the back door. Allison's movements were nervous and her fingers played in midair, tapping out some music only she could hear. When she put our teacups on the table, the smile left her face. "I fucked up, Liz."

Glancing at Cap, I winced at the profanity. "It's okay, don't worry. We can get you help."

"No," she said. "I'm weak. I'm so fu—so bloody weak. They gave me—"

She kept one eye on Cap, who was making conversation with his turtle. "I'd been doing so well. Five months totally clean. But he started me off again. A total stranger. Just showing up like it was Christmas morning. It was more cash than I've seen all at once in my life. Said he wanted to help me get a whole new start. Empower me to control my destiny. But all that money in my pocket and I was hooked again. So much for Santa Claus. Why would someone do that? I thought he was in it for my future business, you know? But he never came back and my guy—Sanjo—he says he had nothing to do with it."

"When did this happen?"

Allison grunted apologetically. "I can't exactly say the old calendar's up-to-date, sis." She tapped a finger on her forehead. "I've been a little, you know, out of it ever since." Something in that gesture of hers took me straight back to when I was four and we were sitting on the stairs, and she was singing some pop song to me and explaining the bubblegum lyrics. This was my *sister*. How many years had we lost? Why had it taken me so long to come looking for her?

I took out a printout of the Rounder.com piece with the photos of Allison and put it on the kitchen table. "Do you think this was it? Was this the day he came over?"

"Oh man," Allison said. "Dude definitely had a camera. I didn't remember that until right this minute. But he was definitely a photographer. He said something about modeling and a real income for once. I know it was bullshit."

Holding the paper at a bit of a distance, she started to read and sucked in air. "Oh, no. I see what they did here. I screwed things up for you. Dragging the Pepper name through the gutter. Exactly why I've left you all alone."

Her face crumpled and she covered it with her hands. "There's more. Oh God, I'm remembering more. Mom and Dad protected you from me and they were right."

"Don't cry, Auntie," Cap said. "If you hold Walker, it will feel better faster." He stopped his game, went to Allison, and put the toy turtle in his aunt's hand.

Though Allison was obviously upset by it, to me my sister's relapse was part of a cycle that I assumed had been recurring ever since she'd left home. I had expected to find her high or sober, having recently been the other. It was no shock that the tabloids had tracked her down. If anything, the remarkable part was that it hadn't happened before. And so in that moment I missed my chance to ask what the man had looked like, or what "more" Allison was remembering.

"Look," I said. "Those pictures helped me find you. I should have come here a long time ago. You don't have to be perfect for me to love you."

"Dad doesn't know you're here," she said.

My ambition had carried me a long way. It had carried me to the pinnacle of fame and success. It had carried me into Rob's arms, where I was everything my father wanted me to be. But in that dark, cold house, with its sour smell and wistful memory of unspoiled summer days, I was, at last, who and where I wanted to be. Not an only child in a flawless family—the sister of an addict. Not a star—an actor. I was myself again.

"It doesn't matter what Dad thinks," I said. "You're my sister."

I wanted to tell Allison about LifeHeartTruth—that I'd supported that charity because I hadn't forgotten her, that they had a place for her to go if and when she was ready. But before I could speak there was a knock at the door. Allison sprang to her feet, suddenly on edge. "I'm sorry, sweetie, but I think you'd better leave." She glanced at Cap. "It's my guy. Sanjo." Her dealer. "Here, why don't you go out this way."

Cap was sliding his turtle down the spout of a ceramic teapot.

"Come on, little man. Time for us to go." I started to lead him through the kitchen.

"Yummy. Uncle Geoff's mints. Can I have one?" I stopped cold and looked over to where Cap was pointing. There on a shelf sat a tin of Curiously Strong Altoids. I stared at it. Cap's child logic sent a wave of nausea through my body. There was absolutely no way Geoff had been here, no chance he was the one who took those photos. *Right?* I showed the tin to my sister. "Allison, are these mints yours?"

Allison was distracted. "What? No, I don't think so. I don't know. You can have them."

"Please?" Cap begged. "Uncle Geoff let me have one after we did the pictures."

It was just a tin of peppermints. They were sold at the counter of every grocery. I refused to let my imagination run away with me. Besides, there wasn't time for that. Allison opened the kitchen door and ushered us out. The seed of paranoia was whisked away into the chilly night air.

Out on the quiet street a blue SUV idled behind our car. The snow was deeper now. I picked Cap up again. As we left, I heard Allison opening the front door and greeting her guest.

Cap and I got in the backseat of our car.

"Please can I have a mint right now, Mommy? Please? Please?"

"No."

"Later?"

"Tomorrow."

"Tomorrow," Cap said. "I'll remember." And I knew he would.

I didn't put it together at the time, but when I decided I wanted Allison in my life, despite the pain and strife that might bring, I was parting ways with the Whole Body Principles. My experience on *The Safe House*, playing Abigail Warren, had changed me. It woke me up to the deep importance of the everyday decisions that comprise a life. I couldn't live by the philosophy that drove my husband's every move. It worked for him. I saw how it worked. But that wasn't a deal I was willing to make.

I had to follow my heart—in my acting and in my relationships. My need to find Allison wasn't practical or logical. It came from emotion, instinct, a sense of what was right. Emotions were real, and Abigail Warren had taught me to live by mine, no matter the cost.

★

The snowstorm had shut down the Kalamazoo airport, our driver reported, but our pilot had flown ahead of it to O'Hare. We drove straight to Chicago, but streets were icy and treacherous, and by the time we got to O'Hare, that airport had also been shut down.

"Six twenty-four South Greenway," I said, without thinking it through. Where would I go from O'Hare but home?

Fifteen minutes later, almost five years after I had sworn never to return, I was in the driveway of my parents' house.

Cap had fallen asleep on the drive, Walker the turtle clutched tightly to his chest. If he'd been awake, maybe we would have gone in, and, for his sake, everyone would have pretended the past five years hadn't happened. What a joyful reunion—my mother hurrying to feed Cap, my father showing me his latest home improvement project. But I couldn't bear to wake him, instead staring at the house. It was a steel blue clapboard, white trim around the windows, black shutters, a great pine out front lending a perpetual Christmas charm. The quaint lines of this house were often pictured in magazine profiles of me, rose-tinting my youth into an American Girl storybook.

In the warm light of the kitchen I spotted a movement—it could only be my mother, setting the table for tomorrow's breakfast as she liked to do. What would she think of it all—the revelation I'd had during *The Safe House*, and how it pulled me toward the sister I'd never known? Back in the den, watching a sports game or an action movie bought on discount at Costco, my father would have none of it. All his work, all his sacrifice, all for me. Just then the front door opened. I ducked down with a little yelp, then watched as my father's arm reached out to flick on the porch light, as he did en route to fixing himself a scotch every night. He'd wired that light himself, the day Aurora got her driver's license and she and I went to a movie by ourselves for the first time.

"This light's for you, Elizabeth," he said. "So you can see your way in at night." But I knew it was for him, his wish to be my beacon, his fear of letting me go. He loved me more than he could ever admit, to me or to himself.

I couldn't do it. I couldn't go in and face his disappointment. "Actually, take us to the Four Seasons, please," I told the driver, and all at once the air rushed back into my lungs.

11

Cap and I took a suite at the Four Seasons. As I put him to bed, I asked him one question, in the same light tone I used to ask him if he'd enjoyed his swim lesson, or if he'd rather read *Corduroy* or *Bread and Jam for Frances*.

"When did Uncle Geoff give you mints? Did he take pictures of you and Leo?"

"Actually, can I have one now?"

"Tomorrow, sweetie. Do you remember when Uncle Geoff gave you mints?"

"They were yummy."

"Was Daddy there?"

"No, Teacher Jana and Jordan and Uncle Geoff and me and Leo. We had a picture party. With cookies. Shhh. It's a surprise. Don't tell." What was happening in that daycare? How far had these lessons gone?

"Okay, Cap. Night-night now." I tucked him in and kissed his forehead. And turned on the bathroom light. And located his missing toy turtle. And gave him one more kiss.

After Cap fell asleep, I stood in the sitting room of the suite, staring out at Lake Michigan, mulling all that had happened. I was dying for a cigarette, but this goddamned presidential suite didn't even have a balcony.

My mind scrolled. Geoff's visit after I met Buddy White. The pictures of Allison after I visited Lexy. Maybe my father was right to think that the Allison exposé was a message to me. The rose, a warning. Allison, a threat. Was Geoff trying to stop me from asking too many questions? And, if so, why? What didn't he want me to know about the Studio? I'd seen and experienced the Practice for myself. I knew it was real and worthwhile. So why all the cloak-and-dagger creepiness? And the biggest questions of all: What photos was Cap talking about? What did Geoff, Jana, and the Studio have planned for my sons?

In two days, Cap and I were due to meet Rob and Leo in New York. I still had no plans to confront him about the scripts I'd found. What could I possibly say? "Your love for me was an act and the show is over?" There was no point to that conversation. What I wanted from Rob was much simpler. I wanted whatever was going on with the boys—the photographs, the training in Whole Body Principles, the *indoctrination*—to stop. I needed Rob to agree that the boys would not be raised to follow any philosophy that they didn't choose.

Cap and I went to New York. (Yes, that was when that famous "Lizzie in a Tizzy?" photograph was taken. The paps caught me turning my ankle as I got out of our car, hence the grimace, but this time, by pure chance, they were right.)

Mercifully, Cap didn't throw up during takeoff, and, as an unforeseen gift, he slept through most of the flight. But I was awake, on edge. Looking back on it now, there had always been parts of the Studio that didn't sit well with me. I mean, channeling emotions as an acting exercise was one thing, but stifling them all the time was kind of ridiculous. I'd always taken it as a theory more than an actual way of living. The One Cell leaders had a flat, robotic effect. It was wildly inappropriate for a child. Also—though this was beside the point—it bothered me that Geoff's girlfriend, Patricia, had seemingly dropped off the face of the earth. It was creepy. I thought about what Patricia had once said to me: that love meant enduring dark moments and sacrifice. What dark moment had come to her? And where had it led her? Because one thing was perfectly clear: No institution was strong enough to interfere with what I knew was right for my children.

Compliance was part of the One Cell way. You were supposed to have faith in the process, which had a proven success rate. If you didn't follow the Studio's lead, it meant that you were your own biggest obstacle. They taught individuality and self-reliance, but demanded total obedience. I knew extricating our children from the Studio wouldn't be well received, to say the least. I had my fingers crossed that Rob was on my side.

The Turtle Bay town house was hands down the boys' favorite of our homes—and not just because Cap loved the name *Turtle* Bay. The neighbors were not the type to meddle, so the boys were able to play freely in the communal gardens behind the house. I liked to see Leo run as fast as he could down the long path. Of course the boys had plenty of space in L.A. and Aspen, but there was something about having other people around, even if all of them were Manhattan bluebloods, music executives, or hedge fund managers. I wanted them to experience being in "public." Our elite private garden was the best we could do.

The minute I laid eyes on Rob, he took me in his arms and held me for a long time. Then he stepped back to look at me, his dark eyes locking onto mine.

"It didn't matter how often we talked on the phone," he said. "It only made me miss you more. I could barely sleep without you. This last week was the worst. See this picture?" He took out his phone and showed me a picture of me holding newborn Cap and Leo in the hospital. "I went to sleep *holding my phone*. That's how crazy I was going without you." His words or a script? It was impossible to say. I could barely summon the appropriate response.

The boys had a bath. Afterward, I listened to Leo's squeals of delight echoing through the house as Rob chased him back and forth down the halls of the top floor. That part I knew was real.

Our chef, Elsie, who'd joined us in New York for the week, cooked us dinner, a big Italian meal with herbs from the garden. The kitchen, on the garden level, opened to the family room with a long farmhouse table, and through the French doors to the backyard we had a view of the replica Medici fountain.

Rob smiled at me, squeezing my hands. "I started going out for runs in the middle of the night. Poor Lewis had to follow me even though I'm sure it was safe. As I ran I chanted to myself: 'I want to do this movie; it won't last forever; Elizabeth will still be there when I go home.'"

If this was a script, it wasn't great; my husband's Cyrano, the mysterious sticky noter Emil, had fallen flat. But Rob's delivery was flawless.

Over dinner, Rob wanted to talk about what we would do when he was done shooting *Istanbul*. We would have all spring and part of the summer free. I was in no state to plan that far ahead, but after he suggested the south of France, I leaned in.

"I have an idea," I said. "Maybe we could go to Fernhills." I watched his reaction carefully. What Buddy White had started to tell me about Fernhills was at the back of my mind.

Rob tensed up. "Fernhills? Why would you want to go there?"

"It's the place where the Studio began. It will be inspirational. We could do a silent retreat together."

"Sure," Rob said noncommittally. "Sounds great."

I pushed again. "How about you take me to see Studio Manhattan tomorrow?" I said. "After all your hard work—I'd love to see how it's progressing." I was still a little bitter that I'd never been able to help with the building when I'd been looking for something to occupy my time.

"Oh. Yeah, well, you wouldn't believe the delays. Construction is interminable." He frowned. "But I definitely want you to see it at some point." His eyebrows slanted up and in. All of a sudden, even next to the warm fire, a chill went through me. I recognized that expression. It was one of his acting faces. I'd seen it in all of his movies, but never before in real life. It was the expression he used when he wanted his character to seem sincere. Or was it an expression of genuine sincerity? Which came first? Was there a difference? Did it matter? Truth, artifice, acting, action; these notions were so muddled it was pointless to draw distinctions. Whatever residual attachment I had to Rob fell away. His truth was an act; he was faithful to that act; and we lived in the drama of his creation.

I put down my wineglass, sat up straight, and went for it. "Rob, did you know that in daycare the boys are learning the Whole Body Principles? Leo cut his finger and didn't even react."

Rob laughed. "That's awesome. He's a natural. I knew he would be."

"But, Rob, Cap and Leo are not even five years old. Children need to experience their emotions. They need to cry and shout and dance."

"And growing up is learning to handle those extremes. Why shouldn't they have the tools? They're not being forced to use them. But I do hear Leo's an exceptional student." I hated his blatant preference for Leo, but I had bigger problems.

"So you knew about this," I said. It was already clear that he had.

"Elizabeth, you're overreacting. Just look at the reality. The boys are doing great. They're blossoming. Why are you so upset?"

His voice was smooth and gentle, as always, but I saw his neck tighten with a spasm of intolerance. I took a deep breath. "Rob, I've thought about it a lot, and I don't want Cap and Leo raised within the Studio. I know how much it means to you, but the boys are too young for the Practice. I want them to have a normal childhood, with playdates and *Sesame Street* and Christmases where they get some but not all of what they want. They should be free to discover the Studio, or any other school of thought, by themselves, as adults, just like you and I did. Not because we force it down their throats. And you should have talked to me before agreeing to it."

The smile faded from Rob's face. He stared at me as if I'd just spoken in a foreign language. "I didn't *agree* to it, Elizabeth. It was my idea."

And now it dawned on me that ever since the day he orchestrated our public coming-out on the streets of Cannes, I had never seen Rob surprised by any aspect of our lives. Not the edits to my movie. Not the boys' training. Even our dialogue had been anticipated and rehearsed. Rob, his agents, and One Cell were directing our lives.

As my father used to say, I had no one but myself to blame. In this relationship I had entered Rob's life. I lived in his houses. I joined his Studio. I pushed my family and loved ones away and accepted his into our lives. Without realizing it, I had been enacting the true role for which Rob had auditioned me on the first day we met. For almost five years, I had been playing the role of his wife. There was no breaking from the script. You don't say no to Rob Mars. I don't think Rob set out to control me. He'd been catered to for so long, he didn't know anything else.

Passion and romance and love and sex, all those elements were supposed to combine to create intimacy. But there was another possibility, a relationship where all the trappings existed, but there was nothing underneath. Rob didn't care to know me, the real me—the me who hadn't been formed exactly for him, the me with opinions and desires of my own, and he had no idea he was missing anything. What could I say to him? I stripped every emotion out of my face and gave him a Stepford smile. Thank you, One Cell.

12

Later that night we exchanged Valentine's gifts—a week late.

"Happy Valentine's Day," I said.

"Happy Valentine's Day, my love. I'll never forget our first Valentine's Day."

As we spoke, the script version of our dialogue typed itself out on the screen in my mind, our words in a generic twelve-point Courier font.

For years, Rob had been playing his part nearly flawlessly. He thought he was the only one who could put on a show? Ha. I'd learned from the best of them. And luckily I already knew my lines.

"Were my eyes sparkling just like they are tonight?"

Rob looked a bit confused. "They were. They were sparkling just like they are tonight." He smiled that megawatt smile, but before he could plow on I stole his next line.

"I never thought I would find someone like you. Someone who fit me perfectly." I could almost see little wisps of smoke coming out of his ears as the circuit boards in his mind overloaded. I'd crashed his operating system, and now his face was a gray screen with a little sad computer icon right in the middle of it.

"Elizabeth, you take the words right out of my mouth." He kissed me. Nice work, Mars. When all else fails, improvise.

We stared at each other with perfectly matched glimmers of love in our eyes. For a moment, I felt sorry for him. To be Rob Mars, the ultimate leading man—it was no cakewalk. What had it been like for him to go on a real, live, unscripted date? To paraphrase Rita Hayworth, they go to bed with Captain Joe and wake up with Rob Mars. How hard was it for him to live up to his own image? So hard, apparently, that it took One Cell, ACE, and an uncredited writer to cobble together the man of my dreams.

The Valentine's present I had for Rob was lame. It was a ticket on the first consumer trip to outer space, with famed airline executive and adventurer Donny Bright. How can an intergalactic flight be considered lame? First of all, nobody knew for sure when the first flight would go up, so for some unstated number of years, all the ticket meant was that Rob would be invited to "astronaut training" and other pseudo-events, any of which a person like Rob could already go to without a ticket, and none of which Rob would bother to attend. Also, it was a little too obvious. What do you get the man who has everything? A trip to outer space. *Here's a theoretical trip to the moon that I bought you with your money. Happy Valentine's Day, honey.*

Rob had a gift for me, too. I'd forgotten about the poster, the artistic image of Cap and Leo hidden back in Bluebeard's chamber that I'd assumed would be my gift. I didn't remember it until Rob ran to the hall closet and came back with a bulky form that was most decidedly not a poster. It turned out to be . . . a saddle.

"Her name is Astra, and she's a beaut," he said. "She's waiting for you in Aspen. Want to go see her? Right after the premiere?"

A horse. Great. But whatever had happened to that photo of the boys? Rob had never given it to me. It was perplexing.

I remember what I wore to the premiere: a gauzy but demure black gown that my friend Saskia Goldman had designed for me. We'd spent New Year's Eve at David and Saskia's chalet in Gstaad. While her three girls and my boys learned to ski, Saskia and I drank hot toddies in the lodge and she sketched out a line I wanted all for myself.

Now, along with the new bangs style that would be dubbed "the Lizzie Pepper" and would make every morning a hell of straightening irons and despair, I was wearing her first creation, understated and elegant, which got so much attention that Saskia started talking seriously about launching her line with me as its model.

I sat in the theater next to Rob, watching him up onscreen. There he was, carrying a briefcase full of stolen cash through the narrow streets of what was supposed to be Berlin but was really Prague, a confident smile on his face. And there he was, shirtless and sweaty, ruthlessly executing the woman who betrayed him (take that, Wendy Jones!). I'd once found it sexy to see him up there, knowing that later that hero would lie next to me in the flesh, a three-dimensional man whose heart would pound next to mine.

But this time, as I watched *The Search for Helen Grant*, the movie that would be hailed as "Mars at his sublime, flawless best," I didn't feel the inner glow of secret, private connection. There was no intimacy. That larger-than-life man up on the silver screen was all I had.

There was an incident when we came out of the theater. Somehow a woman in a wheelchair pushed her way under the barricade and rolled to a standstill in front of us. Security was on her right away—it wasn't the first time this had happened—but Rob put up his hand to stop them.

"Give us a minute, okay?" Then he turned to the woman, stooping down so they were face-to-face. "You're pretty determined," he said.

"I'm so sorry to interrupt, but I need your help," the woman said. Her face was soft, grandmotherly. In spite of her behavior, when she spoke she didn't seem crazy.

"What can I do for you?" Rob asked. "Do you want a signature?"

"My name is Sandy," she said. "My son is missing in Iraq. Can you say a prayer with me?"

I'd seen this before. When confronted with *Son of God* fanatics, mostly Rob said, "Glad you liked the movie," or "Not performing miracles today!" and ducked away. But to my horror he now put his hands on Sandy's head, closed his eyes, and mouthed a prayer. Then he bent down, and whispered something in her ear. A radiant smile spread across her face, and she looked up at him, her eyes glistening. Wow, this one was straight out of central casting.

"Thank you," she whispered. Then, in front of every entertainment news camera in the entire city of New York, she announced, "My son is coming home! It's a miracle."

Yeah, so that happened. My husband: Once he locked into a part, he was in for the duration.

Late that night, after Rob was asleep, I went out to the backyard to smoke a cigarette. I'd been craving a smoke for a long time, but I refused to buy cigarettes. Earlier that evening I'd noticed a pack in the powder room and pinched one. It was my first cigarette in years, and it tasted like dirt, but it took me back. Back to my single days, when I made my own mistakes, and no one gave a shit. Now everything I did was watched—either by the outside world or our zealous staff—everything was perfect, and I was utterly lost. The life that seemed too good to be true was, in fact, too good to be true.

I'd thought I was learning the ropes of Rob's complicated life, compromising to show my gratitude and love, getting used to being a wife and a mother. But all I'd really learned was to bury my head in the sand.

The red tip of my cigarette glowed in the darkness, moving closer with every inhalation. Rob Mars's perfect wife blackens her lungs. *Take that, world,* I thought, *I'm not perfect after all.* I never wanted to be. The perfect Elizabeth Pepper was Doug Pepper's creation and Rob's ideal mate. But I was Lizzie Pepper. Irreverent, sometimes cynical, but always true to my own ideals.

The cigarette was gone, far too soon. I longed for another. But there was nothing now, nothing in the darkness but me and the reality of my situation. My beautiful children. My godlike husband. My sham of a marriage. And then, all the questions I'd pushed under the rug: Patricia's disappearance; the boys' lessons with Teacher Jana; Lexy's fear of the Studio; the pictures of Allison that appeared just when I was starting to ask questions; the much-touted Studio Manhattan that I had never seen with my own eyes. Whenever I started to take notice, I was interrupted, distracted, dismissed, led like a dim-witted cow away from the danger. How many pieces of this puzzle could I ignore, and for how long?

The peppermint tin Cap had found at the cabin. If, just if, everything was a great conspiracy, then that tin belonged to Geoff, and he had exploited information I'd revealed in my 100—that private, sacrosanct ritual. Why would Geoff go to all the trouble to find and photograph my sister? My father's phone call came back to me. He thought someone wanted to use Allison against me. But the photos were already out. The damage was done. Allison's words came back to me: "Oh God, there's more. Mom and Dad protected you from me, and they were right..." Was there another shoe yet to drop?

I picked up my spent cigarette butt and peeled open the white paper.

I dropped the stub of tobacco into a flowerpot and shoved the bit of rolling paper in my pocket. We all have our secrets.

Cap had said that Uncle Geoff gave him mints after taking his picture. Another photo session with a family member. I wracked my brain. Could it have something to do with the poster in Bluebeard's chamber—the Valentine's gift that Rob had never given to me? It didn't seem like a big deal. Unless it was.

I remembered the phone number from the back of the poster. I'm weird like that.

I wanted to call it, then and there.

What was the point in calling? It had to be the number for the photo studio.

Why shouldn't I call? They'd done such a nice job with the photograph. I might want to use them again sometime.

Geoff had given my son mints. A harmless gesture, and yet . . . it felt like candy from a stranger.

Once I had that thought, I couldn't stop myself. I pulled out my phone. Then, thinking twice, I looked in the settings of my phone and switched it to "private browsing." I googled "How to make a cell phone call anonymously," praying that if my phone was bugged they couldn't see what I was googling. I punched *67, to block my number, then dialed the number that I'd seen on the back of the poster. It was eleven o'clock, East Coast time. I expected to get the photo studio's answering service.

"One Cell Promotions," a voice said briskly. I thought fast.

"Yes, hi. Hi! This is . . . Julia Green calling from the PR department at *Glam*. I'm an assistant, and it's my first week actually, so I really, really hope you can help me. My boss asked me to research this picture that came in. It's two boys standing in front of a sunset, and it says 'A world of opportunity lies ahead.' She wants to hire the same photographer for the magazine? Can you help me? I really, really need this job. I'll, like, lose my apartment. My roommate is totally over me and . . . oh my gosh, I'm so sorry to talk so much. Can you please just tell me about this poster?"

"Oh! Well, I'm not sure who sent it to you, but that sounds like our new bus stop ad campaign."

A cold dread started at my neck and spread down my spine. "Oh, it's an ad campaign! That totally makes sense. We're that department. Can you tell me more about it? It's going to be on bus stops?" I said.

"Yes. If you only have one picture, you're missing half of it. There's a companion poster—one that goes facing it."

"Cool, great. Can you tell me what's on the other side?"

"It's a picture of Earth. It says 'One Cell.' They go up across six cities when we launch our fall marketing campaign."

The beautiful picture of Cap and Leo wasn't a Valentine's gift for me. It had nothing to do with me or love. The world of opportunity that awaited my sons—everyone on Earth, as the ad proclaimed—was . . . the Studio.

I hung up.

I already knew that my little boys would never roller-skate down the block or tug my hand in the supermarket, pleading for sweets. They would never make a friend or have a teacher who didn't already have an opinion about their parents, or at least know that they were rich beyond belief. They would never have anonymity or feel normal. These losses weren't Rob's fault, and I had already come to terms with them. They were stuck with who we were and the bizarre corner of the planet that we called home. In theory, the amazing opportunities we could offer made it worthwhile.

But that one image captured all the differences in how my husband and I saw their future.

Later, when Aurora saw the posters, she would say that Rob was exploiting our children, using them, literally, as poster children for his cause. But that wasn't how I saw it at all. Rob would never put our boys' faces on an advertisement. He was as protective as I of their privacy. On its surface, the poster itself did no harm. Nobody would recognize them. They might not even recognize themselves.

The problem was more complex, and it was between me and Rob. It was perfectly natural to him to offer his children for the photo, the way someone might allow an image of their kids at play to be used in a neighborhood bulletin. One Cell was deeply significant to him. But I did not feel the same way. The Studio was not my community. I could not commit them to that world.

We all make choices for our children, and I was particularly careful about mine. Allison was adopted and maybe she was born to be troubled, but the pressure to live up to the Pepper name had driven her to escape our world entirely. And grateful as I was for *American Dream*, I couldn't help thinking about how much I'd loved English literature, and French class, and how for the first twelve years of my life I was certain I'd end up a pediatrician. Dreams change, children don't become their parents, and the greatest luxury we could give Cap and Leo was the freedom to choose their own paths. To make certain choices for them about who they were, well, that would be breaking the one promise I'd made to my younger self.

Rob had conducted the photo session behind my back and had hidden the resulting poster in his private room. He must have known I'd eventually see the posters and most likely recognize the boys. So why the secrecy? I knew the answer to that. Rob didn't want the annoyance of my opinion. I simply didn't matter.

Rob. When I married him, I believed he was the love of my life, and I knew there might be hard times. I was committed to working through them. My parents were still together, for better and worse, and I never thought I would do anything differently.

I had finally found the missing piece that I'd been looking for all these years, the unreachable part of Rob. It was the knowledge that his ambition drove him. He was committed to his work, and faithful to One Cell. Everything else was far down the list.

In a flash, I saw what my life looked like from the outside, what Aurora had tried to tell me. My life wasn't my own. But I wasn't a target; I was an accessory to Rob's vision and goals. As long as I was in his life, there wouldn't be a choice about me and the boys being part of the Studio. It was his way of life. It was more core to who he was than our marriage.

That poster. The dramatic shadows, the rosy sunset, the Hallmark message. I had thought it was a Valentine's present for me. I had let myself believe it was a symbol of family, of true love. But it was so goddamned corny. I could see Aurora gagging. On top of everything else, I had lost my edge.

I slipped back inside and went upstairs to the boys' room. Cap lay stick straight in his twin bed, covers up to his chin, hands neatly clasped on his chest. My little angel. In his matching bed, Leo, as usual, had rotated ninety degrees and was now sideways on the bed, the covers in a twist, his head nearly dangling off the edge. I pulled him back to his pillow, straightening him up. Now the two of them were parallel again, their breath rising and falling in sync as it often did. Their bodies formed such small bumps under the thick down duvets. We hadn't ruined them yet. But their vulnerability terrified me. My job was to protect them, even from a man who loved them and wanted to give them the world.

I didn't care about being a movie star, about being Rob Mars's wife. Not anymore. What I wanted, more than anything, was for my boys to have an imperfect, simple, real-world childhood where they could have friendships that came and went, get report cards, study the secret lives of turtles, and when the day came, they would mourn Mr. Hooper on *Sesame Street*, or his modern-day equivalent.

The only reason I was still in this marriage was for Cap and Leo. But I was wrong. Staying wasn't best for them. It would slowly, insidiously form them. I couldn't sit around for a day, an hour, a minute, with the sense that other forces would shape my sons' lives.

I had to get them away, to start a new life. I wanted a divorce, and I wanted custody. I looked at my phone, next to me on the bed, and remembered how, right after I called Lexy, her number went dead and she was whisked away to Mustique. My phone was being monitored. And Jordan was always with me. And Lewis, a longtime One Cell employee, had the keys to "my" car.

I knew what I had to do. I just had no idea how I could ever do it.

PART FOUR

DAYLIGHT

1

I just want to go on a hike, like we used to," I said into my phone.

Aurora and I had been friends since I was fourteen and if there was anything she knew for certain about me it was that I never had and never would want to go on a hike. My expeditions were strictly armchair.

"I would love to," Aurora said. "I've been missing our hikes. Just don't get us lost like you did last time."

Leave it to Aurora to take a lie and run with it. I had missed her.

"But I need you to know: I'm very happy being part of the Studio. I can't associate with you if you're still talking to that guy—what was his name?"

Aurora instantly picked up on what I was doing. "Buddy. Don't worry. He turned out to be a creep."

The hike Aurora chose ostensibly led to a waterfall, but it hadn't rained much lately in Topanga and everything was dry. The first half of the trail was flat, but it soon became so steep that in places there were chain handholds along the rock wall of the path. My sneakers, which must have been designed for in-gym use, had zero traction and I was sliding all over the place. Aurora set a rigorous pace.

"I get it," I panted behind. "I didn't listen to you."

"I'm your best friend! You ditched me for fame and fortune!"

I stopped. "I know you're joking," I said, "but you're right. I'm sorry. I got swept up in . . . all of it. I thought it was a dream come true. Go ahead. Tell me I'm a shallow bitch."

"I guess it's not entirely your fault. The One Cell Studio plus Rob Mars. That is a hard-core combo. I can't really blame you for getting sucked in."

I'd once accused Aurora of leaking information to the press, but now I suspected the Studio of tapping my phone. Had Geoff tried to frame her—the one friend I had who would worry and warn me about the organization? Had he poisoned me against her?

Though I think there were, and are, many honest, good people in the Studio, I was soon to learn about its dark underbelly. To Geoff, public perception was everything. He had groomed Rob as his poster boy, and he would do anything to maintain that image. Which included me, Rob's perfect wife. To turn me against Aurora was just what Geoff would do to "protect" me.

At the top of the climb, we took a water break on a comfortable perch overlooking the Pacific.

"This feeling in my legs. I don't like it," I told Aurora.

"You prefer to do that weird yoga shit at the Studio?" Aurora teased.

"No, I hate that, too. But this feels more . . . self-inflicted."

Exertion aside, to be outside and perfectly alone—it was amazing. I was free. Free from paparazzi. Free from tapped phones. Free from the watchful eyes of too-polite household employees. A gray "S" of highway was so far below that we couldn't hear its white noise. Even the trees held still. Safe at last, I told Aurora everything.

Aurora, who'd seemed so alarmist all along, was careful not to judge. I now know that she'd been carefully prepped for this meeting by none other than the infamous One Cell rebel Buddy White. Aurora had been told not to scare me away with all she knew about the Studio. It worked; I found her supportive and practical.

And then, when I thought I'd told her everything, I finally said what I'd been thinking ever since I'd found Rob's scripts.

"This is my fault. I got exactly what I wanted: a perfect-on-the-outside husband."

It was the first time I'd admitted it out loud. Rob, whose very touch had given me shivers, was still the enigma he'd been when we first met. The allure of that mystery had transformed into a kind of torture. Giving up the grand lifestyle—that didn't faze me. But I had to accept that the love I'd felt, the love I'd believed in, the love I'd built my life around—it was all a façade. Explaining that, for the first time, I wept.

Aurora put her arm around me. "You loved him. Of course you loved him. It's Rob fucking Mars. You won the heart of the prince of all the land. It's so hard to let go of that."

"Rob Mars." I was crying and laughing. "I'm dumping Rob Mars. Can I do that?"

"Actually," Aurora said, "dumping him might be even cooler than marrying him."

Then I got serious. "But look what happened to Lexy. When she left Rob she walked away from everything. But I have more to lose. Rob will want the boys. That cannot happen. I can't lose them. I'd stay with Rob forever before I'd let that happen."

I know how it sounds. Rob Mars stealing my children! This wasn't a made-for-TV movie (please, I would never). For all the custody issues in all of Hollywood, for all Rob's power and influence, he couldn't keep my children away from me. Except . . . this was Rob Mars *and* the Studio. Lexy seemed to have grown to appreciate her quiet small-town life, but did she have a choice? Geoff's girlfriend, Patricia, had disappeared. *Emotions are a chemical reaction.* Well, there was a chemical reaction going on in my gut, and it told me to be very, very careful. I couldn't just grab Cap and Leo and walk out the door, and Aurora and I both knew it.

"You have to call him," Aurora said.

"I know." I stood up and paced in a tight circle around the summit.

"You don't have to do it right now," Aurora said.

"Give me your phone."

I needed my father's help, but I had no idea how he would respond. After all, being married to Rob was everything he'd ever wanted for me. Not just the famous, rich husband and beautiful children. Rob was my career ticket. That was what my father had arranged for me before I'd even dreamed of marrying a megastar. *The Safe House* was about to catapult me to the next level. Staying with Rob meant success—my father would accept nothing less.

I called him at work—something I'd only ever done to announce that I'd landed a part. I didn't mince words. "Dad, I'm leaving Rob and I need your help."

My father spoke. "I got you into this, and I'll get you out of it." There was an odd garbled sound at the other end of the line, and when he spoke again I could barely hear him. "My baby girl, I'm sorry, for what I did, for all of this . . . Please forgive me, Lizzie."

Tears sprang to my eyes. He hadn't called me Lizzie since I was little. "Of course, Daddy." There was so much to say that I couldn't find another word.

I heard him sigh deeply, and I was almost relieved when his next words summoned his familiar gruffness. "Tell me what you want."

My father, whose ambition on my behalf had both shaped my life and put a wedge between us, was at last ready to listen to me. He'd always cared about me, but for the first time he actually cared about what I wanted. My answer was easy.

"I just want my children." I would move to Bend, Oregon, and give up acting forever if that was what it took. So long as I was with my boys.

"You got it, Elizabeth." I smiled in spite of myself. That was Doug Pepper for "I love you."

Four days later, on a Saturday, my father met me and Aurora at a nondescript office in Santa Monica that his secretary had rented under the name of a client.

As always, Doug Pepper came prepared. "First off, we need to get you to New York as soon as possible," my father said. "You'll start applying to New York schools for the twins immediately."

He explained that unlike California, where the family courts liked to split everything fifty-fifty, in New York, one parent would be awarded primary custody and the other would get visitation. Even though we hadn't spent quite enough time in New York to establish residency, if the New York courts saw that we were serious about staying, they would probably accept the case.

"Second: money. Don't worry about money," he said. "I realize you don't like to mix business and love. However, the prenup I had my lawyers draw up for you is watertight. Aside from your savings from *American Dream* and the proceeds from the sale of your condo, you will have an additional eleven million dollars safely in your Pepper Mills account to get you back on your feet."

Aurora whistled.

I rolled my eyes. "My *dowry*," I said with scorn.

"You'll be thanking me for it when Rob's people freeze your joint accounts," my father said grimly.

"If you don't want it, I'll take it!" Aurora chimed in. "Uh . . . for charity!" she added.

My father wasn't joking around. "You'll need an apartment in Manhattan—for later, not for now. We'll do that in Aurora's name. She'll be your stand-in. Everything we don't want Rob's people to trace will be in her name."

"Thank you, Mr. Pepper. I've always wanted my very own New York apartment," Aurora said. My father didn't even pretend to be amused. Those two never hit it off.

My father turned to the next page of his yellow pad. "This is a serious matter. Rob and his people are not going to let the boys go without a fight. The Studio has an image to maintain, and losing the sons of such a high-profile supporter doesn't look good. We need someone who knows how that place works." He looked up at me questioningly.

"Buddy White?" Aurora suggested. I'd known he would come up eventually. But he was a stranger to me. I had a better idea. There was one person I might be able to trust. She had kept secrets from me, she had envied me, and she had most likely worked against me. But, in the end, after I'd accused her of false friendship and banished her from my life, she'd sent me the key to Bluebeard's chamber. I had to believe in that gesture, to trust that that one, small piece of metal meant more than everything that had come before. Because nobody knew the inner workings of the Studio better than Meg.

But when I said Meg's name, Aurora pursed her lips. "Do you know where Meg is?"

"Back at the Studio?"

"Don't be so sure," Aurora said. "Buddy says that she disappeared after she left your house."

This was one of the popular rumors about the Studio—that, like Patricia, people who caused problems for the organization got locked away in work camps. I knew that people went to Fernhills for silent retreats. It had been described to me as an intense renewal program, one that people freely chose to undertake. (It included a severe fasting program that yielded enviable results. I always cringed when my fellow actors decided they needed to go to Fernhills right before the award season.) Also, Geoff, in more than one lecture, had talked about the forces that had it in for the Studio. "These accusations people make about us—that we're a cult. That we abuse our practitioners! That you are here against your will! Is this your experience?"

"No!" the audience would shout.

Then again, there was the story Buddy White had started to tell me about his wife. She went to Fernhills for a silent retreat, and he didn't hear from her again for years.

Meg had tried to prove her loyalty to me. There was never any affair between her and Rob. I had known that for longer than I realized. I should have believed Meg from the start, but, in true One Cell fashion, I didn't trust my emotions. Now I needed her to help me escape. I needed her, but first we had to find her. If she had gone into a silent retreat, it might be impossible.

We agreed that we would proceed slowly and deliberately. To rush would be to risk everything. I knew what the worst-case scenario was—losing my sons forever. We all left the meeting with action items. My father was rounding up a legal team; Aurora was establishing accounts; and the boys and I took a weekend trip to New York, making sure we were photographed coming out of the Turtle Bay town house. This time, when the paparazzi asked me what we were doing in town, I said, "Well, I've always loved New York. We've been bicoastal for a while now." I'd learned from the best of them: *optics*.

2

Back in L.A., my next task was a long shot, but all I had were long shots. I took Cap and Leo to lunch at the Studio. I hadn't been there for three months, not since I'd called the number on the poster and pulled the boys out of daycare. Now that I was so disillusioned with One Cell, entering the Studio's gates was surreal, like I was on the set of a movie. Were these people innocent, or were they all extras, cogs in a conspiracy of which I was victim? Either way, I had to act as if things had never been better. If I were going to escape, or even assemble the information I needed to escape, I had to make it seem like the furthest thing from my mind.

We sat at my favorite table in the back corner of the courtyard. I knew who the waiter would be—Warren, an old friend of Meg's, the one she had kissed hello the first day I met her.

He put down my chef's salad and two orders of mac and cheese for the boys. As casually as I could, I said, "So, have you heard from Meg?"

He didn't miss a beat. "I'm sorry, I don't know who you mean."

I hadn't expected that response. He totally knew Meg. He knew that I knew that he knew Meg. Everyone knew Meg. "Meg? My former assistant? Your old friend?"

He shook his head. "You must be mixing me up with someone else."

No, I wasn't. I'd seen the two of them chat hundreds of times. "But, Warren, you know I—"

He was emphatic now. "Nope. Sorry." Then I knew. Meg had done something wrong, and now, in the eyes of the Studio, she didn't exist.

Warren hurried away from the table. Instead of eating his food, Cap looked up at me, his dark eyes steady. "Mama, that man is Auntie Meg's friend. I remember."

I faked a chuckle. "He is being so silly, isn't he?"

Cap stared at me, and for a minute I thought he was going to say, "Well, it's not very funny, is it?" But instead he picked up his fork and began to eat. I had less than a minute before this child would understand everything that was going on around him. No doubt he had already seen too much.

I'd given up on getting Warren's help, but when he brought me the check to sign, there was an extra scrap of paper along with it. One word was scrawled on it: "Fernhills." Two pieces of information. One, Meg was at Fernhills, and two, clearly the powers-that-be didn't want me to find out.

In a normal world, I could just go to Fernhills myself and ask to see Meg. Just because Warren was scared didn't mean I had to be. I was a grown-up. A public figure. This was America, for God's sake. I could look for my friend if I wanted to.

Except that I couldn't. I couldn't walk out the front door of my house without being attacked by paparazzi; I couldn't fly commercial under any circumstances; I couldn't take our jet up north without my husband asking why; and I couldn't saunter into Fernhills without all of One Cell speculating as to what I was doing there. I would have to rely on Buddy White after all.

That night I texted Aurora: *so great to c u yesterday! can we do another Fabulous Hike soon?*

As we had discussed, Aurora knew exactly what I was telling her: Meg was in Fernhills.

Buddy White did the heavy lifting. He and his crew helped Meg leave. I heard about it afterward from Aurora (on a prepaid phone, of course). Apparently the Studio never stopped anyone from walking out the front gates. Nor did they withhold mail. The challenge was making contact with Meg, who was voluntarily staying in a yurt with no phones and no access to the outside world. Buddy knew that in order to achieve psychic balance, the Studio would recommend that Meg stay on-site, in silence, with minimal food consumption. This was news to me—the Practice was more extreme than I'd ever known. So many rumors had proved untrue, but where there was smoke, there was fire. Although technically Meg could walk away, or receive or make a phone call, doing so would mean going against the ideals she'd upheld for most of her life.

They didn't know if anyone was reading her mail, so Buddy reached her by sending her friendly letters from a made-up clothing company, "Linus B.," which she'd supposedly "helped" when she worked for me. The idea was that Meg would know these were fake, and, if she wanted to leave but didn't know how, she would pay close attention to the subtext of the letters, which told her things like "Your friends here at Linus B. can't wait to see you again" without giving anything away.

After several of these letters, Linus B. sent Meg a thank-you gift. A token of appreciation for all her "hard work." It was a black cotton motorcycle jacket, with numerous pockets and angled zippers. (My friend Saskia made it, actually. Trust me, it was very of the moment.) Inside a hidden pocket of a pocket was a tiny scrap of paper with nothing on it but a date and time. It was left to Meg to decide to walk out the front gate at that time. If she wanted to leave, she would most likely take up jogging.

Or feign an interest in wildflowers. Or photography. What the escape relied on, more than anything, was Meg's determination. The only chains that bound her were psychological. She had to want to break from the Studio. Meg had to be willing to leave behind the only people and places she had ever known.

Nobody had a clue whether this was what Meg actually wanted until the date of the planned escape, when Buddy's friend drove his food delivery truck to the first intersection outside the entrance to Fernhills. He was prepared to wait there all night, but he'd been there only an hour when Meg, barefoot and wearing Studio robes, walked right up to the truck and asked for a ride. Like my hero Papillon, the amazing convict who escaped Devil's Island, Meg had broken free by almost literally riding out on a bundle of coconuts.

Two weeks after Meg walked away from Fernhills, she, Aurora, and I met at the Sofitel, where Meg had checked in under a false name. I reimbursed her for the hotel bill in cash. We didn't want my business manager to start asking questions. I told Jordan that a Reiki master Saskia adored was in town, working out of a room at the Sofitel. It was an excuse I could employ once a week if need be. I relied on the fact that much as I didn't want to raise any alarms, Jordan didn't want me to feel watched. And so our chess game went.

Aurora had counseled me not to talk to Meg about Fernhills unless she brought it up, and when I saw Meg it was clear to me that this was good advice. She looked different. She was tan, that weathered brown that comes from the real sun instead of a spray-on expert. Her eyes were sunken and sad, and she was very, very thin, her size 00 jeans sagging in the ass. We drank seltzer out of the minibar, and she started talking.

"I don't want you to think our friendship was a lie," she began. "In the beginning, it was exactly what we both thought. I was helping you get to know the Studio. I got paid, but only the same amount I'd always been paid for working as a volunteer at One Cell—less than minimum wage." Meg's words were halting, as if weighed down.

"I'd known Rob for years, but I'd never seen his life up close. The houses, the travel, the food, the clothes—all of it was foreign to me. I grew up believing creature comforts were irrelevant. The core purpose was what mattered. But you were my age, and seeing you live that way—I found myself swept up in it. Dressing up, going to events, borrowing your clothes . . . I'd never even had a glass of wine before."

"Wine is really good," I said.

"Tell me about it," she said, smiling for the first time. She continued: "Then Rob had me coordinate an ad campaign for the Studio—the boys are part of it—"

"I know about it," I said. "I used the key."

"I tried to say no, that I wasn't comfortable keeping a secret from you, but he insisted that he'd surprise you with the news when the time was right. He said you'd be thrilled. I was pretty sure that wasn't true, and I tried to argue with him, but Geoff told me to mind my own business and do my job."

"I'm sorry. You were in an impossible position. I should have trusted you," I said.

"No, you did the right thing. I was being asked to do things that felt wrong. I tried not to let my emotions get in the way, but they did." She turned to Aurora. "Geoff thought you were a bad influence, and I was instructed to take your place. I'm so sorry."

"See?" Aurora said. "This shit is hard core."

Meg went on, "Anyway, you know what happened next. You saw me coming out of Rob's private office—"

"Bluebeard's chamber."

"Yes, and it made perfect sense that you fired me after that. I went back to the Studio and tried to clear my head."

"But you sent me the key! That must have meant you disagreed with Geoff—or at least with what Rob was planning."

"It's more complicated than that. I grew up at One Cell. It was my life. I just couldn't admit that I was on the wrong side. After you fired me, I guess Geoff thought I would want revenge. Or maybe he just thought I would do anything he asked me to do. So he . . ." Meg paused. This was obviously hard for her. "It's . . . it's about your sister, Lizzie."

"Allison?"

Meg took a deep breath, then spoke quickly, as if she were eager to get what she was saying off her chest. "Geoff ordered me to pay your sister a visit. He told me we were reaching out to help her. But he also wanted me to take pictures. I think you know the rest?"

I put my face in my hands. It was as I had feared. Geoff had used my deepest secrets against me. My poor sister had had no idea what she was getting herself into.

"What happened then?" Aurora asked.

"I said no," Meg said. "I refused, but someone must have done it. I can name fifty people off the top of my head who would do anything to get in Geoff's good graces."

The Altoid tin that Cap had found in the cabin. "Actually, I think Geoff himself went," I said. "But for what? What does exposing Allison do for him?"

"Power," Meg said. *Power.* Such a strange concept. I'd never thought about wanting power, being motivated by it, having it, before I met Rob. Meg went on. "Whatever he got from Allison, he'll use to control you." She looked out the window, tears streaming down her cheeks. She had been born into this community, believed in its mission, and she was braver than anyone I'd ever met for letting it go.

Geoff wanted me to stay with Rob, but why? Meg explained that it was in the Studio's interest for Rob to have a model marriage, and to keep it. It was all about image. Rob, as One Cell's most visible advocate, should appear to have it all. Above all, it was what Rob wanted. I chewed over that one for a bit. Was our marriage really what Rob wanted? But I could see it. Rob wanted a family, with children, the same way he wanted nice houses and fancy cars. "Wife" was one of the items he wanted to cross off on his list of goals sought and obtained. Maybe, if I wasn't being cynical, he did feel something for me, even if he didn't trust himself to express it. Without a doubt, he loved Cap and Leo.

"When I drew the line at meeting with your sister, Geoff sent me to Fernhills. For Inner Conflict resolution." A year earlier, Geoff had diagnosed me with Inner Conflict. I suppose it was only my status that kept me from being sent to reform at Fernhills, as Meg had been.

"Is that like prison?" Aurora said. "Buddy told me about it."

"It's intense," Meg said. "We were in a yurt—a big one—twenty-four/seven. They kept it quite dark, and we tried not to talk. During the day we practiced and fasted—just water and some sardines if we were desperate. At night we processed the guided motivation CDs that the Studio sells. Sometimes a crew of us was sent out to work on buildings. The isolation is interesting at first, and some people say it really helps them focus and renew their commitment to the Studio. But after a while I hated it. I lost track of time. And there wasn't much opportunity to rest. I couldn't focus in my practice. All I could think about was food and sleep. I was barely a person."

"How long were you there?"

"Just over six months," Meg said, "but there are some people who've been there for years."

"So Buddy was right. It's really true. People are held against their will. That's completely illegal," Aurora said. "We can shut them down."

"Except it wasn't against anyone's will," Meg said. "I wasn't kept prisoner. I chose to be there. I had a lot to figure out. I didn't belong in your world, and I couldn't obey Geoff anymore. I didn't know what to believe. I *wanted* to be there . . . until I didn't. I was lucky Buddy's guys showed up when I was on work detail. At that point I didn't think I could stand another minute."

"Is Patricia in Fernhills?" Buddy and the other active ex-members had made a big deal of her disappearance, but Geoff liked to say "She still pays her taxes. Guess she has a right to privacy like anyone else."

"There was definitely no sign of Patty." I thought of Patricia often now. She had, I thought, tried to warn me that there was a dark side to the world I was entering. Now that odd, stiff woman was lost to it. Patricia's whereabouts were a mystery I would never solve.

Meg was very clear about one thing. If I was going to escape my marriage, we would have to blindside *everyone*—including Rob. Meg didn't know what might happen if I threatened to leave.

"Lexy let her intentions slip, and look where she is now. We don't want to find out what happens if you cross him. We know for sure that One Cell doesn't want you to leave. That's what Geoff's meeting with Allison was all about."

Meg spoke with conviction. She said that Cap, Leo, and I had to physically escape. Our departure had to be so secret, sudden, and public that neither Rob nor One Cell could stop me.

"Also," Meg said, "if you do get out, don't expect to keep working as an actress."

"Don't be ridiculous," said Aurora. "I'm sure the Studio is all-powerful, but Lizzie is a great actress, and she's totally famous. She'll always have work."

"Not when ACE turns on her. They'll squash your career, if that's what Rob wants. Both ACE and One Cell will do anything for Rob. Once you move forward with this, you can't change your mind."

The Safe House might never see the light of day. ACE had the power to kill it. Hell, movies fell out of production because an executive had a headache on the wrong day. "I'll risk it," I said. It wasn't a hard decision. My boys were more important.

3

My father issued directives from Chicago, and Aurora, Meg, and I sprang into action, setting up the logistics of my exit. We had three months to get everything in order before the Venice Film Festival, where I would make my escape.

"Is all this necessary?" I asked the first time we met in the under-ventilated, windowless waxing room of a hair salon that was a Buddy White–approved safe zone. How real was the danger? It was just so hard to believe One Cell would hurt me or imprison me. That sort of scheme belonged in Rob's movies or the books I loved. True danger was on the slopes of Everest, or in a lifeboat at the whim of the tides, or outside the steep walls of a merciless prison. It was impossible to see myself in rela-tion to any of that. Me! Lizzie Pepper from Chicago! My biggest worries were supposed to be sunspots and bad hair days. I couldn't see Rob, even with all his gloss and movie star perfection, taking part in such a plot. Rob would never let something happen to me. But . . . would he enter a state of denial and let someone else take care of the problem? Yes. And was I a problem? I was about to be.

"People get divorced all the time. Even high-profile people. Can't I just call a lawyer and be done with it?"

"Look, you're not going to be tied up and carried off to Fernhills," Meg said, "but Rob has infinite resources. He can fight you as long and hard as he wants." This was how he would control me—with our children. If he used them, he could make me do anything he wanted, and he knew it.

As per my father, I needed to leave all at once, with a place to stay, money in the bank, and witnesses to make sure the story was told right. My departure, like every other milestone Rob and I had passed, would be a press event. For once, I *wanted* my private affairs in the press. The world would know that I had left; they would see us together, mother and sons, landing in New York—our home. We would control the optics; we would be out of the Studio's reach; and Rob would have to scramble to assemble a legal team. And so we launched Operation Free Lizzie.

I'd never paid much attention to the infrastructure around me. Now I made it my business. I sent an e-mail to Cap's drum teacher, canceling a lesson because I "thought Cap was overscheduled." But I deliberately left it on my calendar. Then, on the afternoon of the lesson, I innocently said to Jordan, "Doesn't he have drum class? It's on the calendar?"

"No, we decided to cancel, remember? You told me Cap's overbooked."

"Oh, of course. Thank you. I completely forgot."

Jordan was reading my e-mail. Confirmed.

I called Aurora and asked her what she thought I should get Rob for his birthday. She made a few suggestions, one of which was golf clubs.

"Hey, that's actually a really good idea. Rob keeps saying he wants to try golf."

A couple of days later I asked Jake if he had any ideas for presents for Rob.

"I think I heard him mention wanting to try golf," he said.

Rob often said he thought golf was a waste of perfectly good grass. Jake was monitoring my phone. To be fair, it wasn't exactly a violation. It was Hollywood protocol that assistants listen in on calls. But Jake didn't say, "I heard you mention golf clubs to Aurora." Privacy was an illusion that we all upheld. By establishing a new barrier of technology around myself, I wasn't just leaving Rob, I was reclaiming the personal space that most people take for granted.

Following my father's instructions, Meg created what she called a "mirror" of my life. I had two phones and two computers—the new ones were in Aurora's name. I lined up a second driver and a second nanny in New York—both of whom had been vetted by Secret Service standards and were hired by "Aurora Janevs."

I started calling Lewis, my driver, directly, to establish a "new normal." I also opened a bank account that our money manager didn't have access to. I made up something about a discount at Barneys that came with new premium accounts and crossed my fingers that it wouldn't raise a red flag.

There were light moments—Aurora showed up to one meeting in a "Run, Lizzie, Run" T-shirt—but for six weeks I had to act as if everything was normal, taking meetings, RSVPing yes for events I didn't plan to attend, taking the boys to lunch at the Studio, all the while secretly receiving my father's updates and instructions in coded e-mails on a disposable phone.

Eventually the boys and I moved to the Turtle Bay town house. Rob, away in Turkey, was unfazed. He liked New York, and had no idea the city was going to be the boys' and my new, permanent home. My father contacted a friend from business school who was launching a new private school in Brooklyn. They registered both boys—under false names—for the incoming kindergarten class. My father helped the school design a private back entrance, which my corporation, Pepper Mills, paid for. I wouldn't even have a chance to tour the campus until after I'd broken free. Meg—who was now on my undercover payroll—rented an apartment in Brooklyn Heights. She scouted out an Episcopal church that I would join the minute I could. These footholds in New York would make up for my previous intermittent presence in the city. We hoped the court would forgive my short-term residency when they saw that I planned to stay.

It felt good to be far from the One Cell stronghold; far from the city that ACE practically owned—a limitless power network that would do anything for Rob. New York felt safer. It was an illusion, of course. No matter where I was, Rob had his allies. But it comforted me to think that after it all went down, if I succeeded, our New York life would distract Cap and Leo from what for them would be the biggest change—that if all went according to plan, I would win full custody. They would see even less of their father than they already did.

It was an awful summer. I barely slept. I lost weight, and my skin broke out in hives. At times, when I was with Aurora or Meg, the detective drama felt like a game, but every night, after the boys and I Skyped with Rob, I went to the bathroom and threw up, aching for my sons, whose perfect world I was about to tear apart.

A few times I almost got caught, and sometimes I lost track of who and what I was trying to escape. Our new driver/bodyguard, Max, was a friend of Aurora's who wasn't on the payroll, and who had signed his life away in confidentiality agreements. One Thursday, I decided to take advantage of Lewis's day off to check out the apartment in Brooklyn Heights that was to be our new home. I threw on a blond wig that was attached to a baseball cap (it was higher quality than it sounds), but Cap refused to wear either the Jedi mask or the fox mask I'd brought for him and Cap. ("Mama, it's just not *appropriate*." The kid was five going on sixty.) Leo ended up wearing them both.

By the time we got downtown, we were being followed. I don't blame Max's inexperience. I should have known it was an impossible idea. The potential repercussions of my recklessness were terrifying. If the paparazzi took pictures of us, someone on Rob's team might notice the new car and new driver. It could blow everything. Rob. Geoff. Lewis. Jake. Liesl. Jordan. The list of people I didn't trust was endless.

There must have been ten black SUVs surrounding us. We had to lose them. In a panic, I texted my father, who suggested I head someplace with security, where the paparazzi couldn't follow.

Doctor's office w underground garage? Office building? Hotel?

k, I wrote back. Then I realized I knew exactly where to go. Rob's project. The New York Studio. I'd never been, but I knew it was on West 17th Street, just off Union Square.

We nearly drove past the construction site—I was expecting a tall building like the emerald Studio in Beverly Hills—I only knew we were in the right place when I saw the Studio's logo on the signage posted along the rent-a-fence. Max pulled up to the gate. The guard recognized me and waved us into an unfinished parking lot. The chain-link fence slammed shut behind us. It wasn't exactly a fortress, but it would have to do. Max pulled over to the side, avoiding the piles of construction materials. An attendant walked toward the car, then, recognizing me, gave a slight wave and went back to his post. Even in New York the One Cell staff knew the drill: They never approached us unless beckoned. I prayed nobody would notice that Max wasn't Lewis.

We were safe. And yet we were hiding in the belly of the beast. Max turned off the car, and, in the backseat with the boys, I hid my tears behind my sunglasses.

It was only that night, safe at home, after the boys were asleep, when I thought to wonder why the project that Rob had been working on so diligently throughout our marriage was still only an empty lot. The site had felt like a refuge because it was so unexpectedly quiet. Where was the hammering and drilling? Why weren't there workers? I called Meg on my safe phone and asked her if she knew anything about the project.

"It was supposed to open last year," Meg said, "but they've been saying it's about to open for the last five years. And now the three Herman-Schmidt brothers, who gave nearly half a million dollars to the fund, are accusing Teddy Dillon of delaying the opening so she can keep raising money. They've raised a hundred million dollars for it already, more than enough for the building, and the Herman-Schmidts are suing her for not using their donation as promised."

How was this possible? If there was one thing I'd never doubted about Rob, it was that he had a good heart. The New York expansion was the embodiment of that—his great project to change the lives of an under-served community. After all those business trips he'd made to check on the project's progress . . . no wonder he hadn't let me get involved. If this was true, that his efforts were an elaborate con, then I'd been played for a fool.

Before we'd left L.A., Pops, the paparazzo who basically lived outside our house, had pleaded for a big-selling image.

"Throw me a bone," he said. "My wife is having a baby next month."

Pops was married. Who knew?

"Let me think about it," I'd said. Pops was a useful friend to have. His telephoto could see through walls. I knew I would need him, I just wasn't yet sure for what.

Now I asked Aurora to meet Pops to have him look into the New York Studio. I couldn't be the one to feed him private information about my husband. If that kind of violation was traced back to me . . . well, not only would the press have a field day but Rob would never forgive me. (These concerns fade after divorce, particularly when one finds out the extent of the lies. . . .)

The irony of asking Aurora to leak information to the press wasn't lost on me. Meg had confessed that she'd set Aurora up as a press leak in order to subvert our friendship. Now Aurora was talking to a paparazzo at my behest. This is what happens when you see the world through the lens of paranoia (even be it by necessity). You bring nightmares to life.

The Venice Film Festival, from which I planned to make my escape, was three weeks away when Pops showed up in New York.

The morning he pushed in front of the other photographers waiting outside our town house, I couldn't help smiling—he may have been a paparazzo, but he was *my* paparazzo.

I was taken aback when he scowled at me. "Thanks for nothing," he growled. Then, seeing the bewilderment on my face, he hissed, "You may have a private jet, but coming here was a big expense for me. *A worthless goose chase.*"

"Later," I hissed, and slid into the waiting car.

A few days later Aurora got the scoop for me. Pops had gone to the construction site. The building was in process. Construction delays were common—no story there. From the footprint he'd photographed, the project seemed to be exactly what Rob had described to me and the Studio had announced to the press.

"But check this out," Aurora said. She handed me a piece of paper that looked like a tax filing. "Pops isn't mad at you anymore. After he saw you, he went back and pulled the public records. One Cell raised *one hundred forty million* dollars for Studio Manhattan to date, and Pops had six different architects look at the plans. They said it can't cost more than eighty million to build, even if they spare no expense. So where is the rest of the money?"

Sixty million dollars, unaccounted for. That was a useful tidbit. "Do you think Rob knows?"

We were in Meg's little pad in SoHo. (When I went to meet her, I always told Cap and Leo I was going to "Aunt Christine's apartment" in case one of them inadvertently mentioned it to Rob. If need be, it would be easy to convince Rob he'd forgotten that my mother had a sister who lived in New York.)

Now Meg, who had been doing dishes, suddenly spoke up. "If Rob has any files about the project, they're in his office in the gym."

Bluebeard's chamber. It really did hold all his secrets.

★

Power. I cared about it now. If One Cell was using Studio Manhattan as a front to collect donations, and I had documents to prove it, it might help me negotiate the divorce somewhere down the line. I wanted a secret weapon. I guess I'd watched too many of Rob's movies, but that night I flew back to L.A., ostensibly because Leo "missed Malibu." Nobody raised an eyebrow. Apparently if Rob Mars's son misses his beach house, it's utterly unremarkable for him to be flown across the country to visit it.

In Bluebeard's chamber late that night, I don't know what I hoped to find. I opened the file cabinet, looking for anything about the New York project, anything fishy. Like a piece of paper that read, "Studio Manhattan is a fraud. We're using it to bilk our practitioners out of millions of dollars." But the files were instead filled with closing documents for houses Rob no longer owned. Old tax forms that certainly weren't worth keeping (except for a 1985 tax filing, where Rob earned a grand total of $14,000— that one was probably worth a pretty penny on eBay).

Then, just before I gave up, I realized I had what I needed. I'd had it all along.

The end was so close, I was almost defiant when I came out of Bluebeard's chamber for the second and last time. I turned on the hallway lights on my way back to my room and practically stormed down the hallway. *It's my house. Go ahead, tell my husband I sneaked into his private office. This ship has sailed.*

4

Rob was coming home to Malibu for two weeks in August, just before we would all fly to Venice for the film festival.

I thought it would be hard to keep up appearances, but it wasn't. We still got along really well. When he came in the front door, with his handsome smile, laden with gifts for all of us, I could see why it had been so easy to fall for him. His scripts told the story of a life that worked. The boys and I had everything we could want. On the surface, there were no dangers or threats, no harsh words or uncomfortable situations. It would have been so simple to go on as we were. To pretend this was all in my head. Because, if you thought about it, it *was* all in my head—in the sense that some other woman, make that thousands of other women, would be more than glad to have my life, every bit of it, no complaints, no problemo. So what if Rob's love was an act? Didn't the happiest of marriages sometimes require the partners to go through the motions of love?

I hated the idea of blindsiding Rob. My reasons for leaving him were, in one sense, so bizarre and abstract. A script I'd found. A mystery man's visit to my sister. My son's reaction to a small cut on his hand. A photo shoot I'd learned about from a phone call with a stranger. If there was a checklist for marriage, I could check everything off. Rob took care of me and our children. Check. He wanted us to be happy. Check. He worked hard, supported us, didn't drink or do drugs, cheat or abuse. Check, check, check, check. He was kind. He was handsome. We never fought.

But the boys and I were prisoners. To make it work, we had to live in his world, follow his plans for Cap and Leo. We could only be the people he wanted us to be. And our fame was unbearably restrictive. My body felt trapped in that house, my spirit suffocating, my self lost. In some alternate universe we could have signed up for couples therapy, learned how to listen and respect each other, and pieced it back together. But I was the only one who had been torn into pieces. Rob was made of granite, a smooth, solid form, impenetrable and unyielding. A statue.

I'd broken up with Justin, my first love, when *American Dream* ended. We hadn't stopped loving each other, but we couldn't stay in Memphis for the rest of our lives (though I will forever long for the balcony of the bookstore café in the center of town, where I enjoyed my last days of anonymity). Justin was heading to New York for a run in *Rent*, and I was off to shoot *The Last Hurrah*. The wrap party was a night of weepy toasts and a clip reel that showed my character growing from a naïve girl into a confident woman. Back then, I wished I felt half as grown up as Lucy McAlister looked. She was headed to St. Lucia, leaving our make-believe town of Linville and her boyfriend, Justin's character, to fulfill her dream of teaching needy children in a tropical paradise. I was leaving to become a movie star. Oh well.

It was such an emotional drain—all those good-byes. The next morning Justin's flight was due to leave before mine. I woke up when he flopped down on the bed next to me, ready to go.

"Don't leave!" I exclaimed, rolling on top of him. "I'm not letting you."

"This isn't the end," he said, kissing me. "We don't have to make a big proclamation. We can just see what happens."

It was tempting. Separating from him was the most painful thing I'd experienced. We could visit, talk on the phone, continue to love each other. But that was not my idea of a relationship.

"We're breaking up," I said. "Long-distance relationships are stupid."

"Lizzie, you are a cold, cold woman," he said.

"That's why you're better off without me," I said, and then, without warning, I started bawling and couldn't stop. Embarrassed, I hid my face in the blanket. And then I heard a funny sound and looked up. Justin was crying, too. I'd never seen him cry (except when his *American Dream* little sister, Sally, died of leukemia, but even then the makeup team had to supply fake tears). It was so unexpected that I was completely startled out of my own tears. I started laughing.

"What?!" he exclaimed.

"Stop," I said. "We're still alive. We have phones. If we miss each other, we'll see each other. That's all there is to it." I stood up and helped him to his feet, and at the door we embraced for the last time, and a week later he was photographed making out with Amanda Forsythe at Bar 66 in TriBeCa. His dead-of-leukemia *American Dream* sister! He'd always denied it, but I'd known he was into her the whole fifth season. She had that pale waif look. Leukemia chic.

My good-bye with Justin may have been young and awkward, but at least we both knew what was happening. Unlike what I was about to do to Rob. The two weeks he was home in Malibu, Rob and I took walks along the water together. I rolled up my jeans and followed him to the top of the bluffs. I held his hand and kissed him back. In the early evenings, when the sun started to go down, I huddled against him for warmth. I wasn't just playing the part. In truth, it was my way of saying good-bye.

He must have sensed something in the air, something in me, a change. One morning we had coffee out on the wide balcony. It was high tide, and the sea crashed hungrily against the rock jetty that had been hurriedly constructed to protect the houses. The beach had all but disappeared, succumbing to erosion in spite of the tens of millions of dollars Rob and his neighbors had thrown into the ocean, begging it to yield. The press had been vicious—criticizing the wealthy beach-house owners for carting in sand to rebuild the beach. Even environmentalists recommended a "managed retreat," letting the ocean slowly reclaim the mansions it so clearly desired.

"I love you, Elizabeth," Rob said, taking both of my hands in his. "I'm sorry for what I said in New York about bringing the boys into the Studio. I believe what I believe, and I won't be bullied by gossip and prejudice to change my mind. But I know how you feel about letting our sons make their own choices."

He paused and licked his lips, an uncharacteristic uncertainty crawling across his brow. He glanced left and right, as if looking for cue cards. "I want to say . . . I just . . ." Was Rob Mars at a loss for words? Had he forgotten his lines? He leaned closer, his voice almost a whisper. "Okay, here's what. Sometimes I think about what it would be like to leave. The industry, the Studio, all of it. We could retire, move far away, live a simple, normal life. It's normal to fantasize about that."

Had he gone off script? Was he improvising? Breaking character? Did he, like Meg, think about leaving the Studio? It seemed real. I almost believed him. I so wanted to believe him. Could MAK, his life scriptwriter, have read my mind? Or was this the real Rob, secretly desperate to escape it all? "What's stopping us? What's stopping us from living that fantasy?" I asked him.

A rush of hope stirred in me. I squeezed his hands. If only Rob would come offstage. If he would leave the Studio. Or back slowly away. Or just agree that we didn't have to be part of it. If he would let go of his plans for Cap and Leo . . . wouldn't that solve everything? He loved me and his sons more than the world. Surely, if I was clear enough and brave enough, he would have to consider it.

The waves beat at the seawall, relentless. You could move sand and you could build walls, but they were temporary solutions, stopgaps, cover-ups. Nothing would stop the ocean. Rob looked at me with eyes that showed hurt, and regret, and frustration at everything he was locked into being, and yet everything he still wanted. Eyes that finally gave me a glimpse into who he really was, and that convinced me that, as much as he was capable, he really had always loved me, and that part of him deep down knew that these were our last few moments alone.

"I can't," he said.

My husband, who could do anything, couldn't do this for me. There was only one option: managed retreat. It broke my heart.

5

A lot has been written about "Lizzie's escape," but it's all a collection of half-truths, best guesses, and completely made-up scenes stolen, as far as I can tell, from old episodes of *Batman*. Here's what really happened.

It all went down, as everyone knows, during the Venice Film Festival, where One Cell had few contacts and Rob and I had a skeleton crew.

Tomorrow held its annual party, this time celebrating its one hundredth issue, at the Cini Foundation on the island of San Giorgio Maggiore. Rob knew the island well—the monastery had been used as a filming location for two of his movies (*Glass Houses* and *The Son*).

The magazine had ferries shuttling guests to the island, but Rob insisted on a private gondola for the two of us. This ended up being the *less* private option, since all the press—who were not allowed onto the island or into the party—had nothing to do but hover around on boats trying to get shots. They swarmed us, our poor gondolier shouting uselessly at the other boatmen in Italian. At some point all you can do is run with it, hence those gorgeous photos of us, kissing in the gondola, silhouetted in front of a spectacular sunset, looking, for all the world, like the last shot of a romance. Oh, it was the perfect final image for our storybook marriage. The only thing missing was the credits scrolling by.

Tomorrow's Venice party was straightforward: a roomful of A-listers enjoying one another. The Venice version was more laid back than their Oscar party. Because it was smaller, there was no VIP area and guests weren't given time slots for their arrival. It was a place where Rob and I could feel almost normal. Except that every time we tried to take a picture in the photo booth, we'd get drawn into a conversation while the photo was drying, and by the time we turned back, our picture had been stolen. The third time we tried, Rob stood blocking the little dispenser slot, arms crossed, daring anyone to sneak past.

Ordinarily, I rode out this sort of event with a mix of boredom and scorn. It was an obnoxious stew of self-congratulatory sycophants. But this time, knowing it was all about to end, I stopped watching the power plays and networking with a cynical eye. Instead, I went for it. I flirted with Matthew Brau, Rob's agent and the head of ACE. I helped Jason See retie his bow tie. I tried to teach the live mynah bird that Celia Montbatten wore perched on her shoulder (part of the dress?) to say "Celia is divine."

In the ladies' room, I ran into my former *American Dream* costar, Wendy Jones, and gushed, "Wendy, I have something to confess. I've always been a little jealous of you. I know it's silly, but, I mean, you're so *gorgeous*. It's *insane*. And on top of that, I have *so* much respect for your art. That's all. I just wanted you to know."

Wendy hugged me, crushing her silicone implants into my shoulder. "I totally get it. It's always been hard for me to have women friends. So many are jealous. But I'm really a girls' girl! Anyway, you were a really good actor, too."

I noted her use of the past tense, but it was basically true. "Thank you," I said, smiling. "I actually just did a part in a little movie. Parker O. Witt. But Rob's work is much more important. I'm just happy to be able to support him."

I floated at Rob's side, leaning in to his shoulder and smiling as he graciously accepted praise and congratulations. Every so often I brushed lint off his lapel or fixed an unruly lock of hair.

"Hold that thought," he said, interrupting a producer who'd come to report on the opening night ticket sales. "Let me kiss my beautiful wife."

"Rob!" I blushed and giggled. We kissed, and then I turned to the producer. "You have to excuse us. We've barely had time together lately. Tonight is a bit of a reunion."

I played my part to perfection. Rob Mars's wife, elegant, supportive, humble, happy, in love—plastic perfection in a plastic world. At the end of the night, for my coup de grâce, I bummed a breath mint off Geoff Anciak.

The next day Rob had seven hours of nonstop interviews for *The Life of Digby Dane* in a conference room at the hotel. Our itinerary had me and the boys on a private tour of a glassblowing studio. On our way out, we stopped by the conference room to say good-bye to Rob. Only I knew how final that good-bye would be.

As I approached, the journalists were sitting in a line of chairs outside the room. There were no cameras, and as we walked past it was quiet but for a few overeager hellos from reporters, hoping for some reason I'd pause to say anything. It was the most polite group of press I'd ever experienced, but I suppose they feared that if they pissed me off, I would put the kibosh on their time with Rob. I smiled politely as I walked past.

Saying good-bye to Rob that day was one of the greatest acting challenges of my life. It had to be the good-bye of a wife who was about to take their sons on a glassblowing excursion and would see her husband again in a few hours. But also, somehow, when Rob looked back at this moment, I wanted him to know everything I was feeling right now. Pain, love, despair. I wasn't heartless; I didn't want to hurt him; I knew he had deceived me because he knew no other way. And yet, I wanted him to know that he left me no choice.

He slouched comfortably in his chair, his shirtsleeves rolled up. When he saw me, he brightened, that handsome smile spreading across his face. Unknowable, he still gleamed as bright and perfect as ever. Unknown, I was lost in the shadows.

I lingered when I kissed him, tears welling in my eyes.

"What is it, Elizabeth? Are you okay?"

And then something clicked, and I knew exactly what to say to him. Emil had drafted it for Rob in the most recent delivery of scripts that I'd found on Rob's desk back in Malibu. I didn't know if Rob had seen the new pages yet, but I took a chance. The lines I spoke fell under the header "Last Words Before a Long Absence."

"There's an e. e. cummings poem I was reading—maybe you know it? 'I carry your heart with me—I carry it in my heart.'"

I looked at Rob. His eyelids fluttered. Was it surprise?

"That's very sweet," Rob said. Did I detect a sadness in his voice? Had he realized that I, his wife, knew that our most intimate moments were scripted by someone who was a stranger to me? I wanted him to understand why I had left. But I also wanted him to know how much I had wanted to believe in us, so the next words I spoke were my own.

"I miss you already," I said. "I feel like I've always missed you; even when we're together I miss you. I want to climb into your heart, but you're always just out of reach." There it was, the truth. I hoped he would remember it. I may have been the one doing the leaving, but he had never been there in the first place.

"I love you too," Rob said. To me, it rang hollow.

Cap, at my side, said good-bye to Rob when I did, but Leo was hiding in the thick hotel curtains, trying to start up a game of peekaboo with

Jake, who was tapping his pencil on his clipboard. We were putting Rob off schedule.

"Come say good-bye to Daddy," I said.

Leo ran to Rob and put his hands on his knee. "Daddy, will you put me to bed tonight?" It was a question he asked at some point every day. He never complained if Rob wasn't home at bedtime, but he liked to know the plan.

Rob glanced up at me for the answer. He never knew our schedule. "Probably not tonight," I said to Leo. There was nothing on our calendar—I should have lied and said we'd both be at the hotel—but if all went smoothly he wouldn't see him again for a long time.

"Bye!" Leo chirped, and started pulling me toward the door.

I knelt down next to him. "Give Daddy a real hug and a kiss, okay?"

Rob would, at least, remember that it mattered to me. Whatever was ahead of us, I resolved that once we were safely gone, the first thing I was going to do was tell him that I would completely support and nurture his relationship with his sons. Little did I know that after that day we wouldn't speak again for more than a year.

Leo climbed into Rob's lap and kissed his cheek. Instinctively, I scanned the room to make sure none of the hotel staff were sneaking a cell phone snapshot.

There were two cars waiting for us. The one Jake had arranged was in the back of the hotel, with Lewis standing by to take us to our glass-blowing appointment. Another one, under a false name, was at the side of the hotel. When the coast was clear, we ducked into the idling car, where our bodyguard/driver Max was at the wheel. He drove straight to the airport.

Fifteen minutes into the car ride, I called Lewis to tell him we were running late.

"Give me twenty, okay?"

A half hour later, just as we were boarding the plane, I called Lewis again. "Actually, I have a headache. We're not going to go today."

Everyone except Lewis thought we were with Lewis, heading to the glassblowing factory. This bought us an unknown amount of time. At some point Lewis would encounter Jake. And Jake would try to track us down. He would text me, and I would respond that I was in the hotel room, resting.

We boarded the plane, my heart racing. People in retreat at Fernhills had no contact with the outside world. Patricia had disappeared. Geoff's threatening image loomed in my head. We had to pull this off, and we only had one shot. If Rob's team realized I was trying to leave, if they stopped me before I succeeded, then they would have optics on their side. Once Rob controlled the story, his people could use their power, money, and influence to fight me for custody of the kids. The case could drag on for years, exposing our lives, dragging Cap and Leo into the kind of mess that would take years of therapy to overcome. I didn't think Rob was capable of harming us, but he was used to getting his way. I thought of Lexy. She had tried, in her own way, to warn me.

I must have squeezed Cap's hand too tightly. He yelped and pulled his fingers out of my grip.

"Sorry, sweetheart," I said.

"Play with Mama's phone?" he asked.

"Sure," I said, handing him my iPhone.

"No, me!" Leo said, and the bickering began. Less screen time for the boys in New York, I resolved. In the months of planning I'd gotten lax.

Papillon—the intrepid Frenchman whose book about his escape to freedom had stayed with me—Papi never had the luxury of escaping via private plane. He braved sharks, quicksand, hurricanes, and inhospitable governments. He befriended fellow prisoners, officers, foreigners, and indigenous people at every turn, winning them over to his right to make a fresh start. He refused to let his prison sentence define him. Once he knew in his heart who he was meant to be, he gave every ounce of strength he could summon to become that person. He was an imperfect man and a hero. If Papi could do it, wearing flour sacks, with his only money shoved in a watertight container where no man could find it, then I could damn well leave my Louboutins behind forever. *Suck it, Malibu*, I thought. *New York, here I come.*

In one of his movies, my husband would have shown up at the last minute, sprinted down the runway, and shouted out his love for me, winning me back just before the plane taxied away. I watched out the window as the pilot waited to get approval for takeoff.

Then—was I being paranoid?—I thought I saw Rob's pilot standing on the tarmac, watching me. Would representatives from the Studio be waiting when I landed in New York? Could I trust the flight attendants? I half expected Geoff himself to burst out of the cockpit like a demon. I instinctively touched my wrist, where there was a panic button with a direct line to Aurora, who was waiting for us at our new apartment in Brooklyn. Obviously involving the police at any point would be a horrible public scandal, but if I pushed that button, Aurora would get help.

This is it, I thought, as the plane touched ground in New Jersey. If the press met the plane we'd be safe . . . and they were there. Pops at the front of the herd, as planned. Before we disembarked, I went to the bathroom, where I pulled off the Truth necklace and flushed it down the toilet. It disappeared with a violent gasp. We were home free. Or so I thought.

6

I've never told anyone about this next part.

The press took photos of us disembarking. They would soon have a story to go alongside the pictures—my lawyers were simultaneously filing for divorce. The local driver was supposed to take me and the boys straight from the airport to our new apartment in Brooklyn. Max was with us, and he was an enormous man. I barely came up to his elbow. I felt safe. It wasn't until we came out of the Lincoln Tunnel and headed north instead of south that I suspected something was wrong.

Max was in the passenger seat, his head skimming the ceiling. I tapped his shoulder.

"Max—where's he going?" It was a little rude, given that the driver was right next to him, but I didn't want to make a direct accusation.

"Turn around, man," Max said. "We're going to Brooklyn."

Staring straight ahead, the driver said, "I have different instructions."

I reached toward the panic button on my wrist.

"Hold on," the driver said. I froze. "Don't worry. You're safe. You've been seen by the press—they're right behind us—and your man Max here isn't going down without a fight. But Geoff wanted me to tell you: You should hear what's going to happen to your sons if you go through with this."

I glanced down at Cap and Leo. Leo was asleep in his car seat, his mouth half open, but Cap stared up at me, perpetual furrow in his brow.

"Do you want the police?" Max asked.

"No, not yet," I said. The police, the panic button, Max, all the safety measures we'd lined up were meant to prevent me from being held against my will. But this was different. If Geoff had something on me, I wanted to know what it was.

Twenty minutes later, Cap, Leo, and I were in a boardroom in a building facing the construction site on 17th Street. Max made sure the room had only one door before he stationed himself outside it.

There was an oval table surrounded by chairs. A small TV was perched on an AV cart at one end of the table.

In walked Geoff and five other men in suits, all business.

"Elizabeth. Casper. Leo." He greeted my five-year-old sons as if they were board members sitting down for an end-of-year finance report.

Leo didn't respond. Sometimes I imagined all adults blended together for him. But Cap asked, "Do you have any mints today?"

"Of course," Geoff said. "Sit quietly and I'll give you one when we're done."

Over my dead body he would. Silently seething, I turned to Cap. "You haven't had dinner yet, but Mommy will get you a treat later."

"Let's cut to the chase," Geoff said. "I wanted to show you this." He used a remote to turn on the TV, and all eyes in the room turned toward it.

Not knowing what to expect, I pulled out my phone. "Here, sweetie," I said, and handed it to Cap. He immediately began to play Turtle-opolis, his favorite. Leo watched over his brother's shoulder.

On the TV screen, the video cut in, and my sister appeared. She was on the sofa in the main room of my uncle's cabin up on Lake Michigan.

"I am Allison Pepper, and yes, my sister is the famous Lizzie Pepper."

Allison laughed, lifted a hand, and studied her fingers. She was high. The film jolted, and I could tell there had been an edit.

Allison continued. "Yes, I have done certain drugs with my sister, Lizzie Pepper." Another jiggle. The interviewer's questions had been cut from the tape so all we could see was Allison's side of the conversation.

"Coke, meth. I'm not proud, but that's the truth."

"Lizzie gave drugs to me and we did them together. Okay?" Allison delivered this last damning sentence in a monotone, and started to stand up as she said, "Now can I—" The film cut out.

Everything was completely clear to me now. The ubiquitous mints. The man giving Allison an amount of money that must have rocked her world. I could imagine him handing her a script, and this tape showed her reciting the lines that he had fed her. (Maybe, like me, she'd memorized her part on the first reading.) This was what Allison had remembered when she told me there was more—that our parents were right to protect me from her. This tape was my worst nightmare. I had never done any drugs, not with Allison (whom I'd only seen that one time since I was a child) or anyone else. It was a lie, yet it would be a PR nightmare. But I refused to be intimidated.

I stood up. "Thank you for that," I said. "We're leaving now."

"You're not as clever as your husband thinks you are," Geoff said. "Unfortunately, this is more than damning to your reputation. It—" He glanced at the boys as if being careful about what he said in front of them. As if he gave a flying fig about my sons. "I'm afraid this tape calls into question your ability to provide a safe and healthy environment for young children. Perhaps they would be safer with their father."

I was such an idiot. Of course this was his game. Custody. My single fear, my whole purpose, was to keep Cap and Leo out of the Studio's clutches. I would do anything to keep custody of my sons and he knew it. I sat back down.

"Does Rob know about this?" I asked.

"Rob is very hurt. He trusts us to support him at this difficult time." Unfortunately, that rang true. Rob would live in denial if it meant having his way.

I had lost. If I left, Rob would fight me for custody. With this video of Allison and all the legal help money could buy, he would certainly win, and Cap and Leo would be lost to me forever. Their image would be used to promote Rob's interests. They would be raised in the culture of the Studio, trained to do endless exercises to suppress their emotions, oblivious to the dark underbelly of the organization. My friends and I, we had tried our very best. Even my father couldn't help me now. My sons and I were free to walk out the door, but it was a false, temporary freedom. It meant nothing. There was no way out. We were up against something much bigger than we were, and we had lost.

The room was silent—everyone watching as I accepted my fate.

"What exactly do you want from me?"

"Very little," Geoff said. "If it were up to me, well . . ." He let his words hang in the air, then went on. "Rob simply would like you to give it some more time. Meet up with him in London. Practice at the Studio. Try to reconnect."

I almost crumbled. Rob was my husband. I believed, in theory, that any marriage went through hard times. I'd never even tried asking Rob to change—to take some time off, to get to know his children, to talk things through with me. We could spend more time together. I would confront him with the scripts. We could start all over again.

Except that Meg had warned me. There was no turning back now. I thought about what my father would do in this situation. Doug Pepper was the smartest man I knew. He'd guided every choice I made before I was married. And Doug Pepper never accepted defeat.

Geoff tapped his fingers impatiently on the boardroom table. Without taking his eyes off me, he flicked open a tin of Altoids. The smell of mint drifted across the table and ignited in me a white-hot fury. This man had photographed my sons. The idea of him giving them candy made me sick. I had to protect them with every fiber of my being. My father and I didn't see eye to eye about my life, but I was still the Pitbull's daughter. In my head, I heard his voice: *I always win.* And suddenly, I knew why he always won. Because he was convinced that he was right. He trusted his instincts. I looked around the room. Everyone was frozen, waiting for my response. Except Cap and Leo, who, blissfully unaware, were having an impressively low-volume fight about whose turn it was on my phone.

I was Doug Pepper's daughter. And I had my own tricks up my sleeve.

"There's something I'd like to show you. Are there security cameras in this room that show the outside of the building?"

Geoff gave a nod. A young man stood up and opened a panel on the wall. It revealed four small screens with different angles on the building entrances. I walked over to the screens. One of the cameras showed the front gate, outside of which ten paparazzi stood, cameras at the ready.

"Can you zoom in on this one?" I asked. The guy complied. Now I could see what I was looking for. There, at the edge of the screen, was Pops. I pointed to his black-and-white image. "Bring this guy up here."

Minutes later, Pops entered the room. I said, "This man has documentation of the donations, the receipts, and pictures of Studio Manhattan. The minute that tape of Allison hits the press, we will release these documents." It was a gamble. And the best acting performance of my life. There had been nothing useful in Bluebeard's chamber.

I stood up. "We're leaving. My sons and I are leaving."

To my amazement, nobody stopped me. I like to think it was my determination, but it may have had something to do with Max the Giant, waiting just outside the door.

While we were en route to our new apartment, Aurora alerted the press. When we arrived, they were already clustered outside the building, shouting, "Is it true that you've left Rob?"

For once I was happy to see them. Their watchful lenses kept me safe.

7

Two weeks later Cap, Leo, and I were comfortable in our new apartment. Gone was Rob's cool, minimalist décor. Gone was Jordan's disturbingly constant presence. Gone were Jake and his notepad of endless obligations. I filled the apartment (prewar! exposed brick!) with flowers and color, and let Cap put amphibian wall stickers in a march around the door of the living room. Everything was on a smaller scale, and the boys' laughter filled the rooms.

What was the beginning of the story for everyone else was the end of it for me. Oh, the media was relentless, but the hardest part was over. I was out.

During the custody battle, the press had a field day. The stories came out, each worse than the next.

One day a man came up to me on the street and wished me strength. "I can only imagine what you're going through," he said. "Call me if you ever want to talk, human being to human being." He handed me his card. Writer. *Rounder.*

Somehow (damn her!) Aurora's "Run, Lizzie, Run" T-shirt was leaked

326

and became a fashion item, reducing the most terrifying moment of my life into a pop culture joke.

Lexy did a photo shoot for *Rounder*. The accompanying article had Lexy saying that she and Rob had an amicable divorce. She thought he would make a wonderful primary caregiver for the boys. I couldn't wait to see what luxury vacation Lexy would be taking next.

Ultimately, I got Cap and Leo. While the lawyers negotiated custody— in my favor—we both kept our sides of the bargain: One Cell sat on the tape of Allison and Pops didn't release the nonexistent documents. Then, as everyone knows, Teddy Dillon (and her brother, Luther, whom I'd never actually seen) absconded with the funds that had been raised for the New York project and were now apparently living happily in Bhutan, which has no extradition policy. Geoff was left to face the Studio's legal woes, and wound up with a fifteen-year prison sentence on federal fraud charges. At the time of this writing, the state sentence was still pending. The Studio is closed for good. ACE immediately bought the Beverly Hills headquarters and had a massive beach party before they put down wood floors in the practice rooms. My ex-husband had no comment. I could imagine Lotus advising him that it would blow over, like everything else. What I couldn't imagine was what Rob told himself.

I can't, and don't, blame One Cell for the failure of my marriage. Ultimately it was one person's fault: mine. I was younger than I knew when I signed on to a life in a megastar's shadow and a love that was too good to be true.

America is still obsessed with the Studio, its Practice, its downfall, and Rob's involvement with it. I don't dwell on it. I simply saw the Studio as his safety net—a place where nothing was improvised, where the end justified the means. It made his complicated life simple, but it would have made our boys' simple lives too complicated. It's hard for me to believe that Rob had no idea what went on with Meg and others at Fernhills. But I guess it's also possible that he would relish the intensity of that experience. He would much prefer enduring a physical, mental challenge—the labor! the darkness! the silence!—to allowing his emotions free rein.

I dream about Rob (me and half of America), but in my dreams he's never singing "Love of My Life" on bended knee or sweeping me into his arms or kissing me in front of a Venice sunset. The Rob of my dreams is mundane. He swats at a mosquito. He drops his car keys. He ties Cap's shoes for him. He plays catch with Leo. Rob went to such lengths to win me with planning and poetry. But the Rob I longed for was at a loss for words.

Nowadays, Rob and I communicate through his new assistant, Marjorie. (Because the Jakes of this world eventually have nervous breakdowns and decide they have to follow their dreams: becoming production assistants.) Rob and I haven't spoken at all, except for one polite hello when we came face-to-face at Sundance last year (which generated two weeks of tabloid drama). He never even called to find out what had gone wrong between us.

We arranged for Cap and Leo to see their father when he isn't working, so long as it doesn't interfere with school and I approve. Through Marjorie, I send frequent notes to Rob about the cute things the boys say, how quickly Cap is learning to read, and how Leo is the social director of his first-grade class. Rob doesn't respond. I wish things were different. I want him to know that I loved him. I sometimes think if only he had publicly renounced the Studio, or if only he'd worked less for those first few years, or if we'd run away to New Zealand, we'd have had a chance to live together, to carve our way, to grow into our marriage, to find each other. But I couldn't be an accessory to someone else's perfect life. And I couldn't let that happen to my sons.

I don't know if Rob and I will ever reconnect. But I do have hope that in some way, though he may never admit it, he understands my side of the story. Our divorce agreement included a confidentiality clause that forbade me to discuss (much less publish) details about our marriage. I chose not to agree to this clause. I crossed it off, and initialed it, as did Rob. To accomplish this, I relied on something I learned when we were married: Rob never reads his contracts. He flips through whatever his lawyers send him while he's on the treadmill, diligently signing all the places with little sticky tabs reading "Sign here." There is a very good chance that this negligence worked in my favor.

But there's another possibility. Behind the page where I crossed off the confidentiality clause, I inserted a new, separate page into the document. It was nothing legal, just a note to my now ex-husband. The note was my attempt to bring us both closure, and it said many things, but the part that is relevant here read, "*You know.* You know exactly why I had to do this. It is hard to live as you do, and I couldn't do it. I need to be in the real world. I need to be free. I couldn't live your story, and I don't want to live the story the press will write for me. I want the freedom to talk about myself. I've spent too much time trying to be what others want me to be. It's my life. I can't sign the right to talk about it away. Please, let's both not have any more secrets."

Did Rob read it? Did he agree with what I wrote? Did he think it was "great"? Is that why he initialed the crossed-out confidentiality clause? Or did he just let it happen? I don't know the answer, but I hope against hope that the reason I own the right to tell my story is that Rob, a man I truly loved, decided to let us each have this freedom. For all his wealth and power, he, more than I, has already had to sacrifice so much.

When everything was agreed upon and signed, and all was said and done, I was free. It was an end, and it was a beginning. Instead of dressing and doing hair and makeup to go get a coffee, now I just throw on a sweat-shirt. The first time I was photographed like that, P. J., my publicist once again, called to applaud my savvy. The second time I wore that sweatshirt, the tabloids declared "Lizzie Losing It," and I learned my lesson.

Without the Studio, Meg needed to find her own identity. At first, we thought it would work for her to stay on and work with me, but when the Studio fell apart, she went back to Fernhills to help her family and friends pick up the pieces. Her boyfriend is also a former practitioner. When last we spoke they were planning a trip to India.

Aurora visits us often, and her organization has been raising money for LifeHeartTruth, so we get to work together on that. She is still my best adviser, my constant text companion, and I was overjoyed to hear that she is expecting a baby girl. It may be selfish, but I love that she's decided to be a single mother—we're already making plans for her girl and my boys and us.

One day Johnny Flaim called. He was sober, allegedly, although every so often he was photographed in Vegas at three in the morning. But on the phone his familiar voice was gentle and full of concern.

"I've been worried about you, girl. Are you safe? Are you free?"

Tears sprang to my eyes and I pushed them away angrily. Why did I feel sorry for myself whenever anyone felt sorry for me? Johnny and I met for lunch at a hole-in-the-wall Lebanese restaurant in the East Village. My car waited outside, an incongruously pristine SUV idling illegally on the narrow street. Johnny spoke carefully, being supportive without probing, and I could see that in the past seven years my bad boy had grown up. Maybe he wanted to show me that, and maybe he thought we could have a second chance. But it felt like we were speaking two entirely different languages.

In 1917, Ernest Shackleton returned from his *Endurance* expedition to England. He had saved all of his men, but Antarctic heroism was of little interest to a country in the midst of a bloody war. Shackleton went on the lecture circuit, tried unsuccessfully to repay his debts, drank a lot of whiskey, and died an early death.

I was no explorer. My adventures were domestic and climate controlled. But my years with Rob Mars had shaped me, sculpting such an irregular form that it was hard to imagine ever fitting next to anyone again. So, *Rounder, Starlight, Sheigh Moi, Glam, Tomorrow*, and every other "news" outlet, for once and for all: The answer is no, Johnny Flaim and I are not getting back together. (Love you, Johnny.)

My movie *The Safe House* went straight to video, all of its potential and all of Parker's hard work for naught. This happens sometimes, and sometimes it isn't because the biggest agency in Hollywood wants to appease its biggest star. The disappointment just thickened my skin. In meetings and in parties I shrugged and said, "It's a tough business, but I'm really proud of the work I did." Besides, I consoled myself, it was just another Hollywood movie about a white savior. No big loss. I recently accepted a part on Broadway, and for now that's quite enough for me.

I am still an actor, and I love working hands-on with O Naturale on our cosmetic line, but mostly I'm a mother. When the boys and I took the subway for the first time, Leo was in heaven. The noise of it frightened Cap, and he started crying for our driver. In the moment I worried that the damage was already done—Cap was never going to be like other kids. But that night I let Max go, and now we take the subway all the time.

Cap and Leo were attending a real school, where they were just like all the other kids. Except for the private exit, down through the lunchroom, where our new babysitter led them out every day for that first year, in disguise, past the food trucks, until the fervor died down.

Cap is intense, like his father. When he is interested in something, he won't give up until he nails it. (He recently traded his interest in turtles for *Matilda*, the musical, and his favorite pastime is belting out the songs while staring at himself in the mirror.) The transition has been harder for Leo. Lately, when he doesn't want to do something, he isn't polite about it. (Though I swear he acts out in front of the cameras like he never does at home.) I try to handle his tantrums the same way every time, no matter if the world is watching. I've knelt down to talk to him while photographers snapped one thousand shots of my butt crack. He's pulled my shirt to the side, exposing my bra. Believe me, the high-waisted jeans and ever-present camisoles are not fashion choices. They are safety measures.

★

Last week the boys and I were on the uptown local, headed to Grand Central on our way to spend Thanksgiving Day with my sister, Allison. As you probably heard, I actually fell asleep for a few minutes. When I opened my eyes, I realized what had happened. Me—Lizzie Pepper—asleep on the subway! It was kind of a miracle.

Allison's sober living facility—a branch of LifeHeartTruth—celebrates Thanksgiving with a turkey buffet. Sitting between my sister and one of my sons, I looked across the table at Chrissy, a mom whose fifteen-year-old daughter, Myla, is Allison's current roommate. I caught Chrissy's eye, and we raised our soda glasses and silently toasted each other.

One year, Rob and I had hosted Thanksgiving in Aspen. His parents and brother were in from L.A.; about a dozen One Cell practitioners attended, and assorted Aspen acquaintances. Aspen was "casual," which meant every guest was outfitted in his or her chic après-ski best. Diamonds and fur vests were rampant. It was a catered dinner for fifty, with an enormous cornucopia of soon-to-be-wasted autumn squash as the centerpiece of the banquet table.

Now Chrissy, Myla, Allison, Cap, Leo, and I barely filled a plain wooden table that was set for eight. Under the florescent lights, other mismatched families sat celebrating. There were posters on the wall with inspirational messages: the Serenity Prayer, the Ten Commandments of Therapy, the kitten hanging on to the tree branch with the words "Hang in there, baby!" The one above Leo's head happened to read, "Feel your feelings." I couldn't help chuckling to myself. That's exactly what I wanted us to do, and it didn't kill me to be reminded. We all need a little rehabilitation sometimes.

The dining room felt ordinary, and special. There was some laughter, some moments of silence when silverware clinked, a reminder that everyone here had gone to a dark, difficult place, where the simple daily ease of a shared family dinner was a hard-won treasure.

It may be oversimplifying to say that my family had sacrificed Allison for my acting career, but I always felt that my achievements were at her expense. We left her to survive alone. We gave up. My family once felt shame and confusion over who Allison was and how we dealt with her. But I am forever proud to have her as a sister, and proud of the family we've rebuilt.

My father is a strong, brilliant man, and I credit him with the person I am today. His strength gave me the confidence to fight the Studio, but (with a little help from my friends) I'm the one who got myself out of a difficult situation, and I'm proud of myself for finally listening to my own instincts.

I wish I could say that my parents and I spent a long time talking about the past, our relationship, and how we could move forward, but that's not really how we are. My dad is never going to be that person. Much as I'm never going to be the daughter he tried to create. We both understand this, and, so long as we don't live in the same state, we get along just fine.

Later that night, back at our Brooklyn apartment, I came across the photo of me on the subway. (Okay, I googled it. I'd never seen myself asleep before.) There I was, without much makeup, my mouth a little open (but not as bad as it could have been), one hand protectively across each boy's lap, completely zonked. Again memories of our Aspen Thanksgiving party came to my head. I remembered the photos (which we sold to *Glam* to benefit One Cell): me, in a brown suede sheath dress that I fit into only after a weeklong juice diet, hair in a too-tight updo, overly made up for the harsh flash cameras, smiling my photo-ready smile. My eyes were blank, my cheeks hollow. Looking back down at the picture of my sleeping subway self, relaxed, oblivious, I couldn't help smiling. It wasn't exactly a normal life, but it was close enough for me.

I left my husband in order to free my sons from a life of extreme privilege and loneliness. I understand why people are curious, but I hope this book answers every question that could be asked. I know that I signed on for the celebrity life, but my sons didn't. If I've earned the right to ask anything of my readers it is this: Please let my children be.

Oh, and one more thing. Call me Lizzie.

ACKNOWLEDGMENTS

Lizzie Pepper

When I talked to publishers about this book, the first question they always asked was whether I had the right to tell this story. They obviously didn't want One Cell's notoriously litigious legal team coming after us all. So, first and foremost, I have to thank my ex-husband's law firm, Harris, Harris, Maxon, and Harris, for hiring the incompetent paralegals who failed to properly review our divorce settlement.

I also want to thank Aurora Janevs and Meg Cheley, who gave me courage; Cap and Leo, who gave me purpose; and Allison, who inspires me every day.

My agent, P. J., who never lost faith in me.

Finally, I want to thank my parents, especially my father, who may always see me as his little girl, but who also gave me the strength to choose my own path.

Love,

Lizzie

Hilary Liftin

In my ghostwriting work I don't usually have the chance to thank people in print, so I am delighted to have at last a place to thank my longtime agent and friend Lydia Wills, whose unflappable wisdom is the bedrock of my career and whose exquisite taste guides my Pinterest fantasies. Without the brilliant Semi Chellas and Esta Spalding, who helped break the outline (Semi jiggling a baby the whole time), I have no idea what this book would have been. My husband, Chris Harris, edited an early draft so heavily that he might be considered the real ghostwriter here. And my other readers: Semi and Esta again, Yasemin Sarikaya, and Katherine Pope gave critical notes out of the goodness of their hearts. Karen Fox, Eric Fox, and Dylan Schaffer gave me pointers on fictional tax and legal matters. And I must give a shout-out to Le Pain Quotidien on Larchmont, my de facto office, where I was supplied with endless green tea and the welcome distractions of other writers.

I am deeply grateful to the following people at Viking: Clare Ferraro and Caitlin O'Shaughnessy, for believing in this book, fighting for it when need arose, and being willing to walk the line. Caitlin, you are the most dedicated, enthusiastic, and just plain fun advocate an author could ask for. Carolyn Carlson and Helen Richard, for taking the reins so expertly. Gina Anderson and Anke Steinke, for devoting many long hours with energy and creativity. Angela Messina, Carolyn Coleburn, Kate Stark, Lydia Hirt, Mary Stone, and the rest of the team at Viking—I'm lucky to have you!

I can't think of a good reason to thank my kids—shouldn't they be thanking me?—but it seems wrong not to put their names here because I am so grateful for them, too. Jozy and Silas.

ABOUT THE AUTHORS

LIZZIE PEPPER is an American actor. Born in Chicago, she starred as Lucy McAlister in the TV drama *American Dream* from the age of seventeen. The show aired on Grand TV for six seasons. Her movies include *The Last Hurrah*, *Man of Her Dreams*, and *The Safe House*. She has appeared on Broadway as Miss Merman in *Compulsion*. Her fragrance, Mode, was named Best New Scent by the International Association of Perfumiers. She is a board member of LightHeartTruth, an addiction recovery center in Malibu. She has more than four million Twitter followers @LizzierPepper. She lives in New York with her two sons.

HILARY LIFTIN is the author of two books, and has ghostwritten and co-written many titles, including nine *New York Times* bestsellers to date. Hilary graduated from Yale University. She lives in Los Angeles with her family. *Movie Star* is her first novel.